S0-AHR-919

For Barbara Lake,

I hope you enjoy the book!

Best,

Angela Barton

9/2006

The Fruits of Atterley

The Fruits of Atterley
A NOVEL

by

ANGELA BANKS

Golden-Banks PUBLISHING

The Fruits of Atterley
by Angela Banks

Golden-Banks Publishing, LLC
6060 N. Central Expressway, Suite 560
Dallas, TX 75206
U.S.A.
http://www.goldenbankspublishing.com

All Rights Reserved. No part of this book may be reproduced or transmitted in any form or by any means, electronic or mechanical, including photocopying, recording, or by any information storage and retrieval system, without written permission from the publisher, except in the case of brief quotations embodied in a critical article or review.

Copyright © 2004 by Angela Banks

This novel is a work of fiction. Names, characters, places, and incidents are either the product of the author's imagination or are used fictitiously. Any resemblance to actual persons, events, or locales is entirely coincidental.

ISBN: 0-9740529-0-6
Library of Congress Control Number: 2003092950

Printed in the United States of America
Cover artwork by Dannelle LeBlanc
Book cover and interior design by Alpha Advertising,
The Writing Shop and Two Hearts Design.

To my parents, sisters, and sister-friends,
who encouraged me to step out into the deep.

Acknowledgments

I am grateful for my beloved parents, to whom I owe my eternal gratitude for raising me well. They taught me to read before I had a full set of teeth and convinced me that my future held limitless possibilities. I would also like to thank my sisters for their support and encouragement—Dannelle LeBlanc, whose artwork graces my cover and whose proficiency at motherhood is a constant inspiration; and Lena, who despite her brilliance and strong-willed self-reliance, will forever be my baby sister. I pray you both will always be quick to tell me who I am and who I am not. Thanks to the editors of my book, Bob Drews and Janis Holmberg, for their invaluable insight and gentle criticism.

Finally, I would like to acknowledge my God for visiting me at my lowest ebb and giving me the gift of writing to prove I was loved.

Author's Note

One of the greatest compliments I have received from readers has been their insistence that such a place as Atterley plantation must have existed, and that *The Fruits of Atterley's* main characters are surely derived from real people resurrected from South Carolina's past. On the contrary, my descriptions of Atterley are based upon a compilation of many antebellum Low Country rice plantations I have researched, rather than on any one in particular.

As much as my literary creations have become real people to me, as far as I am aware, there never was a Gus or Promise, a Hannah or Rebecca, a Zachary or Sir Henry, as they are presented within the pages of this novel. Except for fictionalized accounts of men who were central figures in South Carolina history prior to the Civil War, such as politician Robert Hayne and prominent rice planters John Middleton and Robert Allston, my characters are solely a product of my imagination and of my intense fascination with the complexities of human nature and motivation.

To provide a realistic backdrop for my story, I studied the diaries of South Carolina planters and plantation mistresses, numerous historical documents, and slave narratives. I attempted, as best I could, to remain objective in my portrayal of the South Carolina slaveholders. To characterize them as simply villainous, incapable of human emotion or conscience, and thus vastly different from us, would have been far too simplistic and comfortable, both for me and for others. To weave a believable story that promoted understanding and encouraged self-examination was a far greater challenge. How well I have succeeded in this objective remains for the readers to determine for themselves.

Prologue

When Franklin and Millicent Johanson finally found a buyer for their home in Charleston, South Carolina, they turned their antique store over to their son and prepared for retirement. The couple had long yearned for the peaceful leisure of country living, so they moved to the sleepy, nearby town of St. Andrews Point.

Initially, fishing trips and church picnics were a welcome relief from city life. But after thirty years of purchase orders and bottom lines, the Johansons soon grew restless. After making inquiries about local property available for sale, they cashed in some of their mutual funds and purchased Atterley Plantation—six hundred acres of tired land, a crumbling house, and rusted tin sheds where local teenagers took refuge to extinguish the passions of young love.

Franklin and Millicent spent the remainder of their savings rebuilding the property, intending to open it to the public as a bed and breakfast. Using the plans stored in the local historical society archives, they restored the plantation's main house and gardens to their original condition—when Zachary Riley, Atterley's first master, owned the land. The society also lent the couple family portraits, furnishings that had survived the Civil War and subsequent occupation of Federal troops, and transcripts from their collection of Riley family documents.

The Johansons put these documents on display in the entrance hallway, along with scanned images of the originals. They took great care in decorating the guest rooms, remaining faithful to the style of the antebellum period. From the plantation's initial acreage, over four thousand acres of woods and swampland had been parceled off over the years to different owners, but enough still remained to make Atterley a hunter's paradise. They recreated the plantation's orchards and filled its lake with fish.

Two years after acquiring the property, the Johansons had restored Atterley to its former glory and prepared for the plantation's grand opening on Confederate Memorial Day. The town's residents were thrilled with the prospect of a flood of tourist dollars, and its banks eagerly extended loans to area businessmen for the opening of souvenir shops selling Confederate memorabilia, key rings adorned with dangling sea life, and mugs painted with clusters of yellow jasmine.

The board of directors of the Foundation for the Study of Confederate History made plans for the reenactment of local Civil War battles on Atterley's grounds and organized a parade to commemorate the plantation's opening. A statue of Zachary Riley was commissioned to occupy a place of honor in Anderson Park. Behind it would fly the flags of the United States of America, the state of South Carolina, and the Confederacy. Its plaque was to bear the following inscription:

Zachary Augustus Riley
1796-1869
South Carolina Legislator—Businessman—Southern Patriot.

Their combined efforts to establish St. Andrews Point as a popular tourist destination were aided when Mr. Edmund Manning's article was published in the *Southern Heritage Travel Guide*.

The Rebirth of Atterley
by Edmund Sinderson Manning

Smell the richness of freshly tilled pastureland and visualize the splendor of swaying cypress and gum trees. Hear the echoes of the joyful songs of field slaves as they raise their sickles to the sun during the rice harvest. Taste the succulent fruit from fertile orchards. Imagine the society balls where fashionable ladies and gentlemen exhibit the genteel charms of the well bred.

Atterley's proprietors, Franklin and Millicent Johanson, have painstakingly recreated the splendor of the Old South. Visitors can enjoy the beauty of Atterley's guest rooms at night and an invigorating country breakfast in the morning before touring the grounds on horseback. Atterley offers not only excellent hunting and fishing for the avid sportsman, but also the tranquility of a quiet afternoon on the piazza overlooking the gardens. Suitable for a romantic retreat, or a family vacation, Atterley Plantation will give its guests the opportunity to reconnect with their glorious Southern heritage.

The Riley family papers, featuring the journals and slave records kept by Mr. Zachary Riley, Atterley's first owner, detail the special connection the family had with their land, and the humanity they expressed toward their slaves. Riley's journals reveal a benevolent master who not only gave his slaves a generous food allowance, but also permitted them to hunt and fish on his land without restriction. His notes explain his preference for motivating his field hands with praise rather than punishment. He writes of his wife's purchase of church clothes for their slaves, and of money that was to be set aside to provide for their Christmas celebrations.

Riley also appeared to have been a very attentive master. He kept a careful account of the plantation's acreage and yearly rice production, and his journals also include a detailed description and layout of Atterley's main house. His slave records are unique in that they include the name, date of birth, occupation, and date of death of each one of his slaves, indicating his deep concern for their welfare and personal happiness.

Sadly, the last pages of Riley's journals are filled with grief over the death of his wife and his fears for the future of his beloved Atterley. Unable to adjust to the destruction of his way of life, Zachary Riley died only a few short years after the South lost her battle to become a sovereign nation. For many South Carolinians, the Civil War claimed not only their valiant sons, but their fortunes as well, and during the turbulent years of Reconstruction, the remaining members of the Riley family were rendered destitute and were forced to abandon their property in the state. But

Atterley has been reborn, and the Johansons have ensured that its magnificence is available for all to enjoy.

Buoyed by this enthusiastic endorsement in Manning's article, eager vacationers had reserved all of Atterley's guest rooms prior to its opening day. The *Southern Heritage Travel Guide,* however, was quickly deluged by phone calls and letters from African-Americans angered by Manning's benign characterization of slavery, charging him and the travel guide with racism.

The controversy went largely unnoticed outside of St. Andrews Point. For a nation not ready to confront the diseased roots of its history, the gulf between its black and white citizens was too commonplace to be newsworthy. Instead, only the rotten fruit was plucked, and a compromise was reached. Manning agreed to write a retraction, stating that his article had been written without a complete knowledge of the facts and that he had judged the nature of Atterley's past in light of his own biases.

However, it would have been difficult for Manning to find any conflicting accounts of life at Atterley had he been inclined to look. Often the passage of time paves over history's cracks, creating the picture-perfect image of Camelot. But had Manning known the complete story of Atterley, his article would have been infinitely more interesting.

A good tree cannot bring forth evil fruit, neither can a corrupt tree bring forth good fruit. Every tree that bringeth not forth good fruit is hewn down, and cast into the fire. Wherefore by their fruits ye shall know them.

— Matthew 7:18-20

Atterley's House Slaves
(1850)

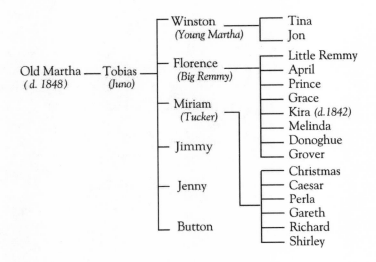

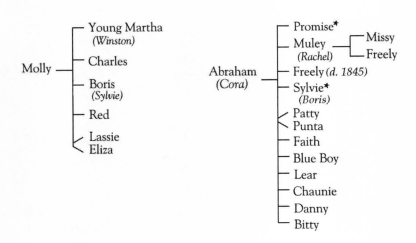

*Abraham & Cora's children who worked as house slaves in 1850.

Book One

CHAPTER 1

Baby Massa

On May 17, 1830, when Augustus Riley finally entered the world, he was two weeks overdue and greeted only by the tortured screams of his mother. Rebecca Riley was a gentlewoman, not used to pain save that accompanying the tightening of her corset strings, and she wrenched the forearm of her nurse, Hannah, so she could have a partner in her suffering.

It was a rather undignified beginning for a child believed to be destined for greatness. Augustus was the firstborn son of Zachary Riley and heir to the fortune his father had amassed as the master of Atterley, one of the most profitable rice plantations along the Waccamaw River in the South Carolina Low Country.

"Shh . . . Shh. Please, Miss Rebecca, be quiet," Hannah pleaded. "He's out now. It's all over." She clipped the umbilical cord and began cleaning off the baby. "Massa says he don't wanna hear no more crying outta you tonight. Juno, go tell him he's got himself a boy." Then Hannah barked orders to the rest of the half-dozen house servants she had recruited to help with the birth, and they obeyed her with rapid efficiency. Rebecca's screams subsided to soft sobs.

Dr. Needham took a handkerchief out of his jacket pocket and let it absorb the sweat beneath his collar. He was relieved that Mrs. Riley's cries had finally stopped. She was so delicate. He hated seeing the agonized thrashings of her body, her face racked with pain. The doctor took the baby from Hannah's arms and cleaned the remaining fluid from his skin. Then his thin fingers probed the child as he began giving him a thorough examination.

Why Mrs. Riley had wanted a slave to deliver her baby he could not comprehend, but after close observation it became clear to him that she coddled her darkies. In that, she was suffering from the same weaknesses of mind and spirit as many of the day's modern women. It was imprudent, like letting a yard dog eat out of your dinner plate.

It was the kind of attitude he expected from a Northern woman, surely, but Mrs. Riley came from a fine Charleston family, and had no excuse for her ignorance. Her husband, however, had not forgotten the scare that Denmark Vesey had given them all nearly ten years ago—when he had almost succeeded in a plot to murder decent white people in their beds. Mr. Riley had sent for him that morning, insisting that he supervise the birth. Thank God Mrs. Riley had married a sensible man, who knew that a white man in South Carolina could put only so much faith in his niggers.

Rebecca gazed down at her son and caressed the butter-soft skin of his back. "Isn't he beautiful, Hannah?"

Hannah wrinkled her nose at the pickled-pink bundle. "Humph. I don't like tellin' tales, so I'm just gonna hold my tongue."

Rebecca was wounded, and she surveyed her baby again with a more critical eye.

Dr. Needham's head shot up. Hannah had forgotten her place, no doubt due to Mrs. Riley's lenience, and since Rebecca's husband was absent, he took it upon himself to put her back in it. "That's your new massa," he told her. "You beg your mistress for her forgiveness or I'll whip your black hide raw." The flurry of activity in the room ceased. Dr. Needham opened his jacket, revealing the curve of the well-oiled whip at his waist. Hannah stood firm, but fear rippled through her body as she watched him unclasp it and hold its handle lightly in his palm.

"No." Rebecca's command came before the doctor had time to raise his arm and strike. "There's nothing to forgive. Negroes, like children, often speak without thinking. Hannah meant no harm. I won't allow you to punish her for so small a thing."

Dr. Needham looked from Hannah to Rebecca's stubborn eyes, unsure of what to do. He would have ignored Rebecca and swung anyway if he had thought Mr. Riley would have approved, but he wasn't sure enough of himself to risk his livelihood on principle alone. Shrugging his shoulders, he put away his whip and began looking around the cluttered room for his black bag.

"Thank you ever so much," Rebecca said. "We'll not be needing your services any more tonight." Her tone softened. "And there's no cause to mention this incident to my husband. He has a great deal on his mind at present, and shouldn't be bothered with trivial matters."

Rebecca lay back against her pillows and congratulated herself on rescuing Hannah. She was a founding member of the All Saints Ladies Benevolence Society and the Winyah Anti-Dueling Association. Her father and brothers had impressed upon her the importance of gentle sensibilities in the fairer sex, and so she took advantage of every opportunity to extend kindness to the less fortunate.

Dr. Needham discovered his bag beneath a pile of crumpled bedcovers. "I don't have time to waste on your nigger anyway," he grumbled. "There's a wench in the quarters who's about to drop her baby. I'll be back in a few days to check on things." He gave Hannah a stern look and managed a weary smile for her mistress before stalking out the door.

Hannah motioned for the others to follow. They did not attempt to disguise their relief, and after giving reverent nods to their mistress and new master Augustus, they retired quickly from the room, eager for the few hours of rest remaining before work began in the morning.

5

As soon as the door closed behind them, Hannah turned on Rebecca. "I ain't no child—as you well know." She thrust out her chin. "I can fend for myself."

"I know, Hannah," Rebecca said softly.

"And I'll thank you not to meddle in my business in the future. Now hand me that baby of yours 'fore he ruins Ole Martha's sheets."

Rebecca lowered her eyes. "I'm sorry. I-I didn't mean..." her voice faltered as she handed him over. "I was only trying to help."

Hannah studied his misshapen head and thin, twisted mouth. *Sure is an ugly baby,* she thought. But all her life, Hannah had been kin to ugly. The closest her mother had ever come to calling her pretty was to say, "You look fine enough, Hannah," when she was dressed in her Sunday best, because the Lord's day demanded absolute obedience to the Scriptures. So Hannah played with Augustus's fingertips and prayed that even if earthly beauty were denied him, he would develop an inner glory and find favor in the eyes of God.

After dressing the baby in a diaper and returning him to his mother, Hannah began changing the sheets, smoothing out the wrinkles with practiced hands. Rebecca unconsciously shifted the weight of her body so she would not impede her progress, hardly noticing the hands that had served her for twenty-two years. Hannah's hands had been the only constant in her world, shielding her from all of life's unpleasantness.

Rebecca's father, the illustrious Dr. Charles Harper, had entrusted her into Hannah's care after her mother had died in childbirth. Rebecca could not remember a moment during her growing up when Hannah had failed her, and she had insisted on bringing her nurse with her when she became Atterley's mistress three years ago.

Zachary had objected at first. Hannah was a towering woman, with a man's back and shoulders, not fit in his opinion to wait on his demure, dainty wife. But because he had little merriment of his own, Zachary loved pleasing, lively things, and he frequently found himself yielding to Rebecca's whims and desires. In the end, it was fortunate that he had given in, for it was unlikely that either woman could have survived the separation.

Augustus's whimpers intensified, and he began shrieking loudly, thrusting his tiny hands and feet against the cotton. Rebecca panicked and looked to Hannah.

"He's just hungry," Hannah said. "Cora should be havin' hers sometime soon. She'll feed him tomorrow, but you gotta nurse him yourself tonight." She pointed to Rebecca's swollen breasts, which had begun leaking a thin fluid—making widening wet rings on her nightdress. Rebecca positioned her baby on her chest and attempted to place her nipple in his mouth. After some awkward fumbling, he found it at last. Mother and child were joined, and he began to suck her milk. Hannah sat down next to the bed, exhausted, and closed her eyes.

"Hannah." Rebecca's voice forced her nurse's eyelids open. "It's so hot in this room, and the flies are circling." Hannah stirred and reached for the large fan of turkey feathers by the bed.

Rebecca tried to relax beneath the swaying feathers. Besides a dull ache between her legs and the soreness from her son's vigorous sucking, she was in no real pain, but she was rather disappointed that her conduct during the birth wasn't more ladylike. Childbirth wasn't exactly like she had imagined.

She had chosen the room with great care seven months ago when she first discovered that she was expecting. It had plenty of light and an unobstructed view of Atterley's gardens. She had decorated the room's walls with silk coverings in muted, inviting colors, giving it a serene, peaceful appearance. She asked Jesse to scour the gardens daily and keep the room's vases filled with their loveliest blooms. And she had called together the house servants and insisted that they give the room's upkeep special attention, and that it be referred to as "the birthing chamber," a command that reduced all but Hannah to fits of laughter as soon as Rebecca left the room.

Rebecca had planned everything to the last detail, but still things had gone awry. She had envisioned her first child coming into the world in a quiet, dignified manner, so she had been both ashamed and horrified to find herself bucking and rearing like a stuck pig—her trembling legs jutting out in all directions.

One such spasm sent her grandmother's crystal vase, filled with freshly cut pink roses, flying across the room and crashing into a wall. Zachary had left his post outside the door and retreated to his study after the first few hours of labor, dismayed by the disorder in the room and the wild appearance of his wife. Rebecca had been hurt by her husband's desertion, but now she was grateful that he had not been present to witness the fullest extent of her disgrace.

Rebecca noticed Hannah's eyes beginning to close. The movement of the fan slowed, until finally it stopped, and Hannah's head rested against the back of the chair. Her baby's mouth stilled, and his body warmed as he lay in her arms in a well-fed sleep. Rebecca pulled him close to her and kissed his tender cheeks and baby lips. "Augustus," she whispered. "Atterley will be yours someday. You will be a great man and a great master—your father's son."

And Rebecca's prayer followed Hannah's to heaven.

CHAPTER 2

The Birth of Promise

It was a warm night, and Dr. Needham fanned himself with his hat as he made his way through the sweet-smelling gardens, thick with heavy-hanging vines. Tramping across the ground that separated the main house from the slave quarters, he reached the rich soil where the highland crops were planted and cursed as his new boots were coated with an unpleasant mixture of damp earth and manure. The ground then began declining sharply as he neared the community of white wooden houses that the field slaves called "the street." A stench filled his nostrils.

A few days earlier, Atterley's floodgates had been opened, covering the rice fields with water to destroy the insects that threatened to devour the budding rice plants. The standing water had an unpleasant odor that the slaves had long become accustomed to and no longer noticed, but although Dr. Needham was familiar with the workings of a rice plantation, he attributed the smell to the unsavory inhabitants of the quarters.

He considered treating slaves beneath his present station in life and would have refused to do so had not the generous salary Mr. Riley paid him been sufficient to assuage his righteous indignation. The dwellings looked virtually identical, but Dr. Needham knew his way. Mr. Riley had instructed him to make weekly visits to all expectant slave mothers to guarantee the safe arrival of the valuable commodities they carried. When he reached his destination, a well-built cabin near the end of the street with an iron knocker and muslin curtains, he mentally prepared himself for the unpleasant task before him and entered.

It was a small room, dimly lit with homemade candles, whose weak light danced against the scoured wooden walls. Iron pots and pans, ordered by size, hung over a stone fireplace that occupied one corner of the cabin, and the smell of slow-cooked rabbit stew hovered in the air. Next to the fireplace stood a table and two chairs built from cypress wood, with decorative strips of iron gracing their backs. The tablecloth was made of pieces of linen and wool sewn together, and a smaller section of the same material lay in front of the doorway, covering the packed dirt floor.

The tidy appearance of the cabin annoyed the doctor, and he slammed the door behind him. It was much nicer than the shack he had grown up in, where his mother had let them run about barefoot and half wild amidst filth and biting ticks. He gratified himself by kicking the rug aside, soiling the floor with his boots.

At the far end of the room was a bed made of pine poles that were pulled together with cords. On the bed's straw mattress lay a quadroon slave girl who looked more like a child than a woman. Beside the bed sat Atterley's blacksmith. Abraham was a full-blooded African, and the blackest black man the doctor had ever seen. The color of the iron cup he held to his wife's lips melted into the rest of his body. It was hot in the cabin, and sweat grayed his bald head, making it glisten in the candlelight like a sparkling black pearl.

Cora craned her neck, reaching for the water to wet her cracked lips. Her body was writhing beneath the covers, but despite her obvious pain, no sound escaped her lips. Her tears had flown freely before Dr. Needham's arrival, but now her eyes seethed with hatred as he approached the foot of her bed.

Although the shade of the doctor's skin was indistinguishable from her own, the social order had determined that Cora was a Negro because her grandmother was, and the lightness of her skin was not enough to escape the curse of black blood in her veins. So she hated Dr. Needham's whiteness. As he stood over her, she was reminded of the drunken men whose flushed, sweaty faces left warm droplets on her body as they strained on top of her in the New Orleans brothel that had been her home.

"You were supposed to be here hours ago," she breathed.

"I was supposed to be just where I was—tending to your mistress," Dr. Needham said. Mercy, he was tired. The contents of his bag wavered in front of his eyes as he pawed through it. "How far apart are her pains?"

Abraham stared at the doctor and said nothing.

"They've been coming every few minutes now," Cora answered for him.

Abraham tipped the cup again, giving her the last precious drops. His silence made Dr. Needham nervous. During his many visits, he had never heard him speak. It was not due to a lack of understanding. There was an intelligent knowing in his eyes, coupled with a quiet defiance that the doctor found infuriating. He threw the blankets on the floor, exposing Cora's swollen body.

As his hands roamed over her skin, Cora clutched her breasts and squeezed her eyes tight to shut out the humiliation of her nakedness. She had learned to detest the touch of white men. Countless numbers of them had taken liberties with her body and fulfilled secret fantasies that they would never have dared attempt with a white woman.

With starched collars, well-tailored suits, and fine manners, the gentlemen had been pictures of propriety. They sipped their brandy as the brothel owner's collection of slave women played instruments and floated about the room in silken dresses, refilling glasses and charming them with pleasant conversation.

As the expensive liquor warmed their bodies and clouded their minds, the men forgot their cultivated wives, their children, and their ministers' impassioned Sunday sermons. They ceased to prefer the company of ladies and desired the services of whores. They chose their fancy, from blue-black

Africans with majestic dark eyes and short-cropped hair, to the palest of the octoroons who could easily pass for white with their blue eyes and thick blond manes.

They made their selections, not realizing that at times they were choosing their own daughters, nieces, or half sisters. Cora had been one of the most popular girls, as had her mother, and her mother's mother before her. She had gray eyes and chestnut hair that fell luxuriously about her shoulders in loose ringlets. In the darkness, her appearance allowed the gentlemen to pretend that she was a white woman, but afterward, their contempt never let her forget that she was still just another nigger.

Grimacing, Dr. Needham conducted his examination, thrusting his fingers inside her. "Push," he commanded, keeping his eyes fixed between her legs. He was careful not to look at her face. When he did, it was too easy to forget what she was—to forget that the only part of her that really mattered was stretched wide open in front of him.

Cora held fast to Abraham's leg. As she bore down, she could no longer contain her screams.

Abraham fingered the iron bracelet around his wrist, his eyes never leaving the doctor. The bracelet had been a gift from his father, an artisan from his village in Africa. Abraham remembered that as his father had placed it on his wrist, he had promised to be with him always—explaining that just as Allah dwells within the bodies of his creations, when a man puts his whole self into his labors, part of his spirit forever remains within his work.

And his father had kept his promise. The bit of iron encircling his wrist had strengthened him, keeping him alive during his capture and terrible journey to America. But it was all that remained from his former life, for the customs and traditions of his people had long since faded from his memory. Like a captive lion whose claws and teeth have been removed to ensure docility, Abraham's proud birthright had been stripped of its potency. The abilities it had given him were unable to secure a future for his children.

The doctor stood up, exasperated. It had been a trying night, and he was quickly losing what little patience he had carried with him into the cabin. His back was throbbing terribly, and despite his patient's efforts, the baby's head had still not appeared. "You hard of hearing, nigger? I said *push.*"

Abraham signaled a warning, scraping the iron cup along the side of his chair, then striking it against the leg, *Creee Dah-Dah, Creee Dah-Dah!*

"Shut that up," Dr. Needham ordered. He'd had just about enough of Riley's no-talking African nigger.

Creeeeee Dah-Dah, Creeeeee Dah-Dah!

Dr. Needham felt the rhythm course through him, gathering in a dark pool of fear in the pit of his stomach.

Creeeeee Dah-Dah, Creeeeee Dah-Dah!

He looked anxiously at the door, wishing he had left it open. "Goddammit, push!" he screamed at Cora, his voice strained with panic. He took hold of her knees and spread them wide. Cora squealed, and hot tears streamed down her cheeks.

Abraham slammed the cup down, *DAT! DAT! DAT!*, and let it fall to the floor. He was on his feet before Dr. Needham realized what was happening. The doctor reached for his whip, but Abraham was too quick for him. It flew violently across the room, and Dr. Needham felt one of the African's work-hardened hands close around his neck.

Dr. Needham was reminded of the chicken his cook had killed that afternoon, how he had laughed while it danced in Fiona's hands after she had wrung its neck. After one swift crack, that jutting chicken head was left to flop loosely against its body, holding empty eyes. The body had fluttered around for a while, blood spurting from the tattered stump where its head had been.

Dr. Needham looked up into the black man's face. Abraham's eyes were flashing down at him like black steel, and he sensed how close he was to death. He wondered if he would have enough time to cry out before the massive man snapped his neck. After calculating the distance from the cabin to the main house, he realized there was no hope of rescue and pleaded for his life.

Abraham relinquished his grip and returned to Cora's side to watch a repentant Dr. Needham attend to his wife. His blood slowed as his finger traced the decorative iron on the back of his chair, *Seeeee-saaah, Seeeee-saaah.* But he felt no great triumph in his victory. He had won just one brief battle with the white man. The war had already been lost.

When the baby came, both husband and wife were relieved that their daughter's hair was curly, and her skin a respectable shade of brown. In honor of the gift given to him by his father, Abraham named his newborn baby girl Promise. But amidst the slave quarters in the middle of that fruitful night in May, there was only a muted happiness, and a restrained joy, because both Abraham and Cora believed in their hearts that their daughter could become no more than they.

Promise's inheritance would be her mother's wounded self-hatred and her father's fragile remembrances of a once-proud heritage. Their baby was birthed into a savage America that offered her no hope, declaring her the possession of another innocent born that night. There was no other legacy her parents could give her.

CHAPTER 3

Foot soldiers and Fairytales

"Augustus, darling, we're waiting on you," Rebecca called out as pleasantly as she could manage that morning. She was accustomed to cloaking herself in cheer. She had practiced her smile on Hannah while she dressed her for breakfast, making sure to show just the right amount of teeth. Hannah had not been fooled, and whirled her eyes back in her head while she buttoned up her dress.

The sunlight streaming through the parlor windows hurt Rebecca's raw eyelids and pierced through the pages at her side, revealing the shadow of her brother's staggered handwriting. Yesterday when the letter arrived, she had at first found Gilbert's words difficult to make out. Although she now knew every sentence by heart, she still could not resist reaching for it once more to convince herself that it was in earnest, and not just another one of her brother's cruel jokes.

Dear Becky,

Do not be alarmed, Father's not dead yet, although the doctor says his prospects have gotten worse. He rarely makes it out of bed anymore. You should not fret about him, though. He has reached a good old age. It is a miracle that he has lived this long. Fortunately, his illness has not yet exhausted his savings, so we will all be well provided for. Of course, Charles will be getting the most, since he is the eldest. It is rather unfair, I think, seeing as Charles has taken over Father's practice and is doing as well as he ever did. But Robert says nothing can be done, so we may as well be resolved.

By the by, Robert says hello. He is at the tavern having the last good drink he will get in awhile, so I am writing for the both of us. I just returned from there myself, so if my writing looks jumbled, that is the reason. Now do not scold us, Becky; there is good cause for us to live it up in these next few days. The Feds asked for two regiments from South Carolina to fight those damned Seminoles, and Governor Butler sent an express to Charleston asking for volunteers. Robert and I have signed up, and by the time you read this we will be on a ship bound for Florida and the glorious battle.

It did not take long before enough men volunteered to fill our quota. The Yanks cannot say that South Carolina has not done her part for the Union, although we have less cause to than anyone—seeing as they tax the hell out of us. You will be pleased to know we are in good company. Robert and I have several acquaintances in the regiment, and we are all looking forward to having a fine time in Florida. There is some friendly wagering among us about who can kill himself the most savages, and the losers will buy the winner all he can drink when we get back to Charleston.

Charles asked me to be certain and tell you not to worry about Robert and me because we have God and right on our side. I told him that you would still worry anyway, being a woman. You cannot be expected to understand a man's excitement at the prospect of a new adventure, but I promised him that I would give you whatever reassurance I could, so there it is. If this does not suffice, you must find comfort in your prayers.

Gilbert

As Gilbert had predicted, Rebecca had spent the night in tearful worry over her brothers' safety, but by the time she had awakened in the morning, she had banished her tears, if not her anxieties. As her husband had reminded her, Charleston's mayor, Robert Y. Hayne, who had formerly been both South Carolina's governor and a United States Senator, would be arriving at Atterley that afternoon, and it would not do for her face to be covered in unsightly red blotches. The Rileys were already a formidable political force in Georgia, and Zachary had lately decided that the time had come for him to adhere to family tradition.

Zachary was born on the Bellebrook plantation outside of Savannah. His father, Mr. Judson P. Riley, had been a patriot of the Revolution, during which his comrades had given him the nickname, "Red Riley," because of his bright orange mane.

Through God's divine grace and guidance, the senior Mr. Riley had prospered in business and at home. He owned four hundred slaves on two cotton plantations, the Bellebrook plantation and the Beaumont plantation five miles to the northwest. He had the good fortune to remain a confirmed bachelor until his mid-forties, and it was then that his desire for an heir inspired him to marry a fine lady twenty-five years his junior. She blessed him with four sons to carry on his legacy and no daughters requiring the hassle of being advantageously married off.

Judson Riley had sent all of his sons to West Point to learn the principles of discipline and duty and a working knowledge of engineering. Zachary was the youngest, and while he was away at school he had followed in the footsteps of his elder brothers—he excelled in debate, was elected to student government, and was offered membership into select societies. And when he graduated, he, too, returned to Georgia to toil at his father's side and preside over the administration of his plantations and holdings.

Once his mental faculties had softened with age and he could no longer balance the entries in his ledgers, Judson Riley had retired and entered political life, where prominence was more serviceable than a sound mind. When he died in the winter of 1821, Mr. Riley left his three eldest sons his plantations to divide between them, and to Zachary he gave one hundred slaves and a large parcel of undeveloped land in South Carolina. Zachary's brothers had already followed their father into Georgia's state legislature, and Zachary believed that Hayne was just the man to launch his political career in South Carolina.

"Augustus, please hurry, dear," Rebecca called again. She wondered why her son couldn't be more like Promise, who had come to the library as soon as she was summoned and was waiting quietly at her feet with her hands clasped in anticipation. She looked down at the little girl affectionately. With the folds of her sky blue dress puffed up around her in soft billows and a matching silk bow in her hair, Promise looked like a sweet black angel. That is, if the Lord's angels could be such a color, and even Rebecca's broad-minded, reformist views about the Negro race were unable to persuade her *that* was possible.

After Rebecca's son was weaned, Cora had returned to the quarters with her baby girl, but Augustus was fretful without Promise nearby, and even Hannah could not get him to sleep through the night. To ensure the comfort of her own child, Rebecca had sent Zachary to Abraham's cabin to make Cora sacrifice hers.

Dr. Needham had advised against it. He frowned upon the boy's affinity for the slave girl, fearing that he would develop the same feebleness of mind as his mother. But when Zachary surrendered to his wife's will and brought Promise back to the main house, Dr. Needham never again spoke against the indulgence of his young patient's unsavory affections. He decided that Mr. Riley paid him handsomely to ensure the health of his child, not to safeguard the future of Atterley. If misfortune resulted from his son's love of

18

niggers, as it undoubtedly would, the doctor took comfort in knowing that he was not to blame.

As the years passed, Rebecca, too, had grown quite fond of Promise. She looked like a darker version of the dolls she had played with as a girl—with cinnamon skin, soft brown eyes, and curly hair that expanded to astonishing dimensions in the South Carolina humidity. Rebecca had been unable to conceive again, so she lavished her dreams of a daughter on Promise—dressing her up in the latest fashions and ordering her clothes from the same stylish shops where she bought her own son's wardrobe.

Her sense of propriety would not let her ignore the unfortunate realities of Promise's race, however, and so she gave the little girl household tasks suitable for a seven-year-old and sent her on errands with a note pinned to her chest that read, "No one better touch this darkey."

Although he was just in the next room, Gus, as Hannah and Promise had renamed Augustus, had not heard his mother calling him, and he continued playing with his toy soldiers. He was deeply engrossed in defeating a formidable tribe of Indians as they threatened to extinguish the fragile flames of American liberty.

During supper last night, his mother announced that his two favorite uncles, whose pockets were always full of change that they willingly donated to his candy allowance, had gone to someplace called Florida to fight in a war. Gus could not comprehend the complexities of war, but he knew enough to know that guns would be involved—conjuring up memories of his mother's history lessons about the Revolutionary War and musket men.

That was enough to make the whole business sound irresistibly exciting. He had begged his mother to let him go to Florida too, even promising to finish his oatmeal from now on, *all* of it, *every bit,* without complaining *even once,* but still she had said no.

Promise made fun of him. "Of course you can't go, silly. I swear, you don't have the sense God gave a flea," she'd teased, in her best imitation of Hannah. "Don't you know anything at all? Boys can't fight in wars."

But Promise had stopped her taunting when he'd told her that he would bring her back some feathers from the head of a real live Indian. "Will you? Will you *really?*" she'd gushed at him then, her eyes shining. Promise had dreamed of those feathers all through the night, and by the time she sat down at the kitchen table for breakfast the next morning, she had envisioned Hannah sewing her brightly-colored collection into hats, creating miniature replicas of the ones her missus wore to dinner parties.

It was then that his mother shattered both their dreams of glory. Gus frowned darkly, remembering her betrayal. She said that he was too little and sick to join the army, and that he would just be in the way. And when Promise was told that there would be no Indian feathers, she vowed to never speak to him again. He had been forced to hand over his dessert to make amends. His uncles were probably having a grand time right now, Gus thought, as he dealt a savage blow to one of his wooden men.

Rebecca was losing patience. "Augustus dear... *Augustus.*" She looked helplessly at Hannah, knitting in the corner.

Hannah laid down her work. "Massa Gus, now I know you hear your mama callin' you," she said with chilling calmness, "so you better get on in here 'fore I come in there after you."

Hannah's words pierced through the fog of Gus's fancies, and he scrambled to his feet, scattering his soldiers about the floor. Seconds later he stood in the doorway, thankful that Hannah was still in her seat. He knew he was in for trouble if she'd had time to get up before he arrived. He gave her a small smile, congratulating himself on his escape.

Promise sat serenely by the edge of the couch, watching the scene unfold with great interest. It was a daily ritual, calling Gus from his toys for reading time—like one of

Hannah's stories, there was a surprise ending each time. Some days, like today, he would arrive with only a little difficulty. On other days, he could be retrieved only after repeated threats, and finally, a whipping.

Boys are impossible creatures, she thought, as she ran her tiny fingers along the French lace trimming of her dress. She loved reading, and she took great pride in knowing that she was the best at it—besides her missus of course. Hannah could not sound out words without moving her lips, and Gus was pretty hopeless all around.

Promise could not remember a time when she did not know how to make sense out of the rows of letters in her missus's collection of brightly-colored picture books. But Rebecca had said that only Gus was allowed to remove them from the library, which Promise had decided was only fair since he needed the most practice.

Rebecca closed the door, and locked it with a brass key from her pocket. "Augustus," she said with more enthusiasm than she felt. "Would you like to choose the first book this morning? It's your turn."

Gus shook his head, stuffed his hands deep inside the pockets of his pants, and rocked back and forth, shifting his weight from one uncertain foot to the other. Rebecca wondered how all of Madame Laremont's lessons on effective motherhood could have resulted in such dismal failure. "All right then," she said. "Promise, you may choose."

Promise needed no further encouragement, and she hurried to the fiercely polished shelves and selected her favorite, filled with castles, magic spells, and best of all, a beautiful princess in a faraway land. Rebecca motioned for her son to sit beside her. He paid no attention and sat down next to Promise instead. He gave her his usual greeting, a vigorous pinch on her arm.

"Ouch," Promise hissed.

Gus stole a glance at the corner of the room to see if Hannah had noticed. She was pretending to be absorbed

21

with her knitting, so Promise retaliated, poking her finger forcefully into the back of Gus's slender neck.

"Ooooooh," he groaned softly, closing his eyes. Promise stared, fascinated, at the bright red circle where her finger had been, while it faded slowly into pink and then blended back into the creamy whiteness of his skin.

"That hurt," he whispered, letting a single tear roll down his cheek.

"You started it."

"Yeah, but you weren't supposed to poke. That's worser than pinchin'."

"Next time don't pinch me then." Promise gave him a sassy smile. "What took you so long anyway?"

"Children." Rebecca rubbed her temples. "If you two do not quiet down, there will be no reading time today."

That would have suited Gus just fine, but Promise nudged him a warning, so he settled down and looked up at his mother, waiting for her to begin.

It was an exciting story, and Rebecca read with a clear voice and perfect enunciation, courtesy of the careful training she had received at the Summerhill Academy for Young Ladies. She was pleased to see that Hannah's fingers had stilled, and that Promise was listening with her usual rapt attention.

Gus was not similarly affected. His mother held his interest until after the delightfully bloody sword battle, when the prince rescued what Gus considered to be a quite stupid princess from a dragon. Then his eyes wandered outside of the open window. His father had not appeared at breakfast, and he wondered if he would catch a glimpse of him before dinner. Perhaps he had gone to town that morning, or perhaps he was riding around Atterley on Roman, the rippling monster of a horse that only his father could mount. Perhaps he was locked behind the doors of his study doing important things with important men just like him.

Gus hated those big, thick doors—thick enough that only the odor of smoke in the hallway betrayed his father's presence behind them—thick enough to shut the sound of his father's voice up inside—thick enough to keep out a little boy's knocking.

CHAPTER 4

The Profiteer

Zachary rode alongside Robert Hayne and his agent, Edward Majors, as they observed the spring planting. Atterley's acreage occupied both the east and west banks of the Waccamaw and was divided into fifteen-acre fields by check-banks. The tides moved a steady flow of fresh water up the river, covering the rice plants and irrigating the land. Zachary used Atterley's best hands to plant his rice, and he was eager to show them off to Hayne. The rows of slaves were making steady progress over the furrows, dropping the seed rice into the trenches before covering them with their feet.

In a boat manned by a black captain and crew, the mayor had sailed from the port at Charleston to the mouth of the Winyah Bay, and then north up the Waccamaw River to visit each of the Low Country planters in succession—his aim being to solicit their help with the railroad. He had already received a dozen favorable responses by the time he reached Atterley.

Hayne had first noticed Zachary at the Nullification Convention five years ago, and had met him briefly at the States Rights meeting the following year. Although he was not well acquainted with Atterley's master, Hayne had decided to petition Zachary anyway, for the other planters thought very highly of him. The pedigree of the Low Country plantation owners positioned them at the top of a rigid South Carolina social hierarchy. They were usually hostile toward outsiders, but they always included the Rileys on their guest lists for weddings and dinner parties.

"You've got some mighty fine land, Riley," Hayne said, "and some good-looking darkies."

Zachary nodded, pleased. "I give them plenty of rations, and as much free time as I can spare without compromising the harvest. And I don't use an overseer. I keep my own books. I don't allow any white trash on Atterley."

Zachary had little sympathy for the poor whites who scratched out a living on discarded patches of land. He turned away the slave speculators who dared pass through Atterley's gates peddling what he considered to be inferior merchandise, and if any of his slaves happened to leave Atterley without a pass, all of the patrollers knew better than to extinguish their frustrations on the backs of his niggers.

Majors let his horse wander away from the two gentlemen toward a fresh-looking patch of grass. Zachary loved nothing more than sharing his ideas about the proper way to run a rice plantation. Since Majors had heard his theories many times, he left him alone to educate Hayne.

Zachary pointed to his head driver, sitting high on his horse. "Henry makes sure my darkies get their tasks done. He does a good job for me, too—likes to use the whip a bit too much, though."

Hayne was incredulous. "That's mighty risky, isn't it—counting on a nigger to watch over other niggers?"

"I keep a close eye on him, but it really isn't necessary. Henry's a good boy, completely loyal. My two under-drivers report directly to him, and I've seen him whip Tucker and Amos raw for going easy on the rest. I don't ride my darkies. They do all the planting and harvesting the African way."

"Too much freedom breeds rebellion, if you ask me. I'm making sure Charleston's free coloreds get fair but firm discipline—curfews, police patrols—and we tax them plenty to cut down on the gambling and drinking. It makes coloreds feel secure when they're kept in line, and ours are a peaceful, contented lot. The last thing we need is for them to get like the North's niggers, lazy and good for nothing, wandering about with no useful occupation to fill up their days."

"Well, that's altogether different," Zachary said, with a slight edge in his voice. He was unaccustomed to being questioned. "You're talking about free coloreds, mulattos mostly, who might start thinking they're just like white men if you don't keep reminding them. My darkies don't have freedom telling them who they are. On Atterley, me and Henry's whip do the telling. A man's gotta run his niggers smart, not strong. I'm good to them, and so they love me—as much as they can and still have the fear of God in them. The proof's in the results. They produce more and more pounds of rice for me each year."

Zachary had not always been so adept at handling his slaves. He had become a wise investor in human capital through a long process of trial and error. At slave auctions he now preferred to buy entire families if at all possible. The Negro race was inherently unstable and had the passions of beasts. He had discovered that splitting up their households was wrought with inefficiencies.

When their women were sold away, the males were rebellious and volatile, breaking tools and refusing to work. In his younger years, he had been forced to shoot dead several of his prime young bucks. The deaths were costly— each slave had been worth hundreds of dollars—but it couldn't have been helped. They were continually plotting revolts, and even the harshest lashes from his whip couldn't remove the resolve from their wild eyes.

Wenches who had been separated from their children gave him almost as many difficulties. They were reluctant breeders, even when paired with his most virile field hands, so he had been forced to impregnate some of them himself. Zachary was well aware that his dark, handsome features and commanding presence made South Carolina's refined society maidens have secret thoughts and desires that would have shocked their mothers and shamed their fathers, so he was rather surprised to find that his advances repulsed their darker sisters.

The women dared not refuse him with their lips, but their bodies fought him hard. They dug deeply into his back, leaving their mark to do the testifying. Over the years, Zachary had had his favorites—those who were happy to make their master their lover as well. At first, he had convinced himself that bedding his slaves was a duty he detested, but soon he found himself awakened at night from dreams of their full, soft mouths and rounded hips. After he had married Rebecca, however, he had realized the need for caution, and he'd been careful not to make any more mulatto babies that only he could have fathered.

The promise of rain turned the sky a soft gray, and the men turned their horses back. Majors appraised the gathering clouds. "We've been getting a good amount of rain lately. Do you think they'll get all the seed in the ground by the end of April?"

"Looking after your commission, Majors?" Zachary laughed. "Don't you worry, it's gonna be a good year. Besides, come rain or come shine, you ship my rice and you'll get your share." The two men had graduated from West Point together, and Zachary trusted Majors more than any other man who didn't bear the last name Riley.

Majors ordered Atterley's supplies—shipping them in from the North and Europe—fabrics and stockings for Rebecca, books, liquors, shoes, and anything else the Rileys needed or wanted. And he paid all of the plantation's bills during the year in exchange for repayment after the harvest, and a commission on the rice crop.

Hayne saw his chance and made his pitch. "Since you'll be having such a good year, Riley, I'm counting on you to buy stock subscriptions when they're issued in October. Baltimore, New York, Philadelphia, Boston—they're all eager for the opportunity Charleston's been given—so we need to move quickly."

Zachary was unconvinced. His loyalty to his adopted state waned whenever it required him to part with his money.

"All of your neighbors to the south have already pledged their support," Hayne added, beginning to wonder if he had made a mistake coming to Atterley. Riley was not a native South Carolinian, after all, and he did have some very peculiar ideas . . .

Zachary noticed seeds of doubt beginning to sprout in the mayor's eyes. He spoke up quickly. "Of course, Hayne, of course. You can count on my full support. It'll be good for everyone if the railroad goes through Charleston."

Hayne turned to Majors. "May I count on you too, sir?"

Zachary gave his agent a playful wink. "From the money you squeeze out of me every year, you can spare a few hundred, surely."

Majors could do nothing besides grunt his assent.

"Good, good," Hayne said. "We'll need four million, or we'll forfeit the charter. It's important that we have a bond with the West, and this railroad will unify us. New friend-ships will be developed, alliances formed. When they see slavery firsthand, they'll realize—they'll know that we're not immoral people."

Zachary nodded. "Mutual dependence, that's the answer."

The three rode up to Atterley's main house, an impressive three-story brick home with majestic white columns and piazzas stretching across its east and west sides. The house stood on high land and its large windows provided an excellent vantage point from which to view the grounds. On the west side of the house, a green lawn sloped downward, stretching toward the river. On its east side, a quarter-mile pathway bordered by moss-covered oaks led to the road. The house was surrounded by flower gardens and perennial shrubbery tended by Jesse, Atterley's head gardener, and his under-gardeners.

The stable boy was waiting for them at the front steps. "'Joy yo' ride, suhs?" Sonny asked. He held the reins while Zachary dismounted. "Did Roman give you any trouble, Massa? He kicked Willy somethin' awful this mornin'."

"No, no trouble at all. Brush him down real good, now. And take a close look at his leg, it feels a little swollen."

"Yes suh, Massa." Sonny nodded to Majors and Hayne politely and led the horses to the stables.

Tobias met the gentlemen at the door. He was a well-groomed, butternut man with just a touch of gray at the temples. He looked very distinguished in the attire Rebecca had chosen for Atterley's menservants—a navy broadcloth coat, ivory vest, and navy plush trousers.

"Have Mrs. Riley join us, Tobias," Zachary said.

Tobias's wife, Juno, captivating and courtly in her navy dress trimmed in silver braid, took their coats and led them into the drawing room. When Rebecca appeared, she looked radiant and cheerful.

"Hayne, may I present my wife, Mrs. Riley. You are acquainted with her father, Dr. Charles Harper, I believe?"

"Oh yes, of course. He's a fine man, very fine. And *you*, my dear." Hayne took Rebecca's hand. "How lovely you've become, although I'm not the least bit surprised. I remember you being a very pleasant girl. It's been so long since I last dined with your father. How is he?"

"Sadly, he's not been well, but I pray that he will be allowed to remain with us for many more years, God willing."

"I'll be sure to pay him a visit the moment I return to Charleston. As time passes, my old acquaintances grow increasingly precious to me."

Rebecca seated herself by Hayne's side and had Juno bring him a thick slice of Molly's raspberry cream cake. She laughed and flirted with him, and delighted them all with a series of humorous stories that she had collected over the years to tell at social gatherings. Hayne found himself swept away by her charms. He wistfully pressed the last moist crumbs with his fork and debated whether he should ask for seconds.

Zachary watched Hayne closely, pleased to observe Rebecca draw him in. He poured the drinks, leaving his wife to explain to Hayne how he had become a self-made man.

When Zachary left his family and friends to make his fortune in South Carolina, he found that his inheritance consisted of nearly five thousand acres of swampland covered with cypress and gum trees and tangled grapevines. The property was situated seven miles north of the Winyah Bay and stretched five miles east to west, from the Pee Dee River to the Atlantic Ocean. Draining and clearing the land was a dirty business, and Zachary's faith had been tested. But even after the Lord allowed a third of his slaves to die from snakebite and disease, he refused to become discouraged.

At this point in her narrative, Rebecca paused and added a spoonful of sugar to her tea to give Hayne a moment to appreciate the pioneering spirit of her husband.

Zachary remained dedicated to his mission, bravely pressing on until his dream was realized. From the plantation's original acreage, 540 were cultivated. He honored the slaves who had laid down their lives building Atterley by giving each one a Christian burial in the land where the orchards now stood.

Although Atterley was not the largest plantation in the area, its slaves produced 1.5 million pounds of rice per year, or over 2,700 pounds per acre—one of the highest yields in the Low Country. Zachary kept a close eye on all of the activities on Atterley, for he had learned to appreciate the value of hands-on management. Last year he had made a clear four hundred dollars profit on each slave who worked in Atterley's fields.

Hayne's heart swelled with pride. Atterley was a symbol of what all could achieve with hard work and determination—a shining tribute to the American Dream. By the time they had finished their second round of drinks, he had decided that his host was just the sort of man that South Carolina needed. Zachary had made a powerful new friend.

CHAPTER 5

By Bread Alone

"Now ain't this a shame." Hannah shook her head at the afternoon's half-eaten dinner congealing on the dining room table. She marveled at the ingratitude of white folks.

Molly had lumbered ungracefully around the coop that morning chasing plumped-up chickens to cook for Zachary's guests. Promise had shelled the peas with her usual painstaking diligence and insisted on dropping them one by one into the bowl to hear them go *plunk*. Young Martha had given the silver and crystal extra attention. Juno had set a beautiful table. And Hannah had strained her nerves—dividing her time between minding Gus and fussing at Jenny to get some gumption and stop plucking the chickens like they could feel it.

But it had all come to nothing. Zachary and his visitors had gone to the Planters Club on the Pee Dee for dinner, and they didn't plan to return until after supper. Rebecca had been too consumed with thoughts of her brothers to touch her dinner. Gus had finished his creamed potatoes and apricot jam, then busied himself mixing the rest of his food into unpleasant looking piles until his mother became disgusted enough to excuse him from the table.

Hannah smelled the white gardenias that Jesse had picked for her. "Thought you'd be needin' a little somethin' today, Miss Hannah," he'd said when he gave them to her.

Jesse had spent a lifetime nurturing the earth, and it had equipped him to properly love a woman. He understood that even the strongest patches of grass on Atterley's lawns would wither away and die without consistent fertilizing. He had learned that the fluctuations of Mother Nature's ever-changing seasons could not be subdued by force, but could be mastered through patience and adaptation. He could sense from the curve of a stem, the touch of a petal, the turn of a leaf, when his flowers were crying out for warmth or nourishment. So without a word of complaint from Hannah, Jesse knew she was having a bad day. The flowers' heavy fragrance made her feel better, and she abandoned the mess in the dining room and went in search of Promise.

She found her in the sitting room, curled up in her little pink satin sewing chair, practicing her stitches. The chair was last year's Christmas present from her missus, and it was tucked snugly beside the davenport so Rebecca could have company while she worked on her embroidery. Gus sat in the far corner, surrounded by his soldiers, looking miserable. He had struggled in vain to match his father's pace as he strode past him and out the door, walking and talking with the two men at his side.

Gus had wanted to show him the bit of wood that he had carved into a hunting dog. It was almost perfect. Yes, maybe he had cut the nose a little too thin and it had fallen off, but the rest was still good enough to tell what it was, good enough for his father to know what he wanted for his birthday, but he hadn't even stopped long enough to see it.

"Promise, you may as well carry the rest of that food out to your mama and them. Ain't no use in it all goin' to waste."

"Can I take the chocolate cake, too, Maum Hannah? Muley sure does like Molly's chocolate cake." Promise's younger brother had won Hannah's heart and earned his nickname with his boldness and complete absence of decorum.

Muley was creamy beige in winter, honey golden in summer, and beautiful all year round, and like most lovely children, he possessed a strong sense of entitlement to special

34

treatment. He thought nothing of loitering around the main house whenever he had a free moment, harassing Hannah for tidbits. Promise found that she could successfully negotiate the many sweets denied her on his behalf.

"All right. Tell Molly to pack it up with the rest."

"Tell me *what?*" Molly's voice echoed through the house. "I didn't say you could give away my *damn* cake!"

"Stop hollerin'!" Hannah yelled back. "Miss Rebecca's napping!"

Molly tore herself away from her frying fish long enough to make an appearance in the doorway. "I-ain't-packing-up-*nothin'*," Molly snapped. "And *nothin'* includes my cake."

Molly looked like an overstuffed brown leprechaun. Her red hair was damp against her face, and her green eyes rattled as she glared at Hannah. The family's desertion of her perfectly fine dinner had put her in a foul mood, and she felt very put out. "Why you tryin' to give me extra work—fixin' it so I gotta cook again? This food'll keep just fine 'til tonight. They can eat it then."

"You know good and well that if that food stays within easy reach of your fat fingers, not a bit of it'll be around come suppertime," Hannah said. "Massa could feed all of Atterley twice over on what you gobble up everyday."

"I can eat as much as I please, Missus said so," Molly shot back. "And how 'bout *you,* while we're giving out blame? How 'bout you handing my suppers over to them free niggas that come 'round here scratching at the back door—beggin' for scraps like Massa's dogs? You ain't fooling nobody—talkin' 'bout we got leftover this and leftover that. You just wanna excuse to send that gal to the street to visit that white nigga mama of hers."

Promise began to cry. "You stop talkin' about my mama. My mama isn't white."

"Now see whatcha did," Molly hissed. "You went and made her cry. Don't cry, gal," she told Promise in her sweetest stirring-pudding voice. "It ain't no concern of *mine* if you wanna go out to the street and see your white nigga mama.

'Til Hannah starts lettin' you carry my good meals out there witcha."

Jenny had been standing in the hallway since the commotion began, watching the exchange wide-eyed, wondering if she should intervene. She was small for eleven, and had her mother Juno's modesty, but not her noble bearing. She weighed her fear of the two commanding women against the poignant message in Reverend Wickerson's sermon the previous week, "Blessed be the Peacemakers." At last, the reverend's preaching won out. With the broom trembling in her hands, she advanced. "The Lord's Word says that man shall not live by eating bread alone. That means we gotta share," she offered.

"Shut up, gal," Molly snorted. "You don't have no kinda sense. This is grown folks' talk."

"M-m-my mama isn't wh-wh-white," Promise sniffed.

As usual, Hannah got her way. Molly, grumbling, retreated to the kitchen. She packed the food snugly into baskets and covered them with cotton cloths to keep out roaming flies. "Jimmy, go get the seed wagon so that gal won't drop these baskets. Hang that woman. Givin' away my good dinner," she muttered.

"Go on and change out of your clothes, Promise," Hannah said. "Miss Rebecca don't want you smellin' up your good dresses."

"I wanna go, too, Maum Hannah," Gus begged. "Can I, Maum Hannah? Can I? Please, Maum Hannah. Can I?"

"No."

"Why not, huh? Huh, Maum Hannah? Huh? Why not?"

"You'll tire yourself out, that's why."

Dr. Needham had advised that Gus not overly exert himself. While Promise seemed resistant to colds and fevers, Gus had been continually ill since birth. The doctor blamed Gus's condition on Cora, whose milk nursed both children, explaining that some white children's stomachs were too delicate for nigger's milk.

Rebecca had scoffed at the idea, but Dr. Needham's diagnosis that Gus's illness was the result of Cora's nursing was correct. When Cora was told to care for Rebecca's newborn, it seemed to her as if all the evils of slavery existed in the tiny form of the future master of Atterley, and she bitterly resented being forced to nourish her own captivity. Whenever she was left alone with him, Gus was painfully neglected. She ignored his cries and attended instead to the needs of her own child.

Only Hannah suspected the truth before it was too late and agreed with the doctor that Gus be removed from Cora's care. He still suffered lingering effects from the deprivation he had endured at her hands. He was painfully thin and several inches shorter than Promise. While she was allowed to run unrestrained over Atterley's grounds, Gus spent his days being schooled by his mother or following Hannah around the house.

"You can help Molly clean the fish if you want," Hannah suggested.

"I don't wanna help Molly. I wanna go with Promise."

"Didn't say you could help me no ways," Molly said, with one hand on her hip and the other turning the sizzling catfish.

Gus's shoulders slumped, and he studied the floor, crushing a small clump of dirt beneath his shoe.

Hannah began to feel sorry. "I'll tell you what. You can go with Promise if Jimmy goes with you—that way he can carry you back if you tire yourself out."

Gus pulled at Jimmy's pant leg. "Will you go with us, Jimmy? Will you?"

"I can't, Massa Gus," Jimmy said, hoisting the baskets into the wagon. "Massa wants me to meet him at the club. I would if I could—you know that. Don't cry now."

Jimmy, Tobias and Juno's youngest son, was a tall, strapping boy of fifteen. Zachary had moved him from his parents' home to a small room in the main house for use as an all-purpose errand boy. Jimmy was an unsettling combination of fire and ice. He was "near white," with skin as fair as Cora's and frigid blue eyes that didn't suit his good nature and warm smile.

He leaned down and whispered in Gus's ear. "Cheer up, now. I know it's real hard on you, havin' to stay cooped up inside like you do, but I'll bring you back the antlers from that buck I found last week. It should be picked clean by now. Bet you'd like that, huh?"

Gus brightened a little. Jimmy was always nice to him. He always made him feel like he was somebody important.

Jimmy mussed up Gus's hair. "Aw, why don't you let him go on and go, Hannah? He hasn't had a bad cold in nearly a month, ain't that right, Massa Gus?"

"Yeah, yeah. I ain't had one in nearly a month, just like Jimmy says."

Hannah took another deep sniff of her gardenias. "Fine," she said, defeated. "But you come straight back the moment you get tired, hear?"

Gus nodded happily.

"Promise, you remember to walk slowly, and rest if Massa Gus needs to. I'm expecting you to watch out for him."

And Promise gave Hannah her solemn pledge that she would.

CHAPTER 6

Father Abraham

Outside the north entrance to the main house was a cluster of fair-sized brick homes called "the circle," where the house servants lived. Grapevines and fruit trees bordered Molly's home beside the large kitchen garden. Molly had six children—Young Martha, Charles, Boris, Red, and two already plumped-up twin girls, Lassie and Eliza. With their brassy hair and light sprinkling of freckles, the two looked like pretty bits of sunshine as they trotted between the furrows of the garden, pulling weeds and gathering vegetables in baskets.

"Hey there, Promise!" they chimed, waving handfuls of turnips and collards.

Next to Molly's house was the kitchen building, used to prepare the food for Rebecca's formal dinners and lawn and garden parties. Behind the kitchen building were the plantation's storage shed and the smokehouse, where hams and sausages were cured.

Tobias and Juno lived on the other side of the garden with Tobias's mother, Old Martha, and their youngest girls, Jenny and Baby Button. The couple's oldest son, Winston, was Atterley's coachman. He and Young Martha were to be married that summer, and Winston had built his own home behind his parents' in preparation for his new bride.

Tobias and Juno's teenaged daughters, Florence and Miriam, served as Atterley's seamstresses. They did all of Zachary and Rebecca's mending and tucking, and transformed the expensive fabrics Rebecca ordered from Europe into curtains, bedcovers, and table dressings.

Florence lived in a house trimmed in red calico with her husband, Big Remmy, the head carpenter, and their four children—Little Remmy, April, Prince, and Grace. Miriam lived next door to her sister and had decorated her home in blue and white gingham. Her husband, Tucker, was one of the plantation's under-drivers who helped Atterley's head driver, Sir Henry, oversee the field hands. The couple had two children, Christmas and Caesar.

Klangk. Klangk. Klangk. Klangk. Klangk. Klangk.

The powerful blows from Abraham's hammer bore through the thick hedge that separated the servants' homes from the smithy and carpentry shop. As the clanging of metal on metal sliced the air, Promise forgot her earlier assurances to Hannah and began walking faster, pulling the wagon wildly behind her over the grass.

Gus struggled to keep up. "You're gonna tip it over," he warned, but Promise was too excited about seeing her father to pay him any mind.

When Abraham saw his daughter coming, he didn't cease his work, but altered its flow. His teeth gleamed white through the smoke. *Klangk-Klangk. Klangk-Klangk. Klangk-Klangk.*

"I'm coming, Daddy!" Promise's heart sang back. She abandoned the wagon and ran toward her father. Abraham thrust a horseshoe into the barrel at his side. The water hissed forcefully, shrouding him in billowing steam by the time Promise reached him. She hugged him tightly, wrapping her arms as far around his waist as she could, not minding the sweat.

Gus followed behind, dragging the wagon wearily. "Promise," he panted. "Maum Hannah said you were supposed to go slow."

Abraham looked down at him, displeased. He didn't like his master's stunted, sissified son to be always so near his daughter. He plunged an iron poker deep into the coals, making the sparks fly.

Gus jumped. The dark man both fascinated and frightened him. He backed away to watch him from a safe distance.

"You like my ribbon, Daddy?" Promise turned her head so that the gold trim caught the light.

"Pree-ty," Abraham lied. His voice was low and guttural. He allowed the ugly, halting language to defile his tongue and lips for his daughter's benefit, and was rewarded with Promise's beaming smile. She was practically one of them now. His master had stolen his little girl from him and had bound her up in finery instead of chains.

Abraham was only a few years older than Promise when he first realized what it meant to be owned. He had huddled with the others on the raised platform, paralyzed by fear as he gazed out at the endless sea of white faces. The dock was flooded with frenzied buyers, jockeying for the best positions as they waited their turn to examine the captives' naked, greased bodies for any scars or signs of disease.

Zachary's father had been on his way to luncheon at Pennington's and was preoccupied with thoughts of the recent drought when the clamoring mob caught his attention. He looked up and noticed a young boy on the platform. Although Judson Riley had not been in the habit of buying Africans, he had the valuable gift of spotting good breeding stock, and so he reluctantly abdicated the succulent breast of duck and roasted potatoes that were awaiting his arrival at the restaurant and joined the bidding masses. He had named his new acquisition Abraham, hoping that he would prove to be as prolific as his biblical namesake.

Abraham rubbed his daughter's curls affectionately.

"You want me to get you some water from the well, Daddy?" Promise asked him. He handed her an empty gourd, and she dashed off toward the carpentry shop where Big Remmy was sweating in the sun, cutting lengths of wood.

Gus gathered his courage and advanced slowly. "Whatcha workin' on?" he asked softly, peering up at the anvil.

Creeee Dah-Dah! the poker commanded.

Gus jumped backward, and was grateful to see Promise running toward them with the dripping gourd. She watched happily as Abraham drank it down in thirsty gulps. Then he bent down low, letting her kiss his cheek before picking up his hammer, signaling that the day's visit had reached its end.

Klangk. Klangk. Klangk. Klangk. Klangk. Klangk.

For a half mile the children walked on, accompanied by Promise's blissful humming. It was a cheerful, made-up melody to the beat of her father's distant hammering. Gus began wheezing softly as he struggled to keep up with Promise's gait. She took no notice of his torment, and the wagon wheels skipped happily behind her over the ground.

A burning anger that began in Gus's stomach surged upwards and out of his mouth. "Your daddy's a halfwit," he said.

Promise whirled around on her heel. "What did you say?"

"I said your daddy's a halfwit. That's what they call folks who can't talk."

Promise stared at him in shocked silence. Then her eyes narrowed, and her fingers quivered against her leg, *Creeee Dah-Dah, Creeee Dah-Dah!* The wagon handle fell with a thump onto the ground. Her face loomed closer and closer to his, until he could smell the custard she'd had for dessert. Her nostrils had become wide circles, expanding and contracting rapidly. Had not terror affixed him to that very spot, he would have taken off running back to the main house and the safety of Hannah's skirts.

"Augustus Riley, you are a mean, hateful, *evil* boy! How *dare* you talk that way about my daddy!" Gus felt her spittle fly on his face. "He is strong, and good, and all the things that *you* are *not!* In fact, if you weren't such a weak, helpless, pitiful *baby,* I'd knock you into the dirt where you belong!" Gus crumbled in front of her, and Promise, gratified, retrieved her wagon and stalked briskly toward the street.

"I don't feel so well . . ." Gus called after her. "Maum Hannah said you were supposed to wait on me."

Promise turned and put a stubborn hand on her hip. "You shouldn't have asked to come if you couldn't keep up. *Maum*

Hannah said you were supposed to wait on me," she mocked. "Why don't you run home and tell on me, then? Just like a little baby would."

"Well, just maybe I will."

"Go on then, *tell* her. That'll do just *fine*," Promise seethed. "Once you tell her what happened, she'll never let you come again."

Gus swallowed. "Didn't say I was *gonna* tell, only that I *could* . . . if I *wanted* to, is all."

"Maybe I should tell her myself." Promise smiled meanly. "After all, we don't want the poor little baby getting sick, do we?"

Gus panicked. "Please don't tell, Promise. I won't fall behind. I'll keep up—*really* I will."

Promise only turned up her nose and walked stiffly toward the quarters.

Gus trailed behind and wished bitterly that he hadn't been so disagreeable. It was impossible for him to catch up to her now. He stuck his hands in his pockets and told himself he didn't care that her dress was beginning to disappear over the next hill. "Stupid girl," he muttered. He kicked the ground with his feet, taking pleasure in the ugly scuffmarks it was making in his brand new shoes.

CHAPTER 7

White Nigga Mama

Promise didn't pause to catch her breath until she reached the street. With the slaves away at work, the quarters were empty. A wide road separated the two neat rows of whitewashed cabins, and next to each was a small garden.

In the center of the road stood Sir Henry's cabin and the sick house, which was presided over by a group of old women collectively referred to as the Ma'Deahs. During the summer, the sick house was filled with slaves suffering from fever; but at present, the cabin's only inhabitants were Atterley's spring babies and children too young to complete a quarter-task daily.

When the weather was fine, the Ma'Deahs allowed the infants to be set outdoors in reed baskets where they were fed and changed by the older children. The toddlers darted nimbly around the rocking baskets, playing chase and trying to grind up pebbles in the hand mill whenever the Ma'Deahs weren't looking. The old women fussed and fawned over the clamoring brood in shifts. Individually, they would have been woefully inept to accomplish the task required of them, but together they were a perfect medley of razor-sharp tongues and sweet babblings, of unwavering severity and tender mercy.

Muley looked up from tending his charge and spotted Promise. "There go Missy! Ma'Deahs, can I go?" They answered him with a chorus of grunts and toothless smiles, and he dashed off before his tottering basket had slowed to a stop. "Whatcha have, Missy? Whatcha have?" he cried, pulling on his sister's clothes.

"Never you mind what I have," she said, rolling the wagon behind her back and away from his probing hands. Promise was a year older than Muley and continually exercised her privilege of bossing him around. "You stay away, or I'll take these baskets right back to Maum Hannah."

"Awww Missy, don't fuss. I'se just glad to see you is all," he said, smiling sweetly. He linked his arm around hers.

"Then why don't you ever come to the main house to see me? You only come looking for treats."

"Can't never find you, that's why. You're always holed up somewheres in Massa's house with *him*." Muley jerked his head down the road at Gus, who was weaving toward them. His face and neck were moist with sweat, and he was covered with a thin layer of dust.

"Well, I bet you'll look harder for me next time when you hear what I brought. Maum Hannah gave me a cake—a chocolate one, too."

Muley's eyes widened. "Shole 'nouf? I gets first crack at it! You better tell the rest, Missy! I gets first crack!"

Gus approached them cautiously, stealing quick peeks at Promise's brother. He had watched Muley many times, romping past the library windows with the rest of Atterley's slave boys when the Ma'Deahs hadn't commissioned him into service. Gus had often pressed his nose against the window as he watched them thunder by, longing to escape his asphyxiating world of women and join them. But his mother and Hannah had always stood firm, and he took revenge on his captors by covering the polished glass of his prison with snotty smears. "Hey Muley," he said softly.

Muley's eyes stayed fixed on the baskets. "Hey."

Gus's hands sought refuge in the depths of his pockets. "You . . . you gonna go fishin' anytime soon, Muley?"

"Yeah, I guess so," Muley said. *Massa Gus sure is a strange one,* he thought. He couldn't see why his sister bothered with him. He was certainly unworthy of *his* consideration. Muley had noticed bulges in Gus's pockets from time to time that suggested the presence of candy, but he didn't seem like the sort of boy who would readily share it with him, or who would keep his mouth shut if tricked into turning it over.

Gus ran his fingers through his hair. "Maybe I can come with you sometime," he suggested. "Maybe I could help you out—"

"Don't know how much help *you'd* be," Muley said. "Thought you weren't allowed outside noways."

"I'm out now, ain't I?" Gus said.

"Ain't is not a word," Promise interjected, "as Missus has reminded you plenty of times. And Maum Hannah's not gonna let you go anywhere once she hears what a time of it you've had today."

"If she lets me, will you take me along, Muley?"

"I dunno, maybe."

"My pa got me some first-rate fishin' tackle for Christmas. He was supposed to take me fishin', but we ain't even gone yet."

"Ain't is *not* a word, Gus."

"You gots brand new fishin' tackle?" Muley asked, suddenly giving Gus his full attention. "Well *shole* you's welcome! A bunch of us boys is goin' fishin' tomorrow. And then we'll have some good hours of light for huntin'."

"Boy! Really? You sure the rest won't mind me comin'?"

"Naw, just bring the tackle. You think Hannah'll let you out? I don't wanna start no trouble with her. She gave me a whole half pie last week."

"She'll let me—if Promise speaks up for me. You will, right, Promise?"

"Maybe I will, and maybe I won't. Is Mama home, Muley?"

"Yeah, the new babies're comin' soon. I told Mama it better be *boys* this time." The Ma'Deahs had done their conjuring and proclaimed that Cora was going to have twins. With two younger sisters already, Muley believed God owed him restitution.

By the time they were ten yards from Cora's front porch, Gus's insides began to quiver. Cora was giving the cabin another ritualistic cleaning, and the odor of lye flooded out the open door. The afternoon's activity had already taken a toll on him, and now the stench was just too much. His legs began to tremble. He stumbled to the ground, covering his mouth to keep down his dinner.

Promise ran toward him and held onto his body while he gagged. "Let it out. It's all right, Gus. Let it out." She rubbed his back like Dr. Needham did during his spells.

Gus needed no further encouragement and emptied the contents of his stomach onto the dirt.

"Come on, Missy," Muley called from the porch. "Whatcha waitin' for? He'll be fine," he said, beginning to wonder if even store-bought tackle was sufficient compensation to let Gus tag along.

Promise ignored him and smoothed sweaty strands of hair away from Gus's forehead. "You wanna sit under the Blackbird Tree? You'll feel better." She braced him as he rose, and walked with him toward the huge oak.

He sank gratefully beneath its shade. The trunk was deeply scarred with artistic carvings and declarations of love, and it had enough strong branches to seat a dozen or so children comfortably. In the afternoons with its limbs filled to capacity, the Blackbird Tree looked as if it were nestling a flock of squawking blackbirds.

Muley poked his head outside the cabin door. "Missy, I told Mama you was sittin' out here with Massa Gus, and she says you best come inside—so come on. And don't forget them baskets."

Promise heaved the baskets onto the porch and dragged them inside. She found her mother scrubbing the walls fiercely with a soapy brush. "Mama?"

Cora scrubbed on. Her round belly was pressed against the wood, and water had soaked through the front of her dress. Her superior beauty and fair complexion had seemingly destined her for house service, but to Zachary's annoyance,

48

although Cora was well educated and spoke fluent French, she had insisted on enduring the strenuous hours in the fields instead of enjoying the relative comfort of the main house. He would not have permitted the sun to spoil the loveliness that he had paid such a high price for had not Rebecca, threatened by the prospect of such a temptation in close proximity to her new husband, argued that Cora be allowed to work wherever she chose.

Cora was pleased at the change those first days in the sun had made in her skin—bringing a touch of yellow to it and lessening the effect of generations of white men's contamination. Each morning when she journeyed to work with the others, she abandoned her genteel speech and adopted the flowing Gullah dialect of the field slaves. Her soft hands and feet had bled daily until they were covered over with thick calluses, but Cora considered this a meager concession for the restoration of her dignity.

"Mama. Mama, she's here," Muley said.

Cora turned toward them. She was still beautiful, although the years beneath the sun's rays were now beginning to punish her skin. Sweat from her labors gathered in the lines around her eyes, which were a watery red from the harsh soap. With dust in her hair, and dripping brush in hand, she looked like an aging Cinderella whose fairy godmother had never arrived. "I see you've brought more of your Missus's charity," she said, pointing a soapy finger at the baskets. Her mouth was wet with venom, and she wiped her lips with a dry patch on her wrist.

"Maum Hannah let me bring what was left of dinner. There's a cake, and some roast chickens—"

"Can I have some cake now, Mama?" Muley interrupted.

"You can wait until after supper and have your share with the rest."

"But Hannah sent it special for me. Promise said so."

"I did not."

"Did to."

"Did not."

"You're just hot 'cause Hannah likes me best, that's all."

"She does not."

"Does too. When's the last time she gave *you* a whole half pie?"

Cora flung her brush to the floor. "Muley, how many times have I told you not to go trotting up to that house, begging for white folks' scraps!" Her legs quivered, and she held onto a chair to steady herself. "How many times? Because you insist on disobeying me, you will not touch *one thing* in those baskets!"

"But *Mama*, there's a cake!"

"Which you can do very well without. Go check those traps so I can start fixing supper."

Muley stared at his mother wide-eyed, shocked by her cruelty, and then stalked off to ask Gus what Molly was preparing for supper and to demand his assistance in acquiring a portion of it.

"You gonna have some, Mama?" Promise asked.

"No, I am not. Where's your young Massa?" Cora's eyes darted toward the doorway. "His mama told him not to set foot inside a nigger's house, most likely."

"He's just not feeling well, Mama. I left him sitting under the Blackbird Tree."

"I'm glad he didn't have the stomach to set foot in here. I never could tolerate that little boy. Does your Missus ask you how I keep my house?"

"No, Mama."

"You can tell her for me that we do *not* live like animals. I'm sure she'll be quite sorry to hear that. She thinks she did you a favor taking you away from me, you know." Cora reached out to Promise and pulled her close. "Have I told you how your massa came in the night, on her orders, and took you away from me?"

"Yes, Mama."

"But it all turned out right in the end." Cora smiled happily. "I have four, and two on the way, and she has only one, and a sick one at that. Besides, folks say he'll die before long."

"That's not true."

Cora grabbed Promise firmly by the shoulders. "Just because your missus lets you call him by his name you think he's your friend, don't you? Well, he's not." She gave her a good, hard shake. "He's your *massa*, Promise, that's all. Somehow they've tricked you into believing you're somebody special, that you matter to them and to that boy out there, so you won't mind waiting on him, entertaining him, wiping his *behind* for him if they ask you to." Cora saw the alarm in Promise's eyes and softened her grip. "But never mind that. Let me get a good look at you. They don't like you coming to visit your mama, do they?"

"Maum Hannah says I can come whenever I want."

Cora's eyes hardened again. "You like living with your massa and missus, don't you? Come on, you can tell your mama the truth."

Promise nodded slowly, looking longingly at the door.

"That's right, I know you do, because your missus puts you in all those *fine* dresses," Cora said with syrupy sweetness. "Why don't you have one on now, *Miss* Promise? No, you don't have to tell me. Your missus thinks they're too good to wear out here just to see some nigger trash. Or maybe your *massa* has you take them off. Maybe he wants you to save all of your fine clothes for *him*."

Promise began to cry. "I've been a good girl, Mama. I've been good—just like you told me."

Cora's eyes misted over. "I'm sorry, baby. Mama's sorry." She kissed Promise tenderly on the lips. "You love your mama? You love your mama, baby?"

"Yes," Promise answered. She closed her eyes and nestled in her mother's breast. "I love you, Mama."

"You're *my* baby." Cora held her close. "Say you're my baby, Promise. Tell Mama you're her baby."

"I'm your baby, Mama."

Cora didn't release her until Muley returned, carrying a raccoon and two long-eared rabbits. Then Promise ran down the cabin's front steps, letting the empty wagon swing against the porch railing. She was grateful to breathe the pure air outside, and she didn't stop running until she reached the Blackbird Tree.

Gus had napped, and was looking considerably better. "I'm sorry about what I said earlier, Promise, about your daddy being a halfwit. I didn't mean it, honest I didn't."

"I know. It's all right. You ready to go? It'll be dark soon."

"My legs still hurt. Let's rest awhile. We'll be home before supper. I'm not scared of the dark."

"Me neither." She sat down next to him and linked her arm around his.

"How did your mama like Molly's cooking?"

"Fine."

"Muley said I could meet them at the orchards after breakfast. I think Maum Hannah'll let me go if you don't tell her I got sick. You won't tell, will you?"

"No, I won't tell."

They sat beneath the Blackbird Tree until the conch shell blew, releasing the field hands from the day's work. Then the children set off for home.

CHAPTER 8

Summer Holiday

Throughout the late spring and summer months, the Waccamaw planters and their families left their plantations to escape the threat of malaria, leaving their slaves and rice fields in the care of overseers. They retreated with their valuables, comforts, and the majority of their house servants to the safety of Charleston mansions, or to summer homes by the ocean, and didn't return until colder weather had eliminated all danger.

The Rileys' refuge was Crestview, a brightly painted house with an excellent prospect of the water. It was located on the south end of Pawleys Island in the Atlantic, just a short half-mile rowboat ride from the eastern border of Atterley. The Rileys usually remained on the island for the first three months of the sickly season before journeying to Charleston.

It was a seaside paradise, where duty often gave way to the pursuit of pleasure. Zachary spent most of his days hunting, fishing, or horseracing with the other gentlemen in the island's summertime social club, the Waccamaw Hot and Hot Fish Club, although he routinely returned to Atterley to check up on Sir Henry.

When he was away, Gus and Promise's lessons were moved outside to the windblown piazza. Afterward, they played in the ocean while Hannah watched from the shore yelling, "Mind that splashin'," in case some stray droplets somehow found their way up her nose, and drowned her. They were allowed to stay in the water until Gus sneezed, or Molly called them in for supper, whichever came first. While they were at Crestview, Rebecca didn't fret over Gus's health, even when the sea turned his nose a dangerous shade of red, and Hannah didn't fuss over the brittle mass of tangles the saltwater made in Promise's hair.

Household tasks were left undone while Rebecca and Hannah took the children for long walks along the beach so they could dig holes to China or tunnel beneath jutting rocks in search of the remains of treasure-laden pirate ships. Promise made jangling seashell necklaces that she and Gus rattled fiercely from side to side whenever Jenny was around until she begged for one, too, and they had the satisfaction of telling her, "Not now, no way, ask again another day."

In 1838, they celebrated their eighth birthday by the sea. Gus shrieked over the shiny new rifle and speckled hunting dog his father gave him, and dashed off to harass seagulls, and Promise received a silver hairbrush from her missus that Hannah declared was much too extravagant for a little girl.

With Rebecca's father so gravely ill, the Rileys shortened their vacation at Crestview so they could extend their visit to Charleston. Zachary and Rebecca had many friends in the city whom they had last seen during Race Week in February. They were continually called upon to participate in an unending series of amusements—the first to be provided by the Charleston Jockey Club which hosted a debutante ball at Hibernian Hall.

A military parade ending with the firing of three volleys on East Battery marked the Fourth of July. In August, the Cotillion Club sponsored a play at the New Charleston Theatre. The event provided the ideal opportunity to see and be seen in the new French fashions, and the attending families identified themselves to spectators by the colors of their liveries. When the weather chilled, the Wynnewood Society held picnics around Rutledge Avenue Pond, served sassafras beer and lemonade, and took up collections to aid the poor and the orphaned. Every evening when the sky was clear, crowds walked along the Battery Promenade and gathered in the White Point Gardens to hear musicians sing and play.

Rebecca reveled in all of the excitement. She still considered Charleston her home, and while her country neighbors scrambled each year to elevate their etiquette and wardrobes to the sophisticated levels required to blend seamlessly into Charleston society, Rebecca enjoyed showing her friends how effortlessly she made the transition. She kept her invitations to the weddings, dances, and musicals in a neat stack on her bureau, with those announcing the prestigious St. Cecilia Society's formal balls on top. She spent a great deal of time fretting over her invitations, and in her happy confusion, she sought the advice of her less popular acquaintances about which she should attend, and to which she should send her regrets.

Zachary was frequently at the side of Robert Hayne, who ushered him past social barriers that money alone could not vanquish, and into Charleston's inner circles. He had no time for needless frivolity, and he attended only those gatherings that would strengthen his business ties or advance his political ambitions. Whenever he could tactfully excuse himself, he did, and journeyed back to Atterley. When he could not, he sent Majors to the country in his stead.

With her husband occupied by weightier matters, Rebecca developed a deeper relationship with her sister-in-law. Eleanor was her eldest brother's wife, and the casual friendship that had begun through dutiful letter writing had blossomed during their months in Charleston into a new level of intimacy. Through this alliance, Rebecca obtained a faithful listener and bearer of gossip, and a new and more convenient surrogate daughter in Eleanor's little girl, Georgeanna, who could accompany her into shops to be outfitted with new bonnets and miniature parasols.

As women often do when they have more time than imagination, the ladies soon set their minds to matchmaking, and they conspired together to further unite their families through their children. To achieve this objective, Rebecca often compelled Gus to accompany her on their outings. But during that summer at least, the ladies' plan bore no fruit, for Gus projected his intense dislike of formal waistcoats and tight-fitting trousers onto his cousin, for whose benefit he was being forced to wear them.

Promise always found the family's time in Charleston rather unpleasant, and that year was no different. At the Rileys' mansion on Meeting Street, there was no vast acreage to explore, only a small garden. And when Promise was sent out into the city by Hannah or Molly to run errands, there were no smiles and waves from the other Negro children as she passed by, or nods from the older "Aunties" or "Uncles" who knew she belonged to Massa Riley.

The noise and activity in Charleston's streets unnerved her. Everywhere there was rapidity and chaos. Jews, Germans, and Dutchmen owned many of the city's stores, and they stood in their doorways peddling their wares, rattling away at each other in strange tongues. Black slaves darted by her, skimming the fabric of her dress, ever watchful of white faces before disappearing into secret entrances to congregate, sell goods, and buy liquor.

Charleston's free persons of color, or "FPCs," as the city's white citizens called them, were mixed with black, white, and at times Indian blood, and were different from any freedmen Promise had ever seen. They bore little resemblance to those she had observed in the country who had no land of their own and wandered around half starved, hiring themselves out to any white man with spare change in his pockets and work to be done.

Charleston's coloreds had their own small schools where boys were apprenticed by masters, and girls learned to cook and sew. Many freedmen worked as tradesmen—tailors, bakers, and shoemakers who smiled across the counter at Promise and called her "Little Miss" when she handed them her missus's order. Their services were solicited by both white and Negro patrons, which made them prosperous enough to purchase slaves to hire out or help them in their shops.

Other coloreds, whose wealth bought them some of the respect, rights, and privileges of their white neighbors, had inherited their slaves from white fathers and freed black mothers. They excluded darker-skinned blacks from their churches and social clubs and walked the streets dressed like gentlemen and ladies.

It made Promise feel uneasy to see Negroes so content without a master to take care of them. It upset the natural order of things, and she was as eager as Gus to leave Charleston and return to Atterley—where things were as they should be.

CHAPTER 9

Hannah's Tale

A week prior to the Rileys' departure, the elder Dr. Charles Harper roused himself from his bed and surprised the Charleston community by announcing that he would host a dinner at his home to bid his daughter and son-in-law farewell. Unfortunately, sad news reached him just as his guests were preparing to begin their meal. His two youngest boys would not be coming home again.

The commander of their regiment, Colonel A. H. Brisbane, who was a personal friend of Dr. Harper's, assured him in his letter that Gilbert and Robert would have undoubtedly served their country with distinction had they lived to see battle. Sadly, they had succumbed to subtropical disease before firing a single shot.

The doctor read the message silently, and then aloud for the benefit of the entire party. Rebecca rapidly descended into hysterics. After Zachary rose to his feet to escort his wife home, Dr. Harper pressed the rest of his guests to stay. He spoke words of comfort concerning the will of God and the heavenly rest of the righteous, then asked his manservant to reheat the soup.

On the afternoon Gilbert and Robert were laid to rest, the house was filled with visitors. Rebecca retired to her room, leaving Eleanor to serve as hostess. Gus romped wildly around the house to crowd out the solemn stillness that had descended upon it, pausing only to beg his mother from the other side of her bedroom door to *"please, please, please"* let him take off his suit. Hannah took Gus by the nape of the neck and pulled him out into the garden to calm him down. Molly, with an offended snort, released Promise from spooning out the shortbread cookies so she could go, too.

It was a windy autumn afternoon. The swirling gusts took hold of the children's bodies for several blissful seconds at a time, propelling them down lanes and into flowerbeds, loosing their bodies from the ground like the season's leaves liberated from their branches. When the children had tired, they each took possession of one of Hannah's hands and walked happily alongside her as she strolled through the garden pointing out gopher holes and mounds of earth concealing nuts stored for the winter.

Hannah reached a tree that caught her fancy and sat down beneath it. Gus climbed into her lap, and Promise, jealous for her fair share of Hannah, cuddled next to her and laid her head against her shoulder.

"Will I go to heaven when I die, Maum Hannah?" Gus asked.

"Why would you ask me something like that?"

"'Cause I hear 'em talking. I see 'em lookin' at me and shaking their heads. They think I can't hear 'em, but I do. I hear 'em saying that I'm gonna die soon—that Mama better not put away her black dress."

Hannah held him close. "Those folks don't know what they're talkin' about. You're not gonna die for a long, long time."

"Then why do they say so?"

"Sometimes people say things just to say 'em. When you get as old as me you learn not to listen."

"But if I do die, will I go to heaven? I'm always being bad."

"There's no need discussing it, 'cause you're not gonna die," Hannah said.

"Well, I know *I'm* going," Promise said. "Missus says I've never given her a moment's worry."

"Do you think Uncle Gilbert and Uncle Robert are in heaven?" Gus asked.

"Only God knows, Massa Gus," Hannah said. "How 'bout a story before supper?"

Promise beamed. "Can we hear the one about the greedy bear cub that didn't listen to its mama, and got stuck up in the honey tree? I like it when she comes to get him, and he can't even move 'cause he's so filled up with the queen bee's honey—just like Gus when Molly makes her berry cobbler."

"No, this is a new one." Hannah stroked Gus's hair and cradled Promise in her arm. They pressed into her eagerly, waiting for her voice to carry them to a faraway place where anything could happen. The afternoon was cooling quickly, and a restless breeze sent the leaves into a fierce rustling. Hannah's body relaxed against the dark trunk. "This story is about a massa who owned one of the biggest, grandest plantations in the whole world," she began.

"Pa?" Gus asked.

"Of course not, silly." Promise laughed at his foolishness. "She can't be talking about Massa Riley, 'cause Lilborne is twice as big as Atterley—even though Missus says they don't harvest enough rice to pay all their bills. That brooch Mrs. Snead always wears when she comes to tea's not even real—it's only fancy-cut glass."

"Whether it's real or not is not important, Promise, and either way it's none of your business," Hannah said. "It's not nice to gossip. But you're right, this massa's not Massa Gus's daddy. This story is about another massa from a long ways away." She leaned her head back and closed her eyes. "All right now, let's see. This massa had a slave named Moses who he'd bought for a great price. Moses knew it, too, and his head and heart swelled up with pride every time he thought about how much his massa had paid for him. Everybody on Massa's plantation looked up to Moses and asked for his opinion on this or that, and they always did what he said to do.

"One day, Massa called Moses up to the main house and said, 'Moses, I'm gonna test you and see if you're really the

61

bravest, smartest, strongest nigga I've got on this plantation. I wanna see what you're really worth to me.'

"And Moses said, 'Well, Massa, I'm sure I'm the best nigga you got, and if you test me, I'll prove that's true.'

"So Massa told him, 'All right then, Moses. Come with me.'

"Massa got into his carriage and told Moses to drive until he hollered, 'Stop.' They drove on and on for a great while— until Moses couldn't make out where they were.

"Then Massa called out, 'Stop, Moses!' He made Moses get down from the carriage and said, 'If you're the bravest, smartest, strongest nigga I got, you'll get back to my plantation in three days time. If you pass my test, I'll give you a fatted hog and a mule, but if you fail, you get fifty lashes from my whip.'

"Moses wasn't a bit scared of Massa's whip—he was just thinkin' 'bout how good that hog would taste come winter, and how many crops he'd be able to plant with that mule. 'Yes suh, Massa,' he said. 'I'll be there in three days time.' Then his massa drove off.

"On the first day, Moses walked in the direction of where he guessed Massa's plantation was, and by and by he came upon a forest thick with trees. He took a deep breath and marched straight into the forest—"

"Did he have a rifle?" Gus broke in.

"No. He had nothin' besides his bare hands."

"Then why didn't he just walk *around* the forest?" Promise asked.

"No one knows for sure. Moses didn't think nothin' could harm him, most likely."

"I don't think he was so smart then," Promise concluded.

"Me neither," Gus said.

"Well, that's still left to be seen. You two want me to keep going?"

They both nodded vigorously.

"All right. So Moses marched straight into the forest and almost fell into a big hole that somebody'd tried to cover up with branches."

"Like for catchin' rabbits?" Gus asked.

"Yes, just like that. And deep inside the hole was a man who hollered up at Moses, saying, 'Hello there, brother! I'm stuck in this here hole. Can you give me a hand up?'

"'You one of Massa's niggas?' Moses asked.

"'Yes, I shole am!' the slave shouted back.

"Then Moses figured that it'd be best if he passed up that slave—just in case he was being tested by his massa, too. He wanted to make sure to be the first to get back to Massa and show him that he was the best nigga he had. So do you know what Moses did? He jumped right over that hole! Most men would've been scared to risk falling, but Moses was real brave and didn't think nothin' of it. And when he was safe on the other side, he just kept right on walkin'. He didn't look back 'til he'd made his way through the forest to the other side.

"The next day, Moses came to a big river, bigger even than the Waccamaw, and it was runnin' so fast and strong that even Moses was a little scared to set foot in it. And he had reason to be, 'cause in the middle of that river there was a man bobbing up and down in the water, lookin' like he was close to drowning. But Moses was smarter than most, and he didn't try to cross the river himself. He spotted some sturdy pieces of wood lyin' around, tied 'em together with young sapling branches, and made himself a raft to cross the river with.

"When Moses rowed up close to the drowning man, he heard him call out, 'Hello there, brother! Lift me up on your raft 'fore I'm done for!'

"'You one of Massa's niggas?' Moses asked.

"'Yes, I shole am!' the man answered back.

"But Moses went right pass him without lookin' back, 'cause he didn't wanna feel sorry for that drowning man and pick him up—especially since he wanted more than anything to be the first back to Massa's plantation. So he fixed his mind on that fatted hog, and that mule, and rowed real hard 'til he'd reached the other side."

Promise looked concerned. "Did the man drown?"

"Yes, he did. But it's just a story. In a story nobody really dies—you know that."

Gus rolled his eyes. "Don't be a baby, Promise. Go on, Maum Hannah."

"Well now, let's see. After Moses crossed the river, he walked on and on—all that day, and all that night—without hardly stopping to rest. When dawn broke, he realized he'd wandered right into the middle of a great desert that looked like it went on forever. At first he started feeling anxious, 'cause he only had one day left, but then he thought about his reward again, fixed his face like flint, and started walkin' as quick as he could across the piping hot sand.

"After awhile, Moses saw a man lying across the ground, lookin' near death. He was shriveled up almost to the bone, and his lips was cracked open. With all the strength he had left, he looked up at Moses and said, 'Hello there, brother. I've been in this desert for days now. You look like a strong nigga. Can you carry me home on your shoulders?'

"'You one of Massa's niggas?' Moses asked him.

"'Yes, I shole am,' he whispered back.

"As strong as Moses was, he might've been able to carry that man over the desert, but he didn't want anything slowin' him down, so he left him right where he was. Moses wanted more than anything to make it back to his massa's plantation by sundown and show him that he was the best nigga he got.

"At the end of the third day, lo and behold, Moses saw Massa's plantation in the distance. He let out a big sigh of relief and started runnin', 'cause he couldn't wait to hear Massa say, 'Well done'—that he had passed his test—to hear him say that he was the bravest, smartest, strongest nigga on his plantation.

"Moses saw his massa standing at the front door of the main house waitin' for him. He puffed out his chest and crowed, 'Look, Massa. I got here in three days—just like you told me. I made it through the forest, I crossed the river, and I passed over the desert. I'm the bravest, smartest, strongest nigga you got.'

"Massa was puzzled and asked Moses, 'But where my other niggas at? I already knew you was a brave, smart, and strong nigga. That's why I left you out there to fetch my other three niggas and bring 'em home.'

"After Moses told Massa that he'd left his three lost niggas out in the wilderness to die, he didn't get no fatted hog, and he didn't get no mule. Instead, Massa gave him fifty lashes to show Moses that he wasn't nearly as good as he thought he was."

Gus and Promise sighed deeply, enjoying the satisfaction that comes with a happy ending. They didn't stir from Hannah's arms until the jeweled sky, steeped in the full-bodied colors of fall, faded into the evening shadows. Then they were ready for their supper. And that night, while they slept the deep sleep of children, they dreamed vibrant dreams of heaven, and of Moses and his massa's test.

CHAPTER 10

The Promised Land

By mid-September, Atterley had turned golden, and was overflowing with the joyful abundance of harvest time. But Rebecca's mourning still left her incapacitated, and she kept to her room. She often called upon Hannah or Promise to search the house for those trinkets she couldn't properly grieve without—the gold snuff box, decorated with bits of jade, that Gilbert had given her as a wedding present; Robert's opera glasses that she had borrowed and never returned the summer her Aunt Beatrice took her on a European tour; the precious locks of golden-blond hair taken from their poor, dead bodies. And at her request, Tobias removed her brothers' portraits from the library and front hallway and positioned them in a colorful cluster opposite her bed so she could gaze at them as often as she liked, and wallow in her remembrances.

Promise steadied herself on the wobbling stool Hannah had set before a basin of water, and handed Jenny a soapy breakfast plate. "Reverend Wickerson talked real nice about Missus's brothers—about how they died serving their nation and all. I wish Missus had been there. It would've made her feel better."

"Yeah, he cried and everything," Jenny observed, in solemn awe of the reverend's talents. "It went along real well with his preaching. It made all those Scriptures come to life—

like when he talked about walking through the valley with death shadowing behind you. I told Missus about it. I hoped it would cheer her up some. It didn't seem to work though . . . but of course the reverend's got such a knack for putting things."

Juno burst into the kitchen. "Have you seen my linen sheets?" Her usually composed face was flushed. Strands of hair had escaped her tidy bun and were swaying restlessly against her back. "Missus wants them. She says those cotton ones are making her sweat, and Massa promised to come back from the fields and sit with her while she eats her dinner. She's babbling on and on about how the heat's ruining her curls when it's those crying fits that've done it. It took me nearly two hours to arrange that woman's hair." Juno wagged her finger at her daughter. "Girl, don't just stand there staring at me, *move!*"

Jenny left the kitchen in a scrambling search for the linen, and Promise slipped away after she had finished the dishes—before Hannah appeared to give her something else to do. She went looking for Gus and found him sitting in his father's study, playing with an ink blotter. "You wanna go to the lake?" she suggested.

"Yeah, I'll race you to Jesse's jasmine!" he shouted, and sprang up from the chair with Promise at his heels.

Since their return from Charleston, Gus had taken to daring her to beat him in footraces, and whether the destination was Jesse's jasmine, Jesse's roses, or Jesse's marigolds, she always triumphed. Promise wondered that he never wearied of challenging her, but on this afternoon, her victory was a narrow one. She had to leap over the last few steps to win. They ran on across the lawn, only slowing as the full impact of the day's heat enveloped their bodies.

Gus was getting stronger. Ever since his mind had wrapped around Hannah's assurances that he was not going to die, his body had begun to believe it. Fresh air, exercise, and his growing friendship with Atterley's slave boys helped, too. In exchange for his companionship, Muley had commandeered Gus's fishing tackle, his six best marbles—the deep blue ones with no chips or cracks—and his carving knife. He had even tried to take possession of Gus's birthday rifle, but although Zachary was of the general opinion that a deal was a deal, he gave his son a severe paddling for letting himself be made a fool of, and sent him to the quarters to retrieve his gun.

After Gus had won Muley over, the other boys accepted him quickly into their ranks, although they did not make allowances for his weaknesses. Gus's favorite game was Stingaree. A line was drawn in the dirt, and the initial "stinger" would stand on one side of the line and throw a ball across the line at the rest—the "ball" being made up of tightly wound lengths of string that Little Remmy had stolen from his mother's sewing box. When a boy was hit, he crossed over the line. If the ball was caught, the catcher became the next "stinger."

Gus found that his unsteady legs were frequent targets for the boys' lightning fast projectiles. At first his body ached after only a half hour of play, but he was learning to force his muscles and lungs to capacity. Yesterday, for the first time, he wasn't picked last when Muley and Andy were choosing up teams for kickball, and poor Uriah and his crooked foot regained their position of dishonor.

Gus grinned at Promise through his sweat. "I can see your underpants," he breathed. Accepting the embarrassed look on her face as his consolation prize, he smiled broadly and pointed to her dress, which was clinging tightly to her skin.

Promise reddened and tried to pull the moist dress away from her body.

"I can see your underpants," he chanted happily.

"I'm gonna tell Maum Hannah, just you wait—you'll get it!" Promise stomped her foot to let Gus know she meant business.

He sobered up quickly. "Gosh, you don't have to make such a fuss," he said, trying not to look frightened. "Just thought you'd like to know, is all." Understanding that drastic measures were required to rescue himself, Gus pulled a rock out of his pocket and held it out for Promise to see. It was a pretty pink color, and dotted with bits of quartz. "I found a bunch of 'em." He shifted the rock from side to side between his fingers so it sparkled in the sun. "It's got diamonds in it, see? Ain't it nice?"

"Ain't is not . . ." Promise began, but she stopped and allowed an appreciative sigh to escape her lips as she watched the glittering rock.

"You can have it—just don't tell Maum Hannah on me, understand?"

Promise eagerly accepted the pretty rock as payment for her injured dignity, and she put her new treasure securely in the side of her shoe.

"That's the only one you're gonna get, though," Gus cautioned her. "I'm gonna be a famous explorer and I gotta save the rest to pay for my trips around the world. I left a few on Pa's desk. He can give 'em to Mr. Majors to sell in Charleston. Maybe they're worth more than the whole rice harvest," he said, imagining himself arriving home to a hero's welcome, with Muley following along behind, carrying bundles of glistening pink riches.

Promise's eyes shone. "Maybe Missus will take mine in exchange for an ermine muff—just like they wear to the theater. Where'd you find 'em?"

"I'm not telling you where. That's for me to know, and you never to find out," Gus said, glad that he'd covered up the hole he'd dug behind the barn with some strategically placed pieces of wood. "Don't you worry, though. I'll scout out enough to make sure you're looked after."

They walked past the highlands, where the slaves grew corn, Irish and sweet potatoes, peas, beans, and other provision crops—with Gus bragging all the while about all that he would do with his prospective fortune. By the time they'd reached the edge of the rice fields, Gus's riches had built Promise her own private castle on Sullivan's Island with plenty of room for Muley, his mother, and Hannah, and a window in the tower so Promise could let down her hair like Rapunzel. And he was the proud owner of an imaginary pack of hunting dogs and a stable full of racehorses that Promise could ride whenever she felt like it.

The children's pace slowed when they reached the lowlands, where there were no trees nearby to catch and carry the wind. The rice fields baked beneath the sun. Its rays reflected off the ground and rose, liquefying the surrounding air. Promise strained to see her mother among the multitude of bodies. The forms quivered in the sun, distorted by the heat.

She spotted her at last, a small speck of white in the middle of the wavering outlines of brown and black. Promise could barely make out the cloth that bridled her mother's hair and sweat, a dark blue dot bobbing up and down over stalks, moving in rhythmic conjunction with the slaves' voices as they sliced down the shoulder-high rice plants with their sickles. Their melody traveled rich and clear through the sweltering sky:

> *Someone stole de fishin' boat from Massa's pond,*
> *Someone stole de fishin' boat from Massa's pond,*
> *Oh, someone stole de fishin' boat from Massa's pond . . .*
> *He look around fuh Johnny, but he good an' gone.*
>
> *Massa had a rooster wid a bright red comb,*
> *Massa had a rooster wid a bright red comb,*
> *Oh, Massa had a rooster wid a bright red comb . . .*
> *Ole Johnny stole dat rooster, an' he took it home.*
>
> *Massa had a bloodhound wid a right sharp nose,*
> *Massa had a bloodhound wid a right sharp nose,*
> *Oh, Massa had a bloodhound wid a right sharp nose . . .*
> *Ole Johnny lef it outside, an' dat bloodhound froze.*
>
> *Massa gots no rooster, didn't hear no sound,*
> *Massa gots no hound fuh huntin' niggas down.*
> *Someone stole de fishin' boat from Massa's pond . . .*
> *He look around fuh Johnny, but he good an' gone!*

It was backbreaking work. Once they finished cutting down a row of plants, the slaves were allowed to take long draughts from the barrels of water at the edges of the fields to extinguish the fire in their bodies. They could tell the time within ten minutes by the position of the sun, and they kept a close watch on the sky, eager for the moment when they could gather around the barrels and eat their afternoon meal of fried fish and cornbread.

Zachary and Atterley's head driver, Sir Henry, were watching them from a small hill that gave them a full view of the fields. They were deep in conversation, pausing from time to time so Sir Henry could let out a shout if any slave lingered too long over the water. Sir Henry's under-drivers, Tucker and Amos, first warned any slow hands, and then if given the signal, would strike the slave with their whips. Whenever Sir Henry's back was turned, however, they prodded idle workers along in low voices that escaped his notice, and they always wielded their whips lightly. When a slave was sick or injured, Tucker and Amos would assign them simple tasks until they were healed.

But there was no reasoning with Sir Henry, and he had never been known to extend mercy. He would've preferred to mete out all of the punishments himself, but he swung his whip with such force that its handle ate through his skin. So more often than he would've liked, Sir Henry was forced to delegate this duty to others until his seeping palms hardened again.

Gus and Promise heard the quick pounding of a dozen bare feet coming down the path. Promise, startled by the commotion, sought shelter behind a nearby tree, but Gus turned to greet the shrieking swarm of slave boys as they barreled toward them, kicking up dust. They were dressed in short pants and loose, cotton shirts that billowed about their bodies like the airy wings of birds. Gus envied their careless freedom, although he had no reason to. In a few short years, the objects of his jealousy would be snared, their wings clipped, and their liberty taken away forever.

For now, the boys were allowed to roam wherever they pleased, and they were in the middle of a game of Limpin' Larry. It was a rousing game where the designated "Larry," who was at present Molly's nine-year-old boy, Red, jolted after the others on an exaggerated, make-believe bad leg until he reached a victim and passed the affliction along.

"I'm comin' for ya, Andy!" Red shouted. "Just like you did me the other day! I'll teach ya!" But Andy was too quick for him. He dodged and ducked just out of Red's reach, until finally, he gave up. Surrendering to practicality, Red lunged at Jonah, who'd been careless enough to get too close. Since the rules of the game prohibited Jonah from making him the next "Larry," Red took a moment to catch his breath while Jonah limped crazily after the rest.

Gus jumped eagerly into the fray.

"Block me, Gus!" Harold squealed, grabbing him by the shoulders and using his body as a shield.

Gus spread his arms wide and shifted from side to side to protect his charge from Jonah's thrusting hands. "You just keep in back of me, Harold."

"You can't catch me, boy," Harold taunted from behind Gus's back.

Jonah went in search of easier prey and grasped at Little Remmy. "I gotcha!"

"You was runnin' full out!" Little Remmy screamed.

"Naw I wasn't! You been got—fair n' square!" Jonah hollered back.

"Since nobody knows for sure, why don't we go on and make Uriah the Larry?" Little Remmy suggested diplomatically. "He's limpin' anyways, ain't he?"

"I ain't gonna be no Larry!" Uriah cried. "I've already been it today and that was the last time I'm gonna be it, too, you just watch!" He hopped around angrily on his good foot. "Just 'cause you's a circle nigga, don't mean you can boss me. 'Sides, I seen Jonah catch you. You's the Larry, L'il Remmy. Ain't no use tryin' to push it off on me!"

"What do *you* say about it, Prince?" Little Remmy asked.

"You're right about it, Remmy. Jonah was runnin' full out."

"That don't mean nothin'," Jonah protested. "You's brothers, so Prince's say don't count no ways."

Muley stepped between them. "We don't got all day. Let Gus decide."

"I catched him—didn't I, Gus?" Jonah demanded.

Gus nodded. "Yeah, you're the Larry, L'il Remmy."

Billy, a fair-skinned boy whose face always began peeling at the end of summer, liberated a thin flake from the tip of his nose. "Wanna come play with us, Gus?" he asked, watching the flake float into the bushes as he released it.

Promise gave Gus a hard look that hollered, "No."

"Yeah, I'm comin'."

"L'il Remmy, you wait 'til we get to that tree there 'fore you start," Muley said. The boys stood beneath the designated tree, daring and double-dog daring Little Remmy to catch them, their bodies poised in a tense state of readiness.

Little Remmy delayed his chase long enough to admire Promise's sweat-soaked dress. "That *sure* is a nice dress, Promise," he said.

The compliment and the strange sparkle in Little Remmy's eyes alarmed her. She stared at the ground in a near panic, wishing him away.

"Come on, L'il Remmy! Whatcha waitin' for?" Gus yelled. Little Remmy gave Promise's dress one last look, and then limped after the others in furious pursuit.

Promise walked on alone past the pastureland and watched the livestock grazing on the seemingly endless acres. She wished her missus would hurry up and feel better so their lessons could resume, and she could have Gus to herself again. As she neared the lake, the grass became moist, dampening her shoes.

The lake was the most beautiful part of Atterley, a lush paradise one hundred yards from the river. Zachary had named it the Promised Land. The water was a clear and uncompromising blue. Small snakes, glowing green, and moist frogs skirted in and out of the lush plants growing along the shore.

Once the workweek was finished on Saturday afternoon, it was hard to find an unoccupied spot along the banks. Men in rolled-up cotton pants and women with their skirts tied in tight knots talked and laughed with their neighbors as they waited in the cool water for the first promising jerk of a fat catfish or pike on the other end of their lines. The children splashed each other and played water games until they were sent to the coast in search of crabs, clams, and shrimp. The woods surrounding the Promised Land were full of ducks, rabbits, deer, and wild turkeys. On Sundays, families laid out blankets and ate early suppers of ash-cooked potatoes; collard greens; griddlecakes; and chicken that had been dipped in flour, simmered in ham-gravy, and fried until golden brown.

Atterley's orchards, a dense ring of peach, pear, and apple trees, bordered the lake. The slaves who had died building Atterley were buried there, providing the trees' roots with a nutrient-rich foundation. Their branches were so heavy with bounty that they groaned under the weight, almost skimming the water. But the orchards' offerings were not fit for humans to eat. Although the fruit looked appetizing, large and firm with vibrant skin, the peaches were bitter, the pears bland, and the apples mealy. Even Jesse could not cajole goodness from that earth, and Molly refused to use any of the fruit for her pies or preserves.

Gus rejoined Promise as she was returning to the main house that afternoon. The heat had made the house's occupants sluggish, and all was quiet when they entered the kitchen. Promise tiptoed towards the stove in search of leftovers, and Gus, puzzled that the house was not buzzing with excitement over the discovery of his rocks, went to his father's study. He peeked inside, and was surprised to see him engaged in a calm discussion with Sir Henry.

"Henry, I want that rice on flats and at my mill by next week, period. No more excuses."

"Yes suh, Massa."

"Majors tells me that Davis's rice has already arrived in Charleston for threshing, so why is it that mine hasn't even left Atterley?"

"Well suh, Massa, they don't have near as much rice as they did last year, not near as much as we gots, no ways." Sir Henry's voice shook. "And I sent Tucker over there after they's rice was all loaded up, to gather some stray stalks. We took off the husks, and that rice was mighty poor qual'ty, mighty poor . . . nothin' like yours, Massa."

"Good." Zachary noticed Gus in the doorway. "Did you want something, boy?"

"No sir," Gus answered, beginning to suspect that someone had stolen into his father's study and carried away his treasure. "I was just wonderin' if you seen my rocks."

"Did you leave those things on my desk? Get in here!"

Gus moved reluctantly into the room.

"How many times do I have to tell you not to come in here when I'm not home? Now I know how that ink got on my papers, you little rascal." Zachary laughed loudly. He was in a good mood. Despite his harsh questioning of Sir Henry, he was quite pleased with the rice crop. "Never mind, look at you. Full of dirt like a boy should be. Henry, you know when I was young, my brothers and I would come home looking just like that many a night—with more dirt on us than we'd left outside. We would've slept out there if Mother had let us."

"My rocks . . ." Gus looked stricken. "What did you do with my rocks?"

"Let's see now. Oh yes, I had Juno throw them out when she cleaned up in here." Zachary puffed happily on his cigar. "Since you like digging 'em up so much, I'll tell you what. I'm gonna send you out to the highland. The ground there's full of 'em, and Amos tells me they're strangling my sweet potatoes." Zachary aimed his smoke at Sir Henry and howled as it formed a perfect ring around his driver's nose.

CHAPTER 11

Preacherman's Service

After three years of unfettered abandon alongside Atterley's slave boys, all traces of infirmity had disappeared from Gus's body. Rebecca rejoiced at the improvement in her son's health, but she despaired over the primitive nature of his companions. She determined that since Gus was no longer in danger of dying, he should begin attending weekly Sunday services at Christ Saints Church before he descended any further into barbarism.

Rebecca chose the Sunday of Preacherman's funeral for her son's induction into civilized society. Preacherman had presided over Atterley's chapel for as long as anyone could remember. White folks used his given name, Jeremiah, but their slaves, who had little use for such formalities when they came to him sick and wearied in body and spirit, called him Preacherman. He was already old when Zachary first brought him to South Carolina, and by the end of his life, Preacherman had shriveled into an ancient gnome with the power of God in his trembling fingertips.

Reverend Wickerson visited each of the Low Country plantations in a rigid rotation and held services at Atterley on the first Wednesday of the month; but on Saturday nights and Sunday mornings, slaves came from miles away to squeeze into the plantation's small chapel and witness Preacherman call fire down from heaven. Although the neighboring planters did not know or care how his miracle-working was managed, they often sent their slaves to Preacherman when they were ailing, bearing pudding and butter-cake offerings. After he died, with his eyes open toward heaven, the plantation owners asked Reverend Wickerson to honor Preacherman's good works by holding his funeral at Christ Saints and allowing their slaves to attend the service.

For Promise, the day of Preacherman's funeral was a mighty glad day. She was finally going to get to go to the pretty white folks' church where God lived. Well, not God *exactly*, but the next best thing. It was the home of the good Reverend Wickerson. She wanted to sit on the blue velvet pews her missus had told her about and hear the ringing of the steeple's big brass bell her massa said he had paid a pretty penny for.

Promise didn't believe God ever visited Atterley's tiny chapel where you had to be careful not to step on the loose plank by the door, and the cracks in the walls let heat inside during the summer and blasting wind in winter. And she saw nothing holy about Preacherman's services—with all the shouting and dancing, jittering and jerking, and cries of desperation for God to "come by here, Lord, come by here." She much preferred Reverend Wickerson's visits, where he served communion and preached inspirational sermons about their heavenly reward, and his wife fluttered her vanilla-scented handkerchief and handed out testaments to any slave who agreed to be baptized.

Hannah was the only one from the main house who regularly went to the quarters to listen to Preacherman, and Promise fought and cried whenever she attempted to bring her along. The field slaves seemed very strange to her, and she wanted nothing to do with any of them besides her mother. The men were a great deal different from her massa, whose stature proved he was a man, for their worth was etched in muscle and grit. Nor could she appreciate the fierce allure of the slave women, which was so unlike her missus's unspoiled beauty, because theirs had been refined by fire.

"Augustus, please hurry and eat so you'll have time to wash up," Rebecca said, wishing her husband would lower his paper a moment and notice her new, scandalously sheer dressing gown.

Gus looked up at his mother, horrified. He faced the day with much less enthusiasm than Promise did, and his mind was filled with evil thoughts unsuitable for a Sunday morning. Not only was he being forced to waste away the whole day at church, but he also had to endure an extra bath!

Usually on Sunday mornings, with Hannah off to see Preacherman and his parents gone to Christ Saints, he and Promise were left in Molly's care. After their carriage passed through the front gates, Molly would spirit one of the field hands inside the back door. Soon a tantalizing bouquet of ham, eggs, pancakes, and buttery biscuits would drift down the hallway and infuse the atmosphere of the library. The fragrance would be accompanied by Molly's giggles, and the raspy whispers of a grateful man who had not had such a good meal in a long while. Afterward, Molly would bring him out to her house so he could thank her properly.

Left to themselves, all sorts of mischief was possible— although Promise was always too scared to do anything daring. Gus made good use of their time alone, however, and regularly prowled through his father's desk looking for change and bits of stray tobacco, or peeked inside his mother's dresser drawers to ogle at her unmentionables.

From time to time, Molly would come back inside to check on them, her moist thighs slapping together gently as she shuffled down the hallway, providing ample warning of her approach. "Y'all look alright enough in here," she would breathe, as she loomed over them with glittering, glassy eyes. Then she would retreat from the room with her back away from them, so they wouldn't see the hooks on her dress undone and her fleshy back exposed.

But from now on, things would be different. Gus peered past the table's centerpiece, filled with a collection of Jesse's yellow buttercups, so he could have a clear view of Promise eating in the kitchen. She was already dressed in her best white dress and was keeping a careful eye on her fork as she navigated it toward her mouth. Her happiness irritated him, and Gus wished he could give her a good, hard pinch. Thinking bad thoughts made him feel better, and since Hannah was not about, he decided to completely relieve himself of his misery by muttering under his breath all of the bad words that Muley had so graciously taught him over the years. It was unfortunate for him that his parents overhead.

Rebecca was shocked. "Augustus Judson Riley!"

Zachary set his paper down with a sigh and came toward his son. He grabbed hold of Gus's neck, pressed his cheek against the table until his breakfast burned into his chest, and dealt him a series of powerful blows on his backside. Then he sat him down hard in his seat. "What in God's name are you teaching him, Rebecca?"

"I have no idea where he could've learned such filthy language, darling."

"You know where he learned it, and so do I. If you'd make him play with Mason's or Davis's boys instead of letting him run wild with my niggers, he'd know how to act in front of decent people."

"But the children won't play with him, Zachary. I'm afraid they think he's rather odd. Dolly had to practically *force* William to invite him over, as a special favor to me. Her son seems to be a sort of leader among the boys—and Augustus came home just *full* of bruises."

"Well dammit, he *is* odd. There's no way around that, and all I want to know is how the hell do we fix him?"

"Darling, please. Remember this is the Lord's day. You're making him cry."

"Stop it, Augustus. You're too old for that," Zachary said. "It's all over now. *Stop crying.*" He was gravely disappointed with how Gus was turning out. To make matters worse, he was beginning to doubt whether Rebecca would ever get pregnant again, and his son was a pretty feeble basket to put all of his eggs in. Gus continued to weep, and Zachary pushed away his breakfast in disgust before leaving the table in search of Juno and a clean shirt.

Rebecca brushed Gus's clothes with her handkerchief, and warm clumps of eggs and hominy fell onto the floor. "Don't cry, dear. You know how much it upsets your father. You're going to have a nice, warm bath, and then you'll feel all better. And I know you'll be on your best behavior today." Then remembering the time, she kissed his cheek hurriedly, gulped the last bit of her coffee, and rushed upstairs to finish getting dressed.

Gus's sobs brought Promise from the kitchen. She sat down next to him, dunked a piece of table linen into a glass of water, and wiped away the food still clinging to his clothes.

"It burns," he remarked sadly, lifting up his shirt so Promise could see the pink circle covering his stomach.

She gave the napkin another soaking and pressed it gently against his skin. "Does that feel better?"

Gus shivered. "Yeah. I wish we could stay here. Why do you wanna go to that stupid old church anyway?"

"I just do, that's all," Promise said, giving the linen a good, hard squeeze. The cool water ran over his belly and soaked the front of his pants.

Gus looked down. "Dang it, Promise, look what you did. Pa better not see me. He'll think I wet myself and I'll get it again."

"Sorry. Church won't be so bad, Gus, I promise. I'll sit next to you in service and keep you company if you want."

"Yeah?"

"Uh-huh. Me and Maum Hannah'll sit right by you and Missus."

"Humph," Hannah grunted as she stood over them, frowning at the puddle of water on the floor. "Looks like you've already had your bath, Massa Gus. Lassie! Liza! Come in here!"

The twins thundered into the room. Lassie and Eliza had left their little-girl sweetness far behind and had become ten-year-old nightmares—ornery and mean as the dickens.

"You two clear off this table," Hannah said.

"But we were hangin' laundry," Eliza protested.

"Yeah. Why don't you make Promise do it?" Lassie pointed at her. "You and Missus don't ever make *her* do nothin'," she said, cocking her head back.

"Promise is going to church, and besides, the laundry would've already been done if you two hadn't spent the whole morning bickering."

"But I'm missing my new scarf," Lassie complained. "Quinny bought me that scarf 'cause I'm the prettiest girl on Atterley, *including* Liza, and that's why she took it and won't give it back."

"I didn't take it, and you better stop lying on me, or I'll make you eat those words," Eliza threatened. "I already told you—I saw one of Massa's dogs runnin' around with your ratty old scarf."

"And just how would one of Massa's dogs get hold of my scarf?" Lassie asked, her eyes narrowing.

"I wouldn't know," her sister smirked. "The same way they got the hat that Missus gave me 'cause I did such a good job on the silver."

Hannah grabbed hold of Gus's arm. "I don't care who's got what. This room better be clean by the time I come back downstairs, or you're both gonna get a taste of my switch."

Hannah fixed Gus's bath and sat outside the door while he undressed. She hummed to herself as he settled into the water.

"Do you like church?" Gus asked her through the door.

"Well now, sometimes I like it real fine. You in yet?"

"Yeah."

She came into the room and poured a stream of water over his back. "Reverend Wickerson's job is to make all the stories that Missus reads you outta the Bible easy to understand. Most say he does a good job of it."

"Like David fighting Goliath, and Daniel gettin' thrown into the lion's den?" Gus asked.

"Maybe so." Hannah sat down by the tub so she could observe his progress. "Mind you, wash those ears good now."

Hannah had a way of making him want to cooperate, and Gus decided to work himself into a good mood, giving his neck and ears a good soaping. "If he preaches about David, or the fiery furnace, or puts a war or two in his sermon, then I guess church won't be so bad."

"That ain't all there is to God, Massa Gus. Reverend Wickerson is probably gonna talk about Jesus, and the cross, and . . ."

"But that's not even the *good* stuff," Gus grumbled. It was all he could do to stay awake whenever his mother read from the family Bible. She always skipped past the exciting tales at the beginning and flipped to the back where there were no more floods, giants, or stories about men and women "knowing" each other that made her stutter and turn red.

Hannah smiled. She had been around Gus's age when God had stepped out of the pages of the written Word and made himself real to her. At twelve, she had been snatched out of her bed in the dead of night by a man smelling of stale whiskey, and dragged by her ankles into the bitterly cold night air. The sound of her body clawing the floor startled her mother out of a restless sleep, but before she realized what was happening, Hannah had been pushed into the back of a waiting wagon. At first her mother's cries filled the air, but they grew fainter as the wagon rolled on, until finally the night was still.

It was then that Hannah faced the frightening realization that for the first time in her life, she was alone in the world. Had not fetters securely fastened her to the side of the wagon, she would have thrown herself beneath its wooden wheels. She neither knew nor cared how long her journey would last, or what would be her eventual destination.

Before that night, God had always belonged to her mother, who asked him to "keep her blood down" when Hannah was being bad, or to her little sisters, who sang "Yes, Jesus Loves Me," and still believed in Santa Claus—who was really her big, fat massa dressed up in red flannel. But as Hannah lay beneath the sky that night and looked beyond the stars, God became hers because she had nothing else to hold onto.

It was nearly dawn when she'd been thrust in front of her new owner, Dr. Charles Harper. She stood before him, cowering, covered with dirt, her thick braids stubbornly pointing in all directions. Dr. Harper, after appraising her appearance, bitterly regretted that he had not been able to make the selection himself. But the deed was done, and the doctor was not entirely displeased with the situation. Hannah's master owed him a substantial sum for gambling debts, and he needed a nursemaid for his newborn. A young girl Hannah's age was considered by both sides to be an even exchange, and the matter was resolved to the satisfaction of both parties. Hannah poured all of her love into baby Rebecca to fight off the loneliness, and over time it had helped mend her broken heart.

As she watched Gus bathe, Hannah' humming amplified. The vibrating rhythm filled her chest and throat until it overflowed, and she began singing in a rich, full alto:

> *Jesus, free us from our captors,*
> *Jesus, free us from our captors,*
> *Jesus, free us from our captors,*
> *Lord, set your people free.*
>
> *We'll be safe from Pharaoh's army,*
> *We'll be safe from Pharaoh's army,*
> *We'll be safe from Pharaoh's army,*
> *Lord, set your people free.*
>
> *There's a land of milk and honey,*
> *There's a land of milk and honey,*
> *There's a land of milk and honey,*
> *Lord, set your people free.*

Gus leaned back against the rim of the tub and watched her as she sang. "They gonna sing songs like that in church, Maum Hannah?"

"No, not likely," she laughed. "They don't have any songs like that in your mama's church." Gus's face fell as Hannah handed him a towel. "But there will be a lot of people dressed up real nice. I bet it makes God happy to see his people dressed so fine. It looks like you did a good job. You can get out now."

Gus eyed the church clothes laid out on his bed, and decided that he didn't care a whit about making God happy if it meant he had to put on a suit. With a heavy heart, he got out of the tub.

CHAPTER 12

Lift Every Voice and Sing

Lift every voice and sing 'til earth and heaven ring,
Ring with the harmonies of Liberty.

Atterley's slave families trickled out of the quarters, forming a widening pool as they spilled out onto the road for the hour-long walk to the church. Promise was anxious to be off. Jesse cradled her right hand and Hannah her left.

Her parents were not there. While Abraham still had the pliability of youth, Zachary's father had encouraged him to become baptized, hoping that religion would quash any savage inclinations that lay dormant beneath a civilized surface. But Abraham had refused, and did not waiver in this resolve, despite Mr. Riley's threats or promised rewards. Abraham rejected the existence of any god—the white man's as well as his own. He despised the first, for he believed only an evil creator could have produced such wicked children, and he disdained the impotence of the second. After many unanswered prayers, he had concluded that Allah was unable to prevent the capture and enslavement of those who served him.

And Cora was a conjurer who long ago had given herself over to black magic. Her handiwork could be found from time to time on the grounds—strange circles in the dust, snake skins, black chickens mutilated and drained of blood. The slaves came to her, shamefaced, for spells and healing potions when Preacherman could not or would not help them. Cora's descent into madness had begun innocently enough—the day she went to one of the Ma'Deahs to make her husband love her.

When Zachary had decided that it was time for Abraham to have a woman of his own, he had chosen Cora to be his bride. It was not uncommon for slaves to look more like their masters than the race to which they were assigned, and Zachary knew that Abraham and Cora's marriage would irrevocably establish her as a Negro. He expected his blacksmith to be pleased with his choice, but Abraham did not place the same value on fair skin as his master, and he refused to touch her until the day Cora sold her soul to the devil. After that day, he had stopped sleeping on the floor and joined her in their marriage bed.

Cora rejoiced, believing that she had found true love at last—until she discovered that Abraham's attentions always faded into indifference without steady doses of witchcraft.

It was a hushed pilgrimage as the slaves journeyed to pay their respects to Preacherman. From time to time, groups joined them from other plantations, and the happy sounds of reunion rippled through the multitude, masking the heaviness. Only Promise was continually jubilant. When she could see the church at last, glowing brightly between the trees, her heart began to race. Its large doors were opened wide in welcome. Reverend Wickerson stood on the front steps shaking the hands of his arriving congregation and extending to them a hearty good morning.

Hannah and Jesse followed the others to the rear of the church. "Why are we going through the back, Maum Hannah?" Promise asked, craning her neck behind her. "I wanna go through the *big* doors."

"Hush, girl." Hannah's firm hand grasped her shoulder, guiding her inside.

The Rileys' seats were at the front of the church, and Gus was peering over the back of the pew, watching the slaves scrape the mud off their shoes before coming inside. "There they are, Mama," he cried, waving frantically. "Look, right over there."

"I see them," Rebecca said, yanking the back of his coat. "Please sit down."

Promise waved back. "We have to sit by Gus and Missus, Maum Hannah. I promised him."

Jesse held her fast. "Come on, Missy, we's gonna sit in the balcony with the rest."

"But there's empty seats up there by Gus and Missus," Promise insisted.

"Those seats aren't for us, child. Come on now," Hannah said, guiding her up the rickety stairs leading to the balcony.

"Mama, I wanna sit back there with Maum Hannah," Gus demanded.

"Shh," Rebecca hissed. With her son dangerously near hysterics, she looked to Zachary. He grunted, releasing her to take Gus to the back of the church and up the stairs, joining the other white children already dotting the balcony who had also elected to sit with their mammies.

"When's it gonna be over, Maum Hannah?" he asked, as soon as Rebecca had deposited him with a sigh at Promise's side.

"You don't worry 'bout when it's gonna be over. Just sit still and mind your manners like Promise."

Promise wasn't so disappointed with the seating when she realized that it provided her with an excellent view of the church, and she marveled in awed silence at the splendor surrounding her. The pulpit towered over Preacherman's wooden coffin. An intricately carved crucifix graced its front, and behind it was a row of high-backed chairs reserved for visiting dignitaries. A stained glass window, depicting Jesus looking wonderfully ethereal in all of His resurrected glory, served as a backdrop for the grand piano. On either side of the window were the Lord's Prayer and the Ten Commandments etched in gold lettering on mahogany tablets. The sides of the arched roof sloped impressively upwards, and although Promise's seat was high above the pews, the ceiling's peak still loomed far above her.

The parishioners below stirred restlessly as they waited for the reverend to take his place at the front of the church. Mrs.

Wickerson read the morning's announcements. The Ladies Sewing Circle was hosting a picnic, and they were soliciting help with the pie baking. Mr. Vernon Stanton wanted to sell some of his mares, and an auction was being held on Helmsley on Tuesday next. Mr. John Mason's runaway Negro, Jefferson, was found and returned, and Mr. Mason was offering his thanks to all those in the congregation who aided in the search. This sort of business was discussed for some minutes before Reverend Wickerson entered in dramatic fashion and took his place behind the pulpit.

"Jeremiah was a fine man, a good man," he began.

There was an enthusiastic succession of "amens" and "uh-hums" from the balcony, and the slaves began a gentle swaying.

"He elevated beyond the natural limitations of his complexion to serve as an example to the rest of his race through his steadfast godliness and divine humility. He partnered with myself, and the fine gentlemen present this morning, by lifting the spirits of their Negroes, healing their bodies, and guiding them toward their heavenly home—where I know he now resides. So let us bow our heads in prayer to commemorate the home-going of our dear friend and brother in Christ."

The congregation lowered their heads obediently. After Reverend Wickerson had finished praying, there was another chorus of "amens."

"Brothers and sisters," he said when they had raised their eyes again, "some information has come to my attention recently that has caused me a great deal of concern. I've been told that there is wickedness in our midst that is viler than the fornicator, more insidious than the thief, and more dangerous than swamp fever. It is an evil that threatens to undermine not only the ideals of our community, but also the life's work of the fine man who will be laid to rest this afternoon."

The good Reverend Wickerson paused to allow the church to let out a collective gasp. Promise shuddered and clung to Hannah.

After a sufficient intermission, he continued. "Mr. Melvin Hall, one of the fine editors of the *Georgetown Review,* has informed me that just yesterday afternoon an anonymous article was submitted to him asserting that the institution of slavery was incompatible with Christian living; that our Negroes would be well within their rights to take advantage of their superiority of numbers and overthrow the authority of their masters."

There was a flurry of inflamed whispers from the congregation.

"Fortunately, Mr. Hall is a godly man, and refused to print it. However, since no one would dare state such views publicly, we do not know how widely such abhorrent beliefs are held. Mr. Hall told me that the style and penmanship of the writing indicates that its author is most likely a gentleman. In fact, I am convinced that he is sitting in this church at this very moment."

The parishioners surveyed each other, their eyes dripping with suspicion.

"For this reason, I will use my time with you today to discuss the issue of slavery. At first, I was simply going to remind you that it is the Lord who commands that servants obey their masters as unto Him, but upon further reflection, I believe that an in-depth analysis of the matter is warranted. My sermon this morning is entitled, 'The Nature of the Negro.'"

The reverend put on his reading glasses. "Please open your Bibles to the book of Genesis, chapter nine, and follow along as I read verses twenty-two through twenty-seven." He waited patiently while his flock found the passage and continued when the rustling of pages had stopped.

"And Ham, the father of Canaan, saw the nakedness of his father, and told his two brethren without. And Shem and Japheth took a garment, and laid it upon both their shoulders, and went backward, and covered the nakedness of their father; and their faces were backward, and they saw not their father's nakedness. And Noah awoke from his wine, and knew what his younger son had done unto him. And he said, Cursed be Canaan; a servant of servants shall he be unto his brethren. And he said, Blessed be the Lord God of Shem; and Canaan shall be his servant. God shall enlarge Japheth, and he shall dwell in the tents of Shem; and Canaan shall be his servant."

The reverend drained the water from his goblet and motioned to his wife to refill it. "The descendants of three men—Shem, Japheth, and Ham—have populated the earth. The Negro, as you know, is the descendant of Ham, and as such, he is cursed to be the slave of his brothers until the end of time. To oppose this natural order is to oppose God."

There was hearty approval from Reverend Wickerson's white parishioners and halfhearted murmuring from their slaves.

"Now turn to Genesis, chapter one, verse twenty-six. 'And God said, Let us make man in our image, after our likeness: and let them have dominion over the fish of the sea, and over the fowl of the air, and over the cattle, and over all the earth, and over every creeping thing that creepeth upon the earth.'"

Reverend Wickerson looked over his glasses at his audience. "After Ham sinned against his father, Noah, he migrated to Africa, and his descendants became a mongrel race by mating with animals. In Africa, the Negro lived like an animal for generations, creeping about on all fours, devouring his brothers' flesh like the other beasts of the field. That is why God sent the white man to dark Africa—to rescue the Negro from himself.

"Today the Negro may best be described as a member of the ape family, and so he is what God refers to here in His word as a 'creeping thing,' over which the white man, who has remained a pure reflection of God's divine image, is to have dominion. If you doubt the Negro's true nature, you have only to look at the lifestyle of the native African to witness evidence of his barbarism. It is only the remnants of his righteous origin that allow the Negro to walk about on two legs, to speak our language, and to reason—although he does so on only the basest level."

It was some minutes before Promise understood the full implications of Reverend Wickerson's statements, and when she did, her breath was stolen from her chest and her vision blurred. The truth had been revealed. No wonder Atterley's slaves did not know how to properly worship Him. He was not their God. They could receive His salvation, but they had no claim on His love—that was reserved for the white man alone. She looked to Hannah. Hannah's eyes were closed, and her lips were pressed together, forming a hard, firm line.

Gus's breathing had softened, and his chin rested gently on his chest. Drops of saliva drizzled lazily onto his new suit, and a thin coating of sweat sat undisturbed on his upper lip. He was mildly aware of a stifling heat trapped beneath the starched collar of his shirt.

"Observe, the white man and the Negro are opposites in all things," the reverend continued. "Just as darkness is to light, and sin is to redemption. That is why the Lord has charged the honorable men and women of the South with the duty of caring for these unfortunate beings, just as Adam was given charge over the animals."

There were nods of vigorous assent from the pews.

Reverend Wickerson pounded his pulpit. "Northern abolitionists, and those among us who sympathize with their cause, have forsaken this most sacred charge. If we allow them to have their way—if we do not hold fast to the teachings of our Lord and Savior Jesus Christ—then the Negro will rise up and begin to consider himself our equal. With his animal instincts unfettered, he will come into your homes at night, he will slit your throats, he will defile the pristine virtue of your daughters—creating yet another mongrel race that is neither man nor beast!"

Fear coursed through his audience as they contemplated the horrific possibilities. Hannah hummed softly and caressed Promise's trembling hand with her fingers.

The reverend removed his glasses and wiped a handkerchief across the back of his neck. "Brothers and sisters, care for your slaves as you should. Feed them. Clothe them.

See after the salvation of their souls. But be stern with them. Chastise them. Instill the fear of God into their dark hearts, so they will not be led astray by evil outside influences."

While the reverend preached, Gus's dreams carried him back to that morning. He felt the soothing stream of water from Hannah's pitcher splashing about his shoulders, cooling the hot ring around his collar. He smiled in his sleep, and with Hannah's voice echoing in his head, he began to sing . . .

"We must find and expose all agitators," Reverend Wickerson thundered. "And we must do so without any—" He paused as a small voice drifted from the balcony, rising gently until it reached the beautifully arched roof, where it amplified and descended upon the churchgoers below.

"Jesus, free us from our captors, Jesus, free us from our captors, Jesus, free us from our captors, Lord, set your people freeeeee!"

Gus was startled awake when Hannah reached around Promise and smacked him on the side of his head. He looked about him, sleepily, wondering at all the black faces grinning down at him from above, and the rows of mortified white faces staring up at him from below.

CHAPTER 13

Penance

The good Reverend Wickerson had been a top graduate of one of South Carolina's finest seminaries, so he could usually be depended upon to say something clever in any unexpected situation, but when Gus burst into song, he stared helplessly at his audience, struggled in vain to collect his thoughts, and then sputtered into an embarrassed silence.

The reverend's congregation gaped from him, to Gus's frightened face in the balcony, and then burst into a flurry of excited whispers.

"Disgraceful. Absolutely *disgraceful.*"

"Was that *Riley's* boy?"

"Makes you wonder what's been talked about in *that* house."

"I know the fault cannot be Rebecca's. She runs a Christian home. My husband's people live near hers in Charleston. Excellent family."

"And Riley's honor is above question. I bought some livestock from him. He always gives me a good, honest price."

"Some children are just born with a touch of the devil in them."

"It's too bad they only managed to have one."

"My, yes."

"I've seen him many times running around with a troop of darkies. They were making all kinds of racket, and he was acting just like one of them . . ."

The chatter continued along this line for some time, until Mrs. Wickerson rescued her husband by striking a rousing chord on the piano, signaling the congregation to stand and open their hymnbooks. Rebecca's face was hot. Zachary furrowed his brows and wondered how much it would cost him to get back into the reverend's good graces. Both were grateful that their seats at the front of the church shielded them from most of the probing stares of their neighbors.

Rebecca apologized profusely after the service. "I cannot say how truly sorry I am that Augustus disrupted your sermon, Reverend. He has not been well. One can never predict what effect early sickness can cause. He should not be judged according to the ordinary rules of convention—"

"You know we have always been dedicated to your church," Zachary said. "In fact, I have long had plans for improvements. I have a mighty fine blacksmith and carpenter. I could easily spare them one afternoon to see if there is anything that needs to be done . . ."

Reverend Wickerson graciously accepted their apologies. He could do no less, considering his Christian duty and the Rileys' generous contributions to his church. But he was a proud man, and he would not easily forget the insult.

Rebecca was near tears as they left the church. "Augustus, how *could* you?" she wailed.

Zachary had no patience for questions. He pushed Gus through the crowd in the direction of the carriage, rapped his sleeping coachman, Winston, on the side of his head, and tossed his son inside.

After Rebecca had sent Gus to bed with an empty stomach and an aching backside, she paid a visit to Promise's room. "What did you think of church today?" she asked her. "It was as beautiful as I've said, don't you think?"

Promise's eyes were intent on the floorboards.

Rebecca wondered at her favorite's poor spirits. "I plan to have Reverend Wickerson and his wife for dinner soon—to smooth things over some. Do you want to help serve? You may if you like."

Promise nodded slowly.

"I don't know what has gone wrong with Augustus," Rebecca went on. "I was just telling Mr. Riley how lucky I am to have you. You have always been such a *good* girl."

Promise looked up at her missus, her eyes pleading for reassurance that all of the horrible things that the reverend had said that morning were not true.

But Rebecca was ill equipped to provide such comfort. "Well, I do hope you enjoyed the service . . . although it was not one of his better sermons, I think," she added softly before leaving the room.

Promise studied herself in the mirror. Her reflection did not bring its usual pleasure. Her dress had lost its crisp whiteness. The dust from the road had given it a brown tinge, and moisture from sweat and crying had wrinkled its smooth creases. She picked up her silver birthday brush and ran her hand along the bristles until one of the stiff spikes poked through the skin of her finger. She pulled it back slowly, and watched as the tiny red dot swelled into a fat droplet that rolled over her fingertip and onto the front of her dress.

In her hurry to get dressed that morning, Promise had neglected to empty the water basin. She reached for the soap and rubbed it against the brush until grayish clumps clung to its hard tips. She wet the brush in the basin and began to scrub—grinding the bristles into her arm. She gritted her teeth to keep from crying out as they tore into her flesh. She was pleased to see pale pink skin show itself briefly before the wound was covered by a flood of scarlet that colored the chilled water. With firm resolve, she ground on until Hannah's heavy hand descended upon her, yanking the bloody brush from her grasp.

Hannah moved with lightning speed, and in a few moments she had torn the hem of her housedress and wrapped it tightly around Promise's arm, ignoring her squeals. When the bleeding slowed, Hannah took a deep breath and thanked Jesus. Once her fear left, anger took its place, and she began shaking Promise wildly. "What do you think you're doing? You gone crazy? You tryin' to kill yourself?"

Promise's raw flesh beat against the makeshift bandage, and she began to sob. "Th-th-the reverend sa-sa-said—"

Understanding flashed in Hannah's eyes. "Never you mind what that man said."

"Bu-but—"

"I *said* never you mind. Now take off that dress. I'll soak it so those stains won't set."

Promise did as she was told. Then, still sniffling, she climbed into Hannah's lap and nestled comfortably against her soft belly. Hannah rubbed the side of her leg. "You're the Lord's child—same as them. There's nothin' wrong with you, at least according to God, and his opinion is the only one that matters."

Promise wasn't quite convinced, but Hannah's arms gave her comfort. As her tears fell, Hannah sang softly and pulled her close to her chest, letting her weep. The release of emotion wearied her, and Promise's eyes grew heavy. Only then did Hannah begin to shed her own tears, and she didn't return to her room until she was sure that Promise was released from the day's hurts, escaping into the temporary refuge of her dreams.

Tho' darkness covers all around,
We once was lost, but now we're found.
Oh, guide us with your mighty hand,
Over into the Promised Land.
Yes, Lord Jesus.

Lord, in your pow'ful arms we'll hide,
'Cause death abides on every side.
Oh, guide us with your mighty hand,
Over into the Promised Land.
Yes, Lord Jesus. Oh yeah, Lord.

Reverend Wickerson forgave the Rileys in earnest after Zachary provided Christ Saints Church with a new roof and furnished his wife with a silver tea service. The members of his flock were less charitable. For a month after "the incident," as the Low Country community had christened Gus's outburst that morning, Zachary, Rebecca, and the peculiarities of their son were the principal topics of conversation. Zachary's background was called into question. His political commentary was recalled by the gentlemen and scrutinized for signs of deception. Rebecca observed that her invitations to luncheon waned so that the other ladies could freely discuss the proper way to raise a dutiful child without offending their wayward friend.

Fortunately, the Rileys' redemption was advanced when a more sensational story materialized. Lawrence Hubbard, Dr. Matthew Hubbard's middle boy, had spent the summer with relatives in the North, and despite the Hubbards' efforts to conceal the ugly truth, it had been discovered that while their son was away from home, he had secretly married a Jewess. Dr. Hubbard appealed to the reverend for council, and when word got out that the young man swore that he would rather be disinherited than desert his new wife, Gus's bizarre behavior faded away into insignificance, and Zachary and Rebecca's former status among their peers was restored.

CHAPTER 14

Christmas Company

Promise leaned as far as she dared over the bubbling pot of cinnamon-apple pudding and stirred its contents slowly. She inhaled deeply, letting the sweet-smelling steam flavor her innards.

Christmas had come to Atterley. Molly had been cooking for three days now, going back and forth from the kitchen building to the main house—chopping, basting, and stooping over simmering iron pots. She recruited members of the household staff to help her, and Promise had been happy to donate her services. The moment Molly's back was turned she dipped in and out of each dish, sampling the delicacies like an expectant hummingbird. The whole house was in a state of frenzied activity, preparing for the festivities that were to take place that night, and the aroma of Molly's creations was accompanied by the scent of freshly-cut pine, silver polish, and the remaining whispers of perfume from a parade of holiday well wishers.

Christmas in the Low Country brought with it a variety of holiday amusements. Instead of the usual service on Sunday morning, proud parents watched as their fur-clad offspring gathered on the church steps and sang carols. Bundled passengers went on carriage rides in the woods, while their slaves, dressed up in seasonal embroidery, guided the processions of groomed horses in and out among the trees.

Families had small gatherings at their homes for relatives and intimate friends. Wives watched dancing couples and bickered over which pairings made the best matches, while their husbands talked business in the next room. Young ladies displayed their talents on imported pianos and sang prettily, hoping to catch the attention of a certain young man arguing spiritedly over cards. Children were allowed to stay up late, and they scurried about getting in everyone's way, making caramel candy and decorating trees with wax lights and ornaments.

In the South Carolina Low Country, however, the only event of the season of real consequence took place on Christmas Eve and was hosted by a different family each year. Only a select group of plantation owners had the means to entertain so many families in a manner meeting with the satisfaction of the discriminating guests in attendance, and this year Rebecca had volunteered to receive them at Atterley. She wanted the event to be the grandest party the Low Country had seen since the extravagant wedding reception put on by Mrs. Jennings Mays when she finally found a husband for her eldest girl.

Rebecca collaborated with Molly to ensure that a vast assortment of food was to be served, and in inexhaustible quantities. There was to be a fragrant duck stew with capers and hard-boiled eggs, served with ginger cake; winter-pea soup and crispy rice bread; roast turkeys basted in butter and stuffed with bread crumbs, celery, and oysters; chickens simmered in gravy and covered with a rich cream and wine sauce; broiled fish and scalloped tomatoes; veal cutlets seasoned with parsley, garlic, and dried onion; venison pastries and flaky, fried potato croquettes; spicy English mutton sausages and baked squash; cured hams with apple preserves and stewed spinach; tender roasts with glazed carrots, peppers, and red potatoes; and an endless variety of cakes, pies, custards, and puddings.

Rebecca took as much care in creating the guest list as she did the menu. She kept her deliberations secret, leaving her peers to speculate about who was to be included in the festivities and who would suffer the humiliation of being barred admittance. Each family prayed that they would be among those who would be given a coveted invitation. Those who were not among the upper-echelon invented imaginary prior obligations, and fooling no one, made hasty preparations to remove themselves from the area by the date of the party.

Rebecca summoned Jimmy each morning for a week, giving him a bundle of invitations to deliver. As the days passed, panic descended into the fine homes across the countryside. Imported chocolates and fine wines arrived at Atterley accompanied by cards, "Wishing the Most Felicitous of Season's Greetings to Mr. and Mrs. Zachary Riley," with the sender's name printed in large lettering. Ladies waited tearfully in their parlors with their sewing lying unfinished on their laps, while their husbands paced the floors and peered outside their front windows—hoping to see Jimmy trotting down the lane carrying a precious gold-accented invitation.

"Come help me peel these 'taters," Molly commanded, removing the pudding from the stove.

Promise hopped down and sat across from her at the kitchen table. Behind the mountain of potatoes, she could see only the top of Molly's brassy bun and the edges of her thighs spilling over the sides of her chair. She selected a large, dusty potato and sighed happily. She loved helping with the cooking. It made her feel quite grown up—adding just the right amount of salt to Molly's recipes, turning sizzling fried chicken, and telling Florence and Miriam's little ones to be mindful of popping grease. And Molly always let her wear one of her aprons that could no longer accommodate her ever-expanding waistline. Promise's favorite was the yellow one. Her missus said a lady could never look unbecoming in yellow.

Promise was looking forward to Christmas and her mind was full of questions, but she had no captive audience to satisfy her curiosity and listen to her excited babbling. Molly merely grunted at her from behind the pile of potatoes, and concerned herself only with the tenderness of the veal and whether the soup was scorched. Promise wished Gus had not been ordered away from the kitchen earlier that morning. Molly had managed to maintain her patience with him after he had turned over a barrel of onions and spilled a custard on the floor, but after he had dropped a jar of peach preserves and started a small kitchen fire, she had waved her plump arms wildly in the air and screeched for Hannah to "come get this boy, 'fore I lose my mind!"

Promise circled her knife delicately around the potato, removing the thin brown skin, and dropped it into a bowl. She wiped the starchy juice on her apron and craned her neck around the potato mountain, hoping to catch a glimpse of Gus in the dining room. With just Molly's bun and thighs to keep her company, she wasn't sure her imaginative powers, though formidable, could sustain her until they finished the peeling.

Gus had pouted for a while after he had been banished from the kitchen. He and Promise were having such fun—racing bread boats in oceans of pudding and poking the crispy skin of the turkeys to see the rivers of juice flow out. He felt very wronged by Molly, and had told Hannah so. Molly should have never handed him that jar of preserves while his hands were still greasy with pork fat, and how was he to know that after he wiped them off he'd dropped the rag too close to the fire?

Hannah had failed to see the logic of his arguments, however, and she'd pulled him from the kitchen by his ear. But he hadn't cried. After the commotion he'd caused at church, his father had taken a more active interest in the development of his character, and he no longer permitted tears. It had taken only a few encounters with his cane to drive the point home. By the afternoon, both Gus's ill temper and burning ear had chilled, and he sat watching Hannah polish the silver—surveying his reflection in each piece as she finished it.

Rebecca breezed into the room with Florence and Miriam at her heels. "Augustus, I want you on your best behavior tonight. You're not to make an unpleasant scene at the party. I want you to resist every temptation to make a spectacle of yourself."

"But I'm never naughty on purpose," Gus said. "How can I keep myself from being bad when I always get into trouble by accident?"

This response did nothing to set Rebecca's mind at ease. "Hannah, *please* speak with him," she pleaded. She trailed out of the room again, looking behind her from time to time to give Florence and Miriam a series of commands concerning the window dressings and the best placements for the rugs.

"You better act right tonight, Massa Gus," Hannah cautioned, handing him a pair of shining spoons to make faces into. She gave him a look that said she meant business. "This party means a lot to your mama."

"Can I stay up late?"

"Yes," Hannah said. "Your Uncle and Auntie Harper are bringin' Miss Georgeanna with them, and I expect your mama wants you to stay up and keep her company."

Gus's spirits fell immediately. "But she's gonna take all the fun out of being awake," he complained. "Mama's gonna make me dance with her—I just know it."

He shuddered, remembering their last trip to Charleston. "She holds onto me so tight I can hardly move, and she stinks, too. She smells like three kinds of toilet water and that soap Mama uses all mixed up together. And she never stops talking. I never met a more boring girl in my whole life. She doesn't climb trees, or go fishin', or do nothin' fun. She's worse than the girls in *Sunday school*," Gus added, to let Hannah know just how low his fair cousin had sunk in his estimation.

"I imagine you'll be thinkin' a bit differently about her in a few years. She'll make a man a fine wife someday," Hannah said, rubbing the side of a soup tureen. "In fact, I do believe your mama's got her in mind for you." She winked at Gus and laughed when his face twisted up. "Miss Georgeanna's quite an accomplished young lady. She sings and plays like an angel, and she's got some real fine manners."

Gus rolled his eyes. He didn't consider good etiquette to be a particularly admirable virtue. "Mama made me sit for a whole hour listenin' to her play. Just when I thought she was done, she'd start right into another one. Promise says when she sings she sounds like a cat caught out in the rain, and she does, too. If Mama makes me dance with her, I'm gonna tell her so."

"No, you will not." Hannah set the tureen down with a clatter. "You'll conduct yourself like a young gentleman."

Gus moaned. "Can Promise stay up, too, then? It won't be so bad if she's there."

"Yes, Miss Rebecca said she might. But she'll be in the kitchen, so she won't be around to keep you company, although maybe she should be—you always do act better when you're with her. I remember when you two were still toddlin' around, if Promise was off somewhere you'd cry and cry until—"

"I'm not a baby any more," Gus interrupted. "I only asked because as girls go, she's all right, that's all, better than Georgeanna at least." With that, he stalked out of the room.

Hannah smiled as she watched him go. *Like a little-bitty rooster just getting a few of his tail feathers,* she thought to herself.

The cream of Low Country society arrived at five in a seemingly unending parade of coaches. Gus and Promise watched from the windows as processions of smartly-dressed, pretty slave boys—who were all the same shade of faded, washed-out brown—jumped from their drivers' seats and helped their master-daddies and their masters' wives step down from their perches. The couples entered Atterley in a majestic procession of twos and walked boldly up the front steps toward the beckoning music emanating from inside, confident in their belonging.

If their social position was ever in question, their inclusion at the Riley affair put all doubts to a final, indisputable rest. They were the beautiful people, the chosen ones. For if God had singled out a group of people on which to bestow his favor, surely it must have been they. They were doctors, lawyers, clergymen, politicians, and gentlemen—who were all blessed with enough slaves to keep them living in the manner that the Lord had destined. And they felt entitled to their earthly glory. The law, the church, and Southern society were all in agreement that things were as they should be—and the North was silent. There was no one left to do the questioning.

Georgeanna was the only child among them. She looked like a miniature version of the rest, all silk and lace. The rest of the Rileys' guests had left their children at home. They were too young to appreciate the honor of being asked to spend Christmas Eve at Atterley, and had no objection to staying home with their mammies. There were no tearful pleas for a rapid return on that Christmas Eve, no appeals for bedtime stories, or cries for one last kiss or hug before their parents dashed out the door in a blur of coattails and beaded satin. They could not miss what had never been given.

It was the children's other, darker mothers who minded the inconsequential details of their growing up, and on that night before Christmas, mammies across the Low Country allowed their excited charges to set out cookies for Santa Claus and pick one carefully chosen present to open before being tucked into bed. These children were permitted to remain in the care of their darker mothers until it was time to send them away to the best schools, the right schools, where all of the other beautiful people's children went—where they forgot their darker mothers and learned to take the place that had been reserved for them among the chosen.

Tobias greeted the guests at the door with his usual grave formality. Jenny and Young Martha took their coats. Juno showed them into the drawing room. When the Harpers made their entrance, however, Rebecca received them herself. Less than a year after her brothers' death, the elder Dr. Charles Harper had been laid to rest beside his wife and two youngest boys.

The loss of her father increased Rebecca's dependence on her remaining brother and strengthened her resolve to someday have her niece for a daughter-in-law. After Florence and Miriam served Dr. and Mrs. Charles Harper their drinks, Rebecca sought out Gus. She found him hiding behind the curtains and led him squirming toward her brother's family.

Dr. Harper looked his nephew over doubtfully. Although Gus had grown a great deal in recent years and his cheeks had filled out, developing the ruddy cast commonly found in red-blooded country boys, he still lacked the boldness of reckless youth that tends to inspire affection from older men by reminding them of their own childhood days. Although his wife and sister were holding onto the hope that their children would marry when they were of age, he didn't believe Gus would ever have the gumption to do anything important enough to deserve his daughter, and was convinced that Rebecca would be getting the better part of the bargain.

Georgeanna extended a gloved hand to her cousin and gave him a polite greeting. Sadly, Gus was not so well trained. His arms remained pinned to his side until Rebecca prodded him forcefully from behind. "Now doesn't Georgeanna look lovely, Augustus? Just like a doll in a store window. Isn't that so, dear?"

Gus appraised the style of Georgeanna's dress and decided it had too many frills. Then he determined that her hair, pinned up on top of her head, was most inconvenient for pulling. He gave his mother a withering look to let her know that it would be unwise to further solicit his opinion on the state of his cousin's appearance.

"Augustus has been looking forward to seeing you again, Georgeanna," Rebecca said. "I'm sure you two have a great deal to talk about."

Gus would have promptly left his cousin in search of more stimulating entertainment had not his mother been keeping an eye on him, making escape impossible. Fortunately, Georgeanna was accustomed to conversing at length without requiring much of a response, and she launched into a detailed description of all of the subjects that she was studying at the Summerhill Academy for Young Ladies.

Zachary's brothers had come from Georgia to spend the holidays at Atterley, and it was clear to all those assembled that they were gentlemen of consequence. Judson, Patrick, and Washington Riley were holding court with Zachary in the center of the room, and they let their voices thunder through the main house unashamed. The other company approached cautiously to introduce themselves and perhaps engage them in some sort of dialogue, about the weather perhaps, but they were received with cool civility and then summarily dismissed.

The men paid no attention to their audience as they talked and swapped stories, seeking only to please themselves and each other. Zachary's brothers were quite curious about the plantation's development since they had last visited South Carolina, and were impressed by the success he had made of himself. From time to time, they eyed Gus speculatively, wondering whether he would prove capable of taking his father's place, or if Atterley would someday be passed on to their own sons.

CHAPTER 15

Barrel Wine

G us and Georgeanna were sent to bed at ten, but the dancing, drinking, and merrymaking went on through the night. The noise kept Gus awake, and at midnight he snuck away to Promise's room and tapped softly on her door. "Promise . . . Promise . . . *Promise!* Open up."

Promise opened the door a crack and peered out. "What do you want?" she asked, her tongue still thick with sleep.

"Let's do somethin' fun."

"Huh?" Promise released a gaping yawn and scratched her leg through her nightdress.

"Let's sneak into Pa's study and steal us some brandy."

"Is that what you woke me up for?" She stared at him in disbelief. "Don't be dumb. Somebody'll see us for sure."

"Not if we're real quiet."

"What do you need me for? Why don't you just go and steal some yourself?"

"I could, but I wanted to give you a chance to get in on a good time. But forget I said anything . . . since you're scared."

"I didn't say I was scared. I just don't wanna get caught—seeing as it's Christmas tomorrow. What if Santa comes down Massa's chimney and catches us standing there with a bottle of brandy? I asked him for a new pair of shoes with gold clasps, and Missus says since I've been good all year I'll likely get them."

"Then how 'bout sneaking some wine from the street? There's no way Santa would spot us way down there, and they got barrels of it."

"You can't go to the street, stupid. Everyone'll see you."

"But you could. I'll be waiting for you when you get back, and you can have the first sip."

"I wouldn't taste a drop of that nasty stuff if you paid me."

After some more wrangling, Gus agreed to give Promise half of his Christmas candy if she would go to the quarters and fill up an empty bottle with barrel wine. They tiptoed past Jimmy's room and paused at the side door. "You stand back," Gus told her. "Lemme see if someone's out there." He craned his neck out and saw Sir Henry twenty yards away.

He was easy to spot in his brightly-striped jacket and matching purple hat that Zachary had given him for Christmas. In one hand he held one of Molly's turkey legs, and in the other a bottle of whiskey. He chuckled along with the gentlemen and ladies inside, misting up the air, and took a hearty swig from his bottle whenever they lifted their glasses for a toast. It was a sad, solitary holiday celebration. Sir Henry was too dark and threatening a figure to help serve the Rileys' guests, and he wasn't welcome at the slaves' Christmas festivities.

"Sir Henry's out there, Promise. You gotta go through the kitchen," Gus whispered. They made their way back down the long hallway toward the kitchen. Murmuring words of encouragement, Gus shoved Promise out the door.

When she could no longer hear the music from the main house echoing behind her, Promise began to run, holding the bottle tightly to her chest. The frost on the ground sprang upwards as she raced across it, covering her legs and moistening the hem of her dress. She didn't stop until the shadowy rows of cabins gained distinction, and the pinpricks of orange light grew into flickering bonfires.

Zachary gave his slaves three days to celebrate the holidays, and they were taking advantage of every moment of their fleeting freedom. As she approached the quarters, Promise found herself in the middle of a joyous jubilee. The slaves had left their homes and were congregated in the middle of the street. Sides of beef, fatted hogs, mutton, and fall-off-the-bone-tender ribs crackled over the flames. Peas and rice, spicy beef soup, chitterlings flavored with pepper and vinegar, collard greens and ham hocks, stewed chicken, okra and onion, and plum pudding sputtered in iron pots. Corn and rice bread were baking over the coals.

Fiddlers played intoxicating tunes, and the slaves took turns dancing in the middle of the thick circle of onlookers—kicking the air to the beat of the clapping, stomping ring. Men hoisted small children on their shoulders. Older children crawled under the maze of legs, joined the adults in the middle of the circle, and tried to imitate their rhythmic movements. There were roars of approval whenever a dancer was particularly zealous, and soon a competition ensued, heightening the ecstatic frenzy of the crowd.

Promise spotted her parents; they were enveloped in joy. Cora's hair, usually hidden away beneath a tight scarf, had fallen loose as she twirled in Abraham's arms. Although the night was cold, excitement had heated the air, and Promise began sweating lightly as she searched around her for the barrels of wine. She eyed them at last and hurried toward the nearest one. After dipping her bottle inside, she slunk back into the night in the direction of the main house. She had reached the smokehouse when Sir Henry appeared in front of her out of the darkness.

"Well now, what you gots there?" Sir Henry asked her, weaving slightly. He looked cartoonishly comical in his master's gifts—his hat hung lopsided on his head, and his coat dangled off one shoulder. But there was nothing in Sir Henry's countenance that inspired laughter. His eyes were glazed pink. The bottle of whiskey that swung from his fingers was almost empty.

Promise was too terrified to answer him and tried to walk past.

Sir Henry blocked her path, and like any predator, advanced more assuredly when he saw the fear in her eyes. After years of unharnessed depravity, he now needed baser pleasures to satisfy his appetite and he had developed a preference for little girls. He took a deep drink and touched the lace collar of Promise's dress. The bottle fell from her hands and wine spilled over her shoes, soaking the ground.

"You shole has growed into a *purty* little gal . . . yes suh, you shole has," Sir Henry slurred. He ran his tongue along his whiskey-stained bottom lip. "I 'member when you was just a baby. You'd be out there by the smithy watchin' yo' daddy work."

He let his fingers slide down her dress until they found her prepubescent nipple and stopped. "But you's 'most all growed up now. 'Bout time for Massa to finds you a man so you can make Massa some babies. Maybe I'll ask Massa if he'd give you to me for Christmas . . . whatcha gots to say 'bout that, gal?"

Promise froze. Sir Henry grabbed her arm and pulled her toward him. "You'd like livin' with Sir Henry," he murmured softly. "Massa gives me the best of everythin'. I gets bacon and molasses every day—not just Sundays like the rest of them niggas. Whatcha thinks 'bout that?"

Promise turned her head away from Sir Henry's sour breath and felt his day-old whiskers scrape against her cheek.

"You thinks you's better'n me, gal?" he said. "You ain't no l'il white gal. You's just like the rest of Massa's niggas, and it won't be long 'fore you sees that. And when you gets old 'nouf, I'm gonna ask Massa Riley if I can have you, and if Massa Riley say you's mine, then you's *mine*." He tightened his grip on Promise with one hand, and she felt the other snake up her leg.

Gus had tired of waiting on the back steps for Promise and went in search of her. When he saw her twisting in Sir Henry's arms, he rushed toward them. "Let her go, Henry!" he screamed.

Sir Henry was momentarily caught off guard, giving Gus a chance to pull Promise from his grasp. He was about to scold him for being out so late when a strange presence in Gus's eyes stopped him—an uncompromising strength, birthed by panic— that looked eerily out of place in his eleven-year-old face.

"We was just talkin' out here together, weren't we, gal?" Sir Henry said, backing away. "Ain't meant her no harm . . . w-we was just talkin' is all," he stuttered, before blending back into the night.

Gus led Promise back to the house. "I dropped the wine," she said, looking down at her stained socks.

"It doesn't matter. You can have my Christmas candy anyway if you want." He walked her to her room and lingered in the doorway. "Are you sure you're all right?" He looked at Promise curiously, hoping she wouldn't cry.

She looked troubled. "Gus, do you think I'm just like other niggers?"

"'Course not. How many niggers you know got shoes with gold clasps?"

Promise thought about it for a moment and decided he was right. "Will you stay with me? We can sleep together, just like we used to when you had a bad dream, remember?"

"I don't know. . . Maum Hannah said we couldn't any more."

"Please, Gus. No one'll catch us—not with so many folks here to tend to."

"All right," Gus gave in. He followed her inside and turned away while she changed back into her nightdress. Then he took off his shoes and climbed in bed beside her. "What was Sir Henry doin' to you out there anyway?" he asked, once they had settled beneath the covers.

Promise didn't answer. She only said that she was cold, and Gus gave her more of his share of the blanket.

Hours later, after the Rileys' company had settled into Atterley's guest rooms for the night, Promise heard a rustling outside that startled her awake. "Gus, do you hear that?" She gave him a shove.

He mumbled unintelligibly and rolled over.

In a blinding flash it came to her—Santa was on the roof about to deliver the presents! She hopped out of bed and hurried toward the window, hoping to catch a glimpse of his reindeer. The noise was coming from a large tree outside that was swaying back and forth in rapid motion. There was something in its branches, but the form was sheathed in blackness. Promise couldn't make out who or what it was, and when the cold began to numb her feet, she gave up and crawled back into bed.

She hadn't recognized the form of Sir Henry up in that tree, sitting where two sturdy limbs joined. He was staring into Rebecca's bedroom window with his pants open and pushed down below his waist. His free hand still gripped the swinging whiskey bottle.

CHAPTER 16

Sir Henry's Proposal

When a young girl reaches the broad wasteland that borders her entry into the adult world, her face and body prepare for the crossing over, transforming into a contentious blend of child and woman. As Promise's hormones erupted, her little-girl charm was marred with irregularities. She went to Hannah for comfort, who explained away her horror about what was happening "down there," but dismissed the rest of her woes over the strange mutations of her body as at the very least, unimportant, and at most, a dangerous sort of vanity.

But after five autumns had come and gone, Promise's awkwardness was overtaken by the glory of sweet sixteen. Her features rotated back into alignment, the angles of her body softened and filled, and the hard buds on her chest blossomed.

Sir Henry observed Promise's progress closely as the years passed, watching her as she walked alongside the rice fields with Gus, and his heart gradually softened with a warped affection. When Promise's lively skipping at Gus's side slowed to a ladylike stroll and he had grounds to call her a woman, Sir Henry was true to his word and decided to pay his master a visit to ask for her hand in marriage.

Crouching at the back door of the main house, he pulled off his boots and pounded the heels against the steps until the mud fell onto the ground in thick, smelly clumps. He dug through his burlap sack and pulled out a pair of Zachary's castoffs, neatly preserved in wax paper. The shoes were a size-and-a-half too large, but they were well polished, and Sir Henry slipped them on his feet with a happy sigh. He reserved them for special occasions only—when he stepped onto the hallowed floors of the main house.

"Hello there, Molly." Sir Henry nodded as he entered the kitchen. "Somethin' shole smells good 'nouf in here."

"Never you mind how it smells," Molly said.

"Come now, Molly, there's no cause to be that way, is there?" Sir Henry said, eyeing her crackling chicken hungrily. "We always got on all right, ain't we? Why can't you just let me get a little-bitty taste?"

"Naw, Henry, we ain't always got on all right. You ain't nothin' *to* me, and you ain't gettin' nothin' *from* me. I know you believe you got the right to sneak in here when you think no one's lookin' and pick at my food like the *rat* you are, but you don't, so go on witcha. Go on, now!" Molly waved her thick finger at the doorway. "You just keep walkin' that-a-way. And you stop sniffin' 'round my girls, too, or I'll sic the dogs on ya." She scowled at him fiercely as he retreated from the kitchen, and then went back to turning her chicken.

Tobias spotted Sir Henry in the hallway. "Is there something you wanted, Henry?" he asked politely, looking through him as if he were someone's lost child, or perhaps a wayward dog that had been carelessly allowed inside.

Tobias was looking especially splendid that afternoon, with freshly trimmed salt-and-pepper hair and groomed mustache. At first Sir Henry cowered before him—until he reminded himself that even the butler's fair skin was still too dark to warrant any deference from him. He threw back his shoulders. "I'd like to see Massa," he announced.

"This way," Tobias said, extending a gloved hand. He checked Sir Henry's fingernails slyly. His face convulsed at the sight of the dirt that had taken root beneath them, and he prayed silently that he wouldn't touch any of the furniture. Then he noticed Sir Henry's sparkling shoes, thanked the Lord for small favors, and ushered the shuffling driver into his master's study to make his petition.

When he entered, Sir Henry was startled to see Rebecca seated at Zachary's side, and he was suddenly unsure of himself, shifting his dusty hat from one trembling hand to the other. Rebecca laid down her embroidery and watched the shower of dirt fall lightly onto the polished floor with each transfer.

Sir Henry's request was a bold one. The Low Country planters discouraged their field and house slaves from intermarrying. House servants were lesser extensions of the masters themselves, pedigreed favorite pets not to be sullied by the mongrels in the fields, whose sun-blackened skin and coarse, kinky hair would inject threatening colors and textures into their masters' pristine surroundings. But Sir Henry was convinced that he had earned the honor, and never for a moment did he believe that his petition would be denied. It was for an entirely different reason that he suddenly found his mouth dry, and his armpits leaking sweat.

As Rebecca looked up at him with her lovely hazel eyes, it became difficult for him to maintain control over his faculties. It wasn't often that he had the chance to be so near her, to let his eyes devour every inch of her in the clear light of day. He couldn't help taking advantage of his good fortune, and he gazed longingly at his mistress's hair, soft curls rising and falling gently against her milky white neck as she breathed.

He could only imagine how wondrous it would feel to nestle against the soft patch behind her ear, where he could freely smell the perfumed strands—how it would feel to hold her, cherish her. How well he knew the shape of that lovely neck, its long slope meeting the fullness of her breasts in the front and widening into the delicate form of her back from behind.

Sir Henry had seen it all before, many, many times, and more besides. It was his only secret from his master, and the knowledge that its discovery meant death didn't stop him from creeping into that blessed tree where the blackness of his skin blended into the sky and only his eyes shone expectantly through the branches. There he could watch her at his leisure, and afterward he could hardly wait to get back to the quarters and find a far inferior substitute for his beloved. Often he could not contain himself, and the tree's sagging branches bore witness to his lust for his mistress.

Standing there in the presence of an angel, he became acutely aware of his odor and disheveled appearance. He hoped Rebecca didn't notice the dried blood spatters that covered his coat. The tanned leather looked like the canvas of a gruesome impressionist, transforming the brown into a dusty crimson at a distance. He never washed away the blood that sprayed from the backs of slaves he whipped, but let it collect to catalog his years of faithful service. Sir Henry knew that his mistress might not view his tiny scarlet badges in a positive light—Rebecca was the sort of woman who probably did not appreciate his line of work.

Zachary looked up from his papers and noticed his driver. "They get that trunk fixed, Henry? It looks like rain—my fields better not get flooded."

"They done fixed it, Massa, 'most two hours ago."

"I've been looking over my figures. I had a good year last year, Henry, a damn good year, and this year I'm expecting more of the same."

"Zachary, please—your language," Rebecca said.

"You should be more forgiving of my manners, my dear. That damn good year has paid for all of the jewelry and baubles you love so much. Stanton harvested nearly a hundred more pounds of rice than I did last year, Henry. Did you know that?"

"Yes suh, but I bets his rice didn't fetch what ours did. Most of it probably wasn't fit for nothin' 'sides feedin' hogs. They beat all the work outta they niggas. They's not so 'ficient as us, Massa."

"True. Still, Stanton's a Yankee, and I don't like the idea of him out-producing us. That's never happened before, and it better not happen again."

"Yes suh. This is gonna be a good year, better'n last."

"I'll hold you to that. Well, is there something you wanted?"

Sir Henry was certain that his eyes were firmly fixed on his master before he began. "Massa, you 'member you tole me that as soon as I gets ready, I could ask you for whatever gal strikes my fancy to be my wife?" Sir Henry rubbed the brim of his hat.

"Of course I remember," Zachary said. "It's about time you got yourself a woman to cook and keep house so you won't keep coming around here at night begging for a decent supper." He tapped his ashes and grinned.

"Well, I done made up my mind."

"Who's the lucky girl you've got your eye on, boy?"

Sir Henry cleared his throat. "I be wantin' Promise, suh."

Rebecca, horrified, stared at Sir Henry. Zachary looked at his wife, sighed deeply, and blew smoke rings at the ceiling. He suckled his cigar, rolling the tip around in his mouth in smooth circles between puffs. Usually the motion relaxed him. Over the years he had solved his most pressing difficulties in that very chair, surrounded by a light cloud of sweet-smelling smoke— the appropriate course of action coming to him in a flash of nicotine-induced inspiration. It was rare for him to be so unsure about what to do.

He had no particular attachment to Promise. She was a pleasant, obedient sort of girl, and useful to have around, but it could be arranged so that she spent her days in the main house and her nights with Sir Henry. He wasn't bothered by the difference in their ages. Zachary had long been aware of Sir Henry's preference for young girls, but he didn't object as long as the work got done and the babies kept coming. Besides, he had given Sir Henry his word, which everyone in the Low Country, black or white, knew could be relied upon. But his wife loved that girl, and he would never hear the end of it if he let Sir Henry have her. He chewed at the cigar tip.

Rebecca broke the silence. "You may not have Promise— now or *ever,*" she said in a manner that let both men know that the subject was closed forever. She hated Sir Henry only slightly less than her husband's slaves did and saw no reason to be courteous. "When your master told you that you could have your pick of his slaves, I'm sure he did not intend Promise to be included in that group. Frankly, I'm astonished that you would consider yourself suitable for her. My husband is not the only one well apprised of the goings-on on this plantation—I can assure you of that. You are a vile and violent man, without any redeeming qualities as far as *I* can tell, so just put the idea out of your mind this minute. I would never allow Promise to marry someone who is in every way not her equal. And if you have any thoughts of taking her by force, as I understand you are wont to do from time to time, know that if you do, I'll take a whip to you *myself*."

Sir Henry stood motionless at first. His hat still dangled from his fingertips as he stared at those beautiful eyes that he had adored for so long, staring back at him. Had they held only the sharp glint of anger, though it would have grieved him, he might have withstood it. But Rebecca did not hide the contempt and disgust he saw in them, and that afternoon, from her chair, she stole the remainder of his manhood.

The docile manner in which he placed his hat back on his head, tucked his tail between his legs, and thanked his master and mistress for their time masked his inner turmoil. From that moment, Sir Henry hated Promise with an intense, irrational hatred—but he put the darkness away to reside in the place where his bitterness had accumulated for a lifetime and reserved his vengeance for another day.

CHAPTER 17

Wagon Races and Monkeys' Tails

Promise took no notice of Sir Henry as he strode past her on his way back to the fields. She was sitting across the kitchen table from Gus, stuffing herself full of fried chicken, blissfully unaware of how close she had come to belonging to him.

"I never liked L'il Remmy much anyway," she mumbled between bites.

"You did, too," Gus shot back. He reached for another leg, his lips shining with spicy grease.

"Did not."

"Then how come you wore his sweetheart ring?"

"That had nothing to do with my feelings for L'il Remmy. I just wanted something pretty on my finger, is all. Besides, I didn't wear it long, did I? I threw it in the river, didn't I? Well, didn't I?"

"Only 'cause you caught him kissin' Lassie under the Blackbird Tree and rubbing her on her backside." Gus laughed heartily, remembering how mad Promise had been that day. How she had picked a fight with Jenny to make her cry. How she had been so angry that she had polished the floors three times over. How the whole house had been awakened that night by what sounded like a clap of thunder—only to find Molly sprawled out on the sparkling floor, surrounded by the remains of a midnight snack.

"I didn't care anything about that, and you better not tell anyone I did, either," Promise said. "L'il Remmy should feel real pleased with himself. He's in such *fine* company. Everybody's kissed Lassie by now—she's so darn fast. And Liza's the same way."

Molly had propped open the back door with a discarded shoe to cool off the kitchen, and Promise frowned darkly as she watched the twins argue over the laundry.

"That one's yours!" Eliza was shouting, pointing a furious finger at the last sheet in the basket.

"No it ain't! I took the *first* one out—that means you gotta hang up the *last* one! That's the way we always do it, and you know it!" Lassie screamed back.

"You're always going slower than me . . . on *purpose*, too!" Eliza's auburn corkscrews rattled around her head like Medusa's snakes. "Well, I got you this time! I've been counting, and I've done one more than you, so here!" She grabbed the basket and shoved it at her sister. "Go on, take it!"

"That's a fine thing!" Lassie retorted, shoving it back. "I'm to take *your* word for it, I suppose!"

Young Martha appeared from the side of the house carrying another dripping pile. "There's no need for all that squabbling. There's plenty more here for both of you."

"Plenty for *me*, you mean, Lassie ain't doin' nothin'."

"Liar! *You're* the one always scheming to get outta work, not me!"

"You both better shut up before Mama comes out here," Young Martha warned.

"Lassie's got better things to think about than working," Eliza sneered. "All she does is talk about L'il Remmy this and L'il Remmy that."

"You're just jealous."

"Jealous of what? That skinny, knock-kneed boy? I got bigger fish to fry."

Miriam came out onto her front porch, looking weary and worn with a half-hemmed dress in her hand, and a toddler clinging to her apron. "Girls, please lower your voices. The baby's sleeping."

"Me and Liza are minding our business, not your *babies*," Lassie said.

"Yeah, not your babies," Eliza echoed.

"Is that so?" Miriam said, and trounced off to fetch Molly.

While Promise was preoccupied with dark thoughts about her rival, Gus was consumed with his own woes. "Mama's makin' me start school," he said, "just like she threatened she'd do if I didn't keep up with my studies without her watching over me all the time."

Promise stared past him. "Lassie and Liza are just *trash*, plain and simple," she seethed. "Molly's gotta take her switch to one or the other of them just about every day for letting one of those nasty boys take liberties. And poor Charles and Boris and Red—always having to fight them off. Little good it does. Like Missus says, Molly better hurry up and get them married off before they're too far gone to have a Christian ceremony."

"It was Mrs. Duvall who found him," Gus continued on. "Some Yankee from Connecticut—Mr. Grant, I think. They've already built him a house on Ashby, and he'll stay with them in Charleston, too."

"Andy, Billy, Jonah—they've all had their chance with one of them, and Muley told me he's messed with *both* of them," Promise prattled on spitefully. "I wondered what he meant by 'messed with,' but I was too scared to ask . . . I wish he'd go on and get himself baptized."

Gus finished off the last piece of chicken and wiped his mouth with his sleeve, leaving a long smear on the cotton. "There'll be seventeen of us, I think. And since he's been tutoring the others for a while, I'll have a lot of catching up to do, Mama says. All the Duvalls, the Hubbards, the Masons, the Davises, the Sneads—except Myrtle, she's in England— and the oldest three Stantons, too."

"Of course, I'm not sure Muley was telling the truth about it all. You never know about him—he lies so darn much."

Molly emerged from her house with a smirking Miriam and wielded a broomstick at her daughters. She managed to give them a few hard whacks before they scattered from her, wailing. Then she came into the kitchen and tried to catch her breath, leaning as much of her weight as she dared on the groaning stick.

"Mr. Grant's supposed to be teaching us all sorts of things—Latin, spelling, geography, music, drawing—and Pa says I better learn all of it, 'cause he's gotta pay a share of his fee. It's a whole two thousand dollars a year. Ain't that somethin'? "

"So L'il Remmy can just go *hang* himself," Promise announced. "Ain't is not a word, Gus. Did you say drawing?"

"Yeah, drawing. I think the whole thing's real dumb. He's supposed to make us into ladies and gentlemen, Mama says. I never thought there'd be a day when I'd long for her lessons. You got any more of that peach pie, Molly?"

"You've made it this far without being a gentleman. I doubt if anything can be done about it now."

"For two thousand dollars a year, I'll bet he's sure gonna try," Gus said sadly.

"You have to grow up sometime, you know. You can't just wander around hunting and fishing all day."

"And why not? Only problem is the others gotta work during the week, but one day Atterley'll be mine, and then I'll set 'em all free and we'll go huntin' everyday—there now."

"You can't do that. Goodness Gus, don't you know anything?"

"Why not?"

"First, you can't set anybody free unless the legislature says so. Second, people just don't go around setting their slaves free."

"How come?"

"They just don't, that's all."

"Well, that ain't fair—about the legislature and all. Seems like folks should be able to do what they want with their own Negroes."

"Ain't is *not* a word. Mr. Grant's sure gonna have a time with you."

Jimmy staggered in the door carrying a large crate. He shoved it in a corner and took a few deep breaths before returning to the wagon for the other boxes of supplies. After he finished, he collapsed into a chair and put his head in his hands. "Molly, could you fix me a plate?" he mumbled. "Massa's been sending me all over the countryside, and I haven't eaten all day."

"Sure, Jimmy. I got some ham and cabbage, but my chicken's gone." Molly narrowed her eyes at the grease-speckled pair, and Gus and Promise lowered their eyes.

"That's fine, just fine, Molly. I ain't particular."

"Promise, how come you're never lecturin' Jimmy about how ain't is not a word?" Gus demanded. "Why're you always harassin' me?"

"Because Jimmy is already pretty much perfect. You still have a lot of improving left to go."

"Thanks, Promise." Jimmy smiled. "You're such a sweet little thing. And that puts me in mind, why don't you go get Jenny? I brought somethin' back with me that you two might be interested in." Jimmy took his hat off, leaned back, and propped his boots up on a stool. He had grown into a tall, well-built man, more striking than handsome.

Promise dashed off to fetch Jenny, and Molly set down Jimmy's food and a big slice of pie for Gus. There was only the sound of energetic slurping for the next few minutes. Molly leaned back against her stove, gratified, watching them eat.

Jenny rushed into the kitchen with Promise at her heels. "Jimmy, you got somethin' for me and Promise?" He nodded at the boxes and shoveled another forkful of food into his mouth.

Gus waited patiently until Jimmy had devoured most of his ham and cabbage, and was sopping up the juice with a thick slice of cornbread. "Can you take me with you tomorrow, Jimmy?" he asked, his mouth running with cinnamon and peach.

"Naw, not tomorrow. I gotta go all the way to the bay. I gotta leave first thing in the morning. I'll take you along the day after, though. That's a promise."

"Can I ask you somethin' else, Jimmy?" Gus said, pushing a stray sliver of peach across his plate with his fork.

"Yeah, what is it? How 'bout some more of that ham, Molly?"

"Can I use two of the wagons next Sunday?"

"No, you can't." Jimmy grinned, his laugh lines deepening. "Muley already asked me. You ain't gonna weasel me into *that* again. Last time you boys had one of your races the wheel came off, and I had to go to Massa and explain what happened. I had to say I wasn't paying attention and accidentally rode over that hole Mr. Mason keeps sayin' he don't hafta fill."

"I'm sorry, Jimmy."

"You should be. I don't think Massa believed me, but he let me go—though he said that if any of the family'd been hurt, he would've had to whip me. Who won, anyway?"

"Jonah. Prince beat Billy, Muley beat Andy, I beat Red, and Jonah beat Harold. Then Prince beat Muley and Jonah beat me. Then Jonah beat Prince. *That's* when the wheel fell off. Then Prince started complaining that it wasn't fair, 'cause when Jonah beat Harold, Jonah started before I said 'go,' and Prince said that's why Jonah beat Harold in the first place. But Muley said Prince should've said 'foul' back then. So everybody pretty much agreed Jonah won.

"Every fella had to give Jonah their first kill that week, but I had to give him my first two, 'cause I got more chances than they do to go shootin', and 'cause Pa gets some of what they bring home anyway. But I sure hated turning over that big fat turkey, and Jonah just kept grinnin' at me, telling me he'd let me get a taste of one of the legs after his mama cooked it up. The rest of the boys only gave him rabbits, squirrels, and such. Jonah said it was real funny that no one managed to shoot himself a deer until after they had squared up with him. Do you think it's right I should've had to give him two, Jimmy?"

"Who cares?" Promise said. "You almost got Jimmy in trouble. I'm *glad* he won't let you have the wagons. All that racing's nonsense. I had half a mind to tell Missus on you last time, and I'll have a *full* mind to if you do it again."

"You know what your trouble is, Promise? You're no fun, and you're too smart for your own good. That's why L'il Remmy wanted Lassie and not you." Gus sneered at her before spreading his mouth wide to hold his last hunk of pie.

"You're just saying that 'cause you think it'll hurt me. You think I cared about that stupid L'il Remmy, who incidentally, is the only boy I know stupider than you. But like I already told you, I don't care a bit."

"Don't mind him, Promise," Jimmy said. "I like smart girls, myself."

"'Course, you like all kinds of girls, don't you Jimmy?" Molly laughed. "I hear Stephanie's expecting. Wasn't she your favorite? But I don't suppose you'd know anything about that, though," she teased, nudging him playfully.

"I'm sorry to say no, Molly, I can't claim the honor." Jimmy grinned good-naturedly and picked a bit of ham out of his teeth. "Massa's been keeping me so busy runnin' all over South Carolina these last few months that I haven't had the chance to make my regular rounds. Anyway, you know that you're my favorite girl, Molly." He gave her an irreverent slap on her thigh, and she blushed like she used to years ago—when such attention from a man would've promised something more.

The girls found their presents at last—some silk handkerchiefs tucked in the corner of one of the wooden crates. They squealed with delight.

Jimmy watched them, pleased. "Mr. McFarland gave 'em to me—said they'd shipped more than he'd ordered. He told me I could give 'em to my lady friends, and I couldn't think of any young ladies I'd rather give 'em to than you two. Besides, they're all so mad at me by now, it'll take more than some handkerchiefs to set things right."

"I can't wait to take one to service," Promise gushed. "Everyone will stare, they'll be so jealous. Goodness Jenny, won't we look grand?"

"We should just take a few for ourselves and share the rest with the others," Jenny suggested.

"You can go on and do whatever you want with *your* half. I'm gonna use each and every one of *mine.*"

Hannah appeared and put a stop to all of the excitement. "Jenny, you stop playing in those boxes and start unpacking them. Promise, clean out that fireplace. Massa Gus, you help her." They stirred into action.

Hannah claimed Gus's seat. "How you been, Jimmy? Haven't seen you around for a few days."

"Don't I know it. I haven't been back here but to eat and sleep—except last week when Mr. Mason wanted to buy some of Massa's cattle. Massa sent me to Grosemont to get his offer. Mr. Mason wrote down his price, and right after I came back with it, Massa wrote down his. Then out I went again, and so on, and so on.

"I must've gone back and forth a dozen times before I looked at those papers. They were fifty dollars apart, with each of 'em only movin' a dollar on every run I was making. At *that* rate it could've gone on forever." Jimmy scowled. "Hell, I just got me a few of my own papers and changed those numbers faster than they did—finished work early *that* day."

Molly gave a slight nod toward Gus. "Maybe you should watch yourself—talkin' so free in front of *some* folks."

"Aw Molly, he's all right. Ain't you, Massa Gus?"

"Sure, Jimmy."

"That wasn't right," Jenny said, looking concerned. "You were messing with Massa's business."

"Well, I suppose he was messing with *my* business—sending me back and forth like some fool, when I got gals waitin' on me with bright smiles, and some sweet—"

"Jimmy!"

"What? Come on, Hannah, the boy's old enough to—"

"And what about Promise and Jenny?"

"Oh yeah. Sorry, I forget."

Juno stuck her head in the doorway. "Massa wants you, James."

Jimmy groaned and put his hat back on. "Damn. I can't get one moment's peace."

"Remember, you must be respectful," Juno cautioned. "Massa trusts you. That's why he calls on you so much. He's been very good to you."

"Mama, if this is his way of being good to me, I'd be dead if he treated me any better." He rose slowly to his feet. "See y'all later. Remember, Massa Gus, day after tomorrow. I'll let you know what time as soon as I can." He gave Molly a quick kiss on the cheek. "Sure was good," he told her, before following his mother out of the kitchen.

Gus removed the grate from the fireplace, and Promise swept the piles of ashes into a pail.

"So did you kiss him?" Gus asked.

"Who?"

"L'il Remmy."

"None of your business," Promise said. She dunked a cloth in water and squeezed it out.

"Come on, tell me. I won't tell anyone, I promise."

She leaned into the hearth, wiping it down. "Why do you wanna know?" her voice echoed behind her.

"I just do, that's all. I wanna know what it was like."

Promise reappeared. Black soot coated her arms up to the elbows. "I guess I kissed him once," she said, blushing.

Gus leaned back on his heels, surprised. "Really? How was it?"

"It was all right, I suppose. You're not doing your share."

"I can't, you're taking up all the room. So were you scared?"

"Kind of." Promise rubbed the dark, slippery grease between her fingers. "Give me the soap."

"How'd it happen?" he asked, handing her the soft mound.

"He just kept coming closer and closer, until there he was, and there was nothing else to do but . . . you know."

"Was it a long one or a short one?"

"Gosh Gus, I don't know. It was a short one, I think."

"I didn't like it at all when I kissed Kitty Stanton."

Promise sat up straight. "If you kissed Kitty, why'd you say you wanted to know what it was like?"

"I don't know what it's like to kiss L'il Remmy."

"You're being smart. I've done my part. You have to finish the rest," Promise said, handing him the blackened cloth.

"Don't be cross. I just wanted to check and see if I was doing it right—to see what a girl thought about the whole thing. The boys are always talking about kissing and other things, but I don't see what the big deal is."

"So what was yours like?"

"She tasted like green apples."

"Really?" Promise giggled. "So is she your girl now?"

"Naw. Dang, it stinks in here." Gus emerged from the fireplace. His face was covered in black, greasy smears. "Did L'il Remmy taste like green apples?"

"Of course not, stupid. What other things?"

"What?"

"You said you boys talk about kissing and other things. What other things?"

"Like . . . the things Jimmy talks about . . . you know."

"No, what? Go on, tell me," she pressed.

"If you don't already know, I'm not gonna tell you."

"Fine. Be that way. I've finished my share and I'm going."

"No, stay." Gus reached for her, and she darted away from his black fingertips. "All right. I'll tell you if you tell me something first," he said.

"What?"

"You swear you won't get mad?"

Promise sat back down. "Yeah, I swear."

"You sure, 'cause you always say that and you always get mad."

"I won't this time. Now go on and ask me."

Gus took a deep breath. "Do Negroes have tails?"

Promise stared at him, stunned. "What?"

"William says Negroes have tails. He says he's seen 'em. I've been dying to ask somebody, but I've been too scared to so far."

"What do you mean by tails?"

"Tails . . . like monkeys got . . . you know."

"No, I do *not* know, and that's the *stupidest* question I've ever heard!" Promise shot up on her feet.

"I knew you'd get mad," Gus said. He held the cloth by its tip and swirled it around in the grimy water.

"What do you expect when you ask me something like that?"

Gus sat silently for a moment. "So . . . are you sayin' you *do*, or are you sayin' you *don't?*"

"You're even *stupider* than I thought, Augustus Judson Riley! If Mr. Grant manages to make a gentleman out of you, he'll earn every penny of his two thousand dollars!" Promise kicked the pail and smiled wide when the water flew out, covering Gus's face and clothes.

Gus wiped the water away from his eyes and watched her backside closely as she stalked out of the room—straining to see if he could detect any hint of a tail.

CHAPTER 18

The Lesson

Mr. Grant circled the desks of the schoolhouse, weaving pretty patterns around the stooped over backs of his pupils. "Number five . . . *De-vo-tion,*" he said, making a delicate tick mark on his notepad. The first class wrote busily on their slates in grating unison.

Once their teacher's piercing gaze had passed them by, the older students ceased their independent study, passed notes, and fraternized with their neighbors using the imperceptible gestures devised by children trained not to speak until spoken to.

The carefully folded letter George Stanton had given Gus to deliver to his girl, Ruthie, hadn't reached its final destination. Gus was near panic as he struggled to complete his essay on the political propaganda in Virgil's *Aeneid* before Mr. Grant reached the end of his spelling list.

"Number six . . . *Temp-ta-tion.*"

Gus had been given an entire week to work on the assignment, but he had only just managed to finish reading it that morning. Without forcing him to endure her usual speech about making proper use of his time, Promise had come to his room before he left for school on a mission of mercy to help him decipher the most difficult passages. She had explained it all very patiently—without making him feel dumb like she usually did—until at last, he understood.

In the brightening, peachy-pink light, Promise's whisperings had made Mr. Grant's lectures on symbolism, structure, and theme make sense, but it had all left him now. The others in the sixth class had already turned in their work, and Gus looked enviously at the neat pile of papers sitting on the corner of Mr. Grant's desk, wishing his was among them.

"Number six . . . *Temp-ta-tion*," Mr. Grant repeated generously for those students whose pencils still hovered confounded in midair.

Promise was being much nicer to him lately. Maybe it was because he was rarely around the main house any more—with school, Muley, and the others taking so much of his time. He had finally worked up the nerve to ask Jimmy about the tail, and he had almost fallen out of the wagon laughing at him. Afterward, he had sworn to Promise that he knew she didn't have a tail all along, that it had all been a joke. That seemed to improve her opinion of him, that he was only being cruel, playing another one of his pranks, that he was not just an ordinary imbecile.

Still, Promise had already told Molly, and Molly, of course, had told everyone. Jimmy had to go to her on his behalf before she would allow him back in the kitchen. It was all William's fault for telling him about the tail in the first place, and so he had ambushed William before school and given him a good whipping for causing him so much trouble. That had resulted in his latest, and most violent encounter with Mr. Grant's ruler.

There had been many more races, in carts that Little Remmy had built in exchange for a share of his allowance. And Promise had not only kept quiet about his activities, she had even watched some of the races, cheering mostly for Muley, and sometimes for him—until the day she saw Red break his foot, sticking it out to round a corner, and she'd run screaming back to the main house.

"Number seven . . . *Cor-rup-tion*."

In return for Promise's help that morning, he had promised to get her whatever she wanted from the new library that afternoon. The Winyah Library Society, headed by his mother and Mrs. Duvall, took newspapers from Boston, Philadelphia,

New York, even as far away as London, and subscribed to all the important periodicals. And there were plenty of books there, too, "*hundreds* of them," Promise had gushed blissfully.

Gus's scribbles blurred before his eyes. He consistently got the lowest marks in his class, and still his father was setting him up for more failure, sending him off to the South Carolina Military Academy at the Citadel without concerning himself about how he was going to graduate when he couldn't even finish a simple essay. He had only been accepted because of his father's friendship with key members of the Board of Visitors. Zachary had passed by Marion Square and observed cadets and graduates of the military school training the Palmetto Regiment to fight the Mexicans. He had decided then that the Academy was just the sort of place to give his son some discipline.

"Number eight . . . *For-ni-ca-tion.*" There was a burst of embarrassed titters before Mr. Grant's glares commanded silence.

William stopped balling up a piece of paper between his fingers long enough to peer over Gus's shoulder. His smile notified the others of Gus's difficulties, and waves of excited flutterings rippled through the sixth class. Tim Mason, Gus's self-proclaimed best friend, craned his neck in his direction to offer help. Melvin Stanton's eyes bulged out at him from behind thick glasses, making Tim shrink back, afraid of being told on.

The girls across the isle had been passing around pretty Annabel Snead's card from fat Ronald Mason. It reeked of pomade, and had "You're Sweet" written inside. They had been taking turns being shocked by Ronald's *gall*, when Kitty paused from the fun long enough to scowl at Gus's detractors, demonstrating the unswerving loyalty any respectable girl showed her sweetheart after proclaiming that she was *dead gone* over him.

William launched a spitball at Melvin. His aim was bad, and it hit Sam Hubbard instead. Sam, thinking it had come from Bernard Snead, whose name had replaced his beside Katie Mason's on the Sweetheart Tree behind the church, retaliated by kicking Bernard's legs fiercely from behind.

"Number nine . . . *Abom-i-na-tion.*"

Gus noticed none of it. He madly scribbled on, straining to recall what Promise had taught him that morning as she crouched over him. She'd read aloud, following the words with her fingers, her other hand resting firmly on his shoulder. Every now and then her arm brushed against his, and their shoulders touched each time her finger snaked beneath the next page, flipped it over, and laid it down smooth.

Gus couldn't conjure up a single thing she had told him during those hours, but he did remember that she looked rather pretty in the weak light of the lamp. He wondered what his father would do to him if he failed to turn in another assignment on time and began to feel sick. He ground his heels into the floor and struggled to scrawl a haphazard conclusion.

"Number ten . . . *Dam-na-tion,*" announced Mr. Grant. After making the final check mark on his paper, he made his way back to the front of the class and seated himself at his desk. "First class, please pass your papers forward."

Gus watched helplessly as Mr. Grant collected the spelling tests. Then he picked up the pile of essays. He flipped methodically through them, crossing off each student's name from his roll book as he went. Gus stared down at his horribly illegible, half-finished paper and prayed—hoping against hope that for once, his teacher would not notice its absence. But it was not to be.

"Augustus Riley." Mr. Grant set the papers down with a sigh and removed his glasses. "May I ask why you have failed to turn in your essay?"

CHAPTER 19

Huntin' Party

Promise hovered outside the sparkling schoolhouse waiting for Gus. When its whitewashed doors opened at three o'clock, the children began tripping out. They looked at her curiously before departing for home in chattering clusters or atop bouncing, pretty ponies. After the doors had opened and closed for the last time, she began to worry, looking anxiously at the sky.

The air was warm and heavy against her skin, and distant thunder was already echoing from the south. The storm was coming quickly. "Gus must have gotten in trouble again," she muttered, wondering if they would be able to make it to the library and back home again before the green-gray sky fulfilled its promise of rain.

Gus's horse was growing skittish, lashing her tail at the advancing clouds. She tugged on the reins, testing the strength of Promise's grip. Promise wrapped the strips of leather around her wrist. "Easy Milo, easy."

There was an unsettling stillness in the air as the sky swelled and filled. The stretches of quiet were interrupted from time to time by the groans of the black clouds rattling the earth, warning those below of the water about to break. It would be foolish to try going to the library now, she decided. They would do well to make it home without getting soaked.

By the time Gus emerged from inside, the road was deserted, but he looked so somber that Promise didn't have the heart to be difficult. "Rain's coming," she said. "You wanna just go home?"

"Yeah. I feel real bad that we can't go today, Promise. I didn't foul things up on purpose. I'll take you the next day it's clear, and I'll get you whatever you want—just like I said I would." Gus handed Promise his books and held out his red knuckles for her to examine. "Mr. Grant sure laid into me. I thought he'd never let me leave. I had to write my essay over while my fingers were swelling up."

"They hurt?"

"A little bit. They'll be good and fat tomorrow. But that's nothin' compared to what Pa's gonna do to me when he finds out I got in trouble at school again."

"Mr. Grant didn't like your paper?"

"He didn't get a chance to like it. I didn't finish." Gus mounted his horse, extended his hand down to Promise, and seated her in front of him.

A thin bolt of lightening glimmered across the sky, and Promise closed her eyes, bracing herself for the coming thunder. "Hurry, Gus, it's gonna be a big one." Milo set off at a quick trot, as eager as Promise to be back behind the safety of Atterley's gates.

The rain began falling in heavy, solitary drops, landing in perfect circles on Promise's clothes and the tip of her nose. She shivered, and leaned back into Gus's chest.

He felt her hair brush his cheek, and realized that he didn't feel like hurrying. He felt inexplicably good, like when his belly was full of something warm. He wanted it to last, and pulled back on Milo's reins as much as he dared.

"Maybe Mr. Grant won't tell on you," Promise said.

"Oh, he'll tell. He'll do anything to get in good with Pa and the others, and stopping by to complain about me is a surefire way to do that. After Sam's marks started improving, Dr. Hubbard let Mr. Grant have half-day use of two of his Negroes to wait on him and clean house. So I'm definitely gonna get it. And to top it all off, he gave me another essay to write. The book's in there."

Promise looked through the stack. "*A Serious Call to a Devout and Holy Life, Adapted to the State and Condition of All Orders of Christians,* by William Law?"

"Yeah, that's it."

"I haven't read this one. It's dreadfully long, isn't it? Usually religious writings are so boring, but some can be quite inspirational. Ever since I read *The Temperate Soul,* Maum Hannah only has to tell me once to finish Molly's fried eggplant. Why doesn't Mr. Grant ever let you read a wonderfully romantic novel?"

"He thinks novels are trash. Besides, I don't think Mr. Grant's what you'd call wonderfully romantic." Gus shrugged. "It's all the same to me. What's Molly fixin' for supper? She had Charles kill a pig this morning. Is it ribs, or maybe chops?"

"I don't know. Chops, I think. You keep getting yourself in trouble, Gus, and I won't have to go to the library. You'll bring the library home to me."

"That's not funny."

"I know. I'm sorry." Promise covered his books with the folds of her dress to protect them from stray droplets. "How about I read it for you and write your essay, and you just copy it over?"

"Naw. Mr. Grant'll get suspicious if it's too good. I think I can get through it all right if you help me."

As they approached Mr. Mason's plantation, Promise admired Grosemont's main house. It was tall and white, with majestic columns and black shutters, but usually she gave the house only a cursory look. Mr. Mason had a big, black dog, as black as his shutters. Whenever she walked past Grosemont's gates, it stuck its muzzle through the bars and barked at her, its saliva dripping down the iron and onto the ground in sticky puddles.

Today the dog was on her side of the gate, growling up at her from the end of Tim Mason's leash. Tim was huddled in a circle with Bernard, William, George, and Sam, who also had their hunting dogs with them.

"Hey, Riley!" William called out. "I see Grant finally cut you loose, huh?"

"Yeah."

"I bet he worked you over real good."

"You should know. You get it 'bout as much as I do. What're you boys doing out here anyway? It's gonna start raining hard any minute."

"We're gonna take the dogs tracking in the rain. It'll be good practice for 'em," Tim said.

"Practice for what? No law says you gotta go huntin' in the rain," Gus said.

"Practice huntin' niggers. You never can tell what a nigger'll do—they don't just run off on sunny days, you know," William said, laughing at him.

"Why haven't you been riding patrol with us, Augustus?" Tim asked. "We've been havin' a wallop of a time, haven't we boys?"

George let out a long, low whistle. "Sure have."

"Didn't my pa tell your pa we were meeting up in front of the church at three each Saturday?" Sam asked.

"Yeah, he told me."

"We waited on you almost an hour the first week. You could've told us you weren't coming."

"My pa said I could either join up with you guys or go huntin', so I went huntin'."

"What Riley *means* to say is he didn't come 'cause he was too busy havin' fun with his pa's niggers." William sneered at Promise, and she fixed her eyes on the ground.

"I'd just rather go huntin' is all." Gus shifted a little and rubbed the reins.

"But riding with the patrollers *is* huntin', Augustus," Tim said. "It's the best kind. We haven't seen anybody shot yet, though. 'Course we've only been at it a month so far."

"When Jefferson ran off again, we were right there when they caught him. He could've shot and killed the lot of us," Sam said.

Gus's jaw dropped. "Who'd he shoot at?"

"He didn't shoot at anybody, *exactly*. The patrollers said he didn't have a gun with him, but he *could* have. That's the fun of it—you never know what one'll do 'til he's cornered."

"It wasn't too much fun if you ask me," Bernard murmured. "Jefferson's *always* runnin', and he never goes far. Everybody knows where he's at—hid by his Injun gal beneath her floor. All we had to do was go right through the door and round him up."

"Your pa should've given him a good whuppin', Tim," William said. "That'll stop all that runnin'."

"Naw. Pa says it don't do any harm. Jefferson does good work, and he keeps everybody in practice for when someone runs for real."

"I'll tell you what's fun," Bernard said. "Catchin' niggers off guard and askin' 'em to see their passes."

"But you're only supposed to stop the ones you don't know are all right," Sam said. "Bernard stops everybody, even some of his own pa's niggers. They look at him like he's crazy when they hand 'em over."

"I think it's better to check than not," Bernard said. "The patrollers didn't say nothin' to me about it, so why should I listen to you?"

"Patrollers are just trash, you know that." Tim shook his head at Bernard's ignorance. "Of course they wouldn't say nothin' to you. Our pas pay 'em, so really they're workin' for us, not us for them."

"Y'all catch any without passes?" Gus asked.

"Yeah, some. The patrollers only whupped one of 'em, though," George said, looking disappointed. "Only our groomsman, Ben. The rest they let off with a warning. Fired a few shots just to scare 'em when their backs were turned, though."

"Me and Tim saw a free colored whupped," William bragged. "Wheaton's old nigger. What was his name, Tim?"

"Darby."

"Yeah, Darby. Me and Tim stopped old Darby, 'cause even though he's free now, he's still gotta show us his papers.

He didn't have his, and they whupped him good—didn't they, Tim?"

"Sure did. He was wailin' like you wouldn't believe, Augustus. Just hollerin' up a storm, 'bout how he was free. You should've seen it. It was a sight."

"Pa says if we ride with the patrollers awhile, we can hunt down runaways by ourselves," George said. "He says us boys can do for free what they pay them for."

William sniggered. "'Course he'd say that, since it's your pa's niggers who're always runnin' off, and he's the main one who's gotta keep paying the patrollers to get 'em back."

"That ain't true."

"Is too. My pa says it's 'cause your pa don't know what he's doing. No one from around here would let some no-count trash whup their niggers like your pa does, like letting the patrollers wail on Ben. Your pa don't know any better 'cause he's a Yankee, and Yankees can't tell the difference between good white folks and trash. Trash is all they *got* up there."

"You take that back," George said. His dog bared its teeth, ready to defend its master.

"Don't worry, George. Augustus'll make your family respectable enough when he marries Kitty," Sam teased. "You are planning to marry her, ain't you, Augustus?"

"Hell no," Gus snorted.

"You saying there's somethin' wrong with my sister?" George demanded.

Gus sighed. "I don't have time to sit out here arguing about a girl. The rain's picking up. I gotta get home."

"Why don't you change your mind and go tracking with us, Augustus?" Tim asked.

"I said we gotta get back."

"He couldn't come anyway," Sam said. "He's got his nigger with him."

"Why don't you go drop your nigger off and come on back? We'll wait for you," Tim offered.

"Naw, I got it!" William's eyes flashed like bright lights through the rain. "Riley, bring her along!"

Promise jumped slightly in the saddle, but she didn't move her eyes from the ground.

"What's she good for?" George said. "She'll just be in the way."

"Listen dummy, we'll use her for practice. Why should we just pretend to hunt down niggers when we got a real one right here?"

"That's a swell idea!" Bernard slapped his hands. "We'll give her a head start. When she's good and hid we'll trail her."

Promise reached back and squeezed Gus's leg.

Tim pointed up at her. "I think you're scaring her, look."

William aimed a wad of spit at the big, black dog's nose. "Niggers are always gettin' spooked over one thing or another. So can we use her, Riley?"

"No."

"Why not?"

"Someone might get hurt."

"We won't shoot at her, of course." William sighed, exasperated. "Whoever's got her will fire some shots in the air to tell the rest. And we'll stay in the woods. We won't go near the swamp. Don't you get spooked and run into the swamp, hear, girl? Don't you go runnin' off for real and get yourself hurt. It's only a game."

"No."

"Aw, we won't hurt her, we promise," Tim begged. "Come on, we'll have a whale of a time. My dog's as gentle as a lamb. She won't hurt a fly unless I give her the word." The other boys quickly vouched for the innocuous character of their dogs.

Gus felt Promise tremble. "I said no, and that's all there is to it."

William's eyes narrowed. "You know, maybe *she's* the reason Riley doesn't wanna marry your sister, George. Is she your *girl*, Riley? Maybe that's why you won't let us borrow her."

Gus dug his heels into Milo and rode at William, who backed up against the gate, his dog whimpering into retreat before the agitated, dripping-wet horse.

"Hey, what's the matter with you?" William cried, quivering in front of the animal's steaming nostrils.

"She ain't my girl, but she is my nigger," Gus said. "She only does what *I* say. And I say we're going home."

"Fine...fine! Just back that horse up," William panted, keeping back his tears. "Please. Back it up."

Gus turned Milo abruptly, and they headed for home.

"I'm *not* your nigger," Promise told him. She sat up straight and away from his body. "I *don't* do what you say."

"I know, Promise. I-I was just saying . . . 'cause they riled me so . . . I didn't mean it."

The rain was falling fast. It streamed down their faces, saturating their clothes until they were tight on their skin. Promise was grateful, for the torrents of fresh droplets camouflaged the salty ones streaming from her eyes. She pulled Gus's books out from under the folds of her dress, letting the rain hit them. "I don't do what you say," she whispered.

Book Two

CHAPTER 20

Letters I

In March 1848, Gus enrolled as a cadet in the South Carolina Military Academy at the Citadel in Charleston. Over the next three years, he and Promise corresponded through a series of letters. One hundred and fifty years later, during the restoration of Atterley, the Johansons' workmen discovered these letters in the plantation's main house—inside a cedar box that had been hidden beneath the floorboards. The letters, along with a note Gus had written Hannah after the South's surrender in the Civil War, were inside a worn Bible. Also inside the box were Rebecca's diaries, dating from 1827 to the time of her death in the summer of 1865.

Not appreciating the historical importance of the items, the men didn't show them to the Johansons until their work was completed months later. By that time, many of the letters had been badly damaged, making some passages, and even entire letters, unreadable. Franklin and Millicent made the box's contents available to the town's historical society, which entrusted them to its investigation committee.

The Bible belonged to Hannah—her name was printed on the inside cover in careful block lettering. The committee referenced her name and position in the household in Zachary Riley's journals. Next, they examined the letters in sequence. According to the contents of the writings, Gus and Promise were in the habit of exchanging letters regularly. A large number of them appeared to be missing—whether they were lost or purposely destroyed was unknown. Any passages that were damaged through careless handling were marked with the notation "[unintelligible]." The investigation committee then studied Gus's 1865 letter to Hannah, scrutinized the contents of Rebecca's diaries, and sent the articles to two sets of experts for authentication.

After the committee brought its findings to the general body, the historical society determined that the items should not be released to the public, and they respectfully suggested to the Johansons that they not include the letters and diaries in Atterley's collection of Riley family papers.

Charleston, March 30, 1848

Promise,

Everyday I have been wating for a letter from you. Mama has sent one with a few lines added in from Maum Hannah & I have already goten two from Jimmy. I doute seriusly wether there will be much free time to have any fun here. Each secund of the day has to be ackounted for & there are rules & more rules set down for everythin you can imajin. [unintelligible] We have to be up & awake before 5 in the morning! There are so many drills, marches, & purades. I am always to tiured out to do anything but sleep wen I get the chanse. Superentendent Colcock made it reel clear that there will be no diferenses made based on class but this is not true. The benefishiary cadets are much quiker at dressin themselves & there clothes always seem to be clean & free of rinkles during the inspektions. Havin a rich pa has given me & some other pay cadets a ruf time of it since we are not used to bein orderly. All my free time is used up to keep myself lookin neat. Tell Jenny & yung Martha that I am sendin them some trinkets from this fancy store called Henrietta's for cleanin & pressin my clothes for so long. I wish that I had pade more atention. Tell Molly I miss her cookin. There is nothin even close to it here. Mama told uncle Charles to envite me to dinner on Sunday during general leave & he says there cook is french & much better then Molly but I doute it.

Gus

Atterley, April 8, 1848

Gus,

I have not sat down to write a letter until now because your father has been entertaining an important guest, a Mr. Whitemarsh B. Seabrook, for the past few weeks. Since she has lately been forced to stay in her bed with stomach pains, your mother has depended on me to give Maum Hannah and Molly extra help. Mr. Seabrook is to be the next governor, at least according to the papers, and your father has agreed to obtain the support of a few key legislators. Apparently, they wrote some essays together for the Agricultural Society.

Maum Hannah does not like him. She says he has a quiet meanness about him, but he has always smiled kindly at me when I bring in the coffee. Tobias says Mr. Seabrook never leaves crumbs behind and that he is mindful of his ashes, so he believes that he has the makings of a fine governor.

I hope you dedicate yourself completely to your studies instead of searching for fun. [unintelligible] Jimmy says your performance has improved in the athletic competitions. I suppose that among men athletic skill is paramount, although I fail to see why high marks are not of greater significance. Either way you are severely disadvantaged.

I hope you are not so bad off that you can no longer bear a little teasing. In case you are in a truly sad state, I am prepared to offer any encouragement I can. I know that if you apply yourself, you will do well. I am sure you will make friends, for you will find many kindred spirits among your classmates who equate high birth with virtue, and will welcome you into a brotherhood bound together by familial snobbery. But I must warn you, Gus, if you end up thinking too highly of yourself I will take great pleasure in bringing you down a peg or two. In all seriousness, please take care and try and find ways to make yourself happy.

Promise

Charleston, April 19, 1848

Dear Promise,

I was glad to get your letter, but please do not send back any more of my letters after you have corekted them. Mama's letters are already full of cryin about my english & such. She is afraide they will think I have goten no instruktion at all. She said she will get Mr. Grant dismised & pa says he will get his money back. I cannot help feelin sorry for pore Mr. Grant. It is not his falt I did not pay atention. I am worse off then the cadets who went to the free schools. Pa had to get help to get me in here, but who ast him to? I wish I was in Californya pikin up gold. [unintelligible] I should have snuk away & I wood have snuk the boys away to. We had it planned. They were goin to act like my niggers til we got there & then I was gonna set them free. You could have come to if you stayed out of the way. But I missed my chanse. I am strugglin with my studies. The corses for the fourth class are arithmatic, geography, South Carolina history, & grammar. History will be the hardest. Professor Brisbane expeks to much. We are also bein tought the duties of a private soldier. It seems that I am always readin somethin or another & tryin to force facks & figures into my brane. [unintelligible] *Tell Muley they can use the carts. I hid them beneeth an old sheet behind Jesse's weelbarow in the storehouse. Pa is not lettin me come home for a visit anytime soon. I hafe to stay here. To make the boys wait til Christmas to race wood be selfish I think. When you come to Charleston please sneek some of pa's segars if you can. If you do not I am gonna ask Jimmy.*

Gus

Crestview, July 16, 1848

Dear Gus,

I am sorry to hear you are not doing well in geography. It does not sound to me as if your professor hates you. I think he would be less abusive if you would show him that you are willing to try harder. I will not be joining your parents in the city. Your father has said that from now on I will stay in the country during the entire summer when they journey to Charleston. Your mother protests daily, but he has remained firm. I do not know what I will do without your mother, or Maum Hannah, or Molly. Jimmy says he will visit me often.

He told me that you got sick off those cigars. I hope you learned your lesson. You had no business with them in the first place. Lassie and Liza will be here, and Young Martha, Jenny, and Baby Button. That is something, I suppose. [unintelligible] *They leave in a week. I have tried not to think hard about it.*

Thank you, thank you, thank you for the books! It will make the loneliness easier to bear when I can hide away in my room with some warm milk and drown myself in the pages. Muley has come to visit me and says to write you hello from him and the rest, and to ask you to please send some more of that saltwater taffy when you get a chance. Also, he wants me to tell you that Harold has caught the biggest fish now—a catfish weighing 35 pounds. Muley is standing over me now, and insists that I point out in the letter where I have written down his request. What good it does I do not know, since he cannot read and is not interested in learning how. Please take care, and I hope you feel better soon.

Promise

Atterley, August 14, 1848

My Dear Gus,

The house seems to ache and groan without Maum Hannah wandering about, putting things in order, and your mother's laughter. Old Martha was buried Sunday. [unintelligible] *It is all very depressing. I have been in a sad mood for weeks and I cannot seem to rid myself of my gloom. At times I cry until my eyelids swell up to twice their size. You would laugh if you could see me now. At present, it is all I can do to keep my nose from dripping all over the page. I consider myself blessed to have you to write to so that I may have some consolation.*

Atterley will soon be overflowing with babies. Harold's girl is having a baby for him. And Mama had a boy this time, named Danny. Also, Young Martha has gotten so big now that it is difficult for her to move about, and I have had to take over the cooking. I know it cannot compare to Molly's, but so far I have not gotten any complaints except from Lassie and Liza, who complain about everything anyway.

Boris has asked Daddy for my sister Sylvie. Despite my counsel, she is willing to be his wife. I think she is too young. Boris wants to marry her as soon as possible, because he is anxious to have Sylvie moved from the street to the circle, and I cannot fault him for that. At any rate, they have to wait, because Reverend Wickerson says he will not perform any weddings until the family returns from Charleston.

Promise

Charleston, October 2, 1848

Promise,

Jimmy came to visit me & pretended to be my cousin from Georgia. He wanted to tour the grounds. We are between King & Meeting Street. There is not much to see, just a two-story brick building & a magazine to store arms & ammunitions but he seemed impresed with it. [unintelligible] *He met some of my professors. I almost laughed out loud when they called him sir. Jimmy played it real good, shaking hands & acting like a fine gentleman. He had come before with Pa but I suppose they did not rekognize him clean shaved & with one of Pa's suites on.*

It was my skeme. Jimmy's skin looks white enuf & with those blue eyes of his they did not look too careful at him. Of course do not tell Molly or even Muley just to be safe. I would say tell Maum Hannah, cause she would laugh, but maybe she would be worried, so you best not. I told him he can visit now as often as he wants & we can go out into the city & maybe to a show or a restarant. Wont that be funny? But Jimmy says he is too well known for that.

Mama keeps writing about how I should be calling on Georgeanna. [unintelligible] I will send you my schoolbooks after my exams in November so you can see what has been torchering me so during my time here. After you get through them I will give you an exam so you can see how you would have done at the Academy. I know you would like that. I am improving a little & that makes me glad. You should not be sad about having to stay at Atterley. I think you got a better deal. Say hello to the boys.

PS—I cannot see why a man cannot be a fine man just because he is a negro. I have never met a finer one then Jimmy & I am not just saying so because he brung me some cigars.

Gus

Charleston, October 19, 1848

Promise,

Pa seems happy with the rough living & strict discipline, but he is unhappy that I get no favors with duties, treatment, or advancement over the beneficiary cadets. I am worried too, even though I have improved a lot, especially since examinations are coming quick. I begged him not to see Superintendent Colcock about it. I am having a hard enough time making friends. I have two. Abrams for one & Inglesby for another. And even though they both went to West Point, Pa going to him did not even work. All distinktions are just for merit.

He must have very little confidence in me. It is clear he suspects I will be a failure without the advantage of being his son. He did not care that I have been doing better in my classes. First Lieutenant Leland told him how much better I was doing in mathematics hisself. We went for a walk & Pa did a whole bunch of talking. I was watching the ships docking instead of listening.

[unintelligible] When I read over your letters, especially when you talk about weekends at the Promised Land, I feel comforted with thoughts of home. It is hard not to be miserable. Do you think I am acting like a child?

Gus

Charleston, November 22, 1848

Dear Promise,

I have never studied so hard in my life! Yes, I know that is not saying much. Thank you for your prayers. I have hardly slept for a whole month. The examinations lasted three long days. You will be happy to know I did well enough to stay here—just barely though. Pa seemed pleased, but I can never really tell for certain. Jimmy was smiling so hard when I told him, I thought he would burst. He gave me a new saddle. He must have saved a long time to buy it. I did not want to take it at first, but he ensisted. The superintendent gave our examination results to the board. Two of my classmates were denied promotion and four were discharged. The strongest have survived, and thankfully I am among them!

Gus

Atterley, December 5, 1848

Dear Gus,

Uriah has died at last. Doctor Needham said the disease that was eating away at his bones finally killed him. He lived longer than anyone expected, and that is good, I suppose. At the end he could not even stand, his legs were so weak. The boys were all torn up when they buried him. They told me they knew you would have been here if you could.

I look forward to seeing you for Christmas. When are you coming? Jimmy wants to know because he would like to come and get you. I have been working for months on your present. Everyone is anxious to have you home. They often ask me for news about you and I share as much with them as I can—without betraying your confidence, of course. Molly is getting ready to cook all of your favorites. Muley and the others have gotten together and have something special planned for you. I do not know what. Muley is taking great pleasure in not telling me. [unintelligible]

Promise

Charleston, December 15, 1848

Dearest Promise,

I will not be returning to Atterley for Christmas. Pa and Mama want me to spend my two week furlough with the Harpers. Majors delivered Pa's letter, but he could give me no other justifikation for this change in plans, except that Mama wants me to get to know my uncle and his family better. I understand Mama's motives, but I do not know why Pa does not want me home for Christmas. I am dreading spending the holidays with Georgeanna and her horrid brothers, but I will exercise self-control and bear it like a man.

I hope this has not made you too unhappy. [unintelligible] I must admit, it will not feel like Christmas without you nearby to tease and taunt me.

Pa, through Majors, has sent me more than my usual allowance for the holidays. I have to buy presents for the Harpers, of course, but I will have enough left to buy something special for you from one of the shops Mama likes on King Street. I hope I will find something that will suit your vanity. I wish I could see your face when you open your present on Christmas morning, but Pa seems fixed on keeping me far from all that I care for. Have a Merry Christmas, Promise, and send my hellos to the others. Think of me when you are lighting the tree.

Gus

Atterley, December 31, 1848

Dear Gus,

[unintelligible] Christmas was wonderful, but you were greatly missed. Thank you for the dress my darling, darling Gus! It was lovely, with such marvelously sloping shoulders and tight sleeves! You must have had help picking it out. I have already worn it twice—once for Christmas, and again at Sylvie's wedding. I will send your gifts through Jimmy. The Stantons hosted the Christmas party this year. We all had a very quiet dinner in the kitchen once your parents had gone out. Everyone sends you their love. I hope your holiday was joyful.

Promise

CHAPTER 21

Letters II

Charleston, January 11, 1849

Dear Promise,

Happy New Year! I had thought that Christmas at Redmond would be an awful chore, and in most aspeks it was. Georgeanna's brothers have gotten even worse as they have grown older. Caleb steals his father's liquor and then lets the servants take the blame, and Frank kept trying to set the tail of poor Georgeanna's cat on fire. For Christmas they tried to give me a woman. I do not know if you understand what I mean by that. They took me to a shop outside of town. It looked ordinary enough, but then the owner led us inside a back door and up a flight of stairs. It took a moment before I realized what that place was. I was curious, I admit, but of course I ran out of there as quick as I could.

Since then they have not stopped laughing at me. But what was I supposed to do? Other cadets have been dumb enough to take that chance, but I cannot risk disappointing Pa. If I were caught I would be immediately dismissed from the Academy like Rice was last term.

My aunt was very nice to me, too nice, and she was forever asking questions about Pa's property. She thought she was being clever—that I could not guess why she had such an interest in his money. My uncle was not so welcoming. He was civil, but just barely. I had never stayed at Redmond for so long a time. Truly Promise, I was shocked by how mean the Harpers treated their slaves. Georgeanna's brothers seemed to love whipping them. They waited until midday when the streets were full of noise, so people passing by could not hear the screams. Aunt Eleanor keeps count of every onion and potato.

It was Georgeanna who made spending the holidays in Charleston more bearable. I know you are surprised, so was I. She is really quiet and shy, not vain like I remember, and she is a lot kinder than her mother. She is very nice to her maid and to the rest of the house servants. She likes to go for walks in the city, and I have agreed to join her so she will not be uneskorted. I do not mind—although she still tends to rattle away at times. She admired your Christmas present from a window display. That is how I knew you would like it. Thank you for the scarf, and thank the boys for the collection of arrowheads. I miss you and the others so much.

Gus

Atterley, March 20, 1849

Dear Gus,

You should not let Muley and the others upset you so much. They do care about you, not just about what you can give them. It is only that they are so busy, and do not have a great deal of free time to dictate letters to me. Muley does not come by as often as he used to. He is sweet on Mr. Mason's Rachel and goes to see her when-ever he can.

I do not agree that it is slavery that has separated you from your friends. I believe the culprit is only time and distance. As far as I am concerned, slavery is meant by God for good, just like Reverend Wickerson says, although unfortunately, as you say, it is often abused by masters who are not true Christians and do not treat their slaves as the Lord has commanded.

[unintelligible]

Someday I hope the Negro race will advance to the point where we will no longer need the guidance of white men. Myself and the other house servants have had a superior upbringing, and we would behave properly and do as we should without supervision, but imagine what would happen if the field slaves were all of a sudden let loose to do as they pleased! Who would make them work?

I am happy that you have made such marked improvements and I am astonished that you find yourself actually enjoying your classes. Your mother brags about you constantly to every visitor who passes through Atterley's halls. Your father says little about your progress, I know, but I am sure that he is equally proud of you.

Promise

Charleston, May 2, 1849

Dear Promise,

Mama should not have worried you. I am just fine. It is true there has been an outbreak of yellow fever *in Charleston, but because of it we have been dismissed for the summer.* [unintelligible]

Pa is sending me to Europe instead of letting me come home. I will be leaving on Tuesday. Aunt Eleanor declares that she is coming too with my cousins. She is in concert with Mama—believing that if they throw Georgeanna and me together often enough, love will blossom. It is very tiring. Plenty of the other cadets would be happy to have her attentions, but they are not so well off as Pa, so my aunt continues to push her off on me. At least the trip will give me a chance to work on my French. I'll ship you something disgustingly extravagant once I get over there.

Gus

Atterley, July 18, 1849

Dear Gus,

All is well here. I did have a touch of the fever, but I soon felt better. Your mother wrote that she would never forgive your father if something happened to me. I am sorry you got sick on your way to Liverpool. England sounds dreadfully gray and bland, but Blenheim and Warwick sound marvelous! I wish I could see a real castle—although you did not make your visit sound very romantic.

Muley has asked your father to marry Rachel. He said he would think it over and tell Muley yes or no by the end of the week. I am expecting a positive answer. I am very happy about it, and so is Mama. Rachel is a very sweet girl, and as far as I can tell he has been true to her. Perhaps Muley will make it into heaven after all.

Promise

London, England, August 7, 1849

Dearest Promise,

It is all gray and gloomy here and we cannot go out. I am so tired of the rain. It is not good to think too much, and days like this one make me reflective. I am not sure that I agree with you and my fellow cadets that slavery is so settled a question. The Academy has taught me how, not what to think, and my time oversees has given me a fresh perspective on many things.

Reverend Miles subscribes to the same school of thought as Reverend Wickerson—that it was the white man's duty and moral obligation to save African savages from lives of godlessness. But this does not seem to be an adequate explanation, for if the purpose of enslaving the Negro was to save his soul, why would he still be kept in chains after he has entered into the Christian brotherhood? "For ye are all the children of God by faith in Christ Jesus. For as many of you as have been baptized into Christ have put on Christ. There is neither Jew nor Greek, there is neither bond nor free, there is neither male nor female: for ye are all one in Christ Jesus." If we all are now one in Christ, why would the Lord condone a practice that allows some of His children to reign so absolutely over the others? And if slavery is a happy condition for the Negro, where all of his needs are provided for, and so on, would any white man gladly take his place, even if well fed and kindly treated?

It has also been argued that the Negro is an inherently inferior being—that without the restraint on his behavior that slavery provides, he would act in accordance with the vile baseness of his nature to the detriment of society and himself. You have made reference to that possibility yourself. But I have met many Negroes here who are just like the freedmen in Charleston—except they are entirely free from the taint of slavery—who are well educated and in every way respectable. They have become prosperous through their own efforts and abilities, and are as genteel as any white man I have ever met. How many more could do the same if allowed? Muley? Molly? Jimmy? Hannah? Or some of those now sweating in Atterley's fields? And even if it is true, as it is generally thought, that these Negroes are exceptional members of their race—that their success is more of a testament to their own unique attributes rather than an example of what their entire race is capable of—would it not still be unjust to subject all to slavery if only for the sake of these?

And what of the poor whites, whom my peers despise even more than their black slaves? I have detected no natural superiority in them. How can their baseness of character be explained if both their color and religion work against it? Cannot an argument be made that they should also be enslaved for their own good, based upon the same rationale that is advanced to keep the Negro in bondage? In that case, would not slavery best be justified based on the poverty and ignorance of the individual, rather than their race? But that notion speaks against the most basic principles of our great country, and I cannot think of one reputable man in the North or South who would not be horrified by the idea.

It is true that the Southern economy is dependent upon slavery. Some believe it is not a moral issue at all, but one of state's rights—that the North should not interfere in matters that only concern the Southern states. For me this is the most troubling argument. I do not believe the North would oppose slavery if its own economy were tied to it, and without question, the South cannot continue as it has for generations without the subjugation of the Negro. A white man cannot become rich in the South unless he profits, in some respect, from slave labor. I myself have benefited from the privileges that slavery affords. But the South has created her own dependence, and if the economic prosperity of the Southern states is sufficient reason to justify our enslavement of the Negro race, how is the white man any different from the African savage, who feeds upon his fellow man to ensure his own survival?

I do not know the answers to these questions, but they trouble me greatly, and I pose them to you, Promise, for you are the only person to whom I dare ask them.

Gus

Atterley, September 23, 1849

My Dear Gus,

Really, you spoil me. The perfume is heavenly. Your mother even asked if she might have a few drops when she goes visiting. Do not mind Hannah when she told you the shawl was too expensive. It is the softest thing I have ever laid my hands on. She has become quite attached to it, though she will not admit it. She always wears it when she goes to visit Jesse.

Please, please, please, Gus! Someday you will have to take me to Paris! I wish you could stay a little longer before you go on to Rome so you would have a chance to visit more shops. Your mother and I are in ecstasy. And how in the world did you explain buying all those hats and dresses? They could not have thought they were all for your mother. Everyone is quite envious of me. You better send the others their presents now and not wait until you return, or they will hate you by then.

Promise

Charleston, November 29, 1849

Dear Promise,

I am feeling more and more at home here. The cadets really are a good group of fellows, although not so much fun as the boys at Atterley. [unintelligible] *But I am a man now, and it has long since been time to put away childish things. I have done well on my exams, especially United States history. My weakest subjects were algebra and geometry.*

You will be happy to know that I have joined the Calliopean Literary Society. Our motto is "Sapere audi" or "Dare to know." At the first meeting I attended, John Calhoun himself was the speaker! He was excellent, although quite frail. His words moved me profoundly, and opened my eyes to a new way of looking at the world. Either slavery is a noble institution or it is a great evil. I used to think it was the latter, but now I am not so sure. What do you think? Sometimes I miss simpler days when I had only my heart to lead the way.

Gus

CHAPTER 22

Letters III

Atterley, January 14, 1850

Dear Gus,

Six of Mr. Stanton's slaves ran off on New Year's Day, and still they are not found. The planters have put their slaves on curfews until they are returned, and everyone is on pins and needles. All has gone on the same on Atterley, though. Your father knows none of us will run. But Hannah will not allow any of the house servants to stray from Atterley after nightfall whether we have passes or not—except for Jimmy, of course. There is not a white man in the Low Country who would dare lay a finger on him.

[unintelligible] I do not know why everyone keeps fretting so over slavery. I think you should concern yourself with weightier matters, like your studies, so that you will not compromise your standing in your classes. Whether slavery will ever be gotten rid of, I do not know, but debating over it will not change anything. I cannot see your father, Mr. Stanton, or any of the rest ever giving us up.

Promise

Atterley, March 5, 1850

Dear Gus,

Little Remmy has been chasing Jenny for a while now, until finally she has taken a liking to him. Juno says it is an abomination, as they are such near relations, but she has only herself to blame. She frightened away all of the others Jenny fancied, threatening to set your father upon them, until Little Remmy alone was left. Your mother and I are in agreement with Juno that it is unnatural, but they seem to be getting along well. Little Remmy is always in the main house so he can be near her. Jenny says she has asked Jesus to save his soul and has committed herself to reading to him daily from the Bible. He must care for her a great deal, because her sermonizing has not yet driven him away.

Sir Henry made Billy a cooper and Andy the head plowman, even though he is only twenty. They are both strutting around Atterley like peacocks, but I am glad for them. Muley seems depressed and listless since your father said again that he could not marry Rachel. I have brought him all the sweet things I can think of to make him feel better, but nothing has worked. Daddy gets frustrated with him sometimes. Muley does not seem to share his passion for working in the smithy. I believe Daddy often wishes that I was born a boy so I could be at his side instead of Muley. The twins will soon be old enough to help Daddy, though, and they seem more promising.

Promise

Charleston, April 26, 1850

Dear Promise,

 Calhoun's body was carried in a funeral procession to the Citadel. Senator Mason of Virginia, a cousin of our Mr. Mason, gave the body over to Governor Seabrook, who in turn surrendered it to Mayor Hutchinson. The procession then went down King Street to Hasell, then to Meeting Street, around White Point, up toward Broad Street, and then to city hall. We marched in the parade along with Charleston's civil authorities, firemen, benevolent societies, Masonic lodges, etc. I cannot remember seeing so many people in the city for any occasion.

 I feel very depressed this evening. Calhoun was the greatest statesman this country has ever known, and a true son of South Carolina. His last Senate speech, read for him by Senator Mason, has been printed in all of the papers, and I believe that it was the most inspiring oration I have ever read. Have you read it? If not, I would encourage you to put down your novels and fashion circulars and do so. I believe you would be inspired.

 We are living in an extraordinary age. As Calhoun explained, the movement to abolish slavery has spread so rapidly that the South is now forced to choose between abolition, which is impossible, and secession. If the Union is to be saved, the North must make significant concessions to the South so that she can maintain her safety and honor. Calhoun argued that the Constitution can only be complied with if the South is given an equal right to newly acquired territory, and if the North agrees to strict compliance with the fugitive slave laws. If the

Union may not be saved, the South must be, through, I pray, peaceful dissolution. Georgeanna heartily agrees with me and was a great admirer of his as well.

Gus

Charleston, May 23, 1850

Dear Promise,

Yes, French is still a struggle. This year it is much more advanced. I know you are dedicating yourself to becoming fluent, but please do not send me any more letters written in French. You are still the superior student and it takes me too long to read them. I like my modern history, rhetoric, and architecture classes the best. I believe I will master this year's exams.

During Governor Johnson's term, the Board of Visitors asked him for $15,000 to build another story on the Citadel to make more room for the cadets. Its security as a military post was also a concern. The school is no longer overshadowed by nearby houses that would pose a threat to our defenses if they were overtaken by an enemy. This is fortunate, for many in Charleston are concerned that if California is admitted to the Union as a free state, there will be a shift in the balance of power unfavorable to the South. There is an uneasy feeling in the streets, and many are fearful of the future.

The board has decided that from now on no students who are not state residents will be admitted to South Carolina's military academies. I am in full agreement. As Governor Seabrook says, the academies were designed to train the youth of South Carolina for war. With the political climate so unstable, this aim is more important now than it ever was. The governor has recommended that the state purchase a pyrotechnic laboratory, engineering instruments, and a battery of artillery.

Gus

Atterley, July 6, 1850

Dear Gus,

It is universally believed that your father will be joining the South Carolina legislature next year. Everyone here is talking of it. I think your mother hopes he will not win. Her letters are full of worries over moving to Columbia. Both Hannah and Jimmy say she has not been herself since your father has announced his intentions. But I am happy for him. He has worked very hard for it. I suppose Mr. Majors will run things while he is gone.

Molly is sending you another batch of tarts, since you liked the others so much. I told her that I suspected you had not eaten them all—that you were selling them to the other cadets for more pocket money—but that only seemed to please her more. [unintelligible]

Florence and Miriam have not been speaking for two weeks. Florence believes that Big Remmy has been sneaking away to see Miriam. I do not believe it is true. Miriam is too much of a lady to do such a thing, but Florence is convinced of it and she is threatening to tell Tucker her suspicions. Your mother has pledged to come from Charleston and intervene before things go too far.

Promise

Charleston, August 22, 1850

Dear Promise,

I have recently come to a profound realization. I attribute many of my weaknesses in my younger years to African slavery. Myself and many of my peers were prevented from acquiring the strength of character that comes with self-reliance. I applaud my father's wisdom in taking the appropriate measures to remedy these deficiencies. Because of him, I am developing into a respectable gentleman through strict adherence to discipline and duty.

In answer to your question, I do not know why God has chosen to make the white man the black man's master, but is it for man to question His divine judgment? God has given the white man the responsibility of caring for his slaves, just as he is to care for his wife and children. It does seem unfair, I know, but when we, as His creations, refuse to submit to the authority that God has placed over us, we are out of His divine will, and chaos results.

Of course, Georgeanna feels as I do and understands the importance of staying in the place that the Lord has put you. I blame Mother and myself for not allowing you to find contentment within your sphere. We have done you a disservice. She has pampered you from birth, and I have continued along that line even though I know it is not good for you to grow accustomed to expensive things that do not suit your station in life. But I cannot help it. You are my Promise and I adore you so.

Unfortunately, being a Negro, and of course a woman, you are to be submissive to every other being that God has made in His image. I wish it were not so, but that is the reality.

Gus

Charleston, September 14, 1850

Dear Promise,

Why have you not written me? Nearly a month has passed without my hearing from you. I have waited and waited for a letter from you to arrive, but I cannot wait any longer. Perhaps you have gotten very busy. If this is the case, please write to me as soon as you have a moment.

Gus

Charleston, October 18, 1850

Promise,

Since you still have not written me, I am assuming you are upset because of what I wrote in my letter two months ago. I am sorry if anything I wrote offended you. That was not my intent. Come now, Promise, surely you realize that I am a sincere friend of the Negro and have never rejoiced in his sad position, but I am helpless to change a system that has been in place for hundreds of years. Slavery is the lifeblood of the South. What can I do about it? It is not I who created slavery, and I am helpless to eradicate it. Without slave labor we would all be destroyed.

When the time comes, I am determined to be as good and as kind a master as I can possibly be. That is the best that I am able to do. Father has asked me to return to Atterley after the New Year since he will be in Columbia. I regret that I must leave Charleston where I have made such good friends, but I must take my place and do the will of my father. As the Board of Visitors instructs—prompt, respectful obedience to every command from proper authority is the first duty of a soldier.

Gus

Charleston, November 22, 1850

Promise,

Although you still refuse to write to me, I will continue to be a faithful friend to you. I was selected to be an attendant to the graduates. It was quite an honor. Enclosed is the program from the commencement exercises. The procession began at the Citadel and moved to the Second Baptist Church on Wentworth. There was a prayer, music, salutary address, and more music. And then there were several orations by the premier graduates on such topics as Conscience and Moral Sense and Public Opinion. The gentlemen received their diplomas from the chairman of the Board of Visitors, and the superintendent performed the benediction. There were many important people there—members of Congress, state and federal judges, officers of the army and navy, and of course the governor and the other members of the Board.

After the commencement, the corps hosted a ball, and I was honored to have Georgeanna on my arm. All the other cadets were quite envious of me. I wish you could attend such events. It is sad that it is only your color that prevents you. I read over a rough copy of that letter I sent you. I think I see why you were so angry with me before. Please, please, forgive me and show me your mercy.

Gus

Atterley, January 1, 1851

Gus,

I suppose I should forgive you. Perhaps you have suffered enough. I am sure you believe that it was the brooch you sent me for Christmas that has softened my heart, but that is not true. It is my generous nature along with the spirit of charity that comes with the season.

Promise

Charleston, January 17, 1851

Dearest Promise,

I am glad that you have chosen not to stay angry with me. You know I could never bear that. I will be in great need of your support once I return home. It will be very difficult for me, but I am prepared to fulfill my duties as Atterley's master to the utmost of my ability, to put aside all personal feelings that may cloud my judgment, exercise the restraint and self-control that I have been taught, and become a respectable man of dignity and honor—a credit to my father, my family, and my race.

"Honour and shame from no condition rise; Act well your part: there all the honour lies."

Gus

CHAPTER 23

Homecoming

Promise circled the main house once more with her lips pressed together and her fingertips fluttering against her leg, *Ta-ta Bruum, Ta-ta Bruum, Ta-ta Bruum*. After Rebecca had returned from Columbia, she had seated herself in the parlor, surveyed the room with fresh eyes, and determined that her son couldn't possibly come home and witness the table lamps looking so irregular next to the armoire, and the console a full four feet away from the window.

Rebecca then extended her scrutiny to the state of Atterley's other rooms until the entire main house had been shifted around, revealing hidden imperfections. Yesterday Atterley's walls had appeared a chaste white, or a muted peach, yellow, or blue. Now what had been hidden was exposed—grease, dirt, and jagged scratches from grating furniture.

"Jenny, are you almost finished in there?" Promise called out. Jenny emerged from the library with pale yellow cream resting in moist smears on her face, hands, and arms, making her skin look like it had melted in spots. "You didn't get any on the floor, did you Jenny?" *Ta-ta Bruum*.

"No," Jenny answered, not really sure. "But no matter how much I paint, I just can't cover up those brown stains. The paint runs right over 'em. It won't stick. Maybe we should call L'il Remmy. He'll know what to do."

"Did you try and wash the dirt off first?"

"Noooo . . . you didn't say *wash*, Promise, you said *paint*." *Ta-ta Bruum. Ta-ta Bruum.* "Wash the wall off *first*, Jenny." *Ta-ta Bruum.* "*Then* paint it over."

"Ooooh." Jenny watched Promise's fingers. "Don't be mad, Promise. Just tell me exactly what you want me to do next time so I'll know."

"All right, Jenny," Promise breathed. *Tap-tap, Ta-ta Bruum.*

Button, who after she had turned thirteen had begun throwing fits until the servants stopped calling her "Baby Button," swept the dirt in Zachary's study into a corner behind the bookcase.

"You sweep that dirt out of there and empty it outside," Juno ordered her daughter, looking regal with a white gardenia tucked into her hair.

"But Mama," Button protested, "it's just Massa Gus who's comin'."

"But Massa Riley will be home from Columbia next Friday, so just go on and sweep it out. *Really*, Button." Juno noticed the remnants of Majors's cigar in an ashtray, and she tapped it into a handkerchief. "And when you finish with the sweeping, clean off Massa's desk. Then dust off the portraits in here and in the hall."

"Missus said she wanted me to change her bedcovers," Button said.

"Never mind that."

"But—"

"I *said*, never mind that," Juno repeated serenely, rearranging her flower. She caught Young Martha's arm as she was passing by with a bucket of water. "Missus needs her bedcovers changed."

"I was just about to rest for a bit . . ." Young Martha began. Juno stared at her pleasantly, but her fingers were icy.

Young Martha studied her bucket. "All right, I guess. It won't take long, I suppose."

Eliza had won a coin toss with her sister when jobs were being distributed, and was settled comfortably in the warmth of the kitchen, helping Molly fold piecrusts. "When's Massa Gus getting here, Mama?"

"Don't know. Flour first, before you roll. You're gonna mess up my crusts, Liza."

"Is he gonna be the massa now?"

"I suppose."

Eliza rolled the pin back roughly, making gaping holes.

"Stop . . . Stop!" Molly yanked the dough from her and stroked it against her breast to make amends. "You don't know what the hell you're doin'. You're worse than Jenny."

Eliza lunged for the dough. "I'll fix it, Mama."

"Git."

"Ma-ma!"

"I said git! Tell Promise to come'ere."

"Dammit!" Lassie cursed the blossoming dust clouds and pounded on the rug with her broom. "My back's achin' so bad it's 'bout to give out, and Liza gets to sit in there on her big behind doin' nothin'," she grumbled. She broke her rhythm to swat a passing chicken up in the air in the direction of the coup, where it landed in a frightened flurry. "All so Massa Gus can step on Missus's rugs and dirty 'em up again. I can do that my *damn* self. His mud's no better'n mine."

Florence and Miriam sat around Miriam's kitchen table surrounded by their clamoring children and yards of multicolored, multi-textured fabric. They had been sewing all day—sewing and cutting, hemming and stitching—their hair piled high beneath calico scarves. Miriam, while continuing to deny culpability, had sworn to her sister that she would never again be alone with Big Remmy, and so they had called a temporary truce.

Miriam grabbed her son and one of her nephews by their collars once they had the misfortune to wander too near. "Richard! Donoghue! I told you two to quiet down!" She swatted the boys on their bottoms and sent them away squalling. "Do you think Massa Gus'll do all right?" she asked her sister. "He was just like one of them from the street, remember? An unruly little savage. Tucker's worried he and Amos won't be able to make them mind once Massa Gus's in charge."

"Tucker's right to worry. I'm not ashamed to admit I have *my* doubts," Florence mumbled, her mouth full of stickpins. She jerked her head in the direction of the fields. "Massa Gus'll likely go too easy on those black niggers." She studied her pillowcase and pulled out a row of stitches. "Unless schooling's given him some sense."

Jesse walked mournfully through the hothouse, deciding which of his flowers would be sacrificed to fill Atterley's vases. He made his selections carefully, keeping his clipping shears hidden behind his back until the last possible moment, so as to not needlessly frighten his darlings. "Jesse's sorry, baby," he whispered to an exceptionally vibrant tulip before cutting its lovely green neck and adding it to the pile in his basket.

Hannah watched his sad ritual from a respectful distance. "I gotta get back to the main house in a minute, Jesse. Miss Rebecca's been worryin' me to death. I'll sure be glad to have Massa Gus back. I've missed that boy. He'll be a good massa, kinder than Massa Riley."

"He ain't a boy no more," Jesse told her quietly. "He always had a warm heart like his mama, but when I mate my roses, I never seen they chillun take some of one, and none of the other. Massa Gus must have some of his daddy in him, too." Jesse stroked two zinnias joined by a single stem. "Don't worry 'bout it now," he murmured, positioning his shears, "you two're goin' together."

"Massa Gus has been raised right—he won't forget," Hannah said, offended.

"I ain't sayin' you raised him wrong, Hannah. Just sayin' that some blooms is the purtiest things you ever seen when the sun's shinin'—standin' strong and tall. But when they gets just a touch of cold, ain't long 'fore they wilts away. You never know what kind you gots sometimes . . . not 'til winter come."

Promise caressed a serving tray, putting on a light coat of polish while she caught her breath. Hours after Rebecca had swept through its rooms, birthing confusion with her proclamations, the house was still in disarray. Jenny, Button, Grace, and Christmas needed constant watching. Juno was industrious and efficient, but she insisted upon choosing her projects independently, leaving questions as to what remained to be done. Little Remmy still hadn't finished repairing the staircase and kept sneaking away to visit Jenny whenever Juno's back was turned. Young Martha had not yet relinquished her pregnancy privileges, and was prone to sitting down whenever the mood struck her, until at Hannah's prodding she rose with a weighty groan, supporting her hollow baby belly.

Promise flipped her rag over, covering the tray with generous circles to make it shine. Polishing the silver relaxed her. From her little pink chair, Promise had watched Hannah for years—rubbing and humming, smiling and shining, loving the silver. Now that her own duty-free days of leisure had passed, she understood it was not the silver Hannah had loved, but the solitude. The cool air felt good on her skin. It had taken a great deal of convincing to persuade Tobias to let her leave the windows open in the formal dining room.

"Wide open windows in this weather?" Tobias asked her. "What will Massa Augustus say?"

"Don't be silly, Tobias, it's just Gus," Promise told him, laughing. "He's not Massa Riley. He wouldn't worry over us letting the heat out, wasting wood." Now with her mind cleared, Promise wondered whether or not that was true, and she had to admit that she wasn't really sure who Jimmy was bringing home that day—an old friend, or a new master.

Eliza poked her head into the room. She saw Promise and cut her eyes. "Mama wants you in the kitchen," she said.

"How long's it gonna take you, L'il Remmy?" Jenny asked him, watching the hard waves ripple over his back as he sanded the railing. "If you finish before it gets too cold, we can go walking."

"I'm tryin', Jenny, but it's kinda hard on me when you're standing there looking so pretty," he said sweetly, making her giggle.

"That you I hear, Remmy?" Lassie called from the kitchen. She came toward them, sucking at the juice of her apple before taking another lusty bite. She was weary, full of dust, and feeling especially vicious.

"Hey Lassie," Little Remmy said, fixing his eyes on his work.

"Could you bring me out some water, Remmy?" Lassie took another bite, sinking her teeth in deep. "I'm gonna take me a nice hot bath."

"No, he can't," Jenny said, her voice quivering toward panic. "Can't you see he's working?"

Lassie brushed past her and curled up on the step beneath Little Remmy, giving him a clear view down the front of her dress. "You can answer for yourself, ain't that right, Remmy?

Why don't you tell Jenny you're your own man?" Her voice was low and husky. "How about comin' on home with me?"

He swallowed hard and helpless, and burrowed his eyes into her cleavage.

"You stay away from him." Jenny wrapped her arm around Little Remmy's shoulders. "He doesn't do that any more. L'il Remmy belongs to me and Jesus now."

"Is that right?" Lassie threw her head back and laughed. "That ain't what he was whisperin' to me last week behind the wood shop, was it, Remmy? 'Course, maybe he just didn't have a chance to get to that. He was too busy doin' other things, like lifting up my dress." Lassie saw the shock and pain in Jenny's eyes, and the mortification in Little Remmy's. She sat back, satisfied. "That's right, Jenny. I don't think you've got any idea what L'il Remmy likes doin'—not like I do."

"You're a liar," Jenny said, her eyes filling up. "L'il Remmy's been baptized. Reverend Wickerson dunked him all the way under. I was there. I saw it. L'il Remmy, you tell Lassie she's a liar."

"Don't you dare open your mouth to me, Remmy," Lassie warned him. "Or I'll tell Jenny enough of our little secrets to make you sorry."

Jenny burst into tears and lunged for Lassie, who let her half-eaten apple drop. She hit Jenny across the face with her fist, and as she stumbled to the ground, Jenny wrapped her arms around Lassie's neck, pulling her down on top of her. Little Remmy rushed toward them, and he'd almost succeeded in separating the two when Lassie hooked her foot behind his leg and swung. It was a mighty flip, impressive for both its height and distance, and Little Remmy landed against the staircase. The commotion brought the entire household into the front hallway.

As Jimmy guided the coach through the front gates, he tapped the roof. "Wake up, Massa Gus. We're here," he said.

Gus yawned and stretched his legs. He peered outside. Jesse had planted some magnolia trees and had reshaped the shrubbery. Otherwise, Atterley was just as he remembered it— except that seeing the grounds only in his dreams for three years made its reality even more magnificent.

Majors had given Atterley's slaves time away from the fields so they could properly greet their new master, and they had assembled in a great throng around the front steps. "Massa Gustus's carriage is comin'!" Sonny signaled.

Gus suddenly found himself in the middle of a sea of grasping black hands as his father's slaves extended words of welcome. He made his way through the gathering, greeting by name the men and women whom he remembered, with Jimmy feeding him the names of the others in discreet whispers. A series of happy reunions ensued when Gus saw his old friends. He paused to inquire about their lives and families and reminisce about old times before moving on. Only Muley seemed distant, extending his hand with cool indifference. Gus grew puzzled as he went on down the receiving line. Where were all the house servants? He couldn't find any of their faces in the crowd. And there was one face in particular that he was searching for most earnestly.

"What-the-hell-is-wrong-with-you-two?" she yelled, covering them with oval grease spots. Eliza joined in. She gleefully dodged her mother's weapon and pummeled the pile of arms and legs indiscriminately, sometimes striking her sister, sometimes Jenny.

Button, frightened by the violence, was crying into Juno's shoulder. Juno looked shaken by the display, and alternated between smoothing imperceptible wrinkles in her dress and begging her husband with rattling eyes to intervene. Tobias ignored his wife's glances and stood resolutely in the doorway of the drawing room, a safe distance from the fray. Young Martha hovered behind him, clutching her belly.

Little Remmy clung to the swaying banister and held his head. His vision blurred as he tried to focus on the words coming out of Promise's mouth. "L'il Remmy, do something!" she was yelling. "Lassie's gonna kill Jenny!"

Rebecca stood at the top of the staircase, aghast. "My goodness. What in the world? My *goodness*." Hannah roared down the stairs, resolved to maintain order.

The front door swung open, and Gus entered Atterley's main house for the first time in three years. Jimmy surveyed the scene, smiling. "Welcome home, Massa Gus," he said. He slapped him on the back and howled.

Gus had been a willowy six feet when he'd left home. Since then, his body had filled and hardened, and he had sprouted two inches, matching Jimmy's height. The Academy had chiseled the boyish innocence out of his face—its angles now displayed a quiet, disciplined composure. He had become a younger version of his father, although his features were not so dark, and his eyes were a soft brown instead of Zachary's piercing blue. But they portrayed no softness now. He observed the bedlam as Jenny, Lassie, and Eliza fought at the foot of the stairs.

"What's going on here?" His voice resonated with authority and permeated the entranceway. It was more of a statement than a question, which was just as well since no one found the words to answer him.

The noise halted instantly. Then just as suddenly, there was frenzied movement. The girls scrambled to their feet. Molly lowered her spoon and wiped the sweat off her upper lip. Little Remmy rose unsteadily, holding up the sagging banister. Tobias rushed forward to take Gus's coat. Juno rearranged her flower and draped her arm over her tearstained dress. Button and Young Martha gulped and stared. Rebecca's eyes shone down at him with pride.

It was Hannah's voice that broke the stillness. "Massa Gus!" She came forward, embracing him warmly.

But Promise remained where she was, watching him from a distance. Master Augustus was home.

CHAPTER 24

Massa Gus's Promise

After supper, Promise retreated to her room to study Gus's scraggly notes from Professor Gauthier's lectures. "*Dire,* 'to say, to tell.' *Je dis, Tu dis, Il dit, Nous disons, Vous dites—*" She heard footsteps coming down the hallway. They were a man's, strong and heavy, coming for something they wanted, something they had the right to get. Her mother's warnings flooded her mind—that one day those footsteps would come for her.

"Promise?"

She recognized Gus's voice and fluttered around the room. His low whisper just outside her door made her insides churn, whether from excitement or fear she couldn't tell.

"Promise? Promise, I know you're in there. I can see you through your keyhole. Why won't you let me in?"

She took a deep breath and opened the door. "You're supposed to be a gentleman now, aren't you?" she said. "You should know better than to look through a lady's keyhole."

"W-Well . . ." Gus stuttered, stepping back. "As I recall, you never used to retire to bed this early . . . I didn't think you'd be . . . I had no intention of . . ." his voice trailed off. "What I mean to say is, I'm sorry." He bowed his head to her in apology.

"Do they need my help clearing away downstairs?"

"No, at least I don't believe so."

"Is there something you needed?"

Gus looked at her curiously. "I didn't think I needed a reason to talk to you."

"Of course not. I forgot." Promise turned away from him and returned to her desk. "I belong to you now. You can see me whenever you please. I only wish you'd given me notice so I could've made myself presentable, as any slave should be when greeting her master," she said. "*Pouvoir,* 'can, to be able.' *Je peux, Tu peux, Il peut, Nous pouvons—*"

"It's not necessary that you dress any sort of way for me, Promise, you know that."

Her only reply was a haughty sniff. "*Vous pouvez, Ils peuvent. Prendre,* 'to take.' *Je prends, Tu prends, Il prend, Nous prenons, Vous prenez, Ils prennent . . .*"

Gus observed Promise closely as she pretended to ignore him and continued on with her recitations. She had grown up, although into a very different sort of woman than Georgeanna. His cousin was tall and stately; he had never seen her hair out of its immaculate upsweep, without its adornments of pearls or jeweled clips, while Promise had an untamed beauty. She was small and spirited, and her hair hung loose in wild curls. Her demeanor conformed to no model of feminine behavior to which he had grown accustomed while in Charleston. There was no rule of etiquette to reference to govern his approach, and he found himself uncertain in her presence.

"What's the matter, Promise? You act as if you don't know me any more. You greeted me so formally after I arrived. And at supper you came and went with one dish after another, and never even looked at me. Are you still angry over that letter I wrote half a year ago?"

"No, I am not."

"Then we are friends? Or do you see me only as a master now?"

Promise turned to look at him. He seemed more like the old Gus in the smallness of her room, now that the gentleness had returned to his eyes. "Is it possible to see you any other way?"

He thought for a moment. "I don't see why not. Jimmy does, and Hannah."

"There would be some things we could never share. Can there ever be a true friendship with such boundaries?"

He appeared saddened as he sat down. "I don't know, but we've never been short of things to say to each other before. I've never insisted you abide by the usual formalities with me. That hasn't changed. If it helps any, I promise that I'll never make you do anything you don't want to." Gus put his hand over his heart and was glad to see the harsh lines disappear from her forehead. Then he was quiet as he wrestled with himself.

"I'm worried, Promise," he said finally. "Father said he's depending on me to mind Atterley while he's away—that he's depending on *me*. He's never counted on me for anything, at least that I can remember, and now he's trusting me with his land and his slaves. Majors will help, and he promised Father that he'll come as often as he can to advise me, but the responsibility for Atterley will be principally mine. I can't let him down. I just can't."

"And you won't," Promise assured him.

"I didn't want this. I never asked for it. Often growing up, I wished that Father had another son, one more like him. One whom he could expect things from and know he'd get it, so I'd be left alone to expect things for myself. But now I suppose he thinks I'm enough like him to be a success at this, and I can finally say that I believe I am, too."

"It's true, you have changed," Promise said, secretly admiring the broad expanse of his shoulders.

"I want to be a good master. Smart like Father, and fair. Georgeanna and I have talked a great deal about how we'd treat our slaves. She shares my philosophy about it—that masters should be as compassionate toward their slaves as possible. Father could be a bit hard at times."

"Our slaves? So you plan to marry her?"

193

"Yes. She's made it clear that she'd accept my proposal."

Promise couldn't claim surprise at Gus's fondness for his cousin. She had noticed his affection for her grow in his letters, but still she felt her heart twinge at the news. She attributed her discomfort to her childhood dislike of Georgeanna, but she was determined to mask her prejudices for his sake. "Well then, may I offer you my congratulations," she said brightly. "When did you know that she was the one for you?"

"Oh, the idea's been coming on gradually. There is nothing to think about, really. There's the family connection, of course. Aunt Eleanor and Mother really want the marriage to happen, although I think Uncle Charles likes Father's money much more than he likes me, and Father couldn't care less whether I marry Georgeanna or not. The Harpers are not as rich or powerful as the Allstons or Middletons, as he's always pointing out, but they're perfectly respectable. And then there's Georgeanna herself. She's beautiful, cultured, and pleasant—a feather in the cap of any man. I'd say we're perfectly compatible."

"Have you already asked her?"

"No, not formally. She'll be coming to Atterley in a few weeks. We'll likely get engaged then. And I want to have the engagement party here later in the spring, and there'll probably be another in Charleston this summer. Then while Georgeanna, Mother, and Aunt Eleanor shop to their hearts' content, I'm finished with the whole business until the wedding."

"Have you thought of what you'll say?"

"When?"

"When you ask Miss Georgeanna to marry you, of course."

"Not really." Gus appeared confused, as if the idea of designing a suitable proposal beforehand had never occurred to him.

Promise shook her head, disbelieving. "No respectable gentleman would ask a woman to marry him without having first planned the entire production to the last detail."

"First, there will be no production—just a simple answer to a simple question. And second, whatever gave you the idea that I was a respectable gentleman?"

"Gus, really."

"All right," he sighed. "If you're determined to be so darned serious. I suppose I'll ask her in the usual way. I'll tell her how well I think of her, that I'd be honored if she would be my bride, and so on."

"Oh Gus, that won't do at all," she said. "That's not the least bit romantic."

"But not all women have your romantic sensibilities, Promise. Many are quite practical and want nothing more than a respectable husband, a nice home, and to be well provided for."

"Is that all Miss Georgeanna wants?"

"Yes, I believe so, which most likely accounts for her partiality toward me. And we both want to have plenty of children as soon as possible."

"My goodness, why?"

Gus laughed. "Father wants South Carolina to be full of Rileys."

"And just who do you think is gonna take care of them? I suppose Miss Georgeanna's gonna want to hand them over to Hannah, and I can tell you right now, she's not gonna like that one bit. She's always talking about how she's done with child raising just in case Young Martha gets any ideas."

"Actually, I was hoping you'd want to help raise them. We could take them to the Promised Land and go swimming and fishing—like you and I used to."

"There'd be a lot more to it than that. I'd have to feed and clean up after a whole mess of babies that aren't even mine." Promise stared at Gus as if he'd lost his senses. "So you can just forget about *that* notion. You pledged that you wouldn't force me to do anything I didn't want to, and I plan to hold you to that."

Gus looked hurt. "I see."

"I could teach them their letters if you want," she conceded. "Jenny might not mind doing the rest, but I want no part of it. If they're anything like you were, they'd make me batty."

"You've always been so hard on me," Gus said. "I've changed for the better, don't you think?"

"Yes, of course." Promise reached for his hands. "I was only joking. Not about the children, but all the rest."

Gus squeezed her fingers warmly. "I'm happy to be home, Promise. We have always been such good friends, you and I. It won't be long before things between us will be just like they used to."

"But we're not children anymore. We must be practical. Whatever else you are to me, you will always be a master first."

"Yes, perhaps you're right. I can't afford to compromise my responsibilities, even for . . . but I'll need your counsel, and even a little of your scolding." He held her hands tight. "Let's just say then, that while we are within these walls, I am not a master, and you are not a slave."

Something about his touch, and the way his eyes gazed down into hers, felt very, very wrong, but Promise couldn't bring herself to pull away. "Then what are we?" she dared ask him.

"We are who we are," he answered softly. "I am your Gus, and you are my Promise."

CHAPTER 25

The Planters Club

When Zachary returned home the following week, his first item of business was to initiate his son into manhood. After enduring the same grasping hands that had greeted Gus, Zachary whisked him away for his first visit to the Planters Club.

The male members of the other prominent Low Country families were already assembled there. The gentlemen had just returned from the hunt, and after presenting their kills to their slaves, they entertained themselves with billiards while they awaited the Rileys' arrival. When the silhouette of Zachary's towering frame materialized on the other side of the finely cut glass window, all conversation inside ceased. The men straightened their ties, took deep, soothing puffs from their cigars, and waited.

As he entered, Zachary paused to showcase the superior quality of his cloak before he removed it and handed it to the doorman. "Come, Augustus," he said. Gus composed himself beneath his father's steadying gaze and followed him as he strode through the room.

The men whom his father considered his social and economic equal were the recipients of a firm handshake and personal greeting. Others were the grateful beneficiaries of casual nods of acquaintance, and an unfortunate few feigned indifference as they were strategically ignored. Only wealth and consequence distinguished him from a carnival performer who keeps a collection of props and disguises in the back of his wagon and mesmerizes his audience with smoke and mirrors.

Zachary had already made good use of his election to the South Carolina legislature and had positioned himself for leadership. Every member of the Planters Club had read and reread his moving speech printed in the *Winyah Observer*, attacking South Carolina's prejudice against incorporation.

He had stood firm beside John Middleton, the president of the All Saints Southern Rights Association, arguing that South Carolina should challenge the authority of the federal government by not filling the state's vacant seat in the United States Senate. He had renewed his intimacy with Robert Allston, fellow West Point graduate and president of South Carolina's senate, and had become acquainted with Joshua Ward, its lieutenant governor, who admired his eloquence and unfaltering resolve. It was widely believed that Zachary could easily acquire a state senate seat himself, should he seek one after finishing his term in the house.

But Zachary's roots in South Carolina were shallow. They were not yet deep enough to secure his own future should he be caught unaware and be taken up in a political storm, or to shield his son from scrutiny—especially a son who had in his youth given his peers so many reasons to question.

When the dinner hour arrived, the gentlemen gathered around long tables in two adjacent rooms. At one sat the graying, or already grizzled planters, who talked only of politics, the state of the economy, and their infirmities. At the other were their brash sons, chattering energetically about women and horses.

Before Gus had a chance to make his escape and join the other young men, his father motioned for him to sit at his side. Zachary's future was sure to take him far from the Low Country, and the other planters wanted to see what Gus's contribution to the conversation would be—to decide for themselves whether or not they approved of the man who would be crowned Atterley's new king once his father had abdicated the throne.

"Perhaps the compromise measures and that traitor Clay did us a favor after all," John Mason said, "opening our eyes to the dangers of our complacency. Zachary, you'll be a delegate at the convention in April—do you believe our right to secede will be affirmed?"

"I do. All that remains to be determined is whether we should leave the Union separately, or if we should yield to the Cooperationists and only do so with the support of our sister states." Zachary signaled the servant behind him. "Tell Esther the veal is wonderful."

Plowden Weston, owner of four plantations northeast of Atterley, raised his glass for more wine. "Your family ties in Georgia may prove beneficial in that case, Riley, and Mason's in Virginia," he said.

"Yes, but should we be forced to, we must be willing to secede alone," Robert Allston said. "We'd be fools to place our fortunes in the hands of others."

John Middleton nodded. "The fanatics in the North have poisoned the minds of the rest—those who would be indifferent, or even sympathetic to our way of life. And the government has outright refused to defend the Constitution, believing they have the right to intrude without restraint into the lives of citizens."

"True, and we have no obligation to compromise," Weston said. "The responsibility for saving the Union belongs to the North, not the South. If they have their way, our very safety is at stake. I'll consider nothing they have to say about the rights of our niggers until *their* Negro population outnumbers decent white men."

"There's no cause to be so dramatic. Fanaticism always fades away in time," Grover Snead, owner of Lilborne, pointed out. "We should exercise the fruit of patience. I believe the abolitionists will lose strength. Why should we concern ourselves with a bunch of free niggers, loud-mouthed women, and Quakers? This whole business began in England, and now many there will finally admit that freeing their Negroes was a mistake, injuring the lives of both slave and master."

John Tucker, owner of Litchfield and Willbrook, was indignant. "Are you suggesting that we sit back and do nothing? If so, that's a ridiculous notion," he said. "It's dangerous to take such a weak stand against sin." Tucker was a strict master who denied rations to any of his slaves who missed one of Reverend Wickerson's services. "We should take it upon ourselves to make the North see that our sovereignty should be respected. It's been proposed in North Carolina and Virginia that all Northern goods should be taxed. We'd be well within our rights to take that step—with a complete embargo on any goods coming from abolitionist strongholds. The quickest route to effect change would be to injure their pocketbooks."

"That would most likely impact our pocketbooks rather than theirs," Joshua Ward argued. He was the country's largest slaveholder, owning a half-dozen plantations located in both the Georgetown and Horry Districts, and his mantles were filled with the awards his slaves had received from the All Saints Agricultural Society for their innovations.

"I don't agree," Tucker insisted. "Temporary denial for the greater good will resolve the matter sooner than you suppose, Ward. If I were a betting man, I'd place a wager on it."

Ward shook his head. "An embargo would take too much time. It's impractical. I have a thousand slaves to care for and more to lose than any other man here by such a scheme, so you'll forgive me if I'm less inclined than you to be adventurous."

"I'm in agreement with Tucker this time," said Vernon Stanton of Helmsley. "Benjamin Perry of Greenville has made that very point—that the best course of action would be to become economically independent. Then the whole mess would be solved once and for all. We should put this secession nonsense out of our minds."

"I'm not surprised to hear you say so," Middleton retorted. "If the time did come to take up arms, which side would you be on?"

Stanton's back stiffened. "Are you implying that I'm less than loyal to South Carolina, sir?"

"I am only saying that your connection to the South is by marriage, not blood," Middleton said.

A roar erupted in the other room. The young men had had too much wine, and William Davis was in a fierce battle with one of the younger Allstons over who would be the victor in a four-mile race, his filly, Chesnut, or Allston's Abilene. Sam Hubbard was taking wagers, Tim Mason was declaring loudly that horse racing was sinful, and Bernard Snead and George Stanton were singing a rousing chorus to drown out his protests. At Ward's prompting, one of the servants left his post and shut the door.

"The only real issue is the character of slavery," Zachary said, once peace had been restored. "The North sees it as either a sin or a crime, and they're determined to using any means necessary to eradicate a practice of which they have no knowledge and no legitimate interest."

"You've been rather quiet, Augustus," observed Charles Davis of Aldingham. His mouth turned up at the corners. "How do you view slavery—as a sin, or as a crime?"

The men put down their forks and awaited his answer.

"I would only say that it is essential," Gus answered quietly.

"Are you saying that you'd be willing to fight for the South, should it come to that?" Allston questioned him.

"I would."

The gentlemen grunted their approval.

"All of this philosophical talk is lost on me," Dr. Matthew Hubbard, owner of Catterlen and Mulgrave, said fiercely, his jowls swinging. "If slavery *is* a sin, it is ours alone, and no business of the government's. There's no need to complicate matters with useless theorizing."

Zachary started. "Are you saying you believe slavery is a sin, Hubbard?"

"Truthfully, I don't know. What I do know is that half my capital is in slaves, just like all of you, and I don't take kindly to any party, or any government, that seeks to extinguish half my wealth." He loosed a mussel from its shell, dipped it in butter, and slid it off his fork with his teeth. "So whether slavery's a sin or not is not my concern."

"Well, it's a concern of mine," Joel Duvall, owner of Ashby, said. Like Stanton, Duvall was a Unionist, but he was also a closet abolitionist who had been the author of several anonymous letters to local newspapers over the years, supporting the cause. "I no more look forward to losing my livelihood than anyone else, but slavery can't continue on forever. As the Negro becomes more civilized, the practice seems to me to be increasingly oppressive. I only pray that God will have mercy on us."

"And yet you still keep over two hundred Negroes bound up by this oppression," Mason said. "Save your prayers for yourself. Your conscience must not be tormenting you too badly. The day you take your slaves up North and set them free, I pledge to be the first to follow along behind."

Their wrangling continued into the night. After many hours of feasting on an extravagant succession of courses and draining bottles of choice wines, all of the gentlemen's personal and political differences melted away in a warm sea of alcohol. At the end of the evening, they raised their glasses together in a grand salute to their beloved South Carolina, believing that she would emerge victorious in whatever course of action she chose to take.

The planters had absolute faith in the continual supremacy of their state, for they had absolute faith in themselves—and in their minds, the two were one and the same.

CHAPTER 26

Promise Demands a Favor

Gus's head didn't begin to clear until later that night. He only vaguely remembered mourning the loss of his fine dinner while he staggered into the house propped up by his father. Zachary cursed at him to be quiet, but Rebecca spotted them anyway. Ignoring her reproaches, Gus stumbled past her to Promise's bedroom, who allowed him to collapse, groaning, onto her bed.

When he came to, she was not at all sympathetic. She was profoundly shocked by his condition and continued where his mother had left off. Fortunately, Gus kept fading in and out of consciousness during her lecture and heard little of it. It was an hour and a half before the room stopped spinning, and another hour after that before he could explain himself to her with any clarity.

Once Gus's head cleared and he began feeling more like himself, he sprawled comfortably across Promise's covers, cracking walnuts, while she sat in front of her mirror, weaving her fingers through her hair to straighten out the tangles. "So how does it feel to be drunk?" she asked him.

"Awful."

"Good. Serves you right." She grimaced as she met with an especially nasty snag and was preparing to carefully navigate her way through it when a walnut Gus was opening exploded into pieces. Her fingers lurched forward. "Ouch!" Promise looked down at her freed fingers, wrapped in curly bunches of hair. "When I said you could eat those nuts in my bed, Gus, I didn't give you license to make a giant mess of it."

He swept away the crumbs. "Sorry. I'm just so darned hungry." He finished the last of the nuts. "I'm still starving. You have anything else?"

Promise sighed, opened her drawer, and took out a couple of pears. "Here."

Gus rolled them around in his palm. "Where did you get these from?"

"I bought them from the West Indian traders."

"I don't want you going down to the river to meet them by yourself. It's dangerous."

"I know. Sonny went with me."

Gus raised his eyebrows. "Sonny? Does he always walk with you down to the river?"

"Sometimes. Sometimes Charles goes with me. Why?"

"Never mind." Gus lay back on Promise's bed. He bit into one of the pears, positioned the second on his stomach, and closed his eyes. "If tonight was any indication of what I'll have to endure as the master of Atterley, I'm in for a rough time of it. The old men were merciless—with me and with each other. Every man was continually looking for any weakness in the others that would give him an edge. I wasn't at ease one moment the entire time, at least not until I got enough wine in me to stop caring."

"But you should be used to that kind of thing by now, shouldn't you? I would've thought you'd grown quite accustomed to that sort of rivalry at the Academy. Men can be so cruel to each other, no matter what their age."

"When I left Charleston I thought I'd finally be free to do as I pleased, without anyone to put a show on for, or answer to, especially since Father will be spending most of the year in Columbia."

"Being a man means that you can't do whatever silly thing strikes your fancy any more," Promise said.

"I suppose. You remember I wanted to go to California?"

"Yes." Promise rolled her eyes. "Thank goodness you grew up, got some sense, and gave up on that idea."

"No, I never really did. I only forgot about it for a while. I used to think Negroes had a better time of it, working outside all day, using their hands—because that was what I would've wanted. I used to want to be like Muley and the others. They had no rules to follow, no expectations to fulfill. Then at the Academy I began to be glad I was white, because being a white man gave me a chance to be important. But now I can see that white or Negro, there's no difference—slavery's got us both in chains."

"I think you have the better end of it as far as *that* goes. I hope you don't expect me to feel sorry for you because you've been given the *huge* burden of having to boss folks around. I could do that, *easy.*"

"No you couldn't—if you had to."

"Humph," Promise grunted, figuring she could.

Gus finished the pears and tossed the cores out the window. He propped himself up on his elbows. "Can I have your cake?"

Promise looked longingly at the moist slice she had saved from supper. She had covered it herself with smooth butter-cream. "Oh, all right," she said, handing it over. She moaned as Gus dipped his finger in the frosting.

"Ummm, good."

Unable to bear watching him devour her dessert, Promise went back to wrestling with her hair. "Can I ask you for a favor?"

"You can *ask*, sure. But I don't feel inclined to grant any favors right now." Gus stuffed a forkful of cake in his mouth.

"But I gave you my cake."

"Yes, and it's very good. Thank you, Promise." He smiled wide, revealing teeth coated with butter-cream.

Promise glared at him, incensed.

"You're right," he mumbled, letting bits of cake fly onto her bed. "Being bossy isn't that hard after all."

DAT-DAT-DAT! Promise gave her dressing table a series of violent smacks with her brush.

Gus flew upright. "All right, all right! My God, stop that! Have mercy. My head feels like it's gonna burst. Honestly Promise, those noises you make—just like your father. I swear, sometimes you act truly mad." He wiped the remnants of the cake from his mouth with his sleeve. "You have my attention, if that's what you wanted. What's the favor?"

"Muley wants to marry Rachel."

"Yes, I remember from your letters."

"Are you gonna let him?"

"Father already told him no."

Promise raised her brush high, ready to strike.

"Now don't you start that again. I'd like to oblige you, Promise, I really would. But Father has a rule against that sort of thing, and it makes good sense. If Muley marries one of Atterley's women, the babies will belong here. Rachel's had two for him already. Why should I let him marry her, and keep making Mr. Mason money that should be Father's?"

"Because he loves her."

"I'm sure given time he'll find a way to love someone else."

Promise turned the brush slowly so it caught the light, flashing silver.

Gus eyed it warily and sighed. "Have him come by to see me. I won't promise anything, but I'll think about it."

CHAPTER 27

New Beginnings

During the first weeks of March, the field slaves began preparing the soil for planting. They had plowed the fields under during the winter months, driving the brave spikes that had poked out into the cold beneath the ground again to enrich the soil. Once the dirt on the street lost its hard crunching and the Ma'Deahs allowed the children to play out of doors without first filling their bellies with steaming hominy, Atterley's slaves knew it was time to stretch the winter out of their limbs and ready themselves for new beginnings.

Despite Juno's tearful protests and Big Remmy and Florence's objections to the match, the day the Rileys left Atterley Reverend Wickerson married Little Remmy and Jenny. Juno pleaded with Zachary to intervene on behalf of her deluded daughter, who was so blinded by love that she would marry her own nephew. Zachary was not persuaded. He was in agreement with the reverend that with Negroes, traditional rules of convention concerning marriage did not apply.

Zachary and Rebecca brought a number of Atterley's house slaves with them when they departed for Columbia, and without Molly's clamoring and Jimmy's laughter, the house was quiet. Promise reclaimed her position as manager of the household affairs in Hannah's absence. Gus began to settle into his position as master. He toured the grounds every morning just as his father had, but without his father's discernment. Zachary had left nothing to chance, however, and asked Majors to remain at Atterley to explain the intricacies of rice growing to his son.

"Go on, now," Gus entreated Milo, who had stopped to bury her nose in some tender sproutlings. He followed Majors across the stretch of land that was cleared to plant the provision crops. Gus recognized Harold's tall, wiry build and waved. "Hello there, Harold!"

Harold glanced up from his hoeing and smiled, creasing the shining sweat. "Hello, Massa Gus!"

Majors looked over his shoulder and frowned. "Augustus, you really must keep up and pay attention. They get their rations on Saturday after all their work's done—rice, grits, peas, sweet potatoes, meal, molasses, and pork or beef. Salt and tobacco are given out on the first of the month. The family allowances are in Zachary's records—you won't find any better fed on the Waccamaw. It's a minimal investment when you consider the difference you get in production. They get more than their usual allowance if they haven't been out sick in awhile, or if it's harvest time or hog-butchering time. Of course the trunk-minders, cattle-minders, sheep-minders, and Henry and his under-drivers, get greater portions. Zachary's got it all written down to the ounce. Henry, Tucker, and Amos do most of the measuring."

"Just the three of them? That's a mighty temptation to steal, isn't it?"

"Your father always watched them, of course, or had me to when he was away, but there's been no more trouble since those months about ten years ago when food started disappearing. Your father wouldn't let any of. them have meat or molasses until the thieves were turned in. There were two of 'em." Majors shook his head. "There's no good reason to steal on Atterley, just greed. They were selling it to the trash for pennies on the dollar. Henry came up with the punishment himself—he whipped the skin off their backs and left them hanging upside down for a week. It was unfortunate. You were so young, though, you probably don't remember."

But Gus did remember—two blood-covered bodies swinging slowly over slimy, brownish pools, cooking in the sun, drawing flies. The smell of rotting meat had reached all the way to the main house. He and the boys had gathered around, as close as they could stand, to watch what used to be men hanging from trees. Red had taken Andy up on a dare, and holding his nose, ran up to one of the bodies and poked it with a stick.

Gus had never forgotten that day. It was the only time he had ever seen Muley cry. From time to time the image of those rotting men still visited his dreams. He doubted if he could stomach handing out such a punishment. "I hope to God there's no more stealing," he said.

Majors guessed his thoughts. "I don't blame you, son— that's why I'm a banker and not a planter." He shrugged his shoulders. "But like your father says, if you get tough with 'em once, it's good for the lifetime of the others. There's been no more thievery since then. If their rations are gone before the week's out, they make do with what they can hunt, catch, or grow themselves. They have to be damn fools to starve. They can grow whatever they want in their own gardens, and there's plenty of fish and game. They just have to show their take to Henry, and then bring a share up to the main house."

"Mother told me she gives you a list of the clothes they'll need, and you place the orders."

"Not exactly." Majors chuckled. "Your father checks it over first and takes off what's too extravagant for them. She doesn't know the difference, and they still get all they need. The men each get a suit, and the women calico, for church, and they're given cottons and linens for summer, and woolens and flannels for winter. They get caps, coats, jackets, and shoes once a year. At the end of summer, Henry passes out sticks they cut to the length of their feet. Then Zachary writes their names on them, and I order shoes from the sizes. They wash and mend their own clothes, and the drivers make inspections to be sure they keep their cabins neat and clean. Of course, your mother gets sole discretion when it comes to clothing the house servants, and her seamstresses do the sewing and tucking as far as that goes."

Rows of men jolted over the rice fields, holding onto the bucking handles of their plows as their muscles strained to keep the oxen steady. Calls of "Hoo-yah" and "Woa-naw" sliced the air.

Majors pointed. "They make special shoes for the oxen, otherwise they'd sink into the ground—it's so soft now. After the fields are plowed, the slaves'll walk across them, real slow and careful, and break apart the mounds with their hoes so it's all smoothed out before they dig trenches for the seeds."

"How far apart do they dig 'em? A foot?"

"About fourteen inches. Their tasks are assigned based on how much each slave can do in a day, so their work should be finished by sundown. The men are given three-quarters of an acre of breaking up sods—that's if they're prime. The other men can do somewhere around half an acre, and so can Big Nan, Gloria, and Helen. The rest of the women and the old men will be able to finish a quarter acre with little trouble. The young ones are usually responsible for only an eighth of an acre."

"How will I know who can do what?"

"You won't, but that's what Henry's for. He knows what each one can do and whether or not they're working as hard as they should. If they're not done by the end of the day, he'll take care of it."

Gus frowned. "By whipping them." He studied the fields where so many of his father's slaves had endured a lifetime of hard labor. The vast acreage looked pleasant from his vantage point—all identical pieces of rich brown patchwork bordered by the thin, sparkling line of the Waccamaw.

"Niggers won't work if you don't watch them carefully, Augustus, and punish them good when they slack off." Majors's tone softened a little. "It's not pleasant, I know, but it's the only thing that works with most of them. A few of them will work even when you don't watch them. They take pride in finishing their tasks on time, and finishing them well. Your father's got more than his share of those. Others do all right if you reward them fairly.

"But with some niggers, you have to beat the laziness out of them. There're only a couple of those on Atterley. Your father's got a good eye, and he won't buy them. Once in awhile when he slips up and buys a hardheaded nigger, he'll let Henry beat the tar out of him to straighten him out. Then if he still doesn't mind, he'll sell him off real quick—so he won't turn the others bad, too."

"I think most of the whippings Henry orders are unnecessary. I believe he enjoys making them suffer."

"Henry knows what he's doing, Augustus, better than any white overseer I've met. I used to doubt the wisdom of putting a nigger in charge, but once again, your father's proved me wrong. Henry knows these niggers, the good from the bad, and he won't be soft on them just because your father's not here. He knows better. In fact, he'll likely lay into them harder just to prove that to you."

"But that's just what I don't want. Henry's been allowed to run positively wild. His conduct toward Atterley's women, and children, too, for God's sake—it turns my stomach. I'm definitely gonna rein him in as far as that goes."

"Be pretty bold to try and make changes when this is your first year running things. Henry's gotta have his rewards, and I wouldn't jeopardize the harvest to protect the integrity of your wenches." Majors laughed at the lunacy. "They don't have much of it anyway, and what they do have, they gladly give away." His smile faded. "But if you ever find that out firsthand, you keep it to yourself, you hear—no matter how many curly headed, half-nigger children end up running around Atterley."

Gus blushed.

"No one would blame you. I doubt if there are many white men who've been able to keep themselves from indulging. I'm not saying I have, mind you—I'm only urging you to be careful. Any public acknowledgment of a Negro mistress would ruin you. And remember, whatever happens, I still get my two percent."

CHAPTER 28

A Visit from Muley

It was well past seven when they returned to the main house. Gus was half starved and eager for his supper. He'd had enough of Majors for one day, and he asked that his food be brought to the study. He was determined to muddle through his father's records, but after a quarter of an hour, his head was aching terribly. When Tobias brought in the tray, he gratefully pushed aside the volumes. He had already devoured his soup when he noticed the letter from Georgeanna that Tobias had tucked beneath a saucer.

My Darling Augustus,

Lucy is just finishing the packing now, and we will be leaving in the morning. I can hardly write, for I am trembling with excitement. I have missed you terribly. It has been a great trial being separated from you. I have realized during your absence how indispensable your company is to me, and I hope that you have found mine so as well—although your responses to my letters have been so brief that they do little to satisfy my hunger for your companionship.

But I will not scold you. I know you are very busy at present securing your future, and I venture to say mine as well. You are so strong, so noble, so brave, to be managing things all alone, and I am eager to join you at Atterley and provide you with whatever assistance I can.

Business will keep Father in Charleston. Mother is determined to keep a close eye on us, but I hope with some ingenuity, we can find ways to slip away and be alone. Perhaps it is improper for me to say such things to you, since you have not yet publicly declared your intentions toward me, but I see no harm in it. I hope it will not be long before I no longer need to be concerned with concealing my feelings from you or anyone, for I believe you will soon profess yours before God and man— relieving us both of our hearts' burden.

As much as I honor and adore my family, I eagerly anticipate the day when I will be joined with another.

Your loving cousin,
Georgeanna

The stationary was saturated with her perfume. Gus tossed it aside and cut himself a large piece of mutton. After enduring a month's worth of her letters, he had come to the awful realization that Georgeanna bored him. He wondered how she had managed to keep his attention while he was in Charleston—since her conversation had never deviated from the themes contained in her letters.

He was ashamed of himself for not adoring her and attributed his lack of passion to some defect in his character. And she was coming to Atterley tomorrow, expecting a proposal. Gus poured himself a stiff drink.

Tobias cracked open the door. "Excuse me, Massa Augustus."

"Yes, what is it?"

"Muley's here to see you. May I show him in?"

"Fine."

"Hello, Massa," Muley said, hovering awkwardly in the doorway.

"Hey there, Muley." Gus waved him in and pointed to a chair. "Go on, sit down. How are things? You been up to your old tricks?"

Muley eyed Gus warily. "Naw. Mama keeps me fed good." His frame had changed little since he was a child. He was slim, with sleek, hard muscles, and still baby faced. But his eyes were old and rimmed in darkness. He was only twenty, but in his features there was no hint of the fun-loving boyishness that should have still lingered.

"Oh come on, Muley, I'm not gonna get mad if you sneak a meal now and then. I know things between us have changed, but we were great friends once. I'm not looking to make any trouble for you. In fact, I thought you would've come to see me before now so we could visit some of our old haunts. I have some free time to spare, not much, but some."

Muley didn't meet his gaze. "Pa keeps me pretty busy at the smithy."

"You don't look well."

"I'se fine, Massa."

Gus was startled by the resentment he heard in Muley's voice and forced a smile. "I remember how you used to hate working there. Abraham would send you off to fetch something or another, and you'd come get me instead. Then we'd sneak off into the woods—"

Muley fidgeted in his chair. "Massa, I don't got long. Pa only gave me a half hour."

"I was only saying . . . I could put you somewhere else on Atterley if you want, where you could do something you'd enjoy—"

"No, that's all right. I likes blacksmithin' fine enough. I come to talk to you 'bout Rachel. Missy tole me you was thinkin' 'bout lettin' me marry her."

"Yes." Gus sighed. "I want you to understand my problem, Muley. Like I said before, I still consider you a friend, but I have to do what's best for Atterley, and what's best for Atterley is for you to find a wife here. After I talked to Promise, I asked Mason if he'd sell Rachel to me. I offered him a real fair price, but he refused. Apparently Mrs. Mason is quite fond of her, and not so fond of you."

"Yeah, I know. I already asked Mr. Mason 'bout it—a long time ago. He says I can marry Rachel, but he ain't gonna sell her. No matter what." Muley looked pained. "I told him I'd work for him when I'm done over here, as long as he wants, if he'd just sell Rachel to Massa Riley, but he tole me no."

"So why is it you're so set on her?"

Muley's eyes smiled for the first time since he'd entered the room. "She's the nicest girl I ever met, that's why."

"Yes, but there's plenty of nice girls right here. What about Doris, or Melvin's girl, Nelda?"

The hard edge returned to Muley's voice. "There're plenty of girls, Massa. Just none like her. No girl that's made me wanna save up everythin' I've ever thought, ever dreamed, ever felt, so I can share it with her. No girl that's made me wanna ask God each mornin' to show me how to love her right."

Gus leaned forward, fascinated. "Is that how you, how you know a girl's meant for you?"

"I dunno 'bout other folks. All I know is when I'm with her, when she's talkin' to me, holdin' my hand. . ." Muley's eyes glistened. "She's just the best girl under the sun, Massa. And I'd be real grateful if you'd let me marry her and have her for real."

At that moment, Gus realized that Muley had something he never knew he longed for, and he was envious of his old friend for the first time since they were children. "Muley, you can have your Rachel," he heard himself saying.

Joy and relief flooded Muley's face. "Thank you," he said, grasping Gus's hand. "Thanks, Massa Gus. When I'm done with my work today, can I go tell her?"

"Sure, Muley, sure," Gus told him, and wrote out the pass.

CHAPTER 29

Regarding Georgeanna

"There now." Promise gave Gus's tie a final twist. "Look." She pulled him in front of the mirror. "See? You look very nice. Miss Georgeanna will be thrilled."

"I don't see why I have to be dressed up so formally," he complained. "It's just a small family dinner."

"Yes, but a small family dinner with your future wife requires a fresh shave and a proper tie."

"You're as bad as Mother." Gus draped his arm around her shoulders. "But you're right. I'm forgetting all my big-city manners. And I do look handsome, don't I?"

Promise flushed. "Yes, you do."

"And you look nice as well. You're wearing one of your Paris dresses, I see, and your pearls. Twirl about a little for me. Hmmmm, lovely. If I didn't know better, I'd suspect that you were hoping to show Georgeanna up."

Promise laughed, delighted by his compliments. "I have the best of intentions, I assure you. I just wanted to look as well as I can."

"Then may I say, you have succeeded." Gus's tone was calm, but the expression on his face was a jumbled blend of admiration and desire.

Promise dragged her eyes away from his. "Thank you. Jenny and Button are also dressed very prettily. Even Young Martha has taken extra care. And wait until you see the twins in your mother's old Sunday dresses. They needed a little letting out, but now they fit marvelously. The girls look so elegant."

"I'm sure. I wonder if they'll make it through dinner without destroying the facade, but I suppose that's too much to hope for. Tobias tells me they've been stealing Father's whiskey, giving it to the field hands most likely, or God forbid, drinking it themselves. If only you could've adjusted their manners so easily. "

"Don't be rude. And I'd think that you, of all people, wouldn't be opposed to such goings-on. You've been indulging in your father's liquor a great deal yourself lately. Many times I've heard you go into his study after you leave my room."

"Only when I can't sleep," Gus tried to explain, looking guilty.

"Besides, Lassie and Liza have promised me faithfully to conduct themselves like ladies tonight."

"Promise!" Eliza's screeching echoed from downstairs. "Lassie won't listen to me and set the table right! She's putting the forks down wrong!"

"I am not!"

"Are, too!"

Gus smirked. "There, see? They've started already. The tent is up, and the circus has begun."

Promise groaned. "I better hurry down or the house will be leveled before they arrive."

Just as Young Martha was pulling the pies out of the oven, the Harpers' carriage passed through Atterley's gates. Georgeanna squinted at the fuzzy blue form standing on the front steps of the main house and attempted to navigate her bonnet outside the carriage window. "There he is, Mother. I see him. He's waiting for us." She rippled her handkerchief furiously. "Augustus!"

"Georgeanna, please sit down and be still. That is only Mr. Majors."

She plopped down. "Where is he, then? I've ridden in this horribly uncomfortable carriage all the way from Charleston just to see him, and he sends Majors out to greet us." She attempted to twirl life back into her hair with her fingers. "This country air is horrible."

"Please calm yourself, child. You hair looks fine."

"It does *not* look fine. Lucy did not wrap my hair very well at all. I told you how important today was to me," Georgeanna snapped at her wrinkled nurse. "I ought to take you out into the woods and whip you good. Things have already started off wrong," she wailed, near tears. "What hope is there that they'll turn right? If only Augustus had already proposed. I was so sure that he was going to ask me to marry him after the ball. There was such a beautiful full moon that night. And he had his chance again at Christmas, by the tree, after you and Father had gone to bed. And the night before he left for Atterley, he took my hand and said goodbye so sweetly, but still he said nothing about our future together. Aunt Rebecca goes on and on about how much Augustus adores me, that he just cannot wait to marry me, but he seems to be waiting rather comfortably."

"I know, dear, but you must be patient. You mustn't seem anxious," Mrs. Harper cautioned her. "If only your father hadn't gotten himself into such financial difficulty. If that weren't the case, I'm certain that Zachary, too, would be pushing the match, and you'd be Mrs. Augustus Riley by now."

Georgeanna blushed at the thought. "I love him, Mother. I love him so *very* much. But I must be back in Charleston for the Freemans' ball in two weeks, and I do so want to return engaged. Wouldn't that be marvelous? Do you believe two weeks is enough time for him to get around to asking me?"

"I don't know. Young gentlemen these days like to keep their ladies in suspense."

Georgeanna wrung her hands. "Perhaps there's someone else."

"Even if one of these coarse country girls has taken a fancy to him, you've gotten to him first, my dear. Augustus is yours to secure or to lose. I am in full agreement with your Aunt Rebecca. I am sure he loves you—how could he not?"

"Yes, I believe he does." The lines in Georgeanna's forehead vanished, and she beamed happily. "Oh, how I wish he'd go on with it. When that blessed day comes I'll be the happiest woman in the world."

Gus met them in the hallway. "Hello, Aunt Eleanor, Miss Georgeanna. I hope the roads were fine."

Mrs. Harper gave her nephew a warm kiss on the cheek. "You are looking well, Augustus. Yes, the roads were very fine, thank you."

"Well, *I* wouldn't know," Georgeanna said, her eyes sparkling. "I scarcely noticed anything at all. I thought only of Atterley and of seeing you again, my dear, dear Augustus." She pressed close to him and didn't loosen her grip on his hands until her mother's throat rumbled.

At dinner, Gus smiled up at Promise as she set down the turtle soup. "Thank you, Promise," he said.

"You're welcome, Massa Augustus. Good evening, Mrs. Harper, Miss Georgeanna, Mr. Majors." Promise nodded politely around the table before taking her place with the others along the edges of the room.

Gus blew away the steam and watched the candlelight play on Promise's face. A painting he had seen in Rome came to mind. It was of David, watching the forbidden Bathsheba bathing—her form revealed to him in the moonlight. It was a breathtaking work, and he had lost himself in it—imagining how the Hebrew king had gazed upon her that night until his passions could no longer be contained, and he was willing to murder her husband and lose favor with his God to have her.

Thoughts of Promise had invaded his mind then, too, although it had been Georgeanna's arm that encircled his.

"Look here," Mrs. Harper gasped. "A fly has just landed on the stewed peaches."

Button strained her arms, fanning harder. "Most times Lassie and Liza do the fannin', Mrs. Harper," she breathed. "They're real good at it. Today they made me, 'cause they put out the silverware."

"It's fortunate that they're good at something, since they certainly have no talent for setting tables," Georgeanna reproved airily. "I do not have a spoon."

"Sorry, Miss Georgeanna," Button panted.

Promise stood, transfixed, as she watched sweat gather on Button's forehead. She hadn't dared stop fanning to wipe it away, and it was rolling around her eyes, gathering in a large, itchy drop on the tip of her nose.

"Miss Georgeanna said that she has no spoon for her soup," Mrs. Harper said, her voice rising.

Promise was startled into action. She was moving toward the kitchen when Button hollered, "Lassie! Liza! Miss Georgeanna don't have a spoon!" The dangling drop of sweat flew from her nose and landed in Mrs. Harper's curls.

The twins emerged from the kitchen, smiling sheepishly, with gleaming rings of peach juice circling their mouths. Gus smiled behind his wine glass, Majors snorted his way into a boorish fit of laughter, and Mrs. Harper declared that she had never seen such a display of bad manners in her life.

Mrs. Harper's nerves did not begin to calm until the servants had served the second course, platters of green beans and rice seasoned with spicy pieces of veal. "Tell me, Augustus, do you entertain often?" she asked him. "I would suppose not, considering the exhibition I've witnessed today."

"I've been much too busy to have guests since I've been home."

"Perhaps you should introduce yourself back into Low Country society by hosting a dinner party during our stay," she suggested. "You can present Georgeanna to your friends and neighbors. I'm sure they'll want to become reacquainted with you since you've been away from the area so long. They'll want to hear all about your plans and ambitions—"

"I have no energy for that right now," Gus interrupted, sounding tired. "I was hoping not to have to host some sort of grand affair."

"No one would expect Augustus to host a large dinner party, Mother," Georgeanna said. "Men know little about such things."

"Sounds to me like Atterley's in need of a mistress," Majors observed, dabbing his mouth with his napkin. "You'd do well to have a wife nicely settled here before too long, Augustus."

The ladies smiled brightly at him from across the table. "Indeed, Mr. Majors, indeed," Mrs. Harper said. "And summertime in Charleston would be a wonderful time for a wedding, Augustus. If the date were set in June, or perhaps July, that would give me enough time to order Georgeanna's clothes—"

"Mother, please," Georgeanna blushed.

"Dear, you know perfectly well that nothing in town will do. The ceremony will be at St. Philip's Church, of course, with a grand reception following. And the guest list will take a great deal of planning, we have so many family and friends in the city, but Rebecca and I will tackle it together . . ." Mrs. Harper paused to gape at her nephew. "Augustus dear, there's no need to gulp your wine in that manner. You will make yourself *drunk,*" she said in astonishment.

Before Georgeanna had finished nibbling her last green bean, Promise had decided that she didn't like her. The intensity of her animosity confused her, but because she was unaccustomed to deep introspection, she was unable to discover its source. Promise had not discerned any fault in Georgeanna's character, nor could she deny that she would make an excellent mistress. It was clear that she had been groomed for congenial service.

Gus's intended bride was just as he had described her—continually pleasant and agreeable. She was unwaveringly attentive to him whenever he said anything at all and appeared genuinely captivated when his commentary was particularly insightful. Although she didn't contribute anything significant to the conversation herself, Promise did not have the satisfaction of believing her to be stupid, for she suspected that Georgeanna withheld her opinions purposefully and that she was much more intelligent than she let on.

Georgeanna felt Promise's eyes upon her and returned her gaze—taking notice of the superior quality of her clothing. "You there. Come here a moment," she said, summoning her. She rubbed the sleeve of Promise's dress between her fingers, and became confused as she recalled the quaint Paris shop where she had last seen it. "It looks even lovelier than I remember . . . and those *pearls*. I see your mistress has given you some of her best things," Georgeanna murmured, struggling to mask her envy. "You must be a great favorite of hers."

"Yes, Miss Georgeanna," Promise answered hastily, and retreated back to her station.

"Missus didn't give her that dress," Eliza piped up, eager for excitement. "Massa Augustus did."

Lassie grinned wickedly across the room at her sister. "Of course, she *is* his extra special pet. Missus's hand-me-downs are just fine for Liza and me, but they won't do for Promise, oh no. He even bought her some fur gloves to match. Didn't he, Promise?"

The room was quiet.

"Goodness me," was all Mrs. Harper could manage.

Majors's expression darkened, but he said nothing.

But Georgeanna recovered quickly. "My, how generous," she said. "One of the things I admire most about you, Augustus, is your affection for your darkies."

Gus's cheeks turned red, but he continued eating without a word, seemingly oblivious to the unasked questions that hovered over the dinner table, demanding satisfaction.

In the end, Mrs. Harper and Majors attributed Gus's extravagance to an unwise adoption of his mother's indulgence of her house slaves, but they did not imagine anything more sinister. Had Georgeanna cared for Gus less, she, too, might have so easily explained away his charity, but love had sensitized her heart. She observed Gus and Promise throughout the remainder of the meal—the hasty glances and slight smiles—and she began to suspect that she had not, in fact, defeated all of her rivals.

By the time coffee was served in the parlor, Georgeanna had determined that Charleston could do very well without her for the next month at least. She discussed her intentions with her mother that night, and in the morning they sent word to Dr. Harper that they would not be returning to the city for some time, and that he was to send them enough clothes to accommodate an extended stay.

CHAPTER 30

"Unlike are We"

The next evening when Gus came knocking at Promise's door, he was caught by surprise when she swung it open and wrapped her arms around his neck. "Muley told me you're gonna let him marry Rachel!"

Gus stumbled backwards into the hallway. "Shh, Promise," he hissed. "Someone'll hear you."

"I can't remember when I've seen him look so happy. Why didn't you tell me he'd come to see you?"

"Promise, please keep your voice down. Georgeanna and Aunt Eleanor are still milling about. Come, let's go inside." Gus closed the door behind them and sat down on her bed. "I don't know why I didn't tell you about Muley. Maybe because I wasn't proud of how easy it would've been for me to say no. I probably should have. I was well within my rights. Nobody would've thought less of me, certainly not Father."

"Then that just makes what you did all the more charitable." Promise smiled at him cheerfully. She settled next to him and kissed him lightly on the cheek. "What made you say yes?"

Gus felt the hot imprint of her lips on his skin. "I-I'm not really sure why I said yes," he said, flustered. "When Muley came to me, asking for Rachel . . . I suppose it was the way he talked about her."

"Yes, she's good for him, although they're very different," Promise said. "Rachel's an absolute angel. I believe she's saved

225

Muley from hellfire. Sometimes opposites belong together, I think. Just like Elizabeth Browning writes in her love poem to Robert. 'Unlike are we, unlike, O princely heart! Unlike our uses and our destinies. Our ministering two angels look surprise on one another, as they strike athwart their wings in passing. Thou, bethink thee, art a guest for queens to social pageantries, with gages from a hundred brighter eyes than tears even can make in mine . . .'" she recited dreamily.

Gus smiled. "The notion that opposites attract is all nonsense if you ask me. A husband and wife should share the same mind and the same disposition. Otherwise, there'll be chaos. I have always thought of love as a mild affection, a fleeting feeling soon substituted by children and responsibilities and other weightier concerns, instead of as a raging passion that seems to exist only in romantic poems and novels—and in the minds of those who read them," he said, looking pointedly at Promise. "But Muley's love for Rachel appeared to be neither. It was an assurance, a knowing that a higher authority had already decreed that they belonged to each other—their only obstacle being the interference of man."

Promise's mouth opened wide with astonishment. "Goodness, Gus. What a sweet sentiment—almost as lovely as Elizabeth's sonnets. You have some romance in you after all. I never would have guessed it."

"I would say thank you for the compliment, but I won't, because you should know by now that no man takes pleasure in being called 'sweet'. And please don't excite yourself. My decision to allow Muley to marry Rachel was based on nothing so fanciful as romance. I'm a great deal like him, you know. All of my choices have been made for me, too. Perhaps I let him have Rachel so that he could have some of the freedom I'd like to have myself."

"You're always complaining about one thing or another," Promise said. "Why view things in such a bad light? I'm always considering my blessings, and it makes me content. I have a good massa and missus. I have been educated and am allowed to continue to improve my mind." She hugged his waist and grinned. "And I have a very, very, good friend in you, Gus—who will someday take me to Paris."

Gus laughed. "Maybe you're right. I have been ungrateful."

"Yes. Instead of mourning over the weight of your responsibilities, you should be thankful that God has put you in a position to bless someone like Muley, as you have done."

"That's what I originally intended when I first returned home. I wanted to do some things differently from Father. I was naive enough to believe that I could end the whippings altogether, but I'm quickly discovering that the procedures on Atterley were put in place because they work. I can't risk changing them now. Father's made me responsible for the harvest. I hate to admit it, but Majors is probably right, the slaves won't work without strict discipline—or at least the threat of it."

"Of course they won't. Everyone knows that. I wish they'd all do what they're told so there'd be no whippings either, but you must be realistic. Like your mother says, they're not like us in the house. They haven't been taught decent ways. The field slaves have no real skills—like Daddy, L'il Remmy, or Muley. And you can't trust them with horses, or cattle, or anything important. They're nearly savage—except for Mama, of course. She knows better, although she does her best to hide it. And it's not like you have to whip them yourself. When it has to be done, Sir Henry will do it."

"Henry. That's another thing. I've always hated him—ever since that Christmas night, by the smokehouse . . . I'd sell him if I could, but Father explicitly forbade it. I'm determined to watch him more carefully than he did, though. I went to see him last week and told him that if I heard any more bad reports about his behavior, I'd have him whipped. That seemed to shock him plenty."

"Are you talking about his drinking? Sometimes he comes to the back door at night, drunk and staggering around. I've seen him twice. Once when I was getting wood, and again when I went outside to help Charles after the pigs got into the garden. Jenny's terrified of him."

"No, I'm not talking about his drinking," Gus muttered, remembering the night, many years ago, when he had seen for himself that all the tales he had heard about his father's driver were true. The squeaking protests of Sir Henry's bed had floated freely out of the window. Gus had hidden behind the Blackbird Tree and watched as the cabin door opened and one of Promise's little sisters, freckle-faced Sylvie, then only eleven-years-old, had come out looking shamefaced. Limping like a maimed deer, she'd weaved past him and back to her parents' cabin. He wasn't surprised to read in Promise's letters of Boris's desire to marry Sylvie and move her to the safety of the circle. "Jenny has good reason to be frightened. The next time you see Henry around the house, you come straight inside, you hear?"

The gravity in Gus's face puzzled her. "He wouldn't dare harm any of us, surely. If it's not his drinking that's gotten you worried, what is it then?"

"Nothing. Never mind. Honestly, Promise. How can you know so little about what goes on in the quarters?"

"Why should I?" she asked. "I have no reason to go there besides to visit Daddy and Mama."

Gus smiled. "Because if you don't concern yourself with anyone besides Jenny and Button, you'll never find yourself a husband."

"And who says I should be trying to find myself a husband?"

"You'll have to give up daydreaming about your mythical Prince Charmings and surefooted heroes and marry a mortal man sometime, Promise. He'll build a little house for you in the circle, and you'll have a great many children and get very comfortable and fat." Gus chuckled at her horrified expression. "So is there anyone you have in mind? You must have my permission first, you know. Would you like to present your petition now—while I'm here and in an agreeable mood?"

"Stop teasing."

"What about Sonny? He seems to be a fine enough fellow. Or Charles? Although I don't think Mother would approve of him—you'd begin to smell like hogs."

"*Gus.*"

"Tell me, do you have any feelings for Quinny? Smelling like sheep is preferable to smelling like hogs, I should think."

"You're not the least bit funny."

"But I must warn you, Promise," Gus said, looking suddenly serious. "I won't give my consent unless he's above reproach. If I find any fault in him at all, I'll not let him take you away from me." He reached out and grazed her cheek with his finger, and Promise felt her insides shudder. Then, sensing that he would be in great danger if he stayed any longer, Gus rose, said goodnight, and left the room.

CHAPTER 31

The Ladies Come to Tea

Time passed slowly for Georgeanna, and she was growing desperate. After nearly a month in the country, Gus had still not proposed. In fact, there had been no talk at all of marriage. The evening before he was to take a short trip to Charleston with Majors, she persuaded Gus to go for a walk with her on the grounds.

"Augustus, do you care for me?" she asked, as they strolled by Jesse's swinging ivy.

"Yes, of course."

She rested her head on his shoulder. "How my heart will ache for you while you're away."

"There's no need to be dramatic, Georgeanna. I'll be returning in three days."

"I know, but won't it be wonderful once we're married? Then we'll never have to be apart again." Georgeanna grabbed hold of one of Gus's hands and laid it softly on her breast. "Then we can do all of those delicious things that married people do. I must admit, I've thought of it often and wondered what it would be like to give all of myself to a man— to yield to his every appetite. You've thought about it, too, haven't you?"

"Yes," Gus said under his breath, his voice raspy.

"Perhaps I am overly emotional tonight," she said, caressing his fingers. "Lucy is not feeling well, and she simply refuses to see your Dr. Needham. She insists that Father must treat her, but he cannot leave Charleston. What shall I do?"

"That's no great difficulty. Why don't Majors and I bring her with us to Charleston?"

"Oh, Augustus. That would be such a relief. I knew that you would manage to think of something clever."

"I'm glad to be of service."

"Lucy is so dear to me. She's been with us since I was a child."

"Of course, I understand," Gus said, guiding her around a wet patch of earth. He was feeling quite warm towards her. "The house servants will be happy to assist you and your mother during Lucy's absence. Jenny is very obliging, and Young Martha—"

"Actually, I would much prefer Promise. She could sleep at the foot of my bed like Lucy does, keep my things orderly, and dress me in the mornings. The others can help Mother, but I want Promise for myself."

Gus swallowed. "You want Promise?"

"Yes. She's so handy. You've said so yourself many times." The principal aim of Georgeanna's request was to test Gus's love for her, and so she studied his reaction to her petition closely, hoping that he would agree to offer up Promise for her convenience, placing her fate into her hands.

"No. That's out of the question. Promise cannot be spared." Gus spoke with a firmness that surprised them both.

"But Augustus, she would be such a comfort to me while Lucy's gone. Why would you refuse to grant me such a small favor?"

"You may use the services of the others however you like, but Promise is mine alone. I'll not share her." The words sprang from Gus's lips before he was able to check them.

Georgeanna blanched and released his fingers with alarm. "Of course I'll not insist upon having her, since you feel so strongly about it."

As the two walked on in silence, it was Georgeanna who spoke first. "This is a horrid way to spend our last night together before you leave me for three whole days," she declared with false levity. "Come Augustus, let's not speak of Promise any more tonight. Let's enjoy the evening." She wrapped her arm snugly around his, and for the next quarter mile talked only of the beauty of Jesse's gardens.

Gus breathed a sigh of relief and let her prattle on, mistakenly believing that the matter was settled.

Rumors about Gus and Georgeanna and the likelihood of a marriage had been circulating throughout Low Country society for some time. The young ladies in the neighborhood believed it was quite unsporting of Gus's cousin to snatch him up while he was away at Charleston—before any of them had gotten a fair chance at him. Initially, they had resisted making Georgeanna's acquaintance, but their resentment of her was surpassed by an intense desire to have their curiosity satisfied.

Being well brought up, the ladies understood that if one elects to do a thing, one should do it properly, and so to discover the truth they first conducted a thorough investigation, questioning their servants and acquaintances. Unfortunately, their probing had yielded nothing, and after Gus left the country for the weekend, they decided that the time had come to journey to Atterley to pay their respects and quiz Georgeanna over tea and cake.

After they had exchanged the usual pleasantries, Miss Stanton began the inquisition. "Tell me, Georgeanna, how much longer will you be visiting here?"

Mrs. Harper answered for her daughter. "Only until May, and then Augustus will likely return with us to Charleston."

"Are you certain?" Miss Duvall questioned. "The Rileys have always spent the first part of the summer on Pawleys Island."

"Yes. We have had such grand times there together," Miss Hubbard added.

"The Rileys have a home in Charleston as well, you know," Mrs. Harper replied archly.

"And now that Augustus and I have grown so used to being near each other, we have no desire to be separated again for so long a time," Georgeanna added, ringing the bell for tea.

Miss Middleton noticed Georgeanna's ruby pin. "My, isn't that charming! Did Augustus buy that for you, dear?"

"No . . . it was a Christmas gift from my father."

"I see, how nice," Miss Middleton said, searching the rest of Georgeanna's person for any other signs of a young man's devotion.

"Promise!" Mrs. Harper called. She snatched up the bell herself and shook it with vigor. "Where in heaven is the tea?"

"You know, Georgeanna," Miss Weston said, fingering her gloves, "we've all been expecting an announcement from Atterley about a special event that is to take place, and frankly, we're astonished that after so many weeks, none has come."

Miss Snead nodded in mock concern. "Has Augustus yet expressed his intentions toward you? We very much want to be your friends, Georgeanna. You may safely confide in us."

"Surely you realize that we are not at liberty to discuss such a subject with only newly formed acquaintances," Mrs. Harper said. She bore her eyes into Promise as she entered the room with the tray.

After a slight curtsy to Mrs. Harper and Georgeanna to make amends, Promise began pouring out the tea.

The young ladies had been circling their prey for some time, and it was Miss Stanton who decided to advance and make the kill. "Forgive me, Georgeanna, but I've heard reports that Augustus does not intend to marry you at all— that his affections lie . . . elsewhere."

Miss Stanton's blind arrow had hit the mark, and Georgeanna lost her composure. "That is a vicious lie!"

The violence of her outburst astonished them all, and each lady scrutinized her companions, wondering which one of them had been so fortunate as to unwittingly procure Gus's favor.

"Yes, it must be a falsehood," Miss Stanton said with a slight smile. "But as they say, in every false rumor there is a fraction of truth."

"That's not fair, Kitty," Miss Mason admonished. "Augustus *must* have invited Georgeanna to remain at Atterley for so long a time. I do not believe she is the sort of person who would have remained here on her *own* accord—with the intention of bewitching him into matrimony."

"Yes Georgeanna, please calm yourself," Miss Hubbard said. "We did not say that *we* believed Augustus has no real feelings for you. In fact, *I* suggested that we come to Atterley to hear *your* side of it. I am sure that you know the value of discretion, and of course nothing causes people to be more discreet than when the truth is generally known. It is speculation that sets tongues to wagging."

"Promise," Mrs. Harper said, noticing that her hands had stilled. "Don't just stand there gaping at the guests. This conversation does not concern you. We are waiting for our tea."

Georgeanna's insecurity made her reckless and overly anxious to quash all doubts. "Actually, Augustus and I are already engaged," she blurted out. "He has proposed and I have accepted, but we were hoping to keep our plans private until the summer."

Promise jolted with surprise and spilled tea across the front of Georgeanna's dress. The ladies burst into a flurry of unguarded sniggers.

Mrs. Harper stood up. "You clumsy thing, look what you've done! Quick! Go take Miss Georgeanna to her room and help her change her dress!"

Promise didn't cease offering her apologies as they walked up the stairs, but Georgeanna did not reply. Her face held no expression at all, and her knuckles were frosty as she grasped the railing. After her visitors had left Atterley in triumph, and her mother had gone to bed with a sick headache, Georgeanna asked Sonny to saddle a horse, and she rode out to the fields to call upon Sir Henry.

CHAPTER 32

Abraham's Cry

Lassie burst into the kitchen. "Sir Henry's tied a rope to that leaning oak by Jesse's grapevines! Somebody in the circle's gettin' whipped!"

Eliza followed behind, carrying a jar of preserves from the storehouse. "No one's getting whipped, silly. Tell her, Young Martha."

"But lookit, he's sittin' right out there polishing up his whip," Lassie insisted.

"He's just trying to spook us most likely—letting the rope hang there while he's oiling that whip of his," Young Martha figured. "I wish he'd do his dirty work someplace else."

"He can't be wanting to whip one of us, could he, Promise?" Jenny asked.

"Of course not. Young Martha's right. Don't be ridiculous." Promise plunged an iron skillet beneath the water. "Grace, come away from the window and finish drying these floors before somebody gets hurt."

Sir Henry's heart was glad. Georgeanna had come to him, seeking his advice, his help—treating him like he was a man worthy of respect. "Henry, with Augustus and Mr. Majors gone, you're the only one I can come to," she'd said, before whispering her request in his ear. And how she beamed at him after he'd yielded—spreading those sweet lips of hers! "We're going to be good friends, you and I," she told him, squeezing his hand.

Sir Henry would have done anything for her then, as he watched the hunger swell in her eyes. He recognized the craving. He had seen it many times in the faces of the elegant ladies who came to call on Rebecca—who turned their noses up at him if he happened by, but then stole secret, curious glances at his private parts. The forbidden desire that they would never dare satisfy consumed their fantasies—to be ravaged by a man with just enough animal in him to make the union intriguingly profane.

Sir Henry grinned as he rubbed a thick piece of pork fat over his whip, his darling. She was well traveled and worn, but in one sense, today she would be embarking upon a maiden voyage. She had never sliced into the back of a house slave before. It was a treacherous pilgrimage, but Sir Henry had counted the cost, and with Georgeanna's prompting, he had decided to encroach upon Gus's authority—believing that although Zachary was far from Atterley, his hedge of protection would still shield him from his son's wrath. Sir Henry had grown resentful of his new master. Gus had taken from him one of his most cherished delights, his enjoyment of the quarter's tender little ones, threatening to have Tucker and Amos whip him if he didn't curb his appetite.

Sir Henry looked up at Georgeanna's window, waiting for her signal. When she waved her handkerchief, he went inside. Usually he sent Tucker or Amos to do the fetching. There were always unpleasant scenes, especially the first time a slave was whipped—before they had learned that it would go better for them if they cooperated. The initial struggle spent his energy, tiring him out before the main event. On this day, however, nothing would be done that he would not do himself.

When Sir Henry first entered the kitchen, there didn't appear to be any cause for alarm. He surveyed the room casually, as if he were in search of a button for his shirt or a fresh cup of coffee. But in his eyes there was a peculiar shining, a frighteningly grotesque bloodlust that made Promise's heart jump when they fixed upon her.

"Promise," he said lightly. His tongue wound around her name as he summoned her towards him. *"Promise."*

Promise's bones frosted over and she couldn't move.

"Promise, Miss Georgeanna tole me that you been causin' trouble for her since Massa Gustus been gone. She tole me that you been actin' uppidy, that you ruint her dress. She says you gotta be whupped to remind you of yo' place."

Promise's fingers twitched frantically in the lukewarm water. *Ta-ta Bruum. Ta-ta-ta-ta, Ta-ta Bruum!* "It was an accident. I told Miss Georgeanna I was sorry."

Sir Henry uncoiled his whip to show Promise he meant business. "That may be, but it don't matter. Miss Georgeanna tole me that I gotta whup you, so you best come 'long with me." He stretched his hand out to her.

"No." Promise backed away from him, burrowing her dripping hands into the creases of her dress, soaking the fabric. "I wanna see Miss Georgeanna. Please. I wanna see Miss Georgeanna!"

"Well, she don't wanna see you, so just stop that runnin'," Sir Henry said, growing angry as he lunged for her. "All Miss Georgeanna wanna see is that purty back of yours all cut up, so you quit yo' hollerin' and com'ere!"

"April, go run upstairs and get Miss Georgeanna!" Young Martha yelled. She picked up a broom and went after Sir Henry. "Get on outta here, you!"

"Yeah, you get on out, you nasty black nigger!" Lassie screamed. "You leave Promise alone! Massa Riley never let you whip none of us! You know that!"

"Don't you do it, Sir Henry!" Eliza warned him. "Don't you *dare* do it! Massa Gus'll get you *good* when he gets back!"

"He ain't gonna do nothin'!" Sir Henry pushed Young Martha to the ground and charged at Promise, snatching her by the arm. He dragged her toward the door. "Now y'all hear me, and hear me *good*," he huffed over his shoulder. "None of you best give me no more mess, or you's gonna be next! Ain't nothin' gonna happen to me. Thangs gonna change 'round here. Miss Georgeanna's here to stay, and she likes the way I does thangs! She ain't as soft as Missus is!"

When April burst into the bedroom, Mrs. Harper was sitting at the desk, writing her letters. Georgeanna was still poised in front of the window. "Miss Georgeanna! Come quick! Sir Henry's 'bout to whip Promise!"

Georgeanna didn't answer her. She was captivated—watching Sir Henry tie Promise to the tree outside.

"You should know better than to come into this room without knocking," Mrs. Harper said. "Promise is getting a much-deserved whipping for disrespecting Miss Georgeanna. You've all been shamelessly spoiled, and your bursting in here in so violent a manner is a perfect example of that."

"But—"

"But nothing. This doesn't concern you. Please go back downstairs and tell the others to stop all that wailing. It's not going to do anybody any good."

Promise kept her eyes fixed on the main house while Sir Henry wrapped the ropes twice around her wrists, fastening the ends in tight knots. She fully expected Georgeanna to rush out and save her, waving her arms high, saying there had been a terrible mistake. But no rescue came.

Sir Henry pushed close to her. "I know this is yo' first time, Promise," he said. His voice sounded hoarse in her ear. "So I'm gonna take it real slow." He unbuttoned the top of her dress, his hands trembling as he pushed aside the cloth to expose the soft triangular patch of skin at the nape of her neck.

Promise began to cry, begging Sir Henry in incoherent babblings to please let her go.

He smiled, ignoring her pleas. His fingers found her spine, and he traced its ridges lightly, letting his fingertips bounce over the hard knobs as he continued to undress her.

Word spread quickly—through the circle, the stables, the carpentry shop, the street, the highlands, the fields, the pastureland.

"Sir Henry's 'bout to whip Promise!"

"He's what?"

"He's gonna beat up on that little-bitty thang?"

"Mean ole Henry!"

"What'll Massa Gustus say?"

"She ain't gonna make it!"

"Lord, help her!"

Over the years, Promise had witnessed the desperate plight of the field slaves from a safe distance, as they were tied up like dogs and stripped naked. She had heard their screams many times and busied her fingers to disguise her discomfort. She had stepped over the bloodstained ground after they had been carried away, without offering a prayer on their behalf. She had never shed tears over their lashes, or turned restlessly in her soft bed, bemoaning their fate. Still they grieved for her on her day of atonement, mourning for her lost innocence instead of being satisfied that the harsh realities of their existence had finally pierced through the fortified walls of the main house.

Abraham received the news with despairing acceptance. Many years ago, his spirit had been taken up and packed tight, remaining in the airless heat of the ship that had transported him to America. His arms and legs were arrested by the chains that had held him then—while his brothers sickened and choked to death on their own vomit just a few feet away. His ears still overflowed with the soft moans of the dying and the embittered cries of the living. His nose was plugged up with the stifling smells of sickness, blood, and feces. Before his eyes were the faces of the young virgins from his homeland, who were carried to secret places to be defiled by sailors.

His mind warred against the insanity that overtook countless numbers of the prisoners on that death ship, who lay unmoving in their own excrement, their eyes staring ahead unblinking. They refused to eat, even after their lips were burned with hot coals, and only whimpered pitifully when the sailors' whips cut their backs to the bone—their life running out in thick rivers on the ship's deck. The men and women who succumbed to this quiet madness allowed themselves to be thrown overboard without a struggle, and because their souls' fire had already left their bodies, they made no sound as sharks approached and devoured their still-living flesh.

Because Abraham was still bound by all he had suffered, he had joined his countrymen beneath the enveloping darkness and could not fight. So although his heart was pained, he relinquished his daughter to her fate and restrained Muley from running toward the main house with his hammer.

Sir Henry, with one firm tug, loosed Promise's dress from her shoulders, and it gathered around her waist. He gazed upon her back—it lay bare before him, supple and virginal. Knowing that he would be the first to conquer her made him tremble, and he took a deep breath, disciplining himself to take his time. "Don't worry, I ain't gonna let nothin' happen to yo' purty clothes," he breathed.

Promise looked down and saw her bare breasts exposed in the sun. Tears dampened her face and neck as she strained against the ropes. She closed her eyes to shut out the spectators she imagined were beholding her shame. But there were none. None of the slaves had ventured near, and they had come away from the windows. Atterley was silent.

"Aw Promise, don't mess yo'self up like that, now," Sir Henry said. He rested one hand on Promise's backside and slid the other down her stomach, caressing its contours until he reached her waist. Her dress and underclothes fell to the ground.

Promise convulsed.

His eyes lingered over her body as it quaked, fixing the image in his mind. Then he pressed against her to feel her nakedness.

She felt his hardness and screamed.

"I tole you that you was just a nigga like me," Sir Henry murmured in her ear, letting his tongue touch her earlobe. "You 'member me tellin' you that?" He ran his whip down her back, leaving a thin layer of grease.

Promise was weakened. She had no more strength to twist and writhe his hands away and had no choice but to submit to his touch.

Sir Henry smiled then, satisfied, knowing it was time. He looked up at the window, waiting for the go-ahead. Georgeanna nodded from the other side of the glass, signaling for him to begin.

ONE. The first strike landed. Promise heard the crack, but initially, she felt nothing. Fears of scarring, of the permanent disfigurement that the lashes would bring, filled her thoughts. But by the time Sir Henry had raised his arm to deliver the second blow, a thin line of searing pain exploded over her back, and she was consumed only by her physical agony. She was determined not to scream and clinched her teeth, letting only a groan escape from between her lips.

TWO. The second strike crisscrossed the first. Sir Henry's whip brought torment where the leather broke new ground, but in the places where it found cut flesh, it ignited rippling fire. The remainder of Promise's modesty dissolved. Her anguish birthed fresh frenzy, adrenaline coursed through her body, and her strength returned. She lurched forward and howled.

THREE. Mrs. Harper did her best to ignore the commotion outside. She kept her head down, engrossed in her correspondence, but Georgeanna watched the proceedings intently. She had always prided herself on her abhorrence of base violence and often chastised her younger brothers for their cruelty. Although she was continually threatening Lucy with whippings, Georgeanna had no real intention of following through on her threats, and her nurse had never received any physical punishment at her hand. But watching Promise's torture awakened and gratified a savage part of her, and she found herself wishing that it was her hand that wielded the whip.

FOUR. In the highland, the women gathered around Cora to comfort her. They knew her sufferings well. But she pushed them away. Her distress was mixed with a fierce anger that she held fast to her heart. She pierced her skin, letting her blood roll over her arm and onto the ground while she cast her spells. The women understood, and Tucker turned away, pretending not to notice.

FIVE. Sir Henry smiled as he sliced, watching Promise's wounds deepen into ragged grooves across her back. His strikes were deliberate, there was an art to carving flesh, and he paused a moment after each one to admire his workmanship. The thin rivers of blood wove together as they flowed over the landscape of Promise's body, joining into a heavy stream at her lower back that flooded between her buttocks before dripping onto the ground.

SIX. The field slaves sowed the ground with their tears and sang to cloak Promise's screams:

Lord, we lift yo' name tuh heaven,
Hallelooo-ooo-ya!
Lord, we lift yo' name tuh heaven,
Hallelooooooooo!

Lord, we know you'll see-ee us through,
What a friend we fo-ound in you.

Lord, we lift yo' name tuh heaven,
Halleloooooooooo!

SEVEN. Abraham rolled his hammer handle across his palm and stared into the flames of his forge. The fire haunted him, like the piercing sounds of his daughter's cries. He saw his past, present, and future in those bright flickers—a medley of reds, oranges, and blues that sprang up like ghosts, and then vanished into wisps of black smoke. The tool felt heavy in his hand. He had no words to express all that he had lost—all that had been taken—and he could not lift it.

EIGHT. The house servants kneeled on the kitchen floor, forming a large circle. They clasped their hands as they swayed gently from side to side—their movements slowed only by the slight bumping of shoulders. Young Martha began a prayer, but her voice soon faltered away—silence seemed more fitting. The stillness was interrupted only by an occasional sniffle or an eruption of fresh sobbing.

NINE. Abraham had not cried since he was a child, but he suddenly found himself unable to carry the heaviness any longer. The first tear fell quickly, piggybacking on sweat. It tumbled into the fire, sizzling into nothingness. The others followed after in a rush—each drop carrying hardened bits of bitterness, misery, and fear. The weighty drops cooled the flames that had danced before his eyes, sending billows of steam up toward the heavens.

TEN. Promise's torment was rendering her delirious. Jesse's gardens were spinning past her in blurred streams of color, making her dizzy. Her legs went numb and her mind abandoned her—wandering far from her body and up into the clouds. The escape was only temporary, however, for each scourge of Sir Henry's whip brought her back to herself.

ELEVEN. After Abraham's tears had rolled away his soul's contamination, all that remained was the smallest fragments of hope. With his courage unveiled, he gathered those fragments together and extended his arms upwards—raising his hammer high. He brought it down hard, and then swung again and again—his spirit's petition echoing over the trees. The wind came alive and carried the message through the sky. It was a cry for help—not from the god of his homeland, or the god of the white man, but from the God who hope whispered could save his little girl.

TWELVE. The slaves working in the highlands, and those bent over the waterlogged fields harkened his call. It stirred them, and they ceased their laboring. The cattle paused their grazing and lifted up their heads. The bobolinks stopped bobbing for insects and rose up in fluttering unison.

THIRTEEN. And the Lord heard Abraham's cry and answered his prayer. In His inscrutable wisdom, He had chosen to give man free will, so although He did not snatch the whip from Sir Henry's hands, He sent an angel to steal the breath from Promise, and she slumped forward, losing consciousness.

FOURTEEN. The lash landed ineffectually on Promise's body, and Georgeanna, with some reluctance, waved her handkerchief a second time. Sir Henry's arm stilled.

CHAPTER 33

The Aftermath

Sir Henry cut Promise down with his knife and let her fall, moist and softened like a ripened fruit, to the ground. After he had abandoned her in the dirt and returned to the fields, the slaves ventured out of their hiding places—peeking over bedcovers and creeping from behind onion barrels. The brutality and degradation of the street had come at last to the circle, and its inhabitants gathered around Promise.

They gasped at the mangled flesh of her back. Sir Henry had outdone himself. Florence and Miriam stood stunned, with a dozen frightened little ones tucked in their skirts. Boris and Red leaned openmouthed against their garden hoes. Winston took off his hat and held it to his chest. Jenny and Young Martha pushed past the crowd and wrapped a sheet around Promise's body. Jesse lifted her gently and carried her inside the house. By the time he had laid her down on her bed, his shirt was covered with her blood.

"Sylvie, Grace, go get me some warm water," Young Martha ordered. Then for an hour, she cleaned Promise's wounds, washing away the dirt and mosquitoes that clung to the seeping blood.

"Massa Gus is gonna be plenty mad," Jenny said, watching Young Martha coat Promise's back with ointment.

Lassie nodded. "He sure will. Me and Liza warned that nasty black nigger."

"Massa Gus is not gonna stand for one of his house niggers getting whipped." Eliza shook her head. "No decent massa cuts up his house niggers."

"It-it ain't right. It ju-just ain't right," Button whimpered. She rubbed her runny nose vigorously.

"Of course it ain't right," Young Martha said, unrolling a long strip of muslin. "But Massa Gus ain't gonna do nothin'—you'll see. He's gonna marry Miss Georgeanna, and that means what she says goes, just like Sir Henry said. He ain't gonna go against her for none of us—including her." She jerked her head toward Promise.

"Miss Georgeanna ain't gonna whip *me*. I don't care what Massa Gus says," Eliza vowed.

Lassie's eyes flashed fire. "Hell no, she ain't. Whipping ain't supposed to be for respectable colored folk. Me and Liza's too pretty to get beat."

"You're not at all respectable," Jenny said, her eyes filling with tears. "It should've been you instead of her."

"Don't you start in," Lassie threatened. "Before I lick you again. L'il Remmy ain't here to help you now."

"If Massa Gus lets Miss Georgeanna get away with this, I'm gonna tell Missus," Eliza said. "She'll be fighting mad once she hears what's been going on around here."

Jesse wiped away a tear. "All of you, quiet down now. Give her some peace."

"Jenny, Button, come'ere," Young Martha motioned. "You two lift her so I can cover her up." She wrapped the muslin gently around Promise's wounds.

Promise grimaced and began to mumble.

"What's she sayin', Young Martha?" Button asked.

"She doesn't know, child. Fever's comin' on. All right, y'all go on now. Get out of here so she can get some sleep."

Seeing Promise whipped had brightened Georgeanna's mood momentarily, but it had not brought her lasting satisfaction. She was nervous at supper, and jittery by breakfast, counting the hours until Gus was to return—her mind busily rehearsing how best to justify what she had done. Finally, she suggested to her mother that they have Winston take them to Georgetown so she could find something pretty to wear when she broke the news.

By the time Gus was due to arrive, Georgeanna, looking lovely in a new dress the same color blue as her eyes, was waiting for him in the parlor. She intended to be the first to greet him, having prepared a reasonable explanation for her actions, but she didn't get the chance.

As soon as Gus and Majors stepped through the door, Lassie and Eliza sprang out of the shadows. "Promise's been whipped!" they shouted in ear-splitting unison.

"Whipped?" Gus echoed. His eyes were vacant, not comprehending. "What do you mean?"

"Miss Georgeanna had Promise whipped," Lassie said.

"Yeah, Miss Georgeanna had her whipped, Massa Gus," Eliza said.

Gus stood very still. His coat dangled off his shoulder, lolling sloppily against his back. "She did what?"

"Sir Henry tied her up out back and *whipped* her," Lassie said, gratified by his shock.

Gus's face turned pale, then red. "My God," he whispered.

"We tried to stop him, Massa Gus," Eliza said.

"We sure did, but Sir Henry wouldn't listen. He's gone crazy, ain't that right, Liza?"

"Yeah, and he stripped her naked."

"*Naked*, Massa Gus."

"And he let her hang like that for the whole world to see."

"Is Promise all right? Where is she?" Gus asked.

"Calm down, son," Majors said. "Just calm down."

"Promise is in her room, Massa Gus. And she doesn't look good."

"Not good at all, Massa."

"Miss Georgeanna's got a mighty bad temper, if you ask me."

"*Mighty* bad."

Mrs. Harper hurried down the hallway, her shoes clicking, with Georgeanna following close behind. "What's all this commotion?"

"Oh Augustus, you're home," Georgeanna said, reaching for him. "You look terrible darling, what's wrong?"

Gus didn't answer her. He was thinking only of Promise as he rushed past them toward her bedroom, leaving Lassie and Eliza to smirk at the ladies' alarm.

"Promise . . . Promise are you asleep?" he whispered at her bedside.

There was a slight movement beneath the covers. Her lids were blood-gorged and heavy, and she opened her eyes slowly.

"They told me what happened—what Georgeanna let Henry do to you . . ." Gus choked on his words. "Promise, I'm so sorry."

Tears gathered at the base of her puffed-up eyelids.

"I'm sorry I wasn't here. If I had been, I never would have allowed this." Gus held the sides of her face and circled her cheeks softly with his thumbs until the dammed-up tears overflowed their banks and rolled over his fingers. "Do you . . . do you hurt very badly?"

"It aches," she said, her voice broken, "but not so much as at first. Has the blood soaked through yet?"

Gus pulled back the sheets and craned over her to look. He gasped at the blood-red stretch of back. "Yes, it has," he managed. "Do the bandages need to be attended to?"

"Young Martha said she has to change them once the blood showed through."

"I'll go get her," he said and rose to leave.

Promise held fast to his fingers.

"I'll come back quickly, I promise, and I'll stay with you as long as you want me."

Georgeanna was waiting for him in the hallway. "Is everything all right, Augustus?" she asked, keeping her voice light.

Gus shut the door behind him. "How could you do such a thing?" he asked her. "How could you have Promise whipped, knowing how strongly I'd feel about it?"

"Oh, that. That was unfortunate. I just hated having it done, but it couldn't be helped. Promise was insolent and careless. She spilled steaming tea on my dress, right in front of my visitors, and she wasn't the least bit sorry for it. And I was trying so hard to make a good impression on them—for *your* sake."

"I find it very hard to believe that Promise was ill-mannered toward you, and I'm certain that whatever she may have done was unintentional," Gus said.

"Is that what she told you? Well, *I'm* certain it was on purpose. It was fortunate that I was not badly burned. Promise seems to have a strange sort of resentment toward me."

"She does not. She has shown you every courtesy."

Georgeanna's thin smile vanished. "Augustus, are you saying that you doubt my word? That you are more convinced of her good character than mine?"

"Yes, I suppose I am," Gus said, struggling to control his anger. "And even if Promise had done what you claim, she wouldn't have deserved that kind of whipping. Can't you see that? Henry whipped her like a man. He could have crippled her, or even killed her."

"Now that I've had the chance to think it over, I believe I may have acted too hastily. I was upset. I did so want everything to come off right when the ladies came to tea. And Henry was too hard on her. He was eager to please me— knowing how important I am to his master. If you'll have Promise apologize to me for her behavior, we can just forget the entire incident." Georgeanna linked her arm around his. "There now, shall we have some dinner? It smells wonderful."

Gus pulled away. "How *dare* you ask me to make Promise apologize to you—after you nearly had her killed for a minor infraction. I'll not do it. What's come over you, Georgeanna? How could you have turned her over to that—that *monster?* You let him take her clothes off, for God's sake! I can only imagine what damage you've done to her."

Georgeanna's features twisted. "I believe it's customary for a slave's clothing to be removed when they're to be whipped," she snapped. "You're not angry because I let Henry whip one of your house servants without your permission. You're not so softhearted, so *benevolent* as you pretend. You would not be this outraged if it were Prince, or Caesar, or one of the others who was subjected to the same treatment. I suspect, my dear cousin, that your objection lies not with the punishment itself, or the severity of it, but upon whom it was inflicted."

Georgeanna had hit upon the truth. They both knew it, and it could no longer be denied. "And what if that is the case?" Gus said. "Promise and I were childhood friends. My feelings for her are only natural."

Weeks of enduring her cousin's preference for his slave had taken its toll on Georgeanna, and her emotions could be suppressed no longer. "There's nothing natural about your feelings for Promise! Nothing natural at all!" she shrieked, shaking her hair out of position. "They are perverted and depraved! Your father may be a great man, but *you*. You will *never* be. You are an embarrassment!"

Mrs. Harper heard her daughter's screams and ran toward them, gathering her skirts up in tight fists. "Georgeanna! What has gotten into you, child? Stop it! Stop it right now!" she gasped, as she witnessed her dreams of financial security vanish before her eyes.

But Georgeanna's emotional wounds were as deep as Promise's physical ones, and she would not be so easily bridled. She spoke slowly so Gus would feel the cut of her words. "You are not *fit* to own the name Riley!"

"Perhaps that's true, Georgeanna, but neither are *you*," Gus returned, and stalked past her to find Young Martha.

Mrs. Harper's mouth dropped open as she watched him go, and Georgeanna fell backward against the wall as if she had been struck.

Gus stood over Promise observing Young Martha as she unwrapped the blood-soaked muslin. "It's almost off, Massa Gus," she warned.

"It's fine, Young Martha. He can stay." Promise held a quilt to her chest to cover herself as soon as she removed the last layer. Young Martha put ointment on the bulging stripes with feather-light fingertips.

The grease burned into Promise's flesh. "Oooooh," she moaned, jerking away from her touch.

"Hold still now. I gotta get this on you, girl, or it'll get worse. Massa Gus, you keep her from moving."

Gus took her hand. "Hold on tight if you need to, Promise, but you gotta keep still, hear?"

Promise wept as she shook beneath Young Martha's fingers. When the pain became too much to bear alone, she pulled Gus close and leaned into him, screaming, until the blessed moment when Young Martha closed up the jar and reached for a fresh strip of muslin.

Gus sat next to Promise's bed after Young Martha had gone, pledging to stay with her until she fell asleep. The windows were left open so she could feel the breeze on her back. The gusts cooled the room as they passed through, bringing the scent of hydrangea and honeysuckle. Every now and then a mockingbird ceased its chirping and alighted on the sill to peck at a row of marching ants.

Promise couldn't sleep and she couldn't cry. She lay very still. "You were right," she said finally.

"About what?" Gus roused himself. "I can't remember a time when you've believed me to be right about anything."

"About what you wrote in your letter. When you wrote that your mother had done me a disservice, making me accustomed to things I had no right to. That's why I got so mad—you were right. Two days ago, I thought I was far different from the field slaves, as far as the circle is from the street. I thought I was entitled to certain things—to dignity and justice. Two days ago I would have said there was no real difference between your cousin and myself. Your mother taught me to believe that. My manners, my clothes—they rival Miss Georgeanna's. I've studied French and German and read all the important works. But still, there *is* a difference, and that difference was enough to wash all the rest away in a moment. It was enough to leave me helpless when there was no white face around to protect me, to stand up for me. It gave Sir Henry the right to treat me like an animal, to undress me, touch me, raise my skirts—when he never would've dared raise his eyes to Miss Georgeanna. Your mother brought me up to forget that difference, which makes it hurt even more now that I remember."

Gus kneeled beside her and pushed a stray hair away from her forehead. "That doesn't matter now, because I won't leave you again. Do you believe me?"

Promise nodded and wound her fingers around his.

He leaned toward her slowly, unsure, giving her the chance to move away, but she didn't, and her eyes stared into his, willing. Encouraged, he lifted her chin upwards and kissed her—gingerly at first, and then with the accumulated passion of all the years that he had loved her. With the sights, sounds, and smells of Mother Earth infusing Promise's bedroom, the kiss seemed natural and right, and they were both taken up.

They forgot that man's law decreed that God's black and white children were meant to meet only with violence or animal lust, not love. They forgot that the foundation of their devotion was made porous by its impossibilities and could not withstand the stormy onslaught of societal conventions that was sure to come. But nature forgave their folly and gave them a temporary haven as they indulged their affections in her midst.

The Harpers left Atterley early the next morning. Majors journeyed with them. His business was suffering due to his absence, and he could no longer afford to remain at Atterley, even at the request of his best client. He had hoped that during the trip to Charleston he could do Zachary one final service and appease the Harpers' anger, but to no avail. By nightfall the ladies had returned to town, their hearts and minds brimming with deep resentment, prepared to tell all.

CHAPTER 34

To Have and to Hold

Gus stayed at Promise's bedside throughout the month of May, delaying the seaside pleasures waiting for him at Crestview. He didn't leave her room except to sleep—slipping away at night after her eyes had closed and returning before she had awakened in the morning. They were alone together much of the day. Gus ignored Tobias's knitted brows and insisted upon carrying their meals to her bedroom himself. Only Young Martha interrupted their isolation when she came to tend to Promise's wounds.

There were good times when Promise's spirits were high. Gus would lay next to her, cradle her in his arms, and press his lips against her neck while they made plans for a future together that were as fanciful as Hannah's childhood stories. But there were also fitful nights when her fever returned. Gus would cool her body with dripping cloths, and with gritted teeth help change sheets soaked with sweat and blood.

As Promise's back healed and the scabs began a fierce itching, he distracted her with stories about his years at the Academy. When she persuaded him to lead her to the mirror and let her see the raised skin across her back, he kept his face level when he assured her in hushed tones that the scarring had stolen none of her beauty.

Not long after the Harpers' departure from Atterley, Gus received a letter from his mother, but he waited until Young

Martha had removed the bandages from Promise's back for the last time before he shared its contents with her.

My Dear Augustus,

> *Eleanor has written me and described in detail your horrible treatment of Georgeanna. According to your aunt, you abused your poor cousin dreadfully and assaulted her character—telling her that she was not fit to be your wife. I apologized on your behalf, but Eleanor has not returned any of my letters, and my brother's response was barely civil. Your uncle will be coming to Columbia next month, and I am hoping that while he is here your father will take the opportunity to try and make amends.*

> *In fairness, I have not yet heard your account of the particulars, so I am writing you in hopes that your aunt has grossly exaggerated your behavior, and that you may still find a way to rectify things. Of course Georgeanna was very wrong to whip Promise. I was horrified to hear of it, and you were right to chastise her. Please tell Promise so for me. But Augustus, it was an unfortunate mistake in judgment that should not affect what would have been a very suitable marriage.*

> *Eleanor has also made some scandalous accusations concerning your feelings for Promise, but they do not bear repeating because there can be no truth in them. However, when you behave in such a violent manner it opens your motives up to speculation. Please write to your cousin and beg her forgiveness so that you will not ruin all chance for future happiness.*

> *Your mother,*
> *Rebecca*

While Promise was confined to her bed, Gus left the plantation's concerns to the drivers, but once she had fully recovered, he turned his attention back to his business affairs. One morning, slave speculators came through the front gates of Atterley with their ragtag wares chained to the sides of their wagons. Jesse saw them first and lowered his pruning shears. "Lord, what they doin' here?" he said.

Before long, all of Atterley was wondering what Gus was up to, because it was common knowledge that "Massa Riley didn't fool with that trash." To buy one of the speculators' beaten down, undernourished slaves who were too old, sick, or unruly to be of any use was foolishness, and for any respectable planter to sell one of their slaves to them was unthinkable.

Gus met the men outside. They didn't dare hope for an invitation inside Atterley's main house, so they were not disappointed. He conducted his business with them from the front steps, and then sent Prince to the fields to fetch Sir Henry.

Sir Henry led his horse toward the front of the main house instead of the back—just as Prince had instructed. He was glad that he had taken the time to change into his good shoes. He had suffered a few sleepless nights after Georgeanna and her mother had left Atterley so abruptly, but as the weeks passed without Gus saying anything to him about the matter, Sir Henry had decided that his young master was too afraid of exacting his father's wrath to challenge him.

Although he couldn't imagine what Gus would want with him so early in the morning, Sir Henry figured that he had finally learned who was who and what was what, and was ready to make peace. He dismounted when he spotted the speculators. "One of these niggas been actin' up, Massa Gustus? You want me to fetch him for ya?" he asked.

Gus was leaning lazily against one of the porch columns, fingering a pile of sunflower seeds in his palm. He popped a few in his mouth. "No, Henry, they've come for you," he said. "I'm selling you away from here."

"Wh-What?" Sir Henry looked stunned. "What for?"

"You know very well what for."

"You can't sell me. Who you thinks you is? Yo' daddy said you can't, so you can't. He tole me so hisself."

"My father's not here right now. I am. You shouldn't have done it, Henry. You shouldn't have whipped Promise. You knew better. Come get him, boys," Gus said, tossing the rest of the seeds in his mouth.

Sir Henry held his hands up and backed away. "Wait! Hole on! Don't you care none 'bout what yo' daddy says, Gustus? I'se Massa Riley's right-hand man! His right-hand man!"

While Sir Henry's eyes were fixed on Gus, one of the speculators raised the butt of his whip and hit him on the side of the head. The blow dazed him, but in a moment he had regained his footing, ready to fight. It took four speculators to grab hold of him and pull him in the direction of the wagons.

As Sir Henry struggled, they stripped him of his trappings—his hat with the snakeskin band, his knife, his whip, his coat. After they had chained his wrists to one of the wagons, the men mopped their sweat and stretched their backs before fully securing him.

One speculator gathered together Sir Henry's legs and noticed his feet. "Them's mighty fine shoes fer a nigger ain't they?" he said.

Sir Henry kicked his legs wildly as they pulled his most prized possessions off his feet. "Them's my shoes! Them's *my* shoes!" he hollered.

Then the men fell upon each other—wrestling over ownership of his belongings.

"You ain't gonna get away with this, Gustus!" Sir Henry screamed over the clamor. "When Massa Riley finds out what you done, he's gonna find me and buy me right back, you hear me? He ain't gonna stand for this here!"

"You boys stop that fighting and get this nigger off my land," Gus said. He spat out the black shells and went inside.

There was a celebration in the quarters that afternoon as big as Christmas and New Year's put together, and widespread praise of Gus for freeing them from a tyrant. But Promise, who had watched the entire scene from an upstairs window, was surprised to discover that the sight of the speculators carrying Sir Henry cursing and crying away from Atterley had not gratified her.

The stripes on her back left scars that had gone deeper, and she saw in Gus's treatment of Sir Henry just how impotent the Negro was without the aid of a white man. She told Gus so later while she stroked his hair.

"Would you rather I'd not sold him?" he asked, looking up disbelieving from her lap. "Would you prefer it if I'd kept him here after he hurt you the way he did? After he put his hands on you?"

"No, I've hated him as long as I can remember, and I'm glad he's gone. It's just that Sir Henry was somebody on Atterley, a big somebody, and still it was so easy for you to take away all he had. You believe that you were right to do it, because he was so horrible, and perhaps that's true. I'm only saying that according to Miss Georgeanna, she was right to whip me. Both of you decided what was a fitting punishment, and without having to answer to anyone, you carried it out. It's the same thing."

"It's not the same at all. Don't be ridiculous. I can't understand why you'd waste one moment's thought on that man. I don't care what's been taken from Henry, he deserves it, and he deserves to get some of the same treatment he's been giving out all these years."

"I suppose," Promise sighed.

"What's wrong with you today? Let's go for a walk to the lake. We'll go swimming."

"No, it's too hot, and the fever's going around. You know, Gus, you never gave me my birthday present."

He laughed and settled himself more comfortably in her arms. "Now that sounds more like my Promise. All right then, what is it you want this time?"

"I want schoolbooks for the children. I want to teach them—to give them something that can't be taken away."

Gus sat up. "What're you talking about? What children?"

"Atterley's children. They're wearing brown skins, Gus, but they're children nonetheless, and they have a right to learn the same as the white ones do. I've been reading about a school in Philadelphia that's just for coloreds. I could ask L'il Remmy to build me a schoolhouse next to the chapel. I want to teach the children to read, write, and figure. So one day when the Negro is free—"

"When?" Gus raised his eyebrows.

"One day *if* the Negro is free, they'll have a chance to stand on their own, without your help or anyone else's."

Gus lay back down and closed his eyes. "Assuming they do have a moral right to be educated, Promise, it's still against the law. I know Mother set a poor example where that's concerned, but her actions, which were unwise, would be even more inappropriate for you."

"No one pays attention to that sort of thing, you know that. Mrs. Mason has taught all of her house servants to read, and Mrs. Duvall and her daughters have done the same for any of their slaves who want to learn. All I need is your say so, and then I can do what I please."

"Perhaps so, but you've said yourself how discouraging it's been—how all you've learned can't ease the burden of being a Negro. Why don't I take you to Charleston? You can pick out something nice, anything you want, and I'll get it for you."

"No. I want to use what I've learned to teach the children. It's true, I may never be a real lady like Miss Georgeanna and visit the Grecian ruins, or sit in a London theater dressed in diamonds, or be allowed inside the fine museums Missus talks about—but at least I know they're there. I don't want any more fancy dresses or silk handbags. I want school supplies for the children."

"Fine," Gus grumbled. "I know I'll have no peace until you have your way. Write down what you'll need for your school and I'll give it to Majors."

Promise wrapped her arms around his neck. "Thank you," she said, kissing his cheek softly. "You are an angel."

"And you are a trial, but if I've made you happy, I suppose it's all worthwhile." Gus cradled her neck and laid her down on the bed. His eyes poured over her body, glittering with a dangerous longing. "Do you know what I want for *my* birthday?"

His voice was low, barely audible. Promise watched his lips as they moved, drawing her in, only a few inches away from her own. "No, Gus, not that. It's not right," she said, turning away. "I've told you. We're not married, and we can't ever be."

He caressed her hairline and brows before moving lower, gracing her temples and the bridge of her nose with his kisses. "You're very selective about which rules you choose to follow," he whispered, finding the soft patch behind her earlobe. "I break my rules for you." He slid his hand downward, resting it lightly on her breast. "Won't you do the same for me?" he said, circling his thumb around her nipple.

"Gus, please," Promise begged, beginning to weaken.

"We can do what we like on my say so, remember?" he said, unbuttoning the top button of her dress. "And I say that you belong to me, and I defy either God or man to tell me that I cannot have you." He nuzzled against her neck and traced her collarbone with his lips.

Then he kissed her mouth, soft and deep, while his fingers moved deftly, undoing the remainder of her buttons. "I, Augustus Judson Riley, take you, Promise, to be my lawfully wedded wife." He massaged her hips and smiled down upon her, delighted by her soft curves. His hand slipped beneath her dress. "To have and to hold . . ."

Promise started, frightened by the sensation of his fingers rubbing gently, but insistently, against the tender skin of her thigh.

"For richer, for poorer . . ." Gus's hands roamed freely, searching for and finding her secret places, and all of Promise's unease was forgotten in a moment, as she was carried away on an unexpected wave of pleasure. "In sickness and in health..."

Her lids fluttered open, and she looked up at him, her eyes clouded. "For as long as we both shall live," she murmured, loosening his collar.

CHAPTER 35

No Honorable Man

Since their return to Columbia, Rebecca had forsaken her sitting room in the afternoons, complaining that its windows let in strong drafts that made her body ache. Zachary allowed her to join him in his study, but his wife's ailments had been so frequent over the years that he no longer gave serious consideration to her protests that the spasms below her belly were coming with increasing regularity.

Only Hannah saw the desperation in Rebecca's eyes. She had seen it many times before in the faces of the fine ladies and gentlemen who came to Rebecca's father after darkness had fallen so that their faces would not be recognized in the streets. Dr. Harper would summon Hannah to attend to them, and in time she was able to recognize all the signs and symptoms of those dirty diseases believed to be reserved for Negroes and immigrants—the names of which were never uttered by Charleston high society until they came shamefaced to the front doors of their trusted doctors.

Although Hannah couldn't bring herself to reveal the nature of Rebecca's illness herself, she treated her as best she could with teas made of ground-up olive leaves and kava. Whenever the pain kept Rebecca in bed, Hannah sent Jimmy out into the city to retain another one of Columbia's famed physicians, hoping that he would reach beyond the bounds of Zachary's class and station and stumble upon the correct diagnosis. But they had all come and gone without raising any alarm. After prescribing a new variety of ointments, they cautioned Rebecca not to exert herself before going downstairs to drink a glass of brandy with Zachary and chuckle over the excitability of women.

It was not only her desire for personal comfort that had driven Rebecca to invade the seclusion of Zachary's study. She was losing her husband. It had not happened all at once. She had gone over the past weeks, months, and years in her mind and could not discover one private incident, public indiscretion, or social embarrassment that had marked the moment when he had stopped loving her. She was not as beautiful as she once was, but she had played her part faithfully, and had clung to her youth for as long as she could.

Still, Zachary had withdrawn himself from her slowly, taking pieces of his heart from her hands. The corsets that once enhanced the shape of her body were now necessary to hold it in place. Her voice had lost the girlish lilt that made him eager to do all she asked so many years ago. Her face powder no longer remained where she put it and settled instead into the lowland crevasses around her eyes. The tools in her arsenal were worn from overuse, and she had no more weapons with which to wage war and recapture her husband's affections.

So Rebecca had dug deeper, searching for a flowing foundation of true love to tap into and quench her thirst. But to her astonishment, she discovered that there had never been an underground spring to draw from, now that the surface water had dried up. Her loneliness made her hungry, greedily craving to be near him. She wondered at his indifference and questioned whether he was going elsewhere to satisfy his appetite.

She tried to console herself that perhaps this was to be expected, that perhaps marriage was never meant to nourish the soul. She had not had a mother to show her the way, and she would never have dared share her insecurities with the women in the Ladies Sewing Circle, or in Columbia, where one had no friends, only strategic allies who banded together for the political advantage of their husbands. Rebecca was too embarrassed to mention her troubles to Hannah, and besides, she'd decided, Hannah had only Jesse to love her and so knew little of such things.

Zachary poured over his books. He longed for his former solitude, but he could find no tactful way to broach the subject. He didn't respond to Rebecca's attempts at conversation, but his silence did not offend her. He resisted her suggestions of late night walks and intimate suppers, but she bore his refusals with patience. When he finally had Juno move the rest of his clothes into one of the guest rooms, his wife said nothing. He lit his cigar, his third since the morning, and left it burning in the ashtray—hoping the smoke would drive her out. But Rebecca only coughed once or twice, dabbed her eyes with her handkerchief, and went back to her poetry.

When Dr. Harper came to call, Rebecca met him at the door. "Zachary says that you're to go straight back to his study, Charles. He sounded so serious—of course he always does nowadays. And Charles, when you've finished your business with him, please persuade him to put away his work and bring me out into the city. He'll listen to you."

Zachary was hunched over when they entered, methodically tallying a neat list of numbers. Dr. Harper watched him work, feeling very small at the other end of the miles of desk that separated them. He wanted to throw himself on top of the shiny mahogany, push off, and see if he could he slide across it in time to grab the tick-marked sheet that signified his financial ruin. The corners of his mouth twitched. "This is all very embarrassing for me . . ." he began.

"It's embarrassing for me, too," Zachary lied. "You're a member of my wife's family, and I've considered you a friend, but you're far behind on your loan payments and there's nothing else I can do for you."

"What are you talking about, darling?" Rebecca asked him. "Are you in some sort of financial trouble, Charles?"

"My investments . . . things haven't gone as well as I expected."

"I'm real sorry about that," Zachary lied again, trying his best to look sympathetic. "But all of South Carolina's prospering, so there's no excuse. It's because of your connection to my family that I've given you so long to pay back the five thousand dollars. And of course when it looked as if Augustus and Georgeanna were going to be married, I didn't want the Riley name connected with any sort of financial scandal. But now that it appears there will be no wedding . . . I've given you extensions, you've missed payments—so I'm going to have to take possession of the newspaper and the mill."

Dr. Harper's voice shook. "But the Harpers have owned a part of the *Charleston Examiner* for generations, and the mill's my only reliable source of income."

"What about your medical practice?"

"Father left some debts, and things have slowed recently. There are so many physicians in Charleston." Dr. Harper reddened. "But it's true, my income from my practice would be sufficient if I did not have so many . . . expenses."

"I see." Zachary smirked, looking at Dr. Harper's lavish jacket. His brother-in-law was a big-city dandy who had never done a hard day's work in his life. He leaned back in his chair. "You think too small, Charles. That's your problem. For a long while now, I've wanted to go into the cotton business, and your mill's gonna be a mighty fine start. You should've been thinking along those same lines yourself. There's a cotton man here in the Up Country, a William Gregg. The legislature's likely to grant him a charter to incorporate, and as soon as they do, he's going to sell me some of that stock. Think of it, a cotton factory right here in South Carolina. Just imagine what that will mean for the South."

"Zachary, please," Rebecca said. "Imagine what your actions will mean for my brother. I beg you to reconsider."

Dr. Harper struggled to remain calm. "You can certainly give me just a few more months, can't you? You have no desperate need for the money."

"True, but I'm financially secure only because I'm a practical man. I make my decisions based on cool reason, not emotion. You could've paid me my five thousand dollars three times over on the money you've wasted on trips to Europe, ridiculously extravagant art, and French servants." Zachary smiled meanly. "I have your sister to thank for all of *my* frivolous expenditures—perhaps fiscal irresponsibility is a family trait."

Rebecca hung her head, and her brother stiffened. "You would do well to remember that the name Harper was a well-respected name in Charleston long before the first tree on Atterley was chopped down."

"That may be true, but the Riley name is respected as well, and not just in this state, but throughout the South."

"But I've introduced you to people, Zachary—people with influence."

"And I appreciate that, as I've told you many times. The leniency I've shown you thus far reflects my gratitude. But the tide is turning, Charles, and you're a Unionist, just like your father was. Unless the North backs off its stand, South Carolina *will* secede. Governor Means has made it perfectly clear where he stands."

Dr. Harper was cornered, and he bared his teeth. "Don't test me, Zachary," he warned. "You'll find that in all political factions I still have many allies who will stand up for me, if only for my father's sake."

"Is that so? Well, I've received letters from every one of your partners at the *Examiner* supporting my decision." Zachary shoved several documents in front of him. "It used to be a money-maker, with a greater circulation than the *Mercury*, not just a political platform. Your associates won't risk their livelihoods just to honor your father's memory. A man who has no money has no true allies, Charles, you should know that."

Dr. Harper glanced down at the papers and recognized the signatures of lifelong friends. He stood up quickly. "I must say that I'm stunned by your treatment of me today. My sister had led me to believe that I would be receiving an apology for your son's disgraceful conduct towards my Georgeanna."

"Then I'm sorry to disappoint you."

Dr. Harper's face was hot. "You'll regret the words you've spoken to me today. You'll regret betraying all my kindnesses toward you and taking advantage of my . . . difficulties. No honorable man would sacrifice his loyalty for monetary gain."

"And that's the one thing you're right about, Charles. Loyalty is a valuable commodity, indeed. In fact, mine's worth about five thousand dollars."

CHAPTER 36

Grave News

By the time the final spring rains had fallen, word of Gus and Promise's relationship had reached every household in the circle. They were careless. Gus had begun staying with Promise through the night, and Promise was surprised to discover how easily she surrendered her judgment for the joy of waking up in his arms.

Soon the news reached the quarters. The field slaves thought no less of Gus for his part in the affair. He was a man and a master, and in their eyes, no different from the rest. He was merely following along the path that his father had paved for him.

Promise was a different case altogether. She had always been viewed as an outsider on the street, and her devotion to their master further diminished their estimation of her. Had Gus taken her by force, had she secretly despised him, they would have understood. But it was said that she loved him, and that they could not forgive.

Cora did not take the news well. Initially, she attempted with soft words and reason to persuade Promise to leave Gus's bed, but when this tack proved unsuccessful, she resorted to calling her a disgrace to her race and a white man's whore. Cora's words bruised Promise's heart, but her mother had accused her of compromising her virtue so often during her growing up that the charge had lost much of its sting now that it was based on truth.

It was only Promise's father who provided her with a measure of comfort. Abraham still received her at the smithy with gladness, so she continued to visit him often and tell him about her duties, her studies, her school—everything except the subjects that were principally upon both their minds.

Despite Gus's efforts to lure Promise to the ocean with visions of late-night strolls along secluded stretches of beach, she insisted on remaining at Atterley that summer. It hadn't taken Little Remmy long to build her a modest schoolhouse, and she didn't want to abandon her pupils just when they were beginning to make progress. At first, Promise's only students were the circle's children and her siblings who needed little persuasion to leave the watchful eyes of the Ma'Deahs to "go book learnin' wit Missy." The other inhabitants of the quarters were not so easily won over. It was a long while before the field slaves became convinced that Promise was not sent to them as a spy for their master.

Ignoring the stares and whispers, Promise came faithfully to the street each afternoon after her morning chores were done, carrying her schoolbooks and a brass bell in her satchel. A dozen or so of the circle's brood trailed behind her, dressed in their Sunday best with shining faces and bobbing pigtails, clutching prettily packed box lunches. As soon as Promise's brothers and sisters heard her jangling bell, they ran out to greet them, joining the procession.

Classes began promptly at two, and continued until the slaves returned home from the fields. Promise kept the windows open, letting the curious peek inside during the reading lessons and recitations. As the months passed, some of the slaves overcame their distrust for the sake of their children. They brought them to the front doors of the schoolhouse—scrubbed clean, with grease rubbed on their knees and elbows, and bearing cloth bundles leaking bacon fat. By harvest time, Promise's students numbered twenty-seven.

During the second week of October, as Promise was dismissing her class for the day, she was happy to see Muley waiting for her outside the schoolhouse. She had been worried about her brother. He was hungry again. His marriage had brought him only a fleeting contentment, and before long his restlessness had returned. He said nothing to her for a while, and paced around the room, nervous and uncertain.

"What is it, Muley? What's wrong? Is Rachel unwell? Is it the children?"

He paused, then strode toward her, gripping her shoulders. "I'm runnin', Missy," he said in a rush.

Promise's face crumpled. "What? When?"

"I'm only saying that I'm runnin'. I'm not saying exactly when, 'cause I don't want you slipping up and actin' funny when the time comes around. Just know that soon, real soon, I'll be gone. I'll be gone as far as I can get from here. "

"But why, Muley? Why would you do such a thing to Gus? He's your friend."

"He ain't my friend, and he ain't yours either—no matter what he's got you believin' so you'll give him what he wants."

Promise's eyes filled.

Muley pulled her to him and held her close. "I'm sorry, Missy. I didn't mean it. I'm just all riled up. I can't take it no more. Havin' my every move being tole to me." He grabbed her hands. "So me and Rachel's takin' the little ones, and we're runnin'."

"Why don't you just tell Gus how you've been feeling, Muley? You may not think he cares about you, but he does. He let you marry Rachel, didn't he? He'll give you more free time to see her if you ask him. I just know he will."

Muley laughed bitterly. "What world you been livin' in? You think Massa Gus is some god—going around doing good and grantin' favors? Rachel's no more mine now than she was before. If Massa Gus and Mr. Mason said we couldn't see each other no more, then that's the way it'd be." The beginnings of tears shone in his eyes. "I'm so tired, Missy. Tired of askin' for things a man's got a right to. I've been beggin' for white folks' favors all my life, and I'm done with it."

"But to run, Muley? Rachel and the children may be light enough to pass, but you're not. How do you think you'd even make it out of South Carolina—let alone all the way up North without anyone asking questions?"

"I've met some good white folks that'll help us get North, and Rachel's saved up enough money from her sewing to live on 'til I find work."

"What white folks? How do you know you can trust them?" Promise shook her head. "There must be another way, Muley. You'd be putting yourself, and Rachel and the children, in real danger."

"I can't tell you no more, but I've got it all planned out." Muley reached out and brushed away a tear. "Don't you start cryin', now. You'll get me goin', too. We'll make it, Missy. I promise. I'll have Rachel write you as soon as we get settled somewhere."

"Please, Muley. Let me tell Gus you're unhappy. He'll think of something. He'll make things better for you."

Muley's eyes widened into round circles. "No, Missy. I'm beggin' you. I put all our lives in your hands just by comin' here to tell you all this, but I just couldn't leave without sayin' goodbye—since I may never see you again. You've always meant the world to me—you know that. That's the only reason why I came. You and Daddy are the only ones who know. I ain't even told Mama—she's so crazy nowadays. Now swear to me. Swear to me you won't tell."

Promise gave him her word, but for the next several hours she tried to convince him to reconsider, to persuade him that his condition was not as bad as it seemed. But he would not be moved. By nightfall, she had run out of words—so she laid her head on his shoulder, wrapped her fingers around his, and pressed close to his body to remember the feel of him.

It didn't take long for gossip about Gus and Promise to spread beyond Atterley. Zachary first suspected that things were amiss when he was overlooked during Secession Party elections in July, especially since party leaders had assured him that the position of vice-president would be his for the taking. To add to his confusion, Zachary had the distinct feeling that he was the only one who was surprised by the snub. As the summer wore on, he observed that Allston and Middleton were distancing themselves from him despite his efforts to maintain their friendship, and he found himself left out of key political meetings. By the end of October, he could no longer endure the rebuffs of his fellow legislators, and he went to Charleston to see Majors and find out why his world was crumbling.

"It's not your imagination," Majors told him, once Zachary had gulped down his second glass of whiskey. "There have been some concerns about your loyalty—about your vulnerability to outside influences."

"My vulnerability to outside influences? What's that supposed to mean? One moment my connection to Georgia is touted as an asset, and now it's being used against me? My God, Majors, I—"

"It's not your brothers, Zachary, it's your son. Harper hasn't let up on him, or you for that matter, since the spring. He's been on a campaign to destroy you through Augustus, and so far it's been going pretty well."

Zachary sat very still, letting the news sink in. He had dismissed his brother-in-law as a political nobody, too weakened to hurt him, and he began to question whether he had made a grave miscalculation. "Is this about the newspaper and the mill? I had the full support of his business partners. I made sure of that. And what's my son got to do with all this? Just because Augustus wouldn't marry his brat of a daughter, they doubt my loyalty? Why would they take the word of a Unionist over mine anyway?"

"Charles is a Unionist, but he's from an old Charleston family nonetheless, and he and his wife keep hollering to anyone who'll listen about you and Augustus. Most people didn't pay attention at first—his claims were so outrageous. But since then other information has come to light that raises questions, serious questions, that indicate they've been telling the truth all along. I've known you for years, Zachary. I know you can be trusted, but others—they can only judge based on what they hear. These are dangerous times, and people don't want to take any chances. I would've come to you myself with all this, but since you've always known about everything that went on at Atterley, I thought you knew, and frankly it's not the sort of thing I'd relish telling any man. The details are rather . . . indelicate." Then Majors unburdened himself, telling his old friend all he had heard and personally witnessed concerning his son and Promise—about their love affair, the school, and Sir Henry.

After leaving Majors's office, Zachary went home and told Rebecca to have the household packed up and ready to travel as soon as possible. They were needed at Atterley.

CHAPTER 37

To Bear the Name Riley

"Good Lord, am I glad we's back!" Molly announced, throwing her arms open as she stepped into the kitchen. "Them Columbia niggas sure was an uppity lot. Always puttin' on airs 'cause of who they massa was. *My* massa's the representative of this and that place. *My* massa's the senator so and so. And them free coloreds Massa hired to help out!" Molly shook her head. "They was worse than the niggas. Couldn't none of 'em roast a turkey without dryin' it out, or make a halfway decent crumb cake. It was downright *disgraceful.*"

The travelers had returned, and the men, women, and children of the circle gathered in the kitchen to welcome them home. They straddled stools and dangled their legs over countertops. The little ones curled up in any available lap or crouched beneath chairs, peeking out between pairs of grownup legs.

Molly rubbed her hands together and began rummaging through the cabinets, shooing people out of her way. "I can't wait to fire up my stove. Get outta my way, you! That newfangled thang in Columbia ain't nothin' like my baby here. Lassie, Liza, you two get y'alls broad asses outta those chairs and find me my big iron skillet and my turnin' fork. You two ain't got no excuse to be that damn fat. I know it ain't 'cause you been eatin' good. Promise can cook alright, but she can't burn like me. It must be just plain laziness, and I'm gonna put an end to that right now. You girls get on up, I said! Jimmy, how'd you like me to cook you a better dinner than you've had in all them months in Columbia? Lord have mercy, where'd you gals hide my thangs? I can't find nothin'! Hannah, could you move these mangy children outta my way? Where my saucepans at? And my coffee mill?"

Gus paced the hallway outside his father's study. He knew that the time would come when he would be called to account for selling Sir Henry, and the cold manner of his father's greeting told him that at least some of the particulars were already known to him. He recalled his training at the Academy and prepared himself to stand his ground. He reminded himself that he was his own man now and went over the list of reasons why selling Sir Henry had made good business sense. He breathed in deeply before he went inside. "You wanted to see me, sir?"

"Majors has enlightened me about some recent developments that have concerned me greatly."

Gus braced himself. "Yes?"

"I explicitly forbade you to sell Henry, did I not?"

"Yes sir."

"And yet you chose to disobey one of the principal instructions I gave you concerning Atterley."

"I felt I had no choice. Henry had become ungovernable. The slaves are all very much relieved now that he's gone. He was unnecessarily violent and abusive toward—"

"Whether or not my slaves liked him makes no difference," Zachary interrupted. "You should know that by now. Augustus, I left you in charge because I trusted your sense, your judgment. Clearly, that was a mistake. Henry wasn't perfect, but he was a good boy, and now he's been sold away to God knows where. I promised him that he'd have a home on Atterley as long as he was faithful to me, and you broke that promise. You made a liar out of me."

"But Tucker and Amos have carried on very well without him, and Atterley's rice production has actually—"

Zachary pounded his desk. "I gave you an *order*, and that order should have been obeyed unless you consulted me first!"

"Yes sir," Gus said, his resolve weakened.

"Majors also told me all about your personal indiscretions. I'm sure you know what I'm talking about."

"I-I have no idea what you mean—"

"You know *exactly* what I mean. News of your illicit relationship with Promise has spread all the way to Columbia. Apparently, I was the last to know. So it appears you've turned me into both a liar *and* a fool. In a few months you've destroyed the respect that it's taken me years to obtain. I had a chance to be governor. An office none of my brothers has attained, that my father never even aspired to."

"I never intended—"

"Intentions are irrelevant, can't you see that?" Zachary gave his desk another pounding. "It's not only my future you've injured. Do you think any proper family is going to consent to your marrying their daughter now?"

"I-I'm sorry," Gus stammered, "I tried to . . . I was reckless . . . I want to make things right—to do what's best."

Zachary rubbed his temples. "All may yet be saved if we take a strong stand now. Lines are being drawn, Augustus—hard, unwavering, uncompromising lines. The South is going to secede. It's just a matter of time, and when it does, South Carolina will be leading the charge. That means that whoever leads South Carolina will lead an entirely new nation. I want to show you something. Sit down."

Gus sank into the nearest chair.

Zachary thrust some papers at him. "Do you see these? These are the monthly receipts from your Uncle Harper's mill, minus the expenses, here," he pointed.

Gus looked them over. "It seems to be very profitable," he said softly.

"It seems to be, because it is. I see the Academy has taught you a little something about facts and figures, but you can't learn everything in a classroom. This mill is mine now. I got it fair and legal—for you and my grandchildren. But you've

279

proven to me by the way you've run things here that you couldn't have done what it took to get this mill. You've still got some soft spots. You've got no *guts* when it comes to making tough decisions. You're my son, so you've got them somewhere deep down inside you, and I'm gonna help you find 'em. You should be proud to bear the name Riley—that name should come before anything else. That's why it's unwise to form any serious attachments outside this family, and by family I mean Rileys. So just like I took Charles's mill, you have to be ready to do what you have to for the good of this family."

Gus sat silently, and prayed that his father wouldn't ask him to give up Promise.

"Now Augustus, I understand that a man alone has needs—that it's difficult not to take advantage of . . . of diversions that present themselves, and I'm sure Promise has been very obliging. But discretion is crucial, and any emotional attachment is out of the question. Your actions have done irreparable damage to your authority, can't you see that?"

"I don't think—"

"Did you know that Muley's run off?"

Gus bolted in his chair. "What?"

"Muley has run away. You've neglected your duties, wasting away the hours with a slave girl, and didn't notice that her brother had run off right under your nose. It's clear you had no idea. It appears that I wasn't the only one who's been made a fool of. I'm sure Promise knew all about it, and still she didn't breathe a word of it to you."

Gus shook his head. "You're wrong. Promise had nothing to do with this. She never would've kept something like this from me. She couldn't—"

"She could, and she did. They probably planned it together. Promise's part was to keep you busy beneath her sheets while Muley made off with Mason's girl—who incidentally, he should have never been allowed to marry in the first place. Was that Promise's idea, too? Now do you see what can happen when you make decisions based on emotion? It appears that Promise knows whose side she's on, though."

Crimson flooded Gus's cheeks. He couldn't bear to meet his father's eyes, and he began to wonder if what he was saying about Promise was true.

"Do you remember when you were a child, and you wanted to name the piglets, and I wouldn't let you? You especially liked that little one with the black ears. You might've thought I was being mean, but imagine how much worse you would've felt when hog-killing time came around, and you saw that black-eared hog hanging upside down in the smokehouse. The Negroes—they're not part of us. They're not *family*, boy. It's important not to get too close, because you never know which ones you'll have to send to the smokehouse. The time will come when you'll have to choose between what's best for this family, and what feels best to you. For your sake, and the sake of my grandchildren one day, I hope you choose right. Promise, as fine a girl as you may think she is, still is what she is, and she can never be more."

Gus was in a dismal mood when he came to Promise's room that night. He didn't sit down, but propped himself up against the wall. "Muley's run off," he said quietly.

Promise watched his legs. They were trembling crazily like they used to when he was a child. "When?" she asked, avoiding his gaze.

"According to Father, two days ago. But because Muley rarely went near the fields, Tucker and Amos didn't notice. And Abraham didn't let on, of course. Who knows when I would've finally found out, except Mr. Mason told Father that Rachel and her children were missing, and he put it all together." Gus watched her closely. "You don't seem particularly surprised by the news, Promise."

Her mouth went dry. "I already knew, Gus. I'm sorry."

"Dammit, Promise!" he exploded. "Father said you knew, but I told him he was wrong! I told him you couldn't possibly have known! How could you keep something like that from me?"

"I didn't want to, but he's my brother," Promise cried, frightened by the violence she saw in his eyes. "What was I supposed to do, betray him by going back on my word and telling you? I tried to talk him out of it—to get him to go see you about his troubles, but he wouldn't listen. What was I supposed to do? What would you've done in my place?"

"I don't know, but you didn't do him any favors. If you had told me his plans, I might've been able to stop him without anyone getting hurt. I pray to God Muley gets away, because if he doesn't, I'm gonna have him whipped good."

Promise reached for him. "No, Gus, please!"

He backed away from her. "There's no use begging me, Promise—Father's here. And even if he wasn't, I've bent as much as I'm going to. I've relaxed a lot of rules around here, mainly for your sake, but letting my slaves run off without punishment—that's something I can't do. Actually, a better master would've whipped your father, and you, too, for not coming forward."

Gus leaned back against the wall and closed his eyes. When he opened them, they were glistening in the lamplight. "I've nearly destroyed Father. I've never seen him so . . . so unstable."

Promise flung herself on her bed and began sobbing into the pillow. Gus's heart softened as he watched her weep. He sat beside her and held her in his arms. "Don't cry, Promise. Don't cry now. It'll work itself out. It's been two days. Muley's probably long gone by now. But we've got to face reality and stop living in the fantasy world we've created for ourselves. We must be more guarded. Some things will have to change."

Promise turned to face him. "Yes, they will. I'm going to have a baby, Gus."

Joy lit up his face like a Fourth of July sparkler, and then, just as quickly, scattered into nothingness. He smiled sourly. "Father just finished telling me all about the legacy he wants to leave his grandchildren. Perhaps I should go back and tell him he has one on the way."

For the next several weeks, Zachary agonized over what was to be done with his wayward son. He routinely sought Gus out and repeated his earlier admonitions about responsibility and family honor, but Zachary knew that duty would soon return him to Columbia, so he was restless and worried, and doomed to remain so until Gus's character was permanently fixed.

One night after supper, he was feeling especially troubled. He tucked his paper beneath his arm, filled his tumbler with whiskey, and sat down in front of the fire. The hour was late, and the house was still. He poured over the political commentary, arguing audibly with the editorials. By the time he had reached the advertisements, he was getting sleepy and ready for his bed. He started abruptly as he noticed a posting placed by Georgetown's sheriff. He rattled the ice in his tumbler as he read it:

Slaves found: Mulatto slave, male, will not give name, 5'10", *brown hair, brown eyes. Traveling with mulatto slave, female,* *answers to the name Rachel, 5'4", black hair, green eyes, and two* *mulatto children called by the names Missy and Freely. Owner* *requested to come forward, prove property, pay expenses, and take* *them away.*

Zachary smiled. He plunged his finger into the remains of his drink, held the tip in his mouth, and thought for a moment. Then he called for Jimmy, and congratulated himself as he wrote out his message to John Mason. He had found his answer.

CHAPTER 38

The Sacrifice

Promise glanced up from her book. "Blue Boy, I see you trying to look over Faith's shoulder. Do your own work."

Faith's hands flew over her slate. "I told you he was cheatin', Miss Promise. I *told* you. Mama warned Boy he better not show out and get in trouble in front of Massa's l'il house niggas again, or he'd be in for it."

Blue Boy looked alarmed. "You gonna tell Mama on me, Missy? I just can't remember if 'cat' starts with a *c* or a *k*. Please don't tell. Mama'll whup me for sure, and her whuppins ain't no joke."

"Ain't is not a word, Blue Boy, and during school hours you're to call me Miss Promise like the others. I won't tell Mama this time, but if I see you trying to look over Faith's shoulder again, I'll whip you myself. Do I have to move you back to the front?"

"Noooo, Missy—I mean Miss Promise. I don't wanna sit with them babies no more. Tina keeps makin' eyes at me, and Richard still wets hisself."

"I do not," Richard said, looking down at his pants to make sure.

"You do, too. That's why your mama sews you them long shirts—to hide it when you have an accident."

"You're just jealous 'cause my mama's cookies are made with real sugar, not black nigga molasses, and I got brand new shoes."

"Am not," Blue Boy said, sneaking a peek at Richard's shining shoes.

"Are too," Richard said. "And I'm *not* a baby, either. I'm nearly as old as you, Boy."

"You got one more time to call me 'Boy' 'fore I make you pay for it," Blue Boy said. "I told you circle sissies that I'm *Blue* Boy to y'all. You slip up again, and I'll be waitin' for ya outside."

"Children, that's enough." Promise said. "I'm telling you boys for the last time—*no more fighting*. Whether you come from the circle or the street doesn't make one bit of difference once you walk through these doors."

"Yes it do, Miss Promise," Penny, a seven-year-old with smooth, black plats, said. "They already learned they's letters. And Richard and Perla knowed how to read 'fore they even come here."

"You're to say, 'their', not 'they's', Penny. And it's true that some of you have had advantages over the others, but Faith is the best speller, and Penny, your arithmetic has improved a great deal since you started working on it in earnest. The rest of you can do the same if you continue to apply yourselves, so I'll hear no more excuses. Blue Boy, *cuh-cuh* 'cat' begins with a *c*. Take out your reader and study it over so you won't forget next time."

"It's not so hard, Blue Boy," Tina assured him. "*Ah-ah* 'ant', *buh-buh* 'ball', and then *cuh-cuh* 'cat' begins with *c*. *K* doesn't come 'til later on when you get to 'kit'. I have a trick to remember the hard ones. I'll teach you later if you want."

"Naw. And I wish you'd quit turnin' 'round hasslin' me."

Tina, offended, turned up her pert little nose. "I was only trying to help, is all. Just shows you're only a low-count black nigger like the others—even if you *do* look like us."

"So what? I don't wanna be nothin' like you circle sissies. From now on you best leave me be. I don't need no l'il house nigga helpin' me with *nothin'*."

Promise reached for her switch. "Tina, Blue Boy, be quiet and mind your manners. If I hear one more uncivil word from anyone in this room, I'll take you out back." Her students bent dutifully over their slates, and she knelt beside each one in turn, whispering assistance and encouragement.

Cora burst through the door. Her eyes roamed over the room, casting a frigid shadow over the children as she searched for her daughter. They sprang from their crate chairs, turned over their box tables, and scrambled toward Promise's skirts, fleeing the dark gaze of Atterley's witch woman. Promise's brothers and sisters retreated to safety with the others. They knew better than to be too near their mother when her eyes turned black.

Blue Boy let his slate fly from his hands, and it landed on Promise's toe. "Ouch!" she cried. "Mama, what's the matter? You're scaring the children."

"They have Muley down at the dock," Cora's voice rumbled.

"What? Who has him?"

"Mr. Mason and the others. They've caught him, and they've got him down by the Waccamaw. They're gonna kill him." Cora's face was gripped by a terror that even her magic could not cast out.

"God help us!"

Cora muttered a rapid string of expletives.

"Mama, please! Remember the children."

"You wouldn't listen to me when I told you to stay away from Massa's filthy seed, would you? You had to see for yourself that he'd bring you nothing but trouble. And now you're having his bastard—"

"Mama!"

"But you weren't satisfied with that even," Cora said. "It wasn't enough for you that your child will wear your disgrace on its skin. Maybe now you'll listen—now that they've come for your brother because of you."

The children burrowed into Promise's dress. She wrapped her arms around as many of the whimpering bodies as she could hold and struggled to keep her voice level. "This is all some sort of mistake. I'll go see Gus, Mama. He'll fix everything. He'll fix things. Nothing's gonna happen to Muley."

"Go on then, and run to your massa!" Cora spat on the floor. "Just know that it's *you* who's killed your brother with your whoring!" With that, she stalked out of the schoolhouse and down the street in the direction of the river, murmuring incantations to summon her spirits.

Promise fought back her hysteria and moved as leisurely as she could bear toward the door. "Children, sit down now. Please sit down. Faith, you're in charge."

"Are you going to the river, Missy? Are you gonna go help Muley?" Blue Boy asked.

"Yes, but first I'm going to the main house to get Massa Gus. Faith, gather up my things and put them in my bag. I'll come and get it from you tomorrow. Make sure everyone goes straight to the Ma'Deahs until quitting time. Then take Chaunie, Lear, and Blue Boy home and start supper. Mama may not be back for awhile, you hear?"

"Yes, Missy."

"And Perla, you walk the others back to the circle." Perla rose up dutifully. "No, not now. First I want you all to finish your work."

Chaunie began to whimper. "What's a 'whoring,' Missy? Is Muley gonna be all right? Is he gonna die like Mama said?"

"Of course not. He's going to be just fine. You all listen to Faith, and do what she tells you. No going to the lake, and no going to the river, understand?" Promise shut the schoolhouse door behind her. She resisted the impulse to run until she was sure that the children could no longer see her from the windows. Then she began racing toward the main house.

Cora hurried in the direction of the distant column of black smoke, tracing its source to the riverbank. A crowd of Low Country gentlemen had gathered there around a roaring fire. They were in a jovial mood. After spending the early afternoon drinking at the Planters Club, the men had rowed to the shores of Atterley, tied their boats to the dock, and staggered onto the grounds to enjoy the principal event of the evening.

Cora rushed forward, prowling the fringes of the crowd in search of her son. When she spotted him, she screamed, jolting the men out of their revelry.

Muley looked dead. His hands were tied to a tree branch, and he was swinging back and forth beneath it. Every inch of his skin that wasn't covered in blood was bruised, or had turned a sick yellow from infection.

Mr. Mason came forward, removing his hat. "We got company, boys. You lost, ma'am?" he asked, mistaking Cora for a white woman. He blocked her view of Muley's body. "We got business here that's not fitting for a lady to see."

Cora scrambled past him and wrapped her arms around her son. "You've killed him! You've killed my baby!" She felt Muley's body stir in her arms. He opened his blackened lids with a whimper. His eyes were narrow slits of red; he recognized his mother's wavering form and spread his lips.

"Oh." Mason put his hat back on his head amidst the men's embarrassed titters. "He's not dead . . . yet. I'm sorry. I really am, but your son's a runaway, and he's gotta get what's coming to him—to set an example for the rest. You better get going. Get on now."

Mason's voice was harsh, but his heart was beginning to feel sorry. "Please. Go on. Tim, William, pull her back so she won't get hurt. The rest of you boys, stack some of that wood under this nigger's feet."

"Gus!" Promise flung open the back door to the main house and flew through the kitchen. "Gus!" she hollered, her chest heaving.

He trotted down the hallway. "Promise, what is it? What's wrong?"

"Gus, thank God I found you! They've got Muley! They've got him down by the river! You have to stop them or Mama says they'll kill him!" She grabbed his hand. "Hurry, Gus, please hurry! We'll take the horses!"

Gus didn't look at her, and he didn't move. "I can't help you, Promise," he said.

"What? What do you mean? Of course you can! There's still time if we hurry!"

He didn't answer.

In a flash the realization came. Gus already knew about Muley. He knew, and he approved of what was happening to her brother.

Zachary heard the commotion from his study. He strode toward his son and laid a heavy hand on his shoulder. "Muley has broken my rules—*our* rules, Promise, and he cannot escape his punishment now, I'm sorry. Augustus is in full agreement with me. Isn't that right, son?"

Gus nodded quickly. "I'm sorry, too, Promise, but there's nothing I can do."

Promise dropped his hand and stepped back. "What do you mean there's nothing you can do? Of course there is. You can ride out there with me and tell them to stop. You can tell them to stop before they murder Muley."

Both men were silent.

"Massa Gus, please," Promise said softly. *"Please.* He's my brother."

Gus's eyes were steady, but his hands shook. He hid them inside his trousers.

"All right then, I'll go myself!"

Gus's resolve shattered, and he lunged forward, laying hold of her. "No! You'll get hurt."

Promise struggled to pull away. "They're gonna hurt Muley! I have to go to him. Let me go!"

"Augustus, let her go, son. Let her go."

Gus released Promise with a sigh, and she ran out of the house toward the stables. She snatched the reigns of a filly from a startled Sonny, and rode her bareback down the lawn to the Waccamaw.

After Mason stoked the fire, he held his torch up, letting the flame feast on sky. Then he walked over to Muley and prepared to set him ablaze.

Cora wrenched herself loose from William's grip. She stood between her son and Mason and dropped to her knees. She was desperate, and oblivious to the chuckles of the men surrounding her, Cora pulled at her dress, letting it fall open. Her eyes were fixed only on Mason.

"Please, Mr. Mason," she begged. "Muley's a good boy. He never caused Massa a day of trouble in his whole life until now. If you spare him, I'll make it up to you. I've been taught how to please. You can do what you want with me—just cut my boy down."

Cora cupped her breasts as she wept and held them up as an offering. But the beauty that had so tormented her youth had at last deserted her. Mason didn't see before him an enticing seductress worthy of ravaging. He saw only a work-worn white nigger. Cora had nothing left to tempt him.

Tears squeezed out of Muley's eyes and rolled down his cheeks. He lowered his head and closed his eyes to shut out the sight of his mother humbling herself before his murderers, prepared to bargain her body for his life.

From her horse Promise watched as Mason lit the kindling. "I didn't tell, Muley! I didn't tell!" she screamed.

But Muley didn't hear her. By the time the fire had seeped through the woodpile and began licking his toes, melting the skin, he was already dead. The fire streamed upwards quickly, and the air was filled with the stench of burning flesh.

Promise dismounted and staggered across the ground toward her brother. When the flames reached the rope, Muley's body fell to the ground in a fiery mass. The bonfire sprang high into the air, making pretty reflections in the rippling water of the Waccamaw, and Promise watched the crimson firelight play on her hands while the remains of her brother burned.

CHAPTER 39

Hannah's Hands

"What in the world is going on in this house? Everyone is so somber," Rebecca asked Zachary from across the supper table. With her own reservoir of joy at such perilously low levels, she was accustomed to relying on the felicity of others to boost her spirits. "Why has Augustus not come down? Where is he?"

Zachary sawed into his overdone, dried-out meat. "Please don't look to me to explain the reasoning behind that boy's behavior," he said. "He continues to be a complete mystery to me. At present, I believe he is dutifully stationed outside of Promise's room."

"What in the world would he be doing there? Is she sick? You know, now that I think of it, the poor girl has looked dreadful these last few weeks—but I only supposed that she's been affected by the general gloom that seems to be going around. Maybe that's where Hannah has disappeared to." Rebecca fluffed her rice and nibbled on a few grains thoughtfully. "These are not cooked through," she observed, depositing the remains of the crunchy grains into her napkin.

In all of her years as mistress of Atterley, Rebecca had never been forced to send back any of Molly's meals, but each day for the last two weeks one of her dishes was found wanting. And tonight, the entire supper was inedible. It was most inconvenient, Rebecca thought, depriving her of the pleasure of consoling her friends over moist slices of Molly's famous lemon poundcake while they bemoaned the inadequacy of their own cooks. "Button, go and bring Molly from the kitchen," she ordered. "I want to speak with her."

Molly came into the dining room with her hand on her hip and her eyes ablaze. "You wanted somethin', Missus?" she demanded.

Rebecca looked down at the pile of half-cooked rice, then up at the fierce expression on Molly's face, and decided that the rice was not so badly prepared after all. "Would you fix some tea please, and have Button bring it to Promise's room?" she ventured timidly. "She's not feeling well." Then in a show of good faith, she scooped up a forkful of rice, and wincing, guided it toward her mouth.

"Fine, but that ain't gonna help her forget about how they *murdered* Muley." Molly grunted and glared at her master. "Ain't no *tea's* gonna fix what she got." Without waiting to be dismissed, she barged out of the room.

Rebecca forgot her manners and let her mouth hang open, allowing several grains to fall back onto her plate. "Is that true, darling?"

Zachary gave up trying to choke down a forkful of peas strewn with bits of flaming red pepper. "Yes, it's true. But Muley wasn't innocent. He'd run away and enticed Mason's maid and her children to run with him—putting them all in grave danger. So Mason and I decided that for the greater good, Muley had to be sacrificed."

"Muley's dead? Why did no one tell me? No wonder that child has been staying in her room. You know very well how Promise felt about her brother. He needed to be punished, surely, but to be *killed?*" Rebecca's tears fell, dampening the balled-up linen in her lap. "That's why the servants are in such bad spirits. And how did Mr. Mason know for certain that the fault was Muley's? Couldn't it have been Rachel who convinced *him* to run? You have always had the highest praise for Abraham. How in the world did Mr. Mason persuade you to forsake his son?"

"There was no need for Mason to persuade me. The plan was mine."

"Then your plan was *barbaric*. I wish you had consulted me before deciding to do such a thing." Her declaration surprised them both. Never in their many years of marriage had she opposed him on any serious matter or challenged the merit of his character.

Zachary set his silverware down with a clatter. "You've never expressed an interest in my business before—especially when it involved performing duties unpalatable to your refined sensibilities. And you should know that the deed was done for another purpose, a more personal one—to irrevocably separate our son from your precious Promise, all to no avail it seems. At this very moment he is most likely begging her for forgiveness."

"As he should. I will go to Promise myself tonight and apologize to her on your behalf, if you will not. And why should you wish to separate them? She's been a great source of comfort for Augustus. He's told me so himself. Now that she's in need, it's right that he should return her past kindnesses to him."

Zachary looked at her, disgusted. "Lord, how you baffle me. I can't judge whether you've purposely chosen to ignore what's been going on in this house, or if you're truly as dull as your discernment suggests. Promise has been very kind to him, indeed. She and our son have been sharing a bed now for God knows how long, and Juno tells me that your little angel is expecting his child."

Rebecca gawked at him. "That cannot be. That is not possible. Not our Augustus."

"Not only is it possible, my dear, it has happened," Zachary retorted. "What else can you expect after you've raised Augustus side by side with her—throwing them together at every opportunity? Have you forgotten all of your pretty admonishments to him about God's love for the Negro, without reminding him of the importance of racial distinctions? For my part, I must bear some of the guilt for not taking a firm enough stand with him until it was too late to turn him around. But I am determined that you will own yours as well, since in my opinion, you're chiefly responsible for this fiasco."

Rebecca didn't finish her supper that night. She swayed up to her room in a torpid daze, but her thoughts came to her in a flood. Promise—the baby she had adored, the child she had indulged, the young woman she had praised—had betrayed her trust, seducing and defiling her son, her only child, luring him into sin. And that sin was destroying him, stealing his strength like Delilah, making him unfit for leadership.

She chastised herself harshly for her ignorance. What a fool she had been not to have listened to her husband's warnings. Now he was angry with her, and rightly so. He had tried to guard her against the wiles of the devil, but still she had been steadfast in her defense of her favorite. And it had cost her her relationship with her brother, her friendship with Eleanor, and her son's happiness with dear, dear Georgeanna. The thought of all her faith had cost her made Rebecca's stomach fill with bile.

All of her earlier sympathy over Promise's loss evaporated into insignificance when weighed against the intensity of her own misery. It had all happened right under her nose. Rebecca wondered how many of the house servants had known about the affair—after she had devoted her life to improving the quality of theirs—and she marveled at their ingratitude. She had bucked convention, teaching any who wanted to learn how to read and write, and although state statute dictated that slaves wear simple attire, there was not a better-dressed household in all of the Low Country.

She had not adopted the narrow-minded views of others, but had always had a warm heart for the sad condition of the Negro. She had read the *National Era* faithfully and bawled like a baby over the plight of sweet, abused Uncle Tom in each weekly edition of Stowe's *Uncle Tom's Cabin—Life Among the Lowly*. And in other ways she had been a generous champion of the Negro's cause—secretly sending money to abolitionist organizations in the North.

But all of Rebecca's large-hearted liberalism halted abruptly at her own front door, and although she couldn't determine whether her feelings derived chiefly from hurt or anger, she was quite certain that she had been extremely ill-used.

Gus was living in misery of a different sort. "Promise, are you all right?" he asked, as he listened to her weep. "You have to talk to me sometime, you know. Let me in. I can make you feel better . . . Hannah, could you please tell Promise to be reasonable and talk to me?"

There was no answer. He clasped his hands behind his back and strode over the scuffed-up trail he'd made in the rug outside her bedroom. Promise was testing his patience. He sympathized with her grief over Muley's death, but what was he supposed to do? She had no right to blame him. The whole mess could've been prevented if she had only trusted him, if she had only told him what her brother was planning. She knew what was at stake. How she could hold him accountable for Muley's mistakes was beyond him. She had put him in a difficult position with his father, and he was helpless to come to Muley's aid. The situation required strict obedience.

But Promise had a hold on him—a hold he couldn't shake. He had unwittingly given all of himself over to her and had nothing left to hold onto and save himself. So he felt compelled to go to her again and again, petitioning her for absolution, with full knowledge that she would likely exercise her power to reject him at will.

Promise was doing her best to make it hard on him. She ignored his addresses, even in front of the other servants, and she would not return his gaze when he spoke to her. She seemed intent on further destroying his credibility. Still, he could not think of a way to make her mind that didn't involve threats or violence, and he couldn't bring himself to subject her to either. He had hoped that Hannah would soften Promise's heart toward him, but it soon became clear that she, too, was disappointed in him, and that she would not align with him to assist his redemption.

Promise's bedroom door opened and Hannah came out. Her eyes were red-rimmed. Gus caught just a glimpse of Promise before she shut the door firmly behind her. "Just let her be, Massa Gus," she said, before walking away.

When Hannah went to Rebecca's room, she found her awake and waiting for her—curled up in bed with the covers tucked beneath her chin. "Did you know that there is some type of sordid relationship going on between Promise and my son?" she demanded.

"I know there're some feelings between them," Hannah said quietly.

"I see." Rebecca's lips were tight. "And you saw no need to inform me?"

"Figured it wasn't my business to."

"Not your business?" Rebecca's eyes opened wide. "Not your business to tell me that my son was jeopardizing his future, compromising his respectability? Is Augustus foolish enough to believe himself to be in love?"

"I haven't talked to him about it."

"But you've spoken to Promise. I know that's where you've been. What has *she* to say? Did you know she is going to have a baby?"

Hannah chose her words carefully. "Promise hasn't told me all the particulars."

"You were in her room for hours!" Rebecca cried. "Why are you being so evasive? Certainly you don't approve of their . . . their *obscene* behavior?"

"It's not my place to approve or disapprove."

"Well, it certainly is *mine*. I was hoping that I could depend upon you to talk to Augustus, to reason with him, but since you don't seem to comprehend the gravity of the situation, I'll take care of things myself. I want Promise out of this house, and I'm going to sell her. Augustus doesn't have the authority to prevent me, and I'm sure Zachary will not oppose me."

Hannah's hands trembled. "That ain't right, Miss Rebecca. It just ain't right. Promise is a good girl, and besides, she's with child."

Rebecca's brows arched. "Well now. I see you're more informed than you pretend. Promise is *not* a good girl. She is a wolf in sheep's clothing, and I *will not*, and *cannot* stomach deception."

"Deception ain't nothin' new around here, can't you see that? Even if you can't, I won't let your blindness destroy that child. You and your lady friends are all the same, deceiving yourselves into believing you're so high up that you're free from the troubles of this world, free to whisper about other folks' failings."

"I don't know what you mean." Rebecca stirred beneath the sheets. "That's an unfair characterization, I think. I'm not in the habit of reveling in the misfortunes of others."

"Lie to yourself if you want to, but not to me. I raised you from a baby, and I've seen all your faces. I've heard y'all, time and again, so quick to gossip about the poor little half-white children runnin' around under other folks' roofs, and can't seem to see the ones beneath your own. But be sure those so-called friends of yours got plenty to say when *you* ain't around. Where do you think Jimmy got those blue eyes and white skin from? His mama and daddy ain't nearly that fair. That never seemed just a little bit odd to you? It would've, if you only opened your eyes to see. And Jenny don't look nothin' like Tobias. But she does look like someone else livin' in this house."

"Surely you don't mean Zachary," Rebecca said. Doubt crept into her mind, but she wished it away. "He would never do such a thing. You've gone mad, that's all. You've lost your senses. You're just trying to turn things around to save Promise— after she's destroyed this family's honor."

"I won't let you blame Promise for that. This family's honor's *been* gone—years and years and years ago. You ever wondered about Molly and that red hair of hers? 'Course you haven't. Massa's got his own sister cookin' his meals, and please believe he knows whose blood she's got in her. And Molly knows

299

it, too, but she keeps her mouth shut up about it just like everyone else. She knows what would happen to her if she claimed she was family.

"And Tobias ain't no fool, either. He knows them two children ain't his, but still he opens the door for Massa and takes his coat, and always with a smile. But I've seen enough lies and pretendin' to last a lifetime, and I'm not gonna play my part in it no more. Massa ain't mad 'cause Massa Gus laid down with one of his slaves—not even 'cause she's havin' a baby for him. He's mad because he's fool enough to love her."

"You shut your mouth," Rebecca said. "I'm not listening to any more of your cruel lies. I want you to leave my room this *instant*, do you hear me?" Her eyes were muddled and savage. "I *will* sell Promise, and there's nothing you can do to stop me."

"I ain't leavin'—not 'til I've said my piece. It ain't just Juno who Massa's been with. What do you think's been makin' you sick, Miss Rebecca? Why do you think you couldn't have but one child? Your husband's the worst kind of sinner, and he's brought his judgment right on home to you. You've been aching and bleeding all these years 'cause of him."

Hannah's voice turned dangerously quiet, and it rippled through the air like a rattler's tail. "And I *can* stop you from sellin' Promise. Don't you make me, 'cause I will." Hannah reached for a fluffed-up pillow and hugged it to her chest until her knuckles ached. "Massa's made you sick enough to die, Miss Rebecca, but the way I see it, dying's better'n livin' sometimes."

It had been Hannah's hands that had held Rebecca close when she was a plump toddler and stroked her wispy baby curls when they were damp from tears and tantrum. They comforted her when her favorite china doll, the one with the raven hair and the dress trimmed in handmade lace, had been broken into countless pieces by the careless horseplay of her older brothers. Hannah's hands had carefully poured the pretend tea at her tea parties, and without even a hint of amusement had served shortbread cookies to a table encircled only with dolls. Before she went to bed in the dank servants' quarters, Hannah's hands had first tucked Rebecca comfortably beneath thick quilts and sang sweet hymns to ensure that the demons of the night stayed far away. As Rebecca grew older, Hannah's hands curled her hair into intricate styles for her society parties, and mended all of the imaginary defects in her elaborate gowns.

But now Hannah was desperate and her hands readied themselves to do the unthinkable—to murder the woman she had spent a lifetime loving. The pillow shook in her clinched fingers as she hovered over Rebecca's bed. "You moan and groan 'bout how you only got one child, but me and Jesse's got none, and we ain't ever gonna have none, either. Your daddy saw to that. As soon as I started bleeding he fixed me—'cause he didn't want me havin' a child of my own to keep me from raising you, and 'cause he didn't want any blond-haired, blue-eyed, nigger grandchildren runnin' around in case any of those wild brothers of yours decided to take liberties.

"You, Massa Gus, and Promise are the closest I got to children, and I won't let you harm her. I want you to swear to me right this minute that you won't sell away that poor girl. I want you to swear to me that you'll have mercy on her, and I'll have mercy on you."

Rebecca began sobbing violently as she agreed to Hannah's terms. Then she stretched out her arms, seeking comfort like a child awakening from a bad dream. Hannah let the pillow drop and went to console her, just as she had always done. She held Rebecca close, letting her cry until the sheets were soaked and the morning's light began to dawn.

301

CHAPTER 40

Au revoir

Promise couldn't sleep. Her body begged for rest but her mind rebelled, and she couldn't keep the events of the dark day of Muley's death from invading her thoughts—fanning the last flames down low while smoke from his smoldering remains filled her lungs; gathering up the charred pieces of him burnt to a smooth, shining black; burying him in a shallow grave before he crumbled apart in her hands.

Her mother sat in the ashes after the planters had left, leaving her to tend to her brother alone. Gus, too, had deserted her. All of her steadfast faith in him had been devoured in the fire that had consumed Muley's body. He had sworn to her that he would be her sanctum, her shield from the hazards of being a Negro, but he had failed her without apology.

The rumblings in Promise's belly cautioned her that she was now responsible for another life that was entirely dependent on her for protection, and she wondered if Gus's professed devotion to her would extend to their baby—for even his childhood affection for Muley had not been enough to spare his life. Would he just as easily sacrifice his child to the dictates of prudence and familial responsibility?

And what if he grew resentful of the high price of reckless love, until one morning he awoke to the discovery that he no longer wanted her and decided to find a more convenient, suitable mate? What would become of her and her child if he married another? Promise had heard too many tales of slave women sent away from their homes clutching swollen stomachs, or too-white babies. She knew that any lasting contentment, any permanent peace, could be found only in freedom—without the man whom her heart now both adored and despised.

It had been an hour since she had last heard Gus's knocking. She went to the door and cracked it open. He was asleep, slumped in the chair across the hall, with his head propped clumsily against the wall. Promise stood quietly and watched him breathe, letting her heart yearn while he slept. He didn't look well. He had lost weight, and two days' worth of stubble covered his face.

That part of her that loved him still wanted to cast aside all reason and run to him, kiss him awake, and tell him all of the lies that he wanted to hear. To tell him that she could forget all that had happened, and that things could continue on as before. She was thankful that the uncompromising coldness returned, overpowering her emotions, before he shifted restlessly in his seat and opened his eyes.

"Promise." Gus rose, stretching the sleep out of his limbs. "Good. I'm so glad you've finally come out. Now we can talk. We can get this whole mess straightened out—"

"Massa Gus, I want you to set me free."

His face flinched. "You don't know what you're saying. You're still upset. Perhaps you should get some rest. It's late. We'll talk about this in the morning."

"I don't want to talk about it. I want you to set me free."

He groaned. "Why must you be so difficult? Even if I wanted to set you free, which I don't, I couldn't—you know that. Not without the state's approval. And with so many in Columbia already watching this family's every move, I can't risk another scandal."

"Then sell me to Mr. Majors. He can take me up North and set me free. I'm sure your father would agree that my leaving Atterley would be the best thing for everyone."

"I see you've given this a great deal of thought," Gus grumbled, "but the answer is still no. And you're not to speak of this again. It's a ridiculous notion. You wouldn't be able to come back. Have you considered that? Who put such a wild plan in your head? Did Hannah suggest it?"

"No, she did not. And it's not ridiculous. I'm determined, Massa Gus. You can't make me want you, and you can't make me love you—unless you intend to force yourself on me."

"Of course not. Surely you know I'm not capable of that."

"Truthfully, I no longer know what you're capable of."

"So that is what you think of me!" he exclaimed, surprise in his voice. "I've told you again and again how sorry I am about Muley, but still you're not satisfied. I tell you I love you, and it doesn't make you content. You're determined to be stubborn, to test me. Well, you can just go right back in your room, Promise. You can continue to keep your distance, to shut me out, but let me make myself clear—*I will not let you go.* How could you think I would agree to send you off to God knows where to fend for yourself? You've never been more than one hundred miles from home. What makes you think you could survive one week up North, surrounded by people and places you've never seen before? How would you support yourself and our child? You have a good life here, so be reasonable. The whole idea is absurd."

Gus left her then and went to bed. After the first fitful hours of wrestling with his bedcovers, his eyes finally closed. He slept through breakfast and dinner, and when he stumbled downstairs the next evening in search of an early supper, the house was quiet. There was no one in the kitchen except for Jimmy, surrounded by platters of Molly's leftovers.

"Hey there, Massa Gus," he murmured, biting into a piece of cold chicken. "Have a seat." He pushed a chair toward him with his boot.

"Thanks." Gus sat down and rested his head in his hands.

"You look rough." Jimmy shoved the heaping plates of chicken, red beans and rice, and collards across the table. "It ain't Molly's best, but you look like you'd eat pretty much anything right about now."

"Yeah, you too," Gus replied, noticing the dark rings beneath Jimmy's eyes. "Seems like you need a full night's rest even more than I did," he said, helping himself. "I'm glad you're not mad at me. Everyone else around here seems to blame me for what happened to Muley. They haven't said so directly, but they haven't tried to hide their anger toward me, either." Gus looked dejected. "But Father's had you out traveling for a while. You may not know what's been going on around here."

"I know. Honestly Massa Gus, there don't seem to be a man or woman in South Carolina who's not talking about them killin' Muley, and about you and Promise . . ." Jimmy looked embarrassed. "When they ask me about it I keep my mouth shut, though." He pulled a whiskey flask from his pocket and took a swig. "I've had plenty of practice keeping secrets."

"Did you know she was pregnant?"

"Yeah?"

"The Ma'Deahs say it's a boy."

"So you're gonna have a son, huh? What're you gonna do about it? Maybe you should build her a house in the circle. Things'll get mighty tense around here when she comes due."

"Promise wants me to set her free."

"That so?" Jimmy said, pouring red pepper vinegar over his collards.

"Yeah, that's so."

"Are you gonna?"

"Of course not. She's angry with me now, and riled up about Muley. It'll pass, and then things will get back to normal."

"I'm not so sure of that, Massa Gus. You can't hold her by keeping her here, you know."

"Now you sound just like her. I thought you'd see my side of it. You've seen a bit of the world. You know how hard it is for the Negro in this country—whether he's in the North or South, it doesn't make much difference."

"And you sound just like Massa. He must be real proud about how you've turned out. I suppose he finally got the son

306

he wanted, huh?" Jimmy looked at him sadly, with a peculiar expression on his face. "You know, when I heard about Muley, about how he died, I didn't believe it at first. No matter how things have changed, I've always thought of you as the Gus I knew from a baby—the Gus who used to follow me around all day nipping at my heels. But I'm not gonna ask you how you could stand by and let Massa do that to Promise's brother, 'cause I know how. God never meant for one man to own another, 'cause it turns 'em both into animals."

"Is that what you're saying I am, Jimmy? An animal? I'm an animal because I respected my father's wishes? I'm an animal because I want to protect the woman I love, and protect our baby?"

"I'm sayin' that only animals turn on their own children, and that's what you'll end up doing if Promise's baby grows up in this house. Sure, you'll begin with good intentions. It'll be simple when he's still young, all shiny and new and easy to hide away. But he's gonna grow up someday, and how will you care for him then? You can't give him your name. You can't leave him any property. You'll tell Promise that you'll love him and treat him special, but you can't truly love what you're ashamed of. And you *will* be ashamed of him, Massa Gus, especially since Promise ain't got a man who'll claim him in your stead.

"Soon you'll start to take advantage of your rights over him and use him as you see fit—just like you use the rest. But when he looks at you, you'll see yourself in his eyes, and that'll make you feel guilty enough to give him a taste of freedom. And that'll be the cruelest thing of all—to let him have just a little of what would've been his if fate hadn't called him a Negro. I know what that's like. Everyday when I'm out ridin' in that wagon, I dream of places I ain't ever seen. I dream of going as far from here as those wagon wheels can carry me, and I wonder what would happen if I just kept going . . . if I just kept right on going. But still I always come back—back to this house, and back to Massa. If you really love Promise and that child she's carryin', then you won't let your son grow up being part free and part slave. You'll turn 'em loose and give him a chance to be whole."

A week later, Gus stood behind Promise, watching her as she washed the dishes. The sight of her body, graceful and light, swaying gently as she stared at some distant point outside the window, always made him impatient to touch her. Only a short time ago, he would have crept up behind her and wrapped his arms around her waist. She would suppress her smiles and pretend to be mad at the interruption. Then he would spin her around, kiss her softly, and try to cajole her away from her work. She would protest, but reach for him all the same, letting her wrists dangle off his shoulders, wetting his hair with her hands. But tonight was different. His kisses and caresses were not welcome.

Promise felt his presence and turned.

Gus cleared his throat, hoping his voice did not betray his emotion. "I've sold you to Majors for a dollar, Promise. You can leave Atterley whenever you choose."

"Thank you," she said. Her expression was subdued, but her insides were leaping.

"I've told him to give you some money so you can get established—"

"No."

"You'll take it, or you'll stay here," he said. Then he sighed. "I don't want to fight, and I don't want you to go." He came toward her, extending his hand.

"I'll be leaving before the month's out, as soon as I can get my things together," she said. Then she turned away and went back to her dishes.

His arm dropped to his side. "I hope you'll take that time to think things over carefully. When you do, I'm sure you'll reconsider."

Two months passed as Promise kept putting off the day of her departure. There were mountains of clothes to sort through. She kept only those that were practical—the rest she gave away to the house servants and her younger sisters, along with her handkerchiefs, perfumes, and accessories—which for most of them helped lessen their grief over her leaving.

There were never-ending goodbyes. Promise shed countless tears over her students and fretted over their futures until Jenny and Button pledged to continue their lessons. Molly put aside her resentment for Promise's sake, and marked her last week at Atterley by cooking up a storm to ensure that her gift for creating majesty from food would never be forgotten. Although Rebecca hadn't sold her, she made it painfully clear to Promise during those final months that she no longer loved her. Cora forsook her as well, and kept her distance.

Fortunately, Hannah came to her at night when the loneliness was most acute and whispered a lifetime of wisdom in her ear, and Abraham gave Promise his bracelet—with a new clasp made of melted bits of brass.

When Promise's final morning at Atterley arrived at last, its slaves gathered on the front steps of the main house to see her off while Jimmy and Winston loaded the carriage with trunks. The well wishers fell silent as Gus strode past them. "I want to speak with Promise alone," he said.

He was relieved when she allowed him to take her hands, but then found himself unable to speak. He wanted to convince her why she should stay. He wanted to tell her that he would hold her up proudly as his own, that he would honor her and their child before God and man, that they would be a family. He wanted to plead with her that if she did go, that she remember him to their son. But in the end, a whispered, "goodbye, my Promise," was all he had the strength for. Then he looked into her eyes to see if he saw any love left in them.

With the pathway to freedom opened wide before her, Promise permitted herself a moment to feel. She smiled up at him, and he released her fingers so the tears wouldn't come. "Goodbye, Gus," she said.

"It's time, Augustus," Zachary called from the piazza.

Promise took Majors's arm and climbed inside. The carriage lurched forward. It rolled slowly down the oak-lined lane and out of Atterley's gates. Promise looked back as it turned the corner and rubbed her belly to ease the trembling that made her want to call out to Winston to turn back. She was comforted that her son never need know about her years as a slave and have to battle his soul to forgive. She peered outside the window and strained to see the last slivers of Atterley's main house flickering through the trees.

She thought she saw Gus standing watch on the front steps, and she imprinted his stance and the shape of his shoulders in her mind. Then she closed her eyes to remember the laugh lines in his face and the passion in his eyes, shining down strong in the moonlight.

She hoped that in time her memories of him would bring her a measure of joy, and she decided that when that day came, she would tell her child the whole story of Atterley, the bitter and the sweet, and leave nothing out—so that he would know what sort of man his father was.

Epilogue

Hannah had hoped that Rebecca would find the strength to confront Zachary about all she had learned and hold him accountable for his lies and infidelities, but she stayed by his side. Even if South Carolina's legislators hadn't thought it best to prohibit divorce, Rebecca still would not have deserted her husband. Her life's foundation had crumbled, and in the end she had nothing left to cling to except the comforts of convention. Without explanation, she banished Juno from her bedroom, but otherwise, her life proceeded according to habit. Rebecca was not so charitable with Promise, however. She never forgave her, and would not allow her name to be spoken in her presence.

Zachary was correct when he warned Gus that they were living in dangerous times, that his peers would not tolerate any radical notions that threatened to disrupt the economic and social order. In the years following Promise's departure from Atterley, Zachary struggled in vain to silence the doubts of his business and political allies. But despite his grandstanding in the legislature, scathing political speeches, and secessionist writings, he was never able to overcome the dishonor that Gus had brought to the family.

During that time of uncertainty when the leaders of the new South were beginning to emerge, Zachary found that he was not included among them, as he had always hoped. On December 11, 1860, when the South Carolina legislature elected the state's next governor, Zachary did not get enough votes to receive even an honorable mention in the *Winyah Observer*. Instead, Francis W. Pickens, devoted follower and cousin of John C. Calhoun, was chosen. And although he was one of the signers of the Secession Ordinance, repealing South Carolina's ratification of the Constitution and proclaiming the state an independent commonwealth, Zachary was not selected to be a member of the committee that drafted it.

Gus did his best to make amends to his father. Although he continued to resist his parents' attempts to find him a wife, he proved himself to be a capable manager of Atterley's affairs once he no longer had any emotional sentiments to hinder his decision-making. He wrote to Promise often during the eight tumultuous years before the Civil War, but did not receive a response from her until the first shots were fired at Fort Sumter. Whatever news he learned of her before then was from her letters to Jimmy.

He was relieved to read of her position as a maid for a respectable Pennsylvania family. He rejoiced over the birth of their son, whom Promise named Joshua. Gus followed his boy's development closely, his first teetering steps, his fondness for fishing, and aversion to arithmetic. And his blessings went with them when after seven years of service, Promise left her employer's home to open a small school with her savings.

In May 1861, Gus joined the Tenth Regiment of South Carolina Volunteers, where he was elected second lieutenant of his company. By the fall of that same year, Zachary and Rebecca, along with the other rice planters, fled to the safety of the Up Country, leaving their field slaves behind to manage Atterley. They didn't return until the South's surrender in the spring of 1865.

By that time, South Carolina's railroads had been destroyed, Zachary's mill was burned to the ground, and the *Charleston Examiner* was bankrupt. There was no more Planters Club or Hot and Hot Fish Club. Confederate currency was worthless. Like their neighbors, the Rileys found themselves destitute, with no access to capital or credit. They came home to find Atterley in ruins. When they passed through the empty space where the plantation's gates had been, there was no receiving line to greet them. Union troops had blasted all of the ground's fine oaks, and Jesse's flower gardens were leveled. Slaves and starving soldiers had devoured most of the livestock.

Zachary was forced to swear allegiance to the U.S. government before legal title to his land was restored, but after years of self-governing, the newly-freed slaves had stopped taking orders. The powerful Freedman's Bureau protected their interests, and Zachary was obligated to contract with them to work his land in exchange for a share of his profits from the rice crop. The strain of poverty was too much for Rebecca's already fragile health. During the summer of 1865, she passed away, and Dr. Needham dutifully recorded the cause of death as swamp fever.

The day after his mother's funeral, Gus announced that he and Jimmy were leaving Atterley with no intention of returning. As the years passed, Zachary waited anxiously for Gus to come home, but his prayers remained unanswered. He didn't see or hear from his son again before his death in the fall of 1869. So he left his beloved Atterley to his family in Georgia. The following is a portion of the communication Zachary sent to his brother, Washington, proclaiming his intentions:

I no longer hold out hope that Augustus will come home to be at my side, so I am giving you Atterley. It is not the prize it once was, but it is yours to divide among my remaining nephews as you see fit. I am not afraid of death; in fact, I am eager for it. It has all been horribly turned around. Everything is for the nigger, and the white man has been pushed aside. He has been freed, not for his benefit, I am sure, but to punish the South, and if that was their aim, they have succeeded.

The niggers have abandoned all useful employment. They are lazy and idle and will not work. They live in luxury, stealing and roasting my remaining livestock whenever I am too weak to get out of bed. The extent of sexual immorality I have witnessed is shocking. They will not marry with no one to make them, and they are continually drunk in the evenings. They are disrespectful and full of bitterness. They will not even remove their hats or pull their hands from their pockets when addressing me. They are resentful that even those in the North consider them inferior to whites.

I fear for the sanctity of our Southern ladies with none of us able to protect them from violence. The Bureau always takes the niggers' side of things and refuses to supervise them. But this madness cannot continue forever, and when the North tires of looking after our niggers, we will be forced to band together and take matters into our own hands to restore order.

The house is empty. All of the house servants have abandoned me and have boarded Union boats sailing north. Only Juno remains to tend to me. Often I think of Henry and wish he were here to help me remember better times. He was such a good nigger. He would not have left me for anything . . .

Hannah, like Gus, abandoned Atterley and her former master after Rebecca's death, but she left behind a gift for future generations. Always the consummate storyteller, Hannah hoped that long after Atterley's principal characters had faded from South Carolina's memory, they would be resurrected and remembered. So beneath the floor of the plantation's main house she concealed her mistress's diaries, a collection of Gus and Promise's letters that were in her possession, and Gus's farewell letter, which read:

My Dearest Hannah,

There is nothing for me at Atterley. With Mother gone, the servants scattered, and you and Jesse leaving for Georgia to find his people, I see no future for myself here, only sad memories. I know Jimmy is my brother now, and we are going west to see America. I expect Father will think I am deserting my obligations, and many will call me a traitor, but I have served him and South Carolina to the best of my ability, and have offered up all that was dearest to me, and still my hands and heart are empty. But my life has been spared, and I am grateful for that. I have seen enough of death in these last years to want to make the most of this new chance.

Hannah, I do not know if I will see you again while we are yet on this earth, but you will always be in my thoughts. You have loved me well, and I have adored you so. I have sent word of my plans to Promise. Perhaps when Jimmy and I have satisfied our wanderlust we will settle in Philadelphia. I still hold onto the smallest hope that I might someday be reconciled to her and be a true father to my son. I am finished serving man and selfish ambition. It is my earnest desire that when I meet my heavenly master, he will say to me, "Well done."

I once asked Promise whether she considered slavery to be a noble institution, or a great evil. As I recall, I never received a satisfactory answer, and I have been wrestling with the question ever since. Now that I am truly a man, I am convinced it was the latter. Slavery has shattered this country in two, and now we must somehow join together the splinters so that the sins of our fathers will not be visited upon the coming generations.

Whether we tried to be good to our slaves, or chose to exploit our rights of ownership, the barbarism of slavery was that it gave one man the power to determine if another man was to live in happiness, or in misery, or even if he was to live at all, and that these decisions were made with only our temperament or whims of conscience to guide us. No one is equipped to bear such a burden, and it is no wonder that so many good men have stumbled under the weight. May God forgive us.

"If my people, which are called by my name, shall humble themselves, and pray, and seek my face, and turn from their wicked ways; then will I hear from heaven, and will forgive their sin, and will heal their land."

All my affections and prayers go with you,

Gus

315

A week after Atterley Plantation's grand opening, after the Johansons' guests had gorged themselves at the dinner buffet, paid their bills, and been handed monogrammed gift bags filled with merchants' coupons and free samples, Franklin and Millicent sat down on the piazza to catch their breath. The hired help finished the cleaning an hour early and had been sent home, leaving the couple alone to nurse steaming cups of black tea and revel in the success of their new venture.

Mariah's homemade fruit pies could have used a tad more sugar, perhaps, but the weather had been glorious. Not a drop of rain had fallen. No careless children had spilled gravy on the table linen. No overly enthusiastic newlyweds had created a disturbance during the night. And none of the local media had asked any uncomfortable questions about the past.

A good time was had by all, although there had been protestors, a small group of troublemakers who just wanted to get their faces on television, but the local sheriff's department had made sure none of them got close enough to the grounds to put a damper on the festivities. The Johansons leaned back in their rocking chairs as they rested from their labors, and counted their blessings. The view was breathtaking. The manicured grass, dotted with flowers and greenery, stretched out before them, and the lake sparkled against the backdrop of the South Carolina sunset.

But all things must come to an end, and the close of the day was fast approaching. When the air turned chilly, Millicent held her husband's hand for warmth, and they remained outdoors to marvel at Atterley's untarnished beauty until the last bit of rosy light lingering over the Promised Land dissolved without warning, and the sky was sheathed in darkness.

"I hold that in the present state of civilization, where two races of different origin, and distinguished by color, and other physical differences, as well as intellectual, are brought together, the relation now existing in the slaveholding States between the two, is, instead of an evil, a good—a positive good. I feel myself called upon to speak freely upon the subject where the honor and interests of those I represent are involved. I hold then, that there never has yet existed a wealthy and civilized society in which one portion of the community did not, in point of fact, live on the labor of the other."

—*John C. Calhoun*
"Slavery a Positive Good," February 6, 1837

"Whether we turn to the declarations of the past, or to the professions of the present, the conduct of the nation seems equally hideous and revolting. America is false to the past, false to the present, and solemnly binds herself to be false to the future. Standing with God and the crushed and bleeding slave on this occasion, I will, in the name of humanity, which is outraged, in the name of liberty, which is fettered, in the name of the Constitution and the Bible, which are disregarded and trampled upon, dare to call in question and to denounce, with all the emphasis I can command, everything that serves to perpetuate slavery—the great sin and shame of America! 'I will not equivocate—I will not excuse.' I will use the severest language I can command, and yet not one word shall escape me that any man, whose judgment is not blinded by prejudice, or who is not at heart a slave-holder, shall not confess to be right and just."

—*Frederick Douglass*
"The Hypocrisy of American Slavery," July 4, 1852

ORDER FORM

To order additional copies online, please visit our website: http://www.goldenbankspublishing.com.

To order products by mail*, send this completed form, along with an enclosed check or money order, to:

Golden-Banks Publishing, LLC
Book Orders
6060 N. Central Expressway, Suite 560
Dallas, TX 75206

Number of Books _____ X $24.00 per copy = _____

S & H ($3 for the first book/$2 for each additional copy)   + _____

Shipments to Texas addresses, add 8.25% sales tax   + _____

Total of enclosed check or money order   = _____

Ship to:

_____
Name

_____
Street Address

_____
City, State, Zip

_____
Phone

_____
E-mail

* All international orders must be placed online.